34

Tilda's Angel

TILDA'S
angel

Dick Hedges

The Book Guild Ltd.
Sussex, England

The Book Guild Ltd.
25 High Street,
Lewes, Sussex.

First published 1993
© Dick Hedges 1993
Set in Baskerville
Typesetting by APS,
Salisbury, Wiltshire.
Printed in Great Britain by
Antony Rowe Ltd.,
Chippenham, Wiltshire.

A catalogue record for this book is
available from the British Library

ISBN 0 86332 810 5

'If the doors of perception were cleansed everything would appear to man as it is, infinite.'

William Blake

Dedicated to my wife.

CONTENTS

PREFACE

Because I do not like stories that hide the chief character and make you learn a different setting, and introduce seemingly irrelevant people, in each of the first few chapters – nor TV plays in which you can only establish the era by the vintage of the traffic – I will explain that this is a tale set in my contemporary Kenya, 1991. Kenya is the ex-British Colony half way down Africa on the right-hand side that hasn't had too much trouble since Mau Mau, the one in which the BBC is always filming 'Wildlife'.

It is the story of an old man's drive from Kenya's capital, Nairobi, to the coast, and of the extraordinary happenings upon his arrival at the coast. You are informed by the means of the old man's reminiscences of the especial significance of those final events, particularly as he reminisces about his life-long association with an ex-Army ambulance called Tilda.

The story is not always in exact chronological order. There is no literary reason for this slight disorder, it is simply because different scenes on the familiar road he is travelling trigger different memories which sometimes overlap, and if occasionally he recalls a favourite memory more than once in a different context forgive him his dotage.

You must forgive him too if sometimes he 'goes on a bit' about death as he tries to resign himself to it, without the help of a belief in any dogma, but as he often used to point out, there are plenty of people who have no interest in baseball, for example, nor in football either, many people will not have eaten an egg, let alone an oyster, nor flown, might not even have slept in a bed or even with another, never have nor never will, but death? That should hold universal appeal and maintain the reader's interest for a page or two because no one 'misses out' on that event.

On occasions when an appropriate English word does not come to mind I use the Swahili one, this is certainly not to show off, far from it, because my lack of fluency in Swahili is a constant embarrassment to me after three-quarters of a lifetime spent in East Africa.

Harry Hill, the old man around whom the story evolves belongs to the White Tribe of Kenya. There are over thirty different tribes in modern Kenya. The White Tribe was the last to arrive circa 1890, and is already nearly extinct. Nearly – but not quite. At the last count (1991) there were only three hundred and fifty of the El Molo tribe making them 'the smallest tribe' whereas there are several thousand 'White wog' citizens, influential out of all proportion to their numbers, and all of them intensely proud of their heritage whether they claim it by birth or by adoption.

One of Harry's favourite reminiscences is that of his early association with the ambulance and the 'Diggers' of the Australian 9th Division in Montgomery's 8th Army. Harry could never get it into his head that many of those Desert Rats, particularly the ones he met in the course of his duty as an attached Medical Corps driver are as dead as Ozymandias. A handful of dust under six foot of sand and a name on a Commonwealth Graves Commission cross in the military cemetery on the outskirts of Mersa Murtruh. Neither could he ever come to terms with the fact that these same soldiers' wives and sweethearts are today at best frumpish, lonely old ladies in granny wings in Coogee.

Tilda herself can still be seen on the Indian Ocean shore, she has been carried up again after her fall and is now safely positioned a hundred yards back from the cliff, so she no longer sticks out like a sore thumb, though the salt-laden atmosphere of the coast, unlike the dry Highlands of Nairobi, means Tilda won't last much longer.

Tilda is, to be exact, a K4 World War Two ex-Army ambulance and she is as British as the Grenadiers and as English as Austin was.

When, in the closing chapters of this odyssey, I try to describe Tilda's Angel I fear that my literary ability is inadequate for the occasion, but find a small consolation in echoing Mark Antony, 'For I have neither wit, nor words, nor worth, Action, nor utterance, nor the power of speech, To stir men's

'blood; I only speak right on.'
I'll go along with that.

Dick Hedges
Nairobi
May 1992

1

Before the Start

The scene is easy enough to describe. The Kenyan Indian Ocean's coral reef shore at low tide, north of Mombasa and south of Malindi. The simplicity of chocolate box art, endless silver sands, the perfect set for a tourist office 'come on' video, a lone Giriama fisherman poling his way in his dugout canoe perfectly suspended twixt the blue sky and the green sea.

On the virgin sand, firm and marvellously corrugated from the recent cover of the still receding tide, land-crabs scurry their crooked way to freshly dug holes as a boxer dog with no immediate sign of ownership chases them in a quivering ecstasy of delight.

None of Easter's neap tides bring their banks of weed, to mar this November's high water line. Not one green bottle, nor even a plastic white one, no smudge of oil pollutes this perfect coast. If green days are in forests, then this is the setting for blue days by the sea. Small puffy white clouds scud in Indian file across the horizon, and nearly half a mile of tanker, smaller than a match box, is anchored in the stream off distant Kilindini Harbour.

The persons soon to enter this idyllic set are harder to describe. Their thoughts and hopes and fears that is. Their outward appearance is almost as unlikely and perfect as their background. Built of the stuff from which Wilbur Smith's characters are chiselled bronze-limbed, blond-haired and Rolex-wristed. Although it was actually a Swatch on the wrist of the pilot of the single-engined Cessna that is fast disturbing the tranquillity of the beach. Perfectly at home in the cockpit he glances reassuringly at the instruments sparkling in the morning sun. The Swatch was typical of his well thought out life,

'Twice as functional and one-tenth the price!' His justification was a shade too pat but one guessed it was the superior function rather than the huge saving over a Rolex that appealed most to Oliver about his Swatch.

He descended to two hundred feet and buzzed his house with a swish rather than a roar as he throttled back heading out to sea. He turned above the head of the fisherman in his canoe who didn't even look up so used was he to Bwana Oliver in his 182. Oliver made his usual perfect landing on the deserted beach, coming to rest by the giant trunk of a fallen tree, its few whitened flotsam-like branches thrusting upwards like a mock Moore sculpture in a Texan shopping mall. For a windsock the smooth branches flew a yellow and green *kikoi*. The stump-tailed boxer dog reluctantly abandoned the pursuit of the crabs for the even greater delight of the proximity of his master and bounded up to the plane and waited in an agony of anticipation under the wing of the plane for his master to alight.

It is a strange fact that children of quite ordinary or even particularly plain Caucasians born and bred in Kenya up to the age of nine or so, could be mistaken physically for the children of the Gods of Arcadian days that played around Olympus. Children lithesome as a dream indeed, golden-brown limbed, lit golden hair in tight ringlets, sky blue eyes, wide mouths and ruby red lips. So uniformly beautiful are the young of the White Tribe of Kenya that toddlers playing at pre-nursery schools have been mistaken by their mothers even, and on one memorable occasion in a Mombasa suburb an *ayah* actually walked the wrong child back home to a bridge-playing mother who, legend has it, looked up unconcernedly from her hand and in a quiet voice, 'Sean, how many times must I tell you? Don't just stand there Sean.' Then in the same monotone but now addressing the ayah, 'That's not Sean you idiot – three no trumps. Sean is wearing a red tee-shirt. Try again. No bid.'

Two such children were running naked across the sand to join the boxer dog in greeting their father. They were followed, diligently as always, by their ayah, a woman of majestic proportions and only a shade darker than her two sunburnt charges. Remembering their training well the twins stopped warily some fifty feet from the plane although the engine had

14

by now been shut down. They were well disciplined for whirling propellers but their exuberance had never been suppressed, and they jumped up and down in excitement at a safe distance. 'Daddy, Daddy will you take us up?'

Oliver was by now out of the plane and patting the boxer. 'Sorry,' he said, shaking his head. 'Not today kids. I just came back to collect something.' The twins' mother was by now also running across the beach to greet her husband. A *kikoi* had been thrown hastily round her slightly too thin body. Again blonde hair, this time shoulder length, streamed out behind her.

Oliver's high wing Cessna bore the same 5Y registration as did the legendary fleets of Flying Doctors' planes, ending in this case with CE to give her her name for all time – Charlie Echo. The light aircraft was obviously of postwar vintage but otherwise the view and the ambiance of the scene seemed to have more in common with the prewar 1930s. Dennis Finch-Hatton used to land on that very beach and the passionate Karen ran down a similar coral cliff from a similar verandah to greet him as he stepped from his plane. In fact it was only a couple of miles south of Oliver and Anne Shaw's house where Dennis took off for the last time to spin in at Voi one third of the way to Nairobi. It was on that beach too that a youthful Beryl Markam used to climb out of her single-engined Avian, in sexy white overalls that caused the withdrawn Baroness von Blixen huge pangs of well-founded jealousy, in the days before Beryl's great adventure *West with the Night*, to the ticker-tape welcome of New York.

Conscious of the fact that he was living in such a paradise Oliver constantly played his life style down, 'Oh, come on' he would say to his critics and admirers alike, 'I bet your car cost more than Charlie Echo, she's fifteen years old you know.' A disparaging remark that was probably true, particularly if the car referred to was one of the many Mercedes seen on the roads of Kenya. Then Oliver would continue to justify his life style, 'Anyway it's a necessity for me – cheapest way of getting fresh lobsters to "The Net",' a reference to his well-known Nairobi restaurant 'The Fisherman's Net'. Occasionally when a more lengthy justification seemed necessary he would explain that even a very modest terraced house in any United Kingdom provincial town would probably be worth more than the five acre coastal plot, which Oliver had in fact inherited, and on which his young family now lived in a bungalow which he had virtually built himself.

Oliver's wife, the blonde girl running across the beach, had by now passed her twins and their ayah and reached the plane. She handed Oliver an envelope of photos. 'That's what you wanted?' she questioned.

In a tone of genuine appreciation for his wife's anticipation he replied, 'Clever girl. Yes, for old Harry if I see him. Right?'

'Yes,' she replied. 'I've got some good ones of it and I expect he would like to see the twins anyway.' The twins, containing their disappointment well, like most children trained with the ancient patience of East African ayahs, were now being led back to the little cliff having resigned themselves to not getting a flight that day. With a child trailing behind on each hand the ayah strode purposefully up the short path to return them to their playhouse.

The playhouse stuck out on top of the thirty foot cliff, like a traditional sore thumb, looking very strange rather as if a van had been parked on the edge of the cliff and then abandoned. This playhouse had figured largely in the lives of Oliver, Anne and the twins for the last six months.

One morning, the previous June, after a stormy night Oliver and Anne had found what at first looked like a cargo container washed up by the tide at the bottom of their garden. It turned out to be the wreck of a van-like vehicle, no wheels, no bonnet, a very rusty engine block and two unhinged large opening doors at the rear, on which despite their recent immersion, they could still quite clearly see two large red crosses painted in white circles. Inside the rear compartment were hooks with remains of fishing nets hanging from them, which made Oliver think that it must, until recently, have been used as a fisherman's hut. He assumed the high seas had dislodged it, possibly from further north where the Galana River disgorged huge quantities of topsoil into the Indian Ocean after the rains, turning the sea murram red, up to ten miles off shore. It is lonely country up there in northern Kenya, stretching to the desolate Somali border, thousands of hectares of mangrove swamps, and behind them a scrub desert where even today an occasional elephant herd can still be found.

Oliver decided to convert the wreck into a playhouse for the twins as relaxation from his desk-bound job at his restaurant. A steel rope ratchet winch was resurrected, it had been in Oliver's garage since his father had died sixteen years before. It took a whole weekend – Oliver, Anne, the twins, five fishermen and their watchman, Askari, in Swahili (always referred to as 'Skary' by the twins), to get the old van-like vehicle up the thirty foot coral cliff and on to what Anne proudly called their lawn – a few strings of creeping *Kikuyu* grass trailing in the sand like the wisps of brushed hair across a balding man's scalp. The conversion of the wreck into a playhouse had given Oliver considerable pleasure. No deadline, relatively cheap material, and plenty of cheap labour to do the hard graft like rubbing the paint down for respraying. Oliver had decided to rebuild its outside at any rate, into a genuine configuration of how it should have looked, taking trouble over the cosmetics of the exterior. When he was in Nairobi he would comb the Industrial Area, Godowns, and fly back to Mombasa with a cherished part like a hammerkop building its nest. He was amazed at what some of the Asian-owned secondhand scrapyards still had hidden away, even for pre-second world war vehicles. On his return with an item he would proudly tell his wife, perhaps over the first beer, 'Hey, guess what? Old Kantaria must have over a hundred starter motors for vehicles like the one we are restoring. Think of that! He can't have sold one for forty years. Nairobi would be an absolute Aladdin's cave for some of those vintage freaks in the UK and the States.'

The twins of course were delighted, getting up early every morning to help, or more likely to hinder, with the conversion and they now divided their life equally between the sea and the playhouse, insisting they sleep in it most nights. Some time during those six months he was working on the wreck it dawned on Oliver that he knew the old Army ambulance given up by the sea, from a long time ago. He was almost sure it was the same vehicle that his father's old friend, Harry Hill, had actually driven overland to Kenya, and which he himself had borrowed as a teenager over twenty years ago one weekend when both his father and Harry's son, Simon, were still alive. He remembered getting it stuck on the Ngong hills one night after it fell into a little crater and he had to abandon it and walk ten miles home. He wouldn't forget that in a hurry because there were still buffalo on the Ngong hills in those days. Oliver realized there couldn't be many ex-Army ambulances like that one left in the world, let alone in Kenya but how that particular vehicle had landed up at the coast at the bottom of his garden he had no idea.

Because he still kept in touch with Harry, his father's old friend, who was in fact godfather to the twins, he and Anne decided to show old Harry the snap they had taken of the playhouse.

'Of course,' added Anne, 'he is always asking for pictures of the twins anyway.' It made quite a snap – two golden toddlers in the open walk-through cab with the sparkling Indian Ocean as a backdrop. Oliver slipped the packet in his pilot's briefcase, gave his wife a peck of a 'goodbye again' kiss and faultlessly taxied Charlie Echo downwind for 200 yards, turned into the diagonal offshore wind and was airborne by the time he reached the flotsam tree trunk.

The tiny red and white plane was swallowed up in the blue panorama of the African sky as Oliver took his bearings for Wilson Airport and Charlie Echo got down to the serious business of putting 4,000 feet between her and the top of the 7,000 feet Chyulu Hills that sprawl across the flight path halfway to Nairobi.

Anne and her cherubic twin girls swam in a rock pool left by the ebbing tide. Leaving her *kikoi* on the last piece of dry sand she strode naked into the shallow water with the two little girls splashing and gurgling with delight around her feet. Nearly two hundred yards away their boxer dog panted under the shade of the fallen tree trunk cum air sock on which the ayah was patiently sitting with her inevitable knitting. No one else was in sight as far as the eye could see in either direction. Even the Giriama fisherman had poled himself out of sight – an idyllic scene again.

When Anne had heard her husband 'buzz' the house so soon after she had returned from dropping him off at the airstrip, she knew instantly that he had not returned because he had forgotten the photographs for old Harry. She knew also that they would be his excuse. The real reason for the detour, she was certain, was to allow him to check out from the air if a certain new large white Citroen car was making its way through the two miles of coconut plantations that separated Oliver and Anne's plot from their new neighbour. The new

18

neighbour had, with admirable propriety, called to introduce himself when he had moved in two months previously. Oliver had only met him three or four times but often enough to have taken an instant dislike to him. In Oliver's eyes the new neighbour was a swaggering, over-sexed, typical rich Greek lecher with breath that constantly smelt of garlic. In fact Oliver's men friends at the Malindi Club had already titled and pigeon-holed him as 'The Mafioso'.

To the young wives of that part of the coast he was looked upon slightly differently. The Greek Cypriot had already retired from the nine to five routine, and yet couldn't be much over forty-five, had recently discarded his second wife, was rich, attentive, interesting and with all the time in the world on his hands to pursue leisure. Such a cock caused quite a stir amongst the pullets at the coast.

He found Anne irresistible and already had the times of Oliver's flights to and from Nairobi very carefully worked out. To understand these less idyllic undertones, enter a 'coffee morning chat' held not at one of the wives' house as of old but at a new shopping mall that had just opened ten minutes' drive from Anne's home. Anne has left the twins with the ayah and taken the Volvo to change videos, videos have taken over so completely the Kenyan settlers' cultural and entertainment programme from The Reprint Society books of the early postwar days. Another young wife joins Anne at the restaurant table. She is about Anne's age and they have known each other since boarding school days at Loreto Convent in a Nairobi suburb where, it was sometimes rumoured, mainly by Protestants, that the teaching nuns extracted just a little too much pleasure from caning the bare bottoms of their young and nubile charges. Anne's friend's nose positively wrinkled with anticipation, 'You haven't, have you?'

Slightly annoyed Anne replied, 'No, no of course not but . . . but . . . '

'But what?'

'Well, if you must know, Olly is spending more nights in Nairobi these days and it slipped out that he *has* got a new secretary.'

'Oh, come off it. He's always had a glam Af sec, ever since they were invented.'

Anne paused a little, pleased from the comfort she gained

from her friend's arguments. She knew just what her friend meant 'since they were invented'. A generation or more ago, before independence, the odd DO fending for himself, some two hundred miles from the nearest white woman, or the lonely up-country farmer might take a dusky young Somali girl as a temporary mistress, but most settlers' wives then had little to worry about from competition from African employees. The tribal girls of those days still geared their charms to young men of the tribe and the town prostitutes were a lean and hungry and strangely sexless lot, but since independence a whole generation of African girls had grown up who had learnt exactly what appealed to the rich westernized African, the tourist, and their white bosses alike. They had learned to make the very best of their considerable sexuality and blatantly turned it on full blast at every opportunity. The wealthy African women were often as well-dressed as their counterparts in Paris. The younger, poorer girls at the disco had somehow acquired an ebony image of sex appeal which could compete at its best with the glamour of Thailand itself.

'I don't know,' Anne continued, 'it's just that sometimes I feel I am drinking out a cup that's got a lipstick smear on it.' Anne's friend nodded, as she held her coffee cup up to look for smears.

'So, you intend to get a little lipstick on yours?' The girls giggled at the ambiguous metaphor.

'Not just yet dearie, but I don't see why I shouldn't take him up on his offer to teach me golf. He's bloody good apparently. He says he played to a four in Nicosia.'

'Well,' replied the other, 'he won't think much of our sandpit then,' a reference to Malindi's municipal efforts at a nine-hole golf course.

☆   ☆   ☆

Oliver, approaching his finals, called up Wilson Tower and with a sentence that seemed most appropriate to him, put his retired Cypriot neighbour out of his mind in order to give his undivided attention and concentration to landing. 'Gleesy Gleek Plick' he muttered to himself.

Oliver always kept his old Toyota Land Cruiser at Wilson airport for Nairobi town running. His first stop after he left the light aircraft airport was on the way into town at the new Toyota Kenya parts and spares depot opposite the new Nyayo stadium, a part of the creeping stranglehold on Africa in which a giant UK investment company has profits from the third world to pay their first world shareholders a dividend but that profit depends mainly on gifts and soft loans from the first world to the third world in order to make any profit possible. Oliver recollected that some Rolon critics said 'Give five pence for a starving Ethiop and it ends up in a rich white man's pocket.'

Communism had failed economically, but morally it still fared better than capitalism: what a field day a Marxist cartoonist could have with this economic madness of the third world 'servicing' its debts to the developed world with loans from the same source! The cartoon would show a pious western Sunday school child putting fifty pence on the offertory plate labelled 'for starving African children' and the arch-evil personification of a greedy capitalist, with a stars-and-stripes top hat and dollar-signed green eyes stretching out a claw-like hand to grab the fifty pence.

Before Oliver had flown to the coast the last time, he had been trying to get a by-pass hose for his Land Cruiser, and owing to it being an old model he had been unsuccessful in Nairobi's endless pirate parts shops where there are whole streetfuls of less expensive, non-genuine, fast-moving spares. So he had now resigned himself to the considerable added expense and time-wasting connected with visiting the main franchise holders. He was walking away from the parts counter with his new hose in a plastic bag when he recognized the rear view of an elderly Mzungu. Oliver recognized him at once because he knew him well but Harry was certainly not the person to stand out in a crowd. By comparison with the characters with whom he seemed to surround himself, he was by no means handsome. Not as an old man of seventy-three, nor even at the height of his youth, could he have been called handsome. To start with he was not tall. At five feet eight and a half inches he was only just tall enough not to be labelled 'short'. Trousers always two inches too long from waist to crotch gave him an elephant-like figure from the rear. Round shoulders and a pot belly had never done much for the rest of his figure either. Once, a hundred years ago, as he put it, when he was a youth and played a second-row forward in the scrum he had liked to be called 'stocky'. Now, with a nondescript fairly short grey beard and a few wisps of grey hair he could not even be called distinguished. He was too untidy for distinction. His small beard hid his chin but not the fact that it receded. A big nose and a middle brow and not particularly wide-set ordinary grey-coloured eyes gave him a working-class un-aristocratic appearance. When his wife had been alive such labels as 'tatty round the edges' were often hurled at him by her as a source of abuse for his lack of concern for his appearance. When he was rejected by the Masons, for example, she was convinced it was because he had egg on his tie at a critical interview and such things infuriated her. Of course he would reply to such suggestions, 'There's no such thing as a "classical" or "aristocratic" look, or even a "square-jawed All-American" look. If you put a cloth cap on King George V, wrapped a muffler round his neck, he would look the same as me or any common London paperseller that you see in black and white pictures taken during the Depression. You can't call any specific feature "common". Look at the aristocracy, they haven't got chins either.'

And his wife would reply, a little frustrated, 'All right, all right, I see what you mean but they don't have egg on their ties, or have long, dirty hair, curling up round their collars.'

But as the years rolled by appearances seemed that much less important and Harry's eyes and mouth grew kinder with age even though his habit of using foul language did not. Oliver noticed that Harry's hair still needed trimming as he waited at the service reception area now operated by smart red-blazered black girls with white-teethed smiles who meticulously wrote out the job description of 'work to be carried out' sheets. The smiles made up in part for their lack of technical knowledge. Old hands usually insisted on seeing the Asian foreman himself who always hovered nearby for just that reason but Harry was not asking for technical assistance. He was thumping the counter and unconsciously imitating a UK comedian he had seen on a video recording, by lengthening the central word of the sentence and giving it a sarcastic ring of long suffering, 'Well, why do you call it a "free" service, that's why I want to know? "Free" means for nothing doesn't it? Free service, not three. Look here,' he said, pointing to his owner's handbook:

'First' said slowly, 'service' said exaggeratedly, 'free' said triumphantly.

The sarcasm was totally lost on the attractive African girl behind the counter. 'Yes sir, it's the service that's free but everybody has to pay for the oil.' Harry closed his eyes and looked up at the heavens in a mock prayer for protection from bureaucratic madness. He was still in this stance when Oliver slapped him heavily on the back.

'Harry – just the person. Having problems?'

'Oh, hello Oliver. No nothing special, just the usual. I'm picking up my car after its first free service actually, and just teasing Ruth here for calling 870 shillings free.' The girl took Harry's money and handed him his receipt and the keys to his car. The two men walked across the car park together.

Then from a genuinely interested Oliver, 'How is the new Corolla doing you then, Harry?' knowing if anyone should be able to judge a new car's performance Harry with all his experience of the East African market certainly should.

'It's good. Mind you I always say that there isn't such a thing as a bad car these days. You get what you pay for, even down to that Lada thing or whatever. Yes, you get what you pay for and that's it.' They chatted together.

'Yes,' said Oliver, 'same with most things really as long as there's not too much local purchase content included,' he added with a knowing smile of a person who had lived with local manufacture for two decades. They had both bought kilos of locally-made nails, for example, and the standing joke was that if you got a few nails with both a head and a point, somewhere in the packet, you would be doing well, the majority had either two heads or two points. Then there was a whole decade of 'ball-burning' matches when the broken lit head dropped off into masculine laps every time one attempted to light a cigarette.

Resting his pilot's briefcase on the bonnet of Harry's new car to open it, Oliver said, 'Guess what? Anne gave them to me just this morning to show to you.'

'Oh the kids – good,' taking the envelope of photographs. 'I really must get down to see them for myself again, one day soon. Anne all right?'

'Yes, fine – thought we'd ask you about *that*.' Oliver was leaning over and pointing to the snap of the playhouse. 'You had an old ambulance like that once didn't you?'

Harry's mouth literally dropped open in surprise. He stared hard at the picture. 'Good God, Olly, where on earth did that come from?' Oliver explained his find and renovation.

Harry nodded knowingly. 'It could be – it could just be Tilda – of course it can't be but it *is*. That's typical Tilda all right.' And Oliver wondered if he meant can't be but was, as being typical of Tilda or if he just meant the photo was a typical shot.

Oliver continued, 'That would be the van I borrowed off Simon just before ... before ... ' Oliver stopped in mid-sentence.

'Before he was killed,' Harry helped without giving away anything in the intonation.

'Yes, that's right,' Oliver agreed, thankful for the help, and he continued, 'Hang on to them. Anne's got copies,' as Harry was about to hand the photos back.

'Thanks – say Oliver, what are you doing tonight? Paul and Rita asked me round for a drink and a bite and I know they would love to see you again. Can you make it?'

For a whole long ten seconds Oliver thought of the elderly contemporaries of his father sitting on a verandah in Langata calling the houseboy to bring more ice for the whisky as the sun set over the Ngong hills, and he compared it with the thought of his new twenty-two year old African secretary slipping off the silky white blouse she always wore in deliberate contrast to her ebony black breasts and lighter brown nipples. 'Sure, about seven o'clock OK?' but try as he might he could not put any enthusiasm into his voice.

Harry noticed the tone instantly, a speciality of Harry's and, unlike most other senses which were degenerating with age. He even guessed correctly what sort of an alternative entertainment Oliver had decided to cancel to enable him to accept his invitation. He gave Oliver a very old-fashioned look as he replied, 'Great. See you there then.'

Seven o'clock that evening saw Oliver in his old Toyota pulling into Paul's Langata house. Like all Langata houses it had its own long drive. Oliver was a little ashamed of his original reticence to accept Harry's invitation to spend the evening with his father's old friends, Paul and Rita, because although there was a generation gap all right Paul always deliberately surrounded himself with young overlanders, who camped on his five-acre plot. They were a hugely interesting company. No one had ever suggested that Paul's love of youth was anything but platonic. You couldn't find a straighter character. Paul and Rita were probably the most intellectual people Oliver knew. When his father had been alive Oliver had been introduced to arguments from Descartes and Chardin and Kant at Paul's house. Paul had taken philosophy when he was up at Oxford to go with his degree in Medieval English History, both typically unsuitable for his final career with Aunty Beeb, as he always referred to the BBC, but an interest that proved very pleasant and entertaining for his retirement years when he was respected as one of the elders of the White Tribe. Apart from his academic background he had also lived an exciting physical life. He had rounded the Cape under sail and fought in the Spanish Civil War, rather uncertainly for the Republicans, it seemed. Now as they passed seventy, Paul and Rita, having no children of their own, became everybody's aunt and uncle. Paul's snowy-white long hair and a pipe gave him a sort of Bertrand Russell effect.

The house and gardens, as well as the occupants, seemed to extend a secure and settled feeling. Oliver remembered incidents of years before when his and other's youthful worlds were falling apart with unrequited love or an alcoholic addiction. Or even a drug dependency on marijuana looming, and the world seeming upside down. He and his friends would pop into Paul's at eight o'clock any morning to belong to the changeless scene, impervious to external or internal events, a continual set. Paul, with a week-old *Daily Telegraph* propped up on his boiled egg and Rita saying, 'Look at you now, come in, sit down, have a coffee.' It would always be the same, always, every day, every week, every year, a sheet anchor of stability from the winds that buffeted youth with its divine problems. Often, especially after his father died, Oliver would drop in. You didn't have to say much. You didn't have to stay. You wouldn't be lectured. The 'stable influence' alone was sufficient to cure most ills. Oliver remembered with delight one breakfast visit when Harry's daughter, Nicky, had been there too, one of the most attractive girls that Oliver had ever known.

The sundown drink on the verandah was another ritual. In fact Oliver remembered his father saying, 'Old Paul must spend half his income on whisky – with friends in to help, which he has most nights, he must get through a bottle a night.' Paul's garden, like so many others in Nairobi's northern suburb, had to be judged as amongst the most delightful anywhere in the world. Jacaranda and bougainvillaea cascaded down in undisturbed profusion, whole bulks of colour, often up to one hundred feet in height. These gardens had become a necessary sanctuary from Nairobi's city centre, about ten miles away, which by the last decade of the twentieth century had become, sadly, like all third world capitals, plagued with the failure of all services. No road maintenance, little garbage collection, a trickle of water, intermittent phone and electricity supply. Even the runways and air traffic control at Jomo Kenyatta International Airport, although only a mere five years old, were already suspect.

Nairobi had mushroomed from a railhead camp a hundred years previously. It was then redesigned as a delightful city for 50,000 privileged European settlers in the mid-fifties, but was by now bursting at all its seams to try and supply the needs of over one and a half million predominantly 'on the bread line' Black African inhabitants. The suburbs were very different, the majority were still five-acre plots, with rich Africans, who fortunately had similar tastes for club life and gardens to the not quite so rich Europeans amongst whom they had settled after independence. Langata and Karen sprawled in the sun under the Ngong hills so loved by Karen von Blixen who gave her name to the Karen half of these suburbs.

Three of Paul's many dogs yapped around the Land Cruiser. Oliver noticed Harry's new car parked in the drive and observed that in the vlei behind the house were, as usual, the tents, the sleeping bags and sand mats strewn around the huge trucks – the debris of overlanders.

Knowing everyone would be on the side verandah Oliver called out the usual Swahili 'Hodi' as he entered the open French windows into the living room. 'Hodi' meant not only 'Hi' but also 'I'm coming in – hope I'm not disturbing you – are you about?' to which the reply would be hopefully one word 'Karibu' – 'Welcome'. On this occasion it was shouted by Rita from the verandah. Paul and Rita's large L-shaped living room, with a dining alcove one end, was typical of all the rooms Oliver knew. It radiated warmth – leather-chair warmth, copper and brass warmth because hand polishing was still affordable. Cosy inglenook warmth. Persian carpets on polished floors warmth. Reprint Society books of the fifties wedged into a wall-to-wall library shelf otherwise filled with Africana. However many books did Nevil Shute write? The television without an aerial because the Voice of Kenya was not worth watching, but the actual box necessary for viewing the profusion of videos, mostly pirated from the developed world's TV networks less than a fortnight previously. The fire, laid up by the Shamba boy to be lit later. Langataites were acutely proud of their evenings which, they insist, are cool enough for a fire on many evenings of the year, particularly during the long rains. Or even, nowadays, in the short rains which come in November. 'We are on top of a mountain here you know, higher than some of the Alps,' was a favourite Langata cliché.

Paul, like the gentleman he was, rose as Oliver entered. 'Oliver, super to see you.' Oliver's mood improved even more as he noticed a young overland couple had been invited to the evening. Oliver took one look at the girl with her jeans and tee-shirt and guessed that she was Australian. She was sitting next to her boyfriend, a face that Oliver vaguely recognized. 'Let me introduce Julie, – Oliver. Peter you may have met?' Oliver duly shook hands with the couple. Peter he did now remember from a previous visit two years ago. He got half up to shake hands but Julie remained firmly seated offering a surprisingly long elegant hand which felt definitely unlike the outdoor hand of an overlander which he had expected.

'How do you do,' she said and Oliver instantly knew he had guessed wrong thinking her Australian; her accent was from the turnip fields of Norfolk. Peter and Julie were a part of Paul's income. Paul's place was the Nairobi overland centre and the rent the overlanders paid generated for Paul a modest income in his retirement. 'Enough for my sundowner', as he usually put it, proving Oliver's father right. Paul had arrived in Kenya in the early fifties about the same time as a wave of settlers were flooding into Kenya from the failed Tanganyikan

27

groundnut scheme, but Paul, though of their vintage, was definitely not of their ilk. Harry had arrived in Kenya around the same time as had Oliver's father and the three men had become firm friends. Oliver sipped his first whisky, glanced at the East Anglian overland girl and decided that the evening would be quite bearable.

The word 'overlander' refers to the overland travellers that enter Kenya by surface route – to say 'by road' would not be totally correct. There are many companies who have been operating 'overland' trips for years and such companies usually disgorge up to forty people two or three times a month from the back of their Bedford trucks. In addition to these there are of course the individual overlanders who usually favour Land Rovers. It is the actual drivers of the companies' trucks that Paul entertains who come back year after year, a breed apart, like old salts of the seas but usually younger, usually resourceful and usually modest. Your typical overlander driver is reared on the mechanized farms of Australia, New Zealand or Britain. They wouldn't think twice about using one of their punters' (as they call their passengers) leather belts to help an engine with an engine knock limp into a town. Or think nothing of cutting a square of PVC from a tent to replace a leaking fuel lift pump diaphragm. As well as knowing just how many bottles of Scotch to trade to get a punter with a South African stamp in his passport safely stamped into Tanzania.

Their ability to dig their vehicles through a mud hole called Zaire or even to build their own ferries to float their Bedfords across swollen rivers, are legion. Old Harry, who was once on the fringes of overland himself, still enjoyed their company and their stories. Julie, as Oliver had suspected, was Peter Rolfe's overland moll, a unique sexual association. If a driver stayed faithful to one passenger the whole trip they often stayed bonded together for life in bonds more secure than those of marriage. Julie had apparently just done her second trip with Peter Rolfe so it looked to Oliver like a 'No Entry' situation as far as his chances were concerned, but outside on the verandah watching the sun sink into the Ngongs, and later as the fire flickered on her face, he enjoyed her company for its own sake, almost platonically in fact, despite her strange sexual fascination.

The stories started while they were still seated on the

28

verandah. First, from Paul, while Rita had slipped into the kitchen to check out on the finer points of the forthcoming meal, because she knew the 'burnt-out truck' story by heart; even Oliver remembered hearing it once before. Wrinkles of smile lines animated Paul's genial face as he started on his story. With twinkling blue eyes and a generous girth he now looked more like Pickwick than Bertrand Russell. 'Malcolm MacGibbon, you remember him?' An order, rather than a question, directly mainly to Peter who nodded vaguely. Malcolm MacGibbon had been on the overland for over ten years and so he should be known to most old hands.

'Yes, yes, I remember him – must have done more overlands than Martin,' Peter added to show his knowledge of overland.

'Right,' said Paul, as he continued, 'Several years ago now, sitting at this very table one night, about this time in fact, an "Involvement" driver, remember them? . . . They lasted for a year or two then "Encounter" bought them out, I think. Never heard of them again anyway. It was one of their drivers – Carl, if I remember right. Just the three of us sitting here over a whisky. Rita must have been visiting her sister in Yorkshire.' Rather typical of Kenyan settlers Paul liked to show his familiarity with the UK. 'Well, Malcolm MacGibbon was chatting away as was his wont, a huge Scottish accent he has – do you remember? and the "Involvement" guy, Carl, was on his second trip down – a bit green, you see.' Peter and Oliver nodded politely. ' "You run an RL I see" he says to old Malcolm. "Och, of course I do".' Paul improved his story with a fair copy of an Inverness accent. ' "Well" says Carl, "I've got an RL differential I'll sell you." Malcolm looked up a little more attentively than before because he had just decided that his differential was making a noise and should be replaced before he drove south. "Nae, I dinna need one thanks." "It's not dear," says Carl hopefully. "Anything's dear if you dinna need it laddie." "Well, do you know anyone who might then?" – after a pause – "No, not off the top of my head." And so it goes on. Just as Malcolm is making his farewell gestures to leave he says by the door "I remember now, Jimmy says he can do with a differential for an RL. How much do you want for it?" Carl sits up. "It must be worth fifty quid." – a fair sum especially in those days. "Come on" says Carl. "I will show it to you – it's tied on to my truck." Now I stayed here but I

29

could hear the shout. "You bastard" shouts Malcolm at the top of his voice.' Paul starts to laugh himself as he recalls the incident. ' "That's my own back axle you're trying to sell me. I would recognize it anywhere. You swiped if from the burnt out Bedford just out of Tam, didn't you?" Not waiting for Carl to reply Malcolm continued, "That was my bloody truck all right. I left it there last year after it caught fire when a bloody punter threw his bloody dog-end into the petrol tank of a generator we were carrying at the time". Ha,' laughed Paul, 'you should have seen Carl's face, he had of course "stolen" it from that very wreck.'

That of course started them off. Peter continued by relating the time when a jerry can of diesel had dropped off his roof rack at the start of the Sahara section just out of In Salah and how it had been returned to him at In Guezzam some five hundred miles south and a week later. A Fiat tanker driver pulled alongside the camped overlander to return it. 'Been following your tracks,' he nonchalantly explained. 'Now where else in the world,' asked Peter proudly, 'could you have something returned to you five hundred miles later that you had lost the previous week in the road?'

They settled around a huge round table large enough to seat ten or twelve so that the six of them chose to sit around half of it. Cheggy, a black Jeeves, in a red fez glided in and out with the courses. It was not until they were all seated in large armchairs round the freshly-lit fire that Paul tried to open up the overland conversation again. 'Tell us about your trip, Peter,' he said but Harry butted in.

'Ah, come on, Paul, you've heard it a hundred times before. Hear one overland story and you've heard them all.'

Paul good-naturedly replied with an exaggerated wicked leer, 'Yes, but I like hearing *her* talk. Her "Ah oi loik turnips" accent is so sexy it turns me on.' Peter replied, a little too quickly, to hide his genuine annoyance, 'Christ, will you old fossils never get past it!' Then added thoughtfully, 'Still, it means that I have another forty years of virility ahead of me, I suppose.' But Paul and Harry picked up the cue as if it were yesterday, instead of two years ago that they last retold their favourite joke.

Paul, in the quavering voice of exaggerated age, 'You remember those pills they gave us in the Boer War?'

30

Harry butted in, in the same voice. 'Them to take our mind off the gals you mean?' and Paul concluded,

'That's right. That's them – well, I think they are beginning to work!'

A rattle of laughter went round the four listeners. They had all heard the old joke before. Then Harry said, 'Go on, Julie, tell us your story, as long as it's not one of those sand mat sagas.'

'Don't worry,' said Peter, 'this is different.'

Julie began her story. 'You see, we left Athens for Port Said.'

'Port Said?' queries Harry. All the listeners knew that the Nile-Sudan route to Kenya had been closed for seven years ever since their mutual friend, Martin, had blown up on a landmine.

Peter continued, 'Yes, the "Head Teds" in London seemed to think there was a call for the Nile, so this trip we headed down the Nile as far as Khartoum and then cut west to CAR. It wasn't too bad actually.'

'I see,' said Paul, looking at Julie, 'so you were in the middle of the Med. Go on.'

'Well,' continued Julie, 'somewhere between Athens and Port Said we broke down.' Laughter all round. 'No – the boat, stupid,' said Julie, realizing her ambiguity.

'Ship,' said Harry primly, 'ship for boats, hound for dogs.'

Oliver this time, 'Oh, don't take any notice of him, Julie. Go on, tell us.'

'After the ship had engine trouble in the Med . . .' Julie continued, 'we diverted to Sidi Barrani.'

Harry's next interruption was with genuine interest. His eyes opened wide. He was now fully attentive. 'Sidi Barrani!' The name of a town in North Africa that he hadn't heard mentioned for fifty years. But he interrupted again, more interestedly this time. 'Good Lord, Sidi Barrani, I didn't think they even had a harbour there.'

Julie continued patiently, 'That's right, they don't. We had to take the Bedford ashore on a lighter. It nearly sank as a matter of fact.'

'Swing the lights for a "sand ladder saga",' said Paul.

'No,' said Harry, 'let her continue. Go on,' he said.

'Well, it was like this. About the second day towards Alex on a good sealed road, . . .'

31

'Tarmac you mean,' interrupted Paul.

Indignantly from Julie, now adopting an exaggerated Oxford accent for a sentence. 'Yes, that's right actually – tarmac,' then relaxing into her Norfolk drawl again, 'Well, that evening when we stopped, Peter and me were both getting a bit tired of the grunters – you know, still whingeing.'

That again was a cue for all of them. Even Rita joined in this time. In chorus they said, 'Whingeing Poms.'

The girl continued, 'Actually most of them were Aussies, and they weren't too bad after the crossing. But this particular night we had just had tea.'

'Supper, that is.'

Oliver said rather irritatedly, 'Oh, shut up and let her get on with it.'

'Well, Peter wouldn't come and I badly needed to get away from the grunters so I took a walk on my own.'

☆   ☆   ☆

A blood-orange moon was sinking into the desert ahead of her at least a yard across. The smell of garlic-spiced cooking gave way to the scent of paraffin lights burning in a hundred shop windows and glowing cheerfully in the doorways which opened onto the narrow alley up which Julie was walking; a passage too narrow for motorized traffic. Fresh donkey droppings and betel nut spit were evident on the pathless street. Activity in every open doorway. Scenes mellowed to softness by centuries of repetition. Julie smiled to herself; she would call this chapter of her travelogue 'Where no transistors squawk'. Although she was only about ten minutes' walk from the truck she suddenly felt less secure. She remembered Peter's jesting shouted farewell – 'You'll probably get robbed and raped' and her reply, much more confident than she now felt, 'I should be so lucky.'

There were no street lights as such and even the oil-lit windows which had such a cheerful look, were thinning out as she strode through the little town towards the encroaching desert. Palm trees were perfectly silhouetted against the giant moon. A tethered donkey braying cut into the quietness of the night. Suddenly a strange but familiar smell came to her which reminded her of her first overland – the unforgettable smell of camels, a smell she knew would now accompany them for the two weeks it would take to drive to the outskirts of the Sahara desert. The buildings ebbed and the hard surface of the street gave way to sand, overblown and unswept. She had been walking fairly strenuously for twenty minutes now and was completely out of town. Then she had an eerie feeling that she was being followed. 'Christ,' she thought, Peter would never forgive her if . . . but that's bloody silly, she thought, worrying about how he would feel, how *he* would react to her being raped. How would *she* feel? Probably beaten up and knifed as well! She stopped dead in her tracks. As a child in Norfolk when walking through the woods with her father she had been taught to meet trouble head on – she turned around, she heaved a sigh of relief. Twenty feet behind her she saw clearly in the moonlight the perfect 'Miniature Arab' – a boy of about ten or eleven, for all the world like the shepherd in a kindergarten nativity play. Although she had stopped, the young boy carried on walking towards her and as he passed he reached up to grasp her hand in his with one word, 'Come.'

Mystified but now relaxed, she allowed herself to be pulled gently forward. Rather stupidly, because she felt anything but in charge, she said to the boy, 'Where are we going?'

'I show you,' he replied.

All Julie's audience knew North Africa well and by now she had a captive audience. The little Arab boy pointed into the purple black night where the moon shadows ended. 'You hear it?' he asked. Julie listened intently but could hear nothing. 'See,' he said and he pointed again. She could now just pick out two pinpoints of light. At the same time the hum of an engine. Finally a source of some music but she couldn't recognize the tune. 'See,' said the boy again. 'You wait, it will leave no tracks.'

Julie frowned. 'What? Tracks?' The boy nodded solemnly.

At first the girl thought that the rapidly approaching vehicle was just another 'Mammy Truck', probably having been stuck in the sand and so was a little late getting back to the oasis town. She had even thought about thumbing a lift back to town then she thought that she didn't really want to risk a lift back with a load of Arab males who sounded as if they had been drinking all afternoon. Unusual but what other explanation could there be? She took a couple of steps backwards as if that would distance her from the approaching vehicle, which by now she could see quite clearly in the moonlight. The cab light was on.

This time it was Julie who broke the spell as she looked Harry straight in the eyes. 'Good God,' she gasped 'his bone structure; it was the spitting image of yours.'

'Whose was?' said Harry, taken aback.

'The driver,' replied the girl, 'the driver of the vehicle. His bone structure made him look just like you.'

'That's a good bit,' butted in Peter, 'you didn't even tell me you saw the driver last time.'

'I didn't,' said Julie. 'I mean I didn't tell you, not that I didn't see one.'

'Anyway,' said Peter, 'last time you told me they were all young blokes, not old men.'

'They were.' Julie was beginning to realize how hard it was to explain exactly what she had seen so clearly. 'It's just . . .' She gave up. 'Anyway they had to be Aussies, of that I am certain, like all the pictures you see, with the turned-up bush hats, some of them with beer bottles in their hands, smiling and laughing. Yet, they were wounded I know.'

'Wounded?' queried Harry.

'Yes, I just knew there were wounded soldiers inside and beardless youths in battle dress hanging off the vehicle and drinking beer from funny old-fashioned bottles that had a neck. Do you know the ones I mean?'

'Egyptian Stella beer bottles still have a neck,' said Paul proudly, a confirmation which obviously reassured her as she continued,

'And as it passed I saw a red cross on the side. People hanging on everywhere like a Kenyan Matatu.'

'Tell them what the boy said,' reminded Peter.

'He said "Look, no tracks" – and there weren't! Even as it passed there were no tracks. I saw it quite clearly from the rear – another big red cross on a white background right across the two big rear doors and another little white cross on the differential.'

'That would be the convoy-follow sign,' added Paul knowingly. 'During the war you know, blackout and all that.'

'Tell them what you heard, tell them what you heard, then,' said Peter almost proudly now. A distant look came into Julie's eyes.

'*Waltzing Matilda*,' she said. 'They were singing, they were singing *Waltzing Matilda* as they drove across the desert. It was so real that if the kid hadn't been expecting it, I would have said it was a film crew or something, returning home late. It was all so real. I know the kid was real enough. His last words to me with his hand held out were "Give me one pound".'

From Oliver, 'What's that meant to prove?'

'Well,' said Julie, 'Ghosts don't need to beg surely?'

'I bet wog one's do,' said Paul.

Harry was the first to break up the little party by claiming it was an old man's bedtime. Hasty farewells, and a nod of reassurance to the night watchman and Harry was in his car driving the familiar two miles home, strangely elated and deeply mystified.

During the course of that day he had experienced two – and he searched for the right word in his mind – revelations was too strong and coincidences was too weak. He had been firmly reminded of Tilda twice in one day, when he had rarely thought about her for the past twenty years. Harry thought it through on his way home and concluded that this was no coincidence, something strange was afoot.

He thought again of Oliver's snapshot of the playhouse at the coast. 'Body,' he said to himself, then he thought of Julie's stories – the story of the Bedouin boy, the vehicle that left no tracks in the northern desert, lit up like a Christmas tree 'and Soul' he added, nodding wisely to himself.

Five minutes later he was safe in bed, though he could not sleep. In fact, the more he thought the more worried he became. He shut his eyes and he imagined a skull, his own skull. 'The bone structure was mine?' Harry shuddered involuntarily. The skull in his imagination had rotten flesh and grizzly hair stuck to it. He turned over and told sad stories of the death of kings, 'worms' he said to himself. He hit his head violently, defiantly on the pillow in an attempt to shake out the horror of his imagination. 'But Tilda turning up like that,' he said to himself, 'typical Tilda. So what is there to worry about? Right,' he said to himself, 'if Tilda is about,' and then he thought of an old New Zealand catch phrase 'She'll be right.' With such comforting thoughts he dozed off at last into an old man's restless sleep.

2

The Start

The thought crossed Harry's mind that three score years and thirteen is too 'mzee' to be averaging a hundred clicks down the Mombasa road, but he put the thought aside by reminding himself that one of the still remaining advantages of living in Kenya today is that as a rule the African traffic police do not hassle Mzungus. The cynics, of course, would tell you that this is because the police have learnt from experience that they won't get 'chai' from a white man. Harry still assumed, and again the cynics will say naively, that it was because the police respected the Mzungus and knew that it was very unlikely that a Mzungu would be driving an unroadworthy vehicle. Anyway, Harry told himself, there's no such thing as a top age limit for driving cars in Kenya.

For the first half hour of his journey he desperately tried to evoke such arguments in an attempt to take his mind off his greater problem. The result was a truly confused picture from his vivid imagination. His childhood in the English Midlands flashed past. His first days in Kenya followed them. Anything to stop the terrifying thought that he probably only had hours, let alone days, left to live. It was seven o'clock in the morning after his little dinner party with Paul and Oliver and the two overlanders. 'And Rita,' he added, annoyed at himself for even thinking of the others without mention of her. Then he justified his omission by reminding himself that you don't have to single her out. She subtly dominates everything. She had a charisma which hadn't changed in the forty-odd years he had known her. Harry smiled to himself momentarily. Could he still be in love with her at his age?

Then terror took over his thoughts again. Just over an hour

previously he had suffered a stroke or a heart attack; he didn't even know which, but as he had climbed out of his bath, as he had done every morning for ever, he had felt a stab of pain across his chest. It had got suddenly worse as he stretched for the towel, like a cramp he often got in the calves of his legs but this time in his heart. He couldn't breathe. Gasping for air he stumbled naked to the ground and that was where Joseph found him. As he lay there Harry knew two things instinctively: firstly, he would never of his own free-will go to hospital and if, by a miracle, he got over this attack then a final attack must come again soon.

As he regained a sort of consciousness he knew that his friends and very much his daughter, had she been about, would have been adamant in their insistence that he be rushed to the intensive care unit in the Nairobi hospital. Joseph, his old servant, was seriously concerned. Nearly as old himself he saw the end of an era fast approaching. Joseph was astounded as Harry clawed his way up the dirty clothes basket shakily and with Joseph's help. In fact Joseph spoke the words Harry expected to hear, 'Hospitali, hospitali' was the main theme from Joseph as he lifted his bwana up and into the old bedroom he knew so well, which he had cleaned every day for over a quarter of a century. He pulled Harry's dressing gown off the back of the door and draped it around the old man.

Already Harry's mind was racing in his own imagination. He was fifty-five years, and seven thousand miles away from Nairobi, 1991: it was like the one time he had taken pot. Then as now his mind could not keep up with itself. Now it was flashing like a fast-forward-wind video. He had only taken pot once in his life and that was just to try it out so that he could be on the same wavelength as the younger generation. A mix – he remembered now – a flashing of images.

The last time he was a patient in a hospital – a hospital from a lifetime ago. The thought of those dear distant days not quite beyond recall, when life was fun in summer weather, gave him now a fleeting tiny assurance in the same way that he guessed anyone born and bred in Europe gained reassurance by living amongst ancient buildings, which he himself had not lived amongst for fifty years, yet now he found himself recalling them. The well-trodden cobbles of medieval Munich, the backs at Cambridge, ancient towns strung along the Danube as far as

Budapest whose citizens inherit a purposefulness, and a comfort from the myriads who had passed that way before, radiating an historic warmth sadly lacking in the new towns of today from Sydney to Surbiton, with their megablocks of highrise. Dubai, he thought, precast in a mere four years, from nothing, the typical modern city, sinisterly symmetric: its citizens must yearn for a crooked lane, a mossy bank, a tramcar even.

☆   ☆   ☆

The youthful Harry had been travelling at forty-five miles an hour out of London on the newly-built Barnet by-pass. The motorcycle Harry was riding, and from the tangled remains of which he was carried off to Barnet Cottage Hospital, was another anchor for Harry's teeming, fearful thoughts. At the time he had known that his bike was a secondhand, partly-damaged Brough Superior that he and his cousin had rebuilt, and he also knew that it had previously belonged to some RAF aircraftman who had written a famous book. The writer had been killed on that very bike. It wasn't until many years later, when Peter O'Toole created 'Orance' that Harry became a Lawrence of Arabia fan and avidly read the many biographies about the previous owner of that motorcycle. Even then, he couldn't get completely into *The Seven Pillars of Wisdom*. At the time in question, the bronze head of the Brough, allowing him to cruise at seventy miles per hour all day should the road permit, was of much more interest to him than the philosophy of Lawrence.

An oncoming Luton-bodied furniture van turned across in front of Harry, completely without warning. It was later shown that a decoration, a hanging bauble, in the cab of the furniture van had completely obliterated the oncoming motorcycle from the view of the driver of the van. This incident caused young Harry to start a life-long crusade against hanging ornaments in windscreens. A lifetime later a Nairobi cab driver was surprised when an old man forcibly entered his cab and ripped down no less than three full inflated Christmas balloons that had been effectively blocking out over half the available vision, as they hung from the interior mirror.

Back, by-passing Barnet, Harry swerved violently to his

right in an attempt to miss the van but as he did so the tip of his handlebar grip, not yet of the twist variety, just nicked the rear mudguard of a three-ton tipper truck travelling towards him and threw Harry and his bike into the side of it.

The next thing Harry remembered was a white globe light on the ceiling of the casualty ward of Barnet Cottage Hospital. His first thought on awakening was a terrifying one, that his right hand had been amputated, but it was quickly followed by one of the more wonderful sights of his life to date. Lifting the blanket with his elbow and staring under it, he could just see four pink fingers sticking out from plaster of Paris. He finally emerged from hospital three weeks later, unlike his motorcycle, completely repaired.

When Harry thought about his early motorcycling days such thoughts were invariably followed by what he came to realize was a cornerstone of his fumbling thoughts in metaphysical philosophy – an appreciation of the Web of Destiny, so firmly spun by chance, which meant there could be no such thing as predestination. He thought how he had related both physically and mentally to literally hundreds and thousands of people since that day of his accident. He then asked himself what would have been the situation had his motorbike started at the second kick instead of the third kick that morning so many years ago. And he concluded that the subsequent history of the world would have been altered out of all recognition. Take, for example, the 50,000 people many, many years later Harry took on holiday for a week or two at a time. Imagine where they would have been had they not been with him, and imagine also where those they were with would or would not have been and the infinite variety of different situations which would therefore have occurred. Like the number of grains of sand, doubling up on the chessboard. Each person's life would have thrown waves of difference on every other person they did or did not come into contact with, as a result of Harry's bike starting on the third kick instead of the second. Had it started on the second it would have been a yard or so less far down the Barnet by-pass and would therefore instead of being thrown away from the lorry, would have been thrown under it and Harry would have been killed.

Imagine all the cars and all the bikes of all the world starting or not starting when they did or when they didn't, altering millions of courses of lives and each one trebling up by a million. It looked to Harry like the future could not possibly be predestined as such, and yet on the other hand it was much too complicated to be left to chance. Could any mind alter the web of destiny? He had both read about such theories and discussed them often with his contemporaries. It invariably led to the world-within-world concept and the attempt to understand that all dimensions are infinite.

'No, no, no.' Harry insisted to himself. '*Not* predestination.' Were that theory true, he argued with himself, then every human act, however evil, would be justified. 'The opposite then?' You are the complete master of your destiny? 'I have control' as both rotary and fixed wing skippers confirm as they take command. 'So we help the weaver of the web of destiny – help her weave? Right? – Right?' Harry answered his own doubts, but without conviction: 'And you are not ready for your infinity parade.'

Back to the start of the Mombasa Road already, despite the early hour comfortably full of traffic. He would not go to hospital – why die in a stinking hospital? At least let him die under a panoply of stars, not in the confines of a room, smelling of vomit and sweat.

The first of many potholes, four inches deep and a yard wide, brought him back to the present. Glancing to his left he smiled. What was now a huge industrial area he remembered as old Frank Watson's farm. Harry had sold a Fordson tractor to Frank during his second year in Nairobi. Now there were factories and godowns as far as the eye could see and sadly he noticed them also springing up like mushrooms on the right hand side of the Mombasa road, encroaching on the Nairobi National Park. He sighed, but Nairobi's urban spread was not one of the greatest problems. Nothing like Europe's environmental problems. He remembered an ancient UK uncle telling him how that worthy had milked a cow by hand and how the jets of milk ringing on the bottom of the empty tin bucket could be made to make a tune. 'D' ye ken John Peel' was quoted as being ideal material for maximum effect. Such tranquil yeoman sounds and deeds, where blind concrete cows now stand in

Milton Keynes.

As Harry passed the old Bellevue drive-in cinema site on the outskirts of Nairobi, he was troubled to notice that even at that early hour the demolition squads were already at work. A giant ball, suspended from a giant crane, was already tumbling the massive concrete screen. It reminded him of a giant playing that old bar skittles game that he used to play as a boy, when the ball was suspended from a pole in most of the public bars of the English Midlands. The drive-in cinema, so famed a symbol of the tropical towns of North America and Aussie. Reminiscent of the fifties, across which now-dying screens had flickered so much sadness, so much joy. Now the sprawl of mini-highrise residential monstrosities would take their place instead and the audiences must make do with video on a sixteen inch instead of a fifty foot screen. Then he smiled at his own pomposity. He could almost hear his daughter chiding him. 'Watch it, bwana! Watching vid, in your favourite armchair by the fire in your slippers, is one hell of an improvement to your quality of your life, remember staring through a misty windscreen in a rain-swept drive-in? Even if vid is a bit smaller! I always used to get neckache anyway, and remember how the drive-in 'gents' used to stink in hot weather?' Of course, she couldn't be chiding him; she had been in Australia for the last – Good God – nearly thirteen years, but Harry heard his daughter clearly and he knew that was exactly what she would have said, had she been about.

November, he told himself, is a very good month to tackle the 600-odd klicks from Nairobi to the coast, because the Mombasa Agricultural Show is held in October and most of the potholes are filled in to smooth the way for the presidential escort. In the old days – not the real old days, but when it was all murram – about twelve or fifteen years ago, when Jomo was still alive, the surface would be like a European motorway by late October because if Jomo hit just one pothole, heads would roll. But after twelve years of pragmatic Moi potholes and the collapse of highways were an accepted part of the way of life. In fact potholes were about the only evil it was safe for the man in the street to hate, this he did by stickers in the back of his car 'I – heart crossed out – potholes' – a sign of repressed freedom of speech. Not for the first time Harry realized how much he missed Jomo, a cunning old bugger at times, but nevertheless a

41

great man. Never in his wildest dreams in Mau Mau times thirty-five years before did Harry think he would ever admit to missing Jomo but now in retrospect his death twelve years before did seem like a 'Father Figure' gone.

Surely old Jomo didn't have too much trouble in dying? In bowing out peacefully, mission accomplished? Then suddenly Harry was terrified again as he remembered a mere hour ago when his heart had seemed to stop beating. Now he likened himself to a faltering misfiring petrol engine, about which he could do nothing, going to conk out any minute. Supposing he blacked out now? And so he came back to the old argument with himself, about the safeness or otherwise of old men and women driving, just, he realized, to take his mind off that very problem. Only last month an aging ex-client from Southampton had sent him a cutting from *The Daily Telegraph* which advocated that seventy-five year old wives should keep their hand in at driving so they could still drive themselves about in the statistically probable event of eighty year old chauffeur hubby going first! And what about old Robin down at Voi; he was ten years older than Harry and he still drove himself the hundred miles into Mombasa most weeks, and back the same day after enough whisky sodas to burn out a breathalyser, and what about old George Adamson at Kora? He was doing handbrake turns in his Landie up to the day that he was shot in it! By comparison with those two veteran drivers Harry was an absolute Kijana.

He decided that Kenya, despite many of its appalling road surfaces, and mad drivers, was on the whole a good place to drive. No need to get up so ridiculously early to get to work, as you had to if you lived on the M25 or ten miles out of LA. Come to think of it, he thought, there were quite a few remaining advantages of life in Kenya in the early 90s.

Lord, he thought, one must now add nineteen hundred to the nineties, because there was a lot going on in Kenya in the eighteen hundred and nineties. The Protectorate's birth came later but the lunatic railway line to stamp out the slave trade at the head waters of the Nile – God, how dated that all seemed – who the hell had cared for the head waters of the Nile for the last eighty years? Or the corner of the Empire that the railway was meant to protect.

'Today, today, today,' he said to himself, 'wandering old

fool.'

OK, he thought, for the kids the wide horizons and still the Indian Ocean for holidays. Water-skiing, horse-riding, motor cycle scrambling, learning to fly even. Probably your oppo in UK couldn't afford most of those. It was not necessarily more leisurely – one had to work harder – but then one played harder too.

Then, in an assumed working class accent, he said to himself sarcastically like he had heard so many times before, 'So that the memsahib can enjoy her coffee mornings I suppose?'

But no, he knew it wasn't that. It was so that she could spend more time making the garden a beautiful retreat to improve the quality of life. Then came the same critic's criticism, of the low salary paid to the servants and the economic exploitation. Such starry-eyed idealists, Harry told himself safe in his ripe old age, never seemed to realize that the salaries which the servants did receive were a thousand times preferable to the lack of them if you didn't employ them, so there!

'And in old age, Jasper?' Harry said to himself quoting subconsciously, from a poem long forgotten. Harry was convinced that old age wasn't a particularly pleasant event anywhere, but as you had to endure it, there were plenty of advantages to spending it in Kenya, like what? Like respect. Hooligans in Europe's hypermarkets swirling in the flood of humanity would not think twice about shouldering through the crowd, possibly knocking the elderly out of the way. But the teeming thousands in Africa's townships' streets had a subconscious respect for age which came from their recent tribal past. No matter whether the old people were male or female, black or brown or pink, it was the body that had achieved old age that was important.

Then, of course, there was no need to worry about being cold. There was one big problem, however: sixty per cent of Kenya's population was under fourteen. This meant there were many days when Harry felt that he must be the oldest person in the world. In fact he used jestingly to say that he had to return to Eastbourne once every two years to make sure he wasn't the oldest person in the world! Finally, you could in any case have the best of both worlds, because living in Kenya in 1990 was certainly not like living in a foreign country like Australia just after the Second World War, where if someone emigrated that was it, that was like being dead as far as returning 'home to mum' was concerned.

Today, thought Harry, Europe was just eight hours away from Kenya, and less than a week's pay away at that – return! In fact he thought to himself that if he had mind to travel to London instead of Mombasa he would just have to drive ten miles out to Jomo International which he was now passing and he could be in London about the same time that he would be in Mombasa. So why didn't he? Just jump on a plane to see a Harley Street specialist? He could afford it. No one would miss him. This was a harder question to answer to his own satisfaction. He then realized that in some strange way he was no longer master of his own destiny. It seemed he was being pulled towards the coast. He knew vaguely that the strings were something to do with old Tilda, the new playhouse on Oliver's Mombasa plot, and also connected to the story Julie had told the previous night, but most of all to do with the fact that he was terrified of dying.

He drove automatically; he had been driving all his life. He remembered driving down to the coast with the kids when it was murram. He smiled to himself again. They would play car cricket. 'Your turn, your turn', they would shout with childish enthusiasm. You would take your batting score 'innings' from the make of the first vehicle approaching which you chose, a Volkswagen say. And the two runs for every car and six runs for every truck till you were out which would be when the next Volkswagen approached. This had delighted young Simon when they had been driving to the coast for their 'summer holidays' as they still called the August break. Nicola at that time was still too young to really get the hang of it. These days, Harry told himself, he would make a poor player because he couldn't tell a Nissan from a Honda or a Toyota from a Ford, like European faces to Africans, and African faces to Europeans, 'they all looked alike!'

Reminiscing again he wondered what had happened to the flutes on the side of a Vauxhall bonnet, or the ripples on a Daimler radiator, or the flying A on an Austin, or an illuminated W on the Wolseley that his father had had before the war, and the Flying Standard? the Union Jack on the Standards! But any person of his age could reminisce for ever on the lost identity of most vehicles. 'Belt up,' he told himself, 'you're being boring again. All right,' he said to himself, 'but anybody may have been able to recognize cars in the old days and not now but I bet they didn't do what I did the other day.' One of those shutter-covered front headlight jobs, Porsche probably. Anyway, he thought he saw it overtake the car ahead on a fast road and was just about to do the same thing himself when suddenly, thank God, he noticed it wasn't going, it was coming, but with the headlights shuttered its front looked like its back should have done. He had had to pull in very quickly. 'There, that proves it. You're senile, you can't even recognize a car coming towards you. You shouldn't be driving along here at this speed.' His arguments swayed backwards and forwards. Anything to get away from thinking about the happenings of the previous hour. 'OK clever bonce. In a twelve-valve four-cylinder car is it the exhaust or inlet valves that are doubled up? Don't know, do you?' And yet only five years back he claimed he knew the purpose of every tiny part, every nut and bolt that made up a Toyota, every single part listed in the parts manual.

He could remember working on sleeve-valve Willis Knights, filing tappet adjustments on Ford V-8s, working on De Dion back axle adjustments, scraping white metal bearings, Bendix brakes! Oh, Harry knew it all in the old days. Now he couldn't recognize one car from another. He wouldn't begin to know how you made a car burn clean fuel. But had all that made life worth living? Had his intimate knowledge of motor vehicles improved the quality of life? No, he supposed it hadn't but at least it allowed him to drive automatically as he had been doing for decades.

Then he was worried again. Christ, he thought, my whole life is flashing past like they say it does when you are drowning. No, it isn't, I'm doing it on purpose. Think of your very, very first memory. He did so and as he thought he knew it wasn't his first memory, but he also knew that it was what he always described as his first memory. Nanny with a safety pin, pinning a scarf around his chest, then carrying him out into the cold raw November afternoon in a house he was staying in, to lift him shoulder-high to see the striking Welsh miners marching past on their way from the valleys to London. Harry later learned that many of his contemporaries had drawn their political views from those Depression days symbolized by the marching miners. The gas-lit rooms of his grandmother's house at Christmas, the roasted chestnuts in the fire, the way the great-aunts covered up their mahogany wireless set like a parrot at night by shrouding it in green baize before they took their candles, yes, candles, to bed. Young Henry was later conscious of the fact that he was brought up among privilege. His grandfather kept maids in the attic and coal in the cellars of his large Victorian house perched on a hill overlooking the Grand Union Canal that in Harry's childhood still had horse-drawn barges for God's sake, and then a few years later, there was the dismal blare of the fog sirens and the beat of the new motor engines on board the barges, and skating round them when they were frozen in.

Harry's grandfather had been almost like a Galsworthy grandfather. He really didn't know what the world was coming to. With the carnage of the First World War so recently behind him the mystified old man could offer little philosophical advice to his young grandson, so instead would help him to string willows into bows, and find him lead tips for the arrows, and chicken feathers to bind on to the arrows' tails. The shadow of the Great War, as it was called then, when the barbarians had invaded France for the second time in a generation, loomed over them in Harry's childhood days. There were still gaps – uncles who had not returned. Nanny herself had stopped mentally and sexually in 1916 when her soldier-boy had been killed. Nanny was typical of the First World War widows and of the girls who had seen a whole generation of boys wiped out. Nanny was always indignantly quoting 'And what good came of it, said little Peterkin. Sixty thousand of our boys for a hundred yards of mud, and now all these strikes and unemployment . . .' That was Nanny by day. Nanny by night still wept tears for George whom she had known for just two weeks before he went to Passchendaele. Stolen kisses by the gasworks as cloth-capped young men left in their hundreds of thousands in troop trains never to return, leaving behind a hundred thousand spinsterhoods for life. Their fantasies were based on perhaps two weeks of passionate friendship. Yet the boys had had no regrets; mostly they were actually pleased to be going. From his Nanny the young Harry learned the geography of Picardy, the rivers, the villages, the ridges, the woods even, that were the backdrop to so great a

46

tragedy. He knew the details of most of Haig's big pushes. Later, based on this early knowledge, Harry became quite an authority on the psychology of 'going over the top' and of the First World War in general. He drew his own conclusions from uncles who did return, and from their friends, about the crazy motivations and confused values of the massed armies. On 'going over the top' for example Harry had learnt that by far the worst alternative for the troops was to stay behind in the trench and *not* go over the top, then they would be shot as a coward, but if one *did* go over one had three opportunities. The first was that your number was on the bullet, in which case you would be joining the vast majority; one had to die one day and like the Persian kings of old, a death shared by thousands was a death a thousand times lessened in its horror. The second possibility was a 'Blighty' wound, and just hope it wasn't too bad a one, and the delight of three or six months of convalescence at home. The third possibility, though not necessarily the best one was to come through the offensive unscathed. Eleven out of seventeen did, but then they had to go through it all again at the next big push.

As a child Harry listened to his few uncles that did 'outlive the day and come safe home' talk of the useless carnage of the Western Front. They each finally concluded that 'they wouldn't give you tuppence for a sackful of glory'. One effect of being born in the shadow of the First World War in the shires of England and participating as a youth in the Second World War, was to make one an eternal optimist because later, as a middle-aged man, when columnists and pamphleteers and many folk he mixed with suggested that the world would soon be coming to an end, so terrible they suggested were things at the present, he had only to look back on a time when 60,000 Brits and 30,000 Germans or even 100,000 Jews were being killed every day.

Twenty years on, and he would see for himself a flicker of glory returning to war as the deaths of three or four hundred of 'The Few' could be said to have saved the world from a second Dark Age. Not forgetting his own heroic moment . . . shades of glory! As a Desert Rat parading through the streets of Hanover in 1945, the triumphant celebrations at the end of the longest advance in the whole history of, not just the Second World War – but of *all* war. From El Alamein to The Elbe, the heartland of the Hun. As the massed bands of pipe and drum led the victors through the ruined city, Harry felt that good had triumphed over evil. He was near bursting with pride.

Harry was by now recalling what mainly gave sheer delight in those distant days: unimportant, inexpensive things like toy lorries that steered; bright red Triang toy cranes, and trains, and snakes and ladders, and later L'Attaque and Alma found in the attic, the Edwardian children's board games named after the Crimea battle. He remembered also his grandmother reading him *Doctor Dolittle* from a rocking chair under an apple tree in the garden and begging for just one more chapter to be read aloud, and cigarette cards of cricketers, and boats, and of match box tops. Those were the things of which his life was made. The weekly winter bath: every time he smelt paraffin stoves for fifty years after that he would remember the paraffin stove in the bathroom of his grandmother's house and the smell which was so associated with it. Tin baths in front of the fire had just been replaced with a bathroom in the elevated social circles into which Harry was born. Tin baths were to remain with the lower classes for another thirty years. On occasion the gas-powered geyser would explode as his grandmother tried to light it. On one occasion he and his grandmother had seldom laughed so much in their lives when the old lady rushed out of the bathroom after an explosion of the geyser with her face covered in black soot. 'Lord, Henry, I look like a nigger minstrel.' That was the first reference Harry had heard to black men, who were later to so fill his life.

Only last week he had read in a UK Sunday paper that a box of station personnel staff from a Hornby train set, well-preserved, mind you, had been auctioned for £1,300. Harry could still see the 1/6d price written on the back of the box which contained his model railway station staff which he had loved so much, but he knew inflation stories are tedious even to contemporaries.

'So what' he said, 'so what. What good, what purpose, what reason, why, why, why, why am I to die? Who am I? Why am I? Am I? Yes, I think, therefore I am.'

Harry swerved violently to miss a forty-seater bus with eighty people on board, hurtling into Nairobi. 'Think on the comfort those old arguments of philosophy with Paul and Rita used to give you years ago.' Logic demands that we all sit in the infinite, no end to size, no end to space, no end to smallness. Suns are obviously atoms of a large complex, and atoms suns of a smaller one, but large and small are meaningless words in the context of the infinite as are the thoughts 'older' and 'younger!' Time in the infinite cannot advance which, of course, is irrefutable proof that one must live for ever.

Such abstract thoughts induced no comfort in him now, perhaps he could review this concept later, he thought, but by this time tomorrow, something was telling him, he would be a corpse. 'Oh, come on,' he said to himself. 'This is the old Mombasa road you know so well and this is now. Do you remember the first time you drove down it? In Tilda, about 1956 that would be. With Jenny and Simon before even Nicky was born.' The Kenya Meat Commission factory was belching white smoke onto the Athi Plains in the same way then as it was now. Then there was hardly a building in the twenty miles between Nairobi and the little village of Athi. Now there seemed to be factories, airports, assembly plants, on either side of the road nearly all the way. Then, the tarmac stopped about fifty clicks out, at the Machacos turning and didn't start again till about ten clicks out of Mombasa just before the causeway, apart from that little stretch at Mackinnon Road where they had two or three miles of tarmac, and it was only the other day that he found out why. Mackinnon Road, threequarters of the way to Mombasa from Nairobi, was a Royal Army Ordnance collection depot when they entrained armaments up from the Mombasa Docks and collected them at Mackinnon Road, on the way to Nairobi from the Ethiopian campaign of 1940.

The Mombasa road is a corridor in the true sense of the word, down that narrow strip from Nairobi to Mombasa there is firstly the train track which started from the mangrove swamps of Kilindini in 1896 and reached Nairobi in 1899. Then, as well as that track there was the original caravan track for trade with the interior down which a million slaves had passed, and is now the splendid tarmac road, and then the powerlines, and even a pipeline, carrying up the liquids from the port, particularly petrol and diesel which has done away with one nightmare – the numerous tankers, the bodies of many of which can still be seen at the bottom of most of the steep gradients, lying rusting in the bundu. So there you have it; cars, trucks, trains, electric cables even, and now telephone transmitter beacons on every hill replace the telegraph poles, there is also the light aircraft corridor, all of which pass over or through or under that same narrow stretch of the 320 miles' length from Nairobi to the sea.

Harry could remember his son's first 'cross country' pilots' navigator training, when he had had trouble in finding Sultan Hamud. Harry then remembered many an aeronautical tale when early visitors had actually landed on the Mombasa road and thought nothing of it. Then there had been no landing strips and only a tiny amount of road traffic. Now it was different. Usually 300 tourists in a Jumbo overhead once an hour and transports hurtling north and hurtling south all day and all night.

☆   ☆   ☆

When Harry tried to recall details about himself as an English prep school boarder, and later as an English public schoolboy, he had at first drawn a blank. Then he recalled that in his school days he had been a coward. He also recalled the day that he had stopped being a coward but that came much later. He must save that happy day, and thinking about it, for later or his life's story would be over halfway to Mombasa. And that, he knew, would never do. Then he remembered that while he had been thinking about those very early Christmases he had forgotten altogether about the boxing glove incident. Perhaps that did come later, at least the significance of it did.

Of his many long years of boarding school life in the England Midlands in the early thirties the part about it that Harry hated the most was the awful confinement of prep schools. In those days the children never left the school grounds from when they arrived at the beginning of term till they departed at the end of term. It was like being in a prison. He knew that to thousands of boys and girls of his age, the most glorious sight that they remembered as children was when the trunks appeared from their storage at the school, for packing up for the holidays. Four months' joy and eight months' agony seemed to make most of those children grasp what was going in later life with both hands. They were both eager and appreciative when at last the ordeal was over. Harry reluctantly admitted to himself that he probably did enjoy the last year

50

and a half of his schooling. Then came a super year, apprenti-
ceships, motor cycles, and then came the war.

'Hold it, hold it. What about God and girls?' God? Twice a
day chapel, three times on Sunday, for all of his four public
school years, had half killed God for him and most of his
contemporaries. Next came a formative youth being drafted
into the army together with half the rest of the world in the
Second World War. In those impressionable years talking to
Mohammedans, Buddhists, Catholics, Communists – seemed
to kill the other half of the weak dogmatic God that he had
been presented with, and which had penetrated his mind so
slightly. Maybe there was once, just once, during a Christmas
carol service echoing over the quadrangle: the innocent treble
voices of the public schoolboys on a snowy December night,
maybe once God knocked, but the holidays were imminent and
only creepers like Harley and Co thought about God in the
hols and those boys born of parents already in Holy Orders had
little choice.

It was eight ten am. The southbound milestone. 'Huh.'
Harry half laughed aloud. 'Milestone' – a misnomer indeed for
a kilometre tin sign on an iron post, that would have deserved
and received a gentle tease from Nicky. 'Fossil, fossil.' Years
ago Nicky was always accusing Harry of being a fossil before
she had married, that was, and settled in Oz. 'All right, click
post, reads MBS for Mombasa, 475. S/H Sultan Hamud,
seventy-five clicks. Well, clicks assumed, OK.' He replied to
the non-existent voice of his daughter.

'Well, twenty minutes to Sultan Hamud. Must be time for
"The Bargees and the Toff".' Incredibly Harry was annoyed
with himself for putting so sarcastic a label on to so sincere an
instant of his childhood. 'Christ, sixty bloody years.' He still
hadn't told anybody, not a soul, not even Jenny. 'Oh come on,'
he said to himself, 'anyone would have thought you had
murdered her instead of screwed her.' He held back again. 'All
right, all right, admit you've played it through every time in
your life when you have wanted to turn yourself on. This time,
this last time, let's have it as it really was.' Pat, the bargee's
daughter, would have been a star guest indeed had Harry been
famous enough to warrant a *This is Your Life* show on television. God, he thought, she would be well over seventy by now
too! As the seventy-five clicks to Sultan Hamud reduced to

51

sixty-five he got his childhood erotic scene into some sort of perspective.

Harry's grandfather, towards the end of his life, often used to delight in quoting a travelogue book which his father had given him as a boy. 'Luton – small straw hat-producing village, nearest market town Leighton Buzzard.' Being proud of his immediate environment he would then go on to lecture anyone who would listen. 'In fact, if the Rothschilds hadn't bought Mentmore Towers, and they very nearly didn't – I'm told, the old fellow fancied a place down in Wycombe, but the son, that is the present lord, fancied the Mentmore hounds, so they did, buy it I mean. But if they hadn't then there wouldn't have been any pressure on the track-layers and Bletchley Junction would have been right here, and Wolverton railway works, shouldn't wonder.' One had to assume from his tone that such a course would have been a disaster beyond comprehension. As it was, even Leighton Buzzard station was in Linslade, well outside the town and so the old market town was left to decay, despite the fact that the Grand Union Canal and the main LMS line crossed in the middle of it.

The voice from Nicky in Australia broke into his thoughts again, 'You're being a fossil again, Bwana'. 'All right, all right. The British Railways line to Scotland from Euston – you've heard of Euston, I suppose? It's in London. And the Grand Union Canal? It's still called that, isn't it?' This last sentence to shut up the unspoken criticism. Harry knew again that was exactly what his daughter would have said. Ha, what the hell, get on with it. OK. When Harry was around twelve years old – he always stayed during the school 'hols' at his grandmother's and grandfather's huge house – the very essence of the Victorian era set on a hill in Linslade on the outskirts of Leighton Buzzard, Bedfordshire. God, he hadn't thought of the actual name and address for sixty years. Stoke Road could clearly be seen from 'The Elms' attic window. By the time he stayed there the last of the chambermaids had vacated her accommodation in the roof and young Harry had spent many a happy hour watching the world go by from her one-time window. The farm machinery business which his grandfather ran had been hit by the depression as had most industries all around the world. The attic of Harry's childhood was filled not with saucy white-capped maids but with Victorian memorabilia. There came to mind an electric machine in a wooden box to cure God knows what, two huge brass handles that you were meant to grasp as if you were sitting in an electric chair, and somebody cranked the magneto to send an electrical shock, a remedial medical electric shock, through your body. So what? So, said Harry to convince himself, that was the only electrical gadget in the whole house. Even in 1932, right? Grandfather, he remembered, would not be connected to the mains, even though it would only have cost him half-a-crown an outlet. It was too dear. Anyway, grandfather insisted gas gave a much healthier light.

From the attic window, . . . and now Harry realized he was searching for detail from the past to keep his mind off the present, and to take himself back, back to try and find a clue. 'Jesus H,' he said to himself, 'if Socrates and Descartes couldn't find it, how the hell do you expect me to?' 'No harm in trying,' he argued with himself. Even in his new-found truth Harry couldn't remember exactly how he had felt when he had first met his first love, how sadly he smiled to himself still. Their difference in station was extreme, yet their zest for life was equal enough. She, the eldest of six children, and only just twelve, lived in the *Barnaby Rudge*, a motorized longboat, out of Manchester. Temporarily undergoing engine repair, and docked just outside the Linslade Lock complete with its load of coal. Another barge that had departed from Berkhamsted to tow it onwards was also running late because one of the children on that barge had had to be rushed to Hemel Hempstead with acute appendicitis. The twelve year old Pat and her bargee family had therefore been living in the stationary barge within sight of 'The Elms' in Stoke Road, when young Harry was spending his Easter holidays there.

Harry's grandmother and several of the other ladies in the neighbourhood had a good thing going with the landlady of the towpath pub. They let it be known that they would offer three shillings a day to any of the bargee women who wished to do a day's laundry and these worthy wives had little problem in persuading their husbands to stay around for a couple of extra days with the towpath pub being so handy.

The Jolly Bargee, was both the name of the public house and a well-suited adjective for Pat's mum who was 'doing' for Harry's grandmother. One day her small daughter Pat traipsed up the hill into the garden of the big house. There followed a whole week of clandestine meetings. Pat was a normal typical twelve year old girl, brought up in the hard school of a large family and a small income, unlikely enough material for erotica. Carrot-coloured hair tumbled down to half cover a carbolic soap-scrubbed clean, freckled face, and a tomboy figure not yet a woman's. The solitary boy was earnestly in need of company and the girl was equally in need of the solitude that could be found in the massive house away from her Ma and Pa and her five siblings packed into the four berths of the stationary barge. In fact she later decided that it was the strange security of all that space which had excited her sexually. Harry's grandfather was always in his Leighton Buzzard office till the evening hours, listening to the many reasons why his salesmen were unable to sell the latest Massey Reaper on which he had pinned such hopes.

Pat's mother was at the other end of the house singing as she scrubbed the laundry. Grandmother, too, had popped out to visit one of Harry's aunts who was married to a bank manager and who lived conveniently enough 'down the lane'.

Ten o'clock on a perfect spring morning in 1932, young Harry and his girl friend were chasing each other all over the huge empty house. 'Hey, you ain't allowed in 'ere. I'm on the can,' as Harry pulled up short at the half-open door of the extravagant Edwardian lavatory. The littlest room in his house was, as Pat later told him, about as big as the biggest room in which she lived on the barge, with her family. The high cistern, with chain hanging like a bell rope, was engraved, the closet itself was decorated with grey scrolls of fern, and for a seat in true commode fashion, highly polished mahogany. Something made Harry pull the door open and peep. The twelve year old Pat was perched on the very edge. Her off-white pants in a ring round her sandalled, stockingless feet, a foot off the ground. 'Mind you don't fall in,' Harry laughed.

The innocent Harry noticed a strange or rather different look in Pat's eyes as she jumped off the seat. Then, waddling in an exaggerated form, with her pants still round her ankles she tottered out onto the long passage. As she passed Harry she grabbed his hand and led him down the passage through the next door which led into the gigantic bathroom. Both rooms were at the end of the longest passage that Pat ever imagined could exist. The sun's rays were streaming in the bathroom window illuminating the pink roses on the wallpaper. There was also a white painted screen, Harry seemed to remember. Harry had in fact been remembering that bathroom scene for sixty long years. Almost as if in a tussle the girl pulled Harry down on top of her. Harry was fascinated and he enjoyed the feeling but was totally ignorant of what was going on. Well-educated, middle-class English boys of the thirties knew, to use the euphemism of the day, exactly where babies came from, what they weren't quite so sure about was how they got there. With curiosity rather than sexual desire he noticed the slit between the girl's legs. He rather surprised himself by enjoying her tongue licking his lips which he soon opened. The girl undid Harry's belt and pulled his shorts down. 'Come on' she said, 'come on.' Then angrily, 'I thought you said I was to be your girlfriend,' to which Harry replied,

'Oh yes, oh yes, please be, please.'

In retrospect Harry presumed he must, at that time of his life, have been unable to orgasm but the girl certainly was able to. The thought of that sweet innocent child clinging to his ignorant body, sixty years ago, despite the fact that little more happened, was one of the most erotic thoughts that Harry could conjure up through all of his later life. When he still looked mystified as the body under him started jerking and the girl sat up saying still rather crossly, 'Haven't you ever seen your Ma and Pa at it?' Harry didn't admit it but even when they had both been alive he had never seen his mother and father in the same bed nor anyone else for that matter. A lifetime later Harry found himself frowning. The line between the perverted and the normal is both flexible and fine. Shouldn't he perhaps fantasize over a voluptuous whore, rather than a little girl? *'Honi soit qui mal y pense'* thought Harry with a vengeance. For the Harry on the Mombasa road it was not the childishness that held the erotica but the simplicity and the pleasure of the female dominance, and he the privileged partner.

Sultan Hamud sixty-five. What next? He passed Machacos's turn in his new Corolla at about 170 kilometres an hour. Back

to earth, back to Kenya with a bounce. Some authority had laid a water main across the Mombasa road leaving a trench about three inches deep and two foot wide but he didn't even brake and his Corolla rode over it with the ease of a point to point race horse.

The piston rings for the broken-down Lister engine on the Grand Union barge stranded at Linslade Lock turned up the day after Harry and Pat's lovemaking efforts. Now, a romantic and less innocent Harry promised Pat he would put a candle in the attic window every night he spent at his grandparents' house in the future so that when she passed that way again she would know that he was waiting for her. And he did, right up to his grandfather's death in 1936. For a split second Harry returned to the present and remembering his closeness to death tried desperately to clothe Pat for his final thoughts of her – but she would not be clothed.

The final footnote to Harry's first sexual experience was in the late sixties. On her fiftieth birthday Pat found herself in a Greenline coach going to visit her married daughter who had moved to the new town of Hemel Hempstead. The fifty-year-old housewife noticed that she was passing through Leighton Buzzard, and with a smile she decided to alight, the better to look at the old house on the hill and spent an hour till the next coach – Linslade Lock revisited . . . . That very week 'The Elms' was in the process of being demolished to make way for a highly undesirable housing estate! The beams of the roof were still there, skeleton-like, as the tiles had been removed. The attic window was still in its frame. As she looked up, Pat felt tears coursing down her cheeks, 'God Almighty, what an underprivileged childhood I did have. A bloody bargee's daughter,' she said to herself, 'but by God, I would not have had any part of it any other way.'

☆   ☆   ☆

Harry slowed for an empty trailer returning to Mombasa from Kigali, he could quite clearly see from the number plates. But he himself was returning from Linslade, Leighton Buzzards, Beds.

Looking back on it all, Harry began to realize how much his life had changed, as a child, in so very short a time. By the time young Harry had had his first love affair with the freckled nymph of the barge he was already an orphan, hence the time spent with his maternal grandparents. His father had died suddenly of a cerebral haemorrhage when Harry had been ten and his mother died shortly after, giving birth to a still-born child.

Sympathy naturally poured on the young only child, now orphaned. After that double tragedy, but even at the time, let alone later, Harry really couldn't claim to have suffered as much as one would have expected. He presumed that he loved his parents but he was never close to his mother and later he realized that he never really knew his father. In fact, he had to admit that he had shed more tears when he had learnt that his nanny had been given notice – 'and a sack to put it in,' as she said, about eighteen months before his father had died, when he had first been sent to boarding school. When Harry was called up ten years after his father's death, there were soldiers in his barrack rooms that still used Rolls Razors. The characteristic clack clack of those were the only effect which had really reminded him of his father who used one till the day he died. His talk to his father about razors was one of the few conversations he could recall their ever having had together.

A few years later, a sad one as he recalled, his first year in the great public school system of England, he wrote his first short story 'Lion Rampant' for his house magazine – a veritable masterpiece for a fourteen year old, they said, describing how, with the restraints of parents lifted, one could become rampant, and didn't have to worry about their restrictions which might hold one back. Because of their early demise, so the story went, it meant that your average orphan would have less problems than those with parents still alive who required looking after. An orphan's lifestyle could be completely as they wanted it. A faulty argument, one presumes, but Harry held it sincerely enough and he certainly didn't arrive at that conclusion from any bitterness or lack of sympathy. Harry had felt very sorry for both of his parents who had died so young, such a waste, but he didn't feel any great sorrow for himself. He had, after all, five of the ten uncles whose name was apparently not written on any Boche bullet and who had therefore returned safe home from France. They had families, boys and girls, cousins who almost vied amongst themselves to look after poor

Meg and Stan's boy.

Then there was £6,000 inheritance – an absolute fortune before the Second World War, a part of which was spent on Harry's education. In fact, this access to large amounts of money at an early age probably affected him more than the untimely death of his parents. Spending so much time with his grandparents on his own also moulded his character. They didn't exactly spoil him by over-indulgence but certainly afforded him a more mature environment. A more staid environment, yet with few restrictions which gave Harry a feeling of responsibility above his years, a trait which, he now realized, he had passed on to his son who was ordering men around at fifteen, with no embarrassment to the men and no hang-ups for him.

Harry's childhood holidays of riverbanks and meadows, of barge houses on the towpaths, of bicycles and cinemas, of boarding school and holidays sped past. Now, as Sultan Hamud appeared on the kilometre sign but from which he was still some thirty kilometres away, Harry tried one of the hardest feats of all, when it comes to remembering. One can usually easily recall instances, but very seldom can one recall the atmosphere in which the acts took place, one's hopes or fears at the time. People will say, 'I remember the day I learned to ride a bike' or 'I remember the day war broke out' and so they do, but few will recall with honesty how they felt on that day, of what they were afraid might happen on the next. To recall an incident was hard enough: to recall his emotions Harry found it harder still. He was now trying to remember the second year of the Second World War.

3

Birth and Christening

Harry was in Coventry on the night of November 15th, 1940. Many a detail of that night had stayed with him and he had recounted it often, like the steering wheels being too hot to handle, even with gloves on, as he attempted to drive vehicles out of the burning assembly lines. Of a picture of *The Haywain* in the boarding house he was staying in falling off the wall two nights *after* the raid and waking him in terror from the first sleep he had had in over sixty hours, but how the people he met and how he himself felt Harry found impossible to recall. He would keep remembering instances which hadn't happened at the time at all, but which he had seen on the newsreels, much later, in the fifties, and again, on television, in the sixties when the official reaction was being sought by historians. He certainly didn't appreciate the fact then and he was fairly sure that nobody else he knew did, that Britain, on that November night, was exactly halfway through the time when she stood alone against the combined Axis might, from the fall of France the previous June to the entry of Russia into the war the next April. There was comradeship, there was valour, there was cheerfulness, 'Cheer up mate, there's worse troubles at sea' or 'It must get better, it can't get any worse'.

Harry had been on a welding course the summer that war broke out, so now he found himself, and he wasn't quite sure whether he was sorry or not, in a reserve occupation by day, and a Fire Warden attached to the Civilian Fire Station, by night. Many of his contemporaries had returned from the British Expeditionary Force via the Dunkirk beaches and were now on various training schemes in the Yorkshire Moors or the Highlands of Scotland. Something in him couldn't help but associate that corner of France behind Belgium which the British Expeditionary Force had retreated from, with the same piece of land wherein so much greater carnage had occurred and decimated so many families, including his own, only twenty-four short years before. In 1940 girls certainly didn't look askance at a healthy young man not being in uniform, as they had done in the First World War. There was no white feather nonsense but occasionally he had to reassure himself that there were probably more firemen than soldiers being killed in the UK in those months since there was no fighting on any front.

Vital war workers in reserved industries – Harry tugged his memory chords in earnest – were they respected or not? He was working at the time in a hastily thrown together corrugated iron lean-to, outside the main Austin car factory in Coventry, electrically welding petrol jerrican holders to three-ton Army general purpose trucks. Thinking back about it, he wasn't even sure if the jerrican as such, that he had lived with every day of the last thirty years, had even been invented, let alone named, at the beginning of the war. As far as he remembered, it turned up in North Africa with Yanks and Jeeps. Well, whatever – tool boxes, tow bar brackets, shovel brackets, those little round disks he remembered clearly – he didn't even know what they were for at the time and later found out they were the bridge weight number disks. Racks, for rifles, and all the other requirements the infantry had to hook onto the outside of their troop carriers.

Harry welded such brackets to the trays of Austin army lorries from eight o'clock in the morning till six o'clock at night, with only half an hour off for lunch, 'dinner' as everybody called it, at the Lord Woolton; not a pub, but a sarcastic name given to the British Restaurants after their founder, the Minister of Food, Lord Woolton. He remembered experiencing the warm affinity of everybody being in the same boat and noticing not a little pride on every face. Before the war, for example, even though work was hard to get, few would have stuck it out in an unheated open lean-to in November, but now his fellow workers just kept on their overcoats, gloves even on the particularly cold days. A 'Britain can take it' spirit was at large. People didn't really appreciate that they were the goodies fighting the evil Nazis. At that time it was just a bitter national defence against the onslaught of Germany, but despite it all life was for the most part enjoyable. Many years later when one of the safaris that Harry was taking got bogged down in bottomless mud and several clients had to sleep in the truck without an evening meal, one of the elder Brits who was with the group, said to Harry, 'Don't worry, I haven't enjoyed myself so much since the Battle of Britain' and Harry knew exactly what the client meant.

It was already dark as Harry left work at six o'clock that November evening, raining too. He crossed the road to the bus stop in company with a fellow worker who lived in the same suburb in the Holbrooks area. 'How are you getting on then, young Harry? Finished off those water carriers I saw you working on yet?'

'Yeah – on troop carriers now' almost proudly. The rain dropped off his cap peak on to the back of a woman in front of him in the eternal queue. Then the ghostly blacked out bus appeared – two tiny pin points of light in the dark November evening.

Harry just got on to the bus to hear the conductor say, 'That's it,' which meant that his co-worker had been left behind for the next bus.

Harry immediately jumped off to make room for his mate. 'You've got a wife waiting for you,' he said and his mate jumped on in Harry's place.

'Oh, very civil of you, young Harry. Ta muchly. See you tomorrow then,' as the bus pulled away leaving Harry at the head of the queue for the next one. But the weaver of the web of destiny was also working overtime that night. Harry never saw that co-worker again, for that night Field Marshal Goering unleashed the biggest air raid on any one city in the history of aerial bombardment to date, including Warsaw and Rotterdam.

He remembered he had high tea served by his tireless landlady who seemed to have four children at her heels both day and night, her husband having been called up. Two beautiful kippers, Harry remembered them well, surprisingly fresh, he thought, considering they were about as far from the sea as it was possible to get in the British Isles.

As he left the table in his boarding house the air raid siren warning wailed out. It droned in the night as the first wave of the Luftwaffe bombers were directly over Coventry. The searchlight batteries latticed the sky, the crump of the anti-aircraft guns was non-stop. Before the end of the war Harry had learnt that ack-ack, as they called the anti-aircraft guns, only accounted for a tiny proportion of aircraft destroyed. The guns were fired all night, however, for two purposes. Firstly, to discourage dive bombing and to keep the enemy airplanes as high as possible, but more importantly, to boost civilian morale as citizens lay in their beds and heard the guns, they had the feeling that they were fighting back at the raiders. Harry's first fire call was only a little way up the street from where he worked by day. 'Bit early for work, eh Harry,' joked his fire chief who knew that Harry worked in that area. They were not particularly successful in putting out that early fire which had mainly been caused by incendiaries, which were always dropped first to mark the target for the high explosives which were carried by the following waves of bombers. As the firemen rolled out the red fire engine's hoses towards the hydrant for connection and the water started pouring on the flaming buildings, the silhouette looked like a set-piece of latter-day symbolism of the Blitz of London and other cities. Two black tin-helmeted firemen held a hose and jetted water at tumbling masonry, the red inferno lighting the sky behind it. Walls tumbled within yards of the firemen. The fire chief attempted to open a huge iron gate set in a burning wall, leading into a large cavern of a factory. As it was jammed he axed it open, shouting, 'Come on, we can save some from this end anyway.' He ran into the smoke calling for help to push out some of the vehicles at the end of an assembly line. Four men answered his call and two or three vehicles were rolled out through the gate into the open area by the fire engine. As they rushed back for more a beam crashed right on top of the chief, killing him instantly. His number two called off the hopeless fight. The fire was by now well out of control. 'Come on lads, we can do more good down the road.' Off they drove to fight another fire.

Standing on an empty black tarmac car park lit by the blood-red glow of the burning factory and a burning Coventry behind that, which could be seen, it was said, from over fifty miles away, still wet from the firemen's hoses which had sprayed it to cool it, one of the huge red crosses on her side blistered, is what can best be described as a newly born Army ambulance. The first sounds she heard were the engines of the Junker Ju 88s as they flew back to France with empty bomb racks, and the wail of the 'all clear' siren echoing across the English Midlands as Coventry burned.

Not far out of Sultan Hamud the magic of the Kenyan Bundu was helping to calm Harry's terror as the Corolla's speedo hung around 160 kilometres an hour. Harry actually smiled to himself – 100 *miles* per hour! None of the Europeans would ever think in metric, although miles and gallons had been banished with colonialism. Often from about where he was on the Mombasa road now, one could see Kili itself but today, it being a little overcast, the giant was clothed in cloud. In that direction he could see the nearer Chyulu Hills, huge and gentle. No one could be gloomy for long if they are surrounded by Kenya's vast horizons and the sun is shining. Well, the sun wasn't shining, but at least it wasn't raining.

A wealth of local memories well up – the time the front suspension collapsed on a Singer Vogue whilst he was doing a recce for the Safari Rally; the time his son Simon had run out of fuel flying back from Lamu and he and Jenny had rushed down with four drums of av gas to an embarrassed Simon who had had to put down at the landing strip at Sultan Hamud. Harry fought desperately to keep the order right. Those early days in Kenya were fifteen years ahead of wartime Britain but as anyone over fifty will know, the fewer years one has ahead the more one cherishes the memories of those behind. Harry was over seventy and the memories came flooding back. From Coventry, November 1940, to Port Said, December 1941, try as he might, Harry could only recall very little. He could remember the Bordon, Hampshire, training camp, the first time he had actually slept for any length of time south of London.

The troopship voyage through submarine-infested waters from Southampton via Gibraltar where they welcomed in the New Year 1941 was all in clear focus. He could even remember the name of the Australian sergeant who was talking to them the first day they landed in North Africa, Sergeant Neville. Four of them were sitting at a street-side café in Port Said, Harry and two fellow Royal Army Service Corps drivers whose name he had forgotten. They were still extremely excited at the magic of the North African town. It was a Sunday afternoon, Harry remembered, and they were experiencing the delights of mint tea at the pavement café. Sergeant Neville was in the Australian Medic Reserves and he was drinking beer. The sergeant put down his glass of Stella beer and said, 'Well, the beer don't get any better,' in his huge Australian drawl, 'and I'll swear that the bints in there haven't changed since last time,' nodding to an upstairs window. Harry listened enthralled as the ANZAC history unfolded. Sergeant Neville, now forty-four years old and admitting to thirty-nine of them, had actually trained in Alexandria twenty-six years previously as a tender and eager recruit on his way to Gallipoli.

It is the scents, the aroma of North Africa that you always remember best. The excitement of the bazaars of Alexandria and Cairo, the exotic belly dancers. Life for Harry at that time was the best he had ever known. He didn't even begin to guess this at the time. He would have hotly denied it, if anyone had suggested it, just like when adults tell children that their schooldays are their happiest. He grumbled about the filth and the smells and the lazy wogs with the rest, but a part of him fell in love with the eternity that is Egypt. Even after he left the fleshpots of Port Said and Cairo and was encamped in the desert he could still remember that all was extremely well with the world. The basics of barrack room life pleased him. He was a soldier in the great tradition of fighting men like Napoleon's troops who had been encamped in the same place. More than a thousand centuries looked down on him and later the bell tents he slept in, the queues for food, the hot Egyptian air, the long scented nights, all became sheer delight. None of the complications when other people were dependent on him. Yes, a most worthwhile existence being willing to give up your very life for right against wrong. That, of course, was it, Harry realized later. The backdrop of death made everything stand out before it, clear and bold and beautiful. A simplification, Harry thought, with which Nicky's generation fortunately could not equate.

64

A huge bus appeared in Harry's rear view mirror behind him, as he approached the village of Sultan Hamud. Until then nothing had overtaken him nor did he expect anything would. Most of the fast car owners these days flew to Mombasa.

He left his memory on recall Alex; slowly, to allow the maniac bus to edge past at eighty miles per hour. Originally trained with the Royal Army Service Corps as a driver he found himself attached to the Royal Army Medical Corps and he could remember two instances from his Alexandria days as if it were yesterday instead of half a century ago. The first was base workshops, not a REME base workshop, REME hadn't been created yet, the Royal Army Ordnance base workshops were what were coming into focus. Harry was on a driver-mechanics course for six weeks and the very first casualty, the very first corpse that he saw in fact, was not killed in action at all. He could see the body now, a young ginger-headed boy from the base workshops, miles from the front, who had mistakenly undone the outer ring of smaller nuts that held together the split rim of the Bedford truck's front wheel, when he should have undone the inner ring to change the wheel! The ninety-five pounds pressure inside the tyre forced the rim apart and it hit the boy's gut like a cannon ball, not too much blood, but his legs, Harry remembered, were like a rag doll's. It was after this instance that written orders of the day went out 'for all nuts holding split rims together to be painted red', whereas previously only a few Army workshops had adhered to this very sensible idea. Harry remembered driving hastily to the town of Alexandria looking for the base hospital in a small ten cwt Austin pick-up which was the only vehicle available: a tiny introduction to the three and a half years of active service that followed.

His second memory was also in Alex before his actual involvement with the 8th Army began in earnest and from the same central workshops. A K4 Army ambulance was lined up for repair with many other Army vehicles and most were painted in the light brown sand colour of the 8th Army and bearing the emblem of the Desert Rat on their front wings. An incredible assortment – Humber staff cars, fifteen cwt Morris commercials, Scammell tractors for tank transportation, Sherman tanks, Daimler armoured cars with solid tyres that, it was alleged, could go as fast backwards as forwards, which the

newly-joined Australians used to say used to be just as well –
but they wouldn't be using *that* asset, now that the Diggers had
arrived; Enfield motorcycles for the 'Red Caps', a whole
assortment of the Army's fighting vehicles were there in the
huge base workshop. It was there that one of the vehicles under
repair was an Austin Army ambulance that had come in for a
new water pump. It was probably the first time that Harry had
seen a water pump changed, an easy enough operation to do,
and on the sideways uplifted bonnet Harry remembered seeing
the neat letters painted in white paint 'KATY'. A young
Ordnance Corps mechanic who was working on it told Harry
the story of how that particular ambulance had brought two
officers, a staff sergeant and a nurse back from Tobruk to Alex
and had outflanked Rommel's Afrika Korps on the edge of the
Qattara Depression. Harry often repeated that story long
before Katy gained immortality in *Ice Cold in Alex*.

It was to an identical Austin ambulance that Harry was
finally joined, painted in the same light brown sand colours
with small roll-up canvas doors, small 'blacked out' headlights,
two huge crosses on each side and another one across the rear
doors. Obviously Harry didn't know then, nor ever, whether it
was the same ambulance that his Fire Chief had died trying to
save, and which Harry and his mates had pushed out of the
burning building in Coventry but as time passed he suspected
it may have been.

What a year that was, 1942. Harry had arrived in Egypt
early in the year but it wasn't until June that he saw his first
action. By that time he had been assigned to his Army
ambulance for some three months. Like giant dinosaurs of old
the battle in North Africa had ranged backwards and forwards
across the sands for two years already. Now Rommel was
attacking with the Afrika Korps and Ritchie was defending for
the 8th Army in the area of Tobruk.

Knightsbridge, Harry remembered that name. He remembered also that for several years after the war, every time he
read of or saw Harrods he thought of Knightsbridge. The
Knightsbridge he remembered was a tiny oasis set in the sand
of the northern Sahara and as he sped through Sultan Hamud
Harry found himself wondering about what exactly it is that
makes one place so different from another. The temperature at
Sultan Hamud and the temperature at Knightsbridge, 4,000

miles to the north, are similar. The sky, the vast horizons, the sand around Knightsbridge and the scrub desert around Sultan Hamud are not unalike, yet no one could ever mistake North for East Africa.

A scorching mid-day sun beat relentlessly down on the little cluster of sunbaked buildings, camouflaged perfectly, in the hot sand. Clumps of date palms giving patches of mottled shade, equally to Arab dogs, Arab goats, and Arab children.

Several sandy tracks converged on this oasis named Knightsbridge by the troops. Parked in the shade of another cluster of palms was a convoy of British 8th Army transports. A dozen troop carriers, two track-laying Bren gun carriers and a staff car. Harry were there too, with his Army ambulance, all in the 8th Army sand colouring, all with a Desert Rat on their front mudguards. Like the rest of his contemporaries, Harry did not admit to being happy; it was fashionable always to complain. 'Roll on leave, roll on death, and let's have a bash at the angels' were sentiments often expressed but on balance he had never enjoyed himself so much in his life. Now the very presence of death gave life added dimensions. As he later said, it was like being on a permanent high.

The old campaigners talked wistfully of the open warfare against the Italians when one of O'Connor's battalions would drive back whole divisions of Italians, but nevertheless the British grew to like their Italian prisoners captured so easily, and it slowly dawned on some of the British why it was so easy to take Italian prisoners. They decided it was because for Italian boys in an Italian village not to fight for the Duce was unthinkable and cowardly, and no doubt the signorinas would despise them had they stayed at home. When these same young men went off to fight, however, they found that to die in a distant desert at the hands of men from England, Scotland, Wales, Australia, South Africa, New Zealand that they had never actually met, but whose parents were allied to their parents, made no sense, especially when led by Germans whom they neither trusted nor liked. Surrender and spend your war in captivity, that was a perfectly sufficient sacrifice! Definitely no need to die. So in the early days before Hitler in desperation threw in Rommel to bolster his fleeing allies, the North Africa campaign had always been a fun affair, as wars go, that is.

Many years later when Harry heard about Italian atrocities

in Ethiopia and Libya he was convinced that they must have been perpetrated by a different kind of troops to those he had chatted to in the prisoner of war cages in the African desert. He adamantly refused to believe that they would slaughter women and children in cold blood.

A dispatch rider, handling his Norton motorcycle like a Wembley dirt track star roared along the sandy track towards the oasis. He was riding in from the north. He parked up in the midst of the convoy, carefully lifting the motorcycle rear wheel onto its stand – what ever happened to those types of motor-cycle stands? Nobody in those days would think of propping up a motorbike on one leg as all do now. The dispatch rider approached the captain who was standing outside his staff car and with a smart salute handed over his dispatches.

The young captain with a spotty complexion and a public school accent seemed to be right out of *Journey's End*. He read the orders, nodded and then spoke to the non-commissioned officers that surrounded him.

'The Old Fox seems to be giving the Kiwis a bit of a hard time up on the ridge, counter-attacking strongly up there. They are in a spot of bother so it looks like 'about turn' lads and back up to the hill.' Raising his eyes in the direction of Harry, 'You came in from that ridge this morning didn't you?' Harry nodded eagerly. 'Well, you'll know the best tracks then. You lead off and we'll follow you.' Harry and his medical orderly proudly jumped into the front of his ambulance. Harry switched on the ignition and pulled the starter as he had done a thousand times in the last three months. The engine turned over fast enough but the engine would not start. For a whole two minutes he whirred away on the electric starter motor and the engine didn't even fire, the battery getting flatter all the time.

The captain was naturally irritated when the ambulance refused to start. Some soldiers from the troop-carrying truck behind were ordered out to push her, and pushing a three-ton ambulance through the soft sandy tracks at mid-day in the desert was no joke.

'Try her in second,' cried the captain. At last, two hundred yards from the oasis she started, and keeping her engine running fast Harry edged her onto the desert track through a dry river bed and headed off for the track in the sand for the south. Half a mile out of the oasis he came to a fork. Both tracks led to the ridge towards Benghazi where he knew the fighting was and where they were needed. Having returned that morning by the eastern track and knowing it was badly drifted with blown sand, he swung left to take the westerly route. It was just then that the ambulance engine petered out again. This time it was more serious because there was a fairly high bank of sand on either side of the track and it would be difficult for vehicles to pass. It was mid-day and the tropical sun being directly overhead there was no shadow. The ambulance thermometer gauge showed 110°F in the cab. Harry ground away on the starter motor, absent-mindedly watching a solitary white camel about 200 yards away down the track heading straight towards him. Harry noticed the camel particularly because it was unusual to see just one on its own.

The captain arrived, 'I thought this bloody ambulance was checked out in Alex. Have you flooded her?'

'No sir,' replied Harry.

'Hm, vaporization then I suppose,' said the officer. 'Anyway we can't wait – try and put her off the track into the bank and see if we can get the rest past you then the recovery gantry will have to tow you along behind until she has cooled off.' Harry was both disappointed and surprised – this was the first time in the three months that he had been assigned to the ambulance that she had let him down. He couldn't understand it. She had been much hotter than she was now without any trouble, but all he said was, 'Right you are sir.'

Once again, the soldiers in the convoy jumped out of their troop carrier; sweating and straining in the heat they heaved the ambulance off the sandy track. The second vehicle of the convoy, the troop carrier, was just starting to edge past the broken-down ambulance when fifty feet ahead there was a terrific explosion. Sand volcanoed skywards followed by a huge pillar of black smoke and an incredible blast of hot air.

The camel had trodden on a mine and even the half-starved Arab mongrel dogs could not find a piece of meat from that camel larger than a man's hand. It was fortunate after all that the ambulance had broken down. The track down which they were driving had been freshly mined, possibly by an advance party of the Afrika Korps in the night. The corporal pulled out his map and a compass and worked out a route which would get them to the ridge where the ANZAC soldiers needed them, leaving the mined track well to their east. Driver Hill went back to the ambulance and absent-mindedly pulled the starter. Without a moment's hesitation her engine burst into life. 'Well,' thought Harry, 'that's a bit of luck.' The ambulance engine never sounded sweeter, he slipped her into gear and rolled forward with the rest of the convoy.

Many a wounded soldier bumping about on a stretcher in the back of that ambulance heard from her driver the story of the mined track outside Knightsbridge down which she had refused to go. It was a very encouraging tale when high explosive shells were raining down on all sides. Backwards and forwards from base hospital to the front line and the field dressing stations trundled the ambulance day after day with her cargo of bleeding men, past the blackened hulks of burnt-out tanks and trucks and shot down planes, and nothing seemed to stop her and somehow her driver got the feeling, driving endlessly across the battlefield under the desert sky that she *was* different! The strangest thing of all was that for the next eighteen months until they had finally pushed the Afrika Korps back into Tripoli the ambulance engine never missed a beat again. But Knightsbridge and the Cauldron and June 1942 gave way to a sadder July as Rommel fought the 8th Army back, back, back towards a little railway station called El Alamein.

The engine of old Harry Hill's new Corolla purred equally sweetly as it raced towards the coast. He glanced at his watch, only just gone nine, 'Good God, I'll be in Mombasa soon after lunch at this rate. Perhaps the Tamarind.' Then the terror gripped him again. Lunch, for God's sake? For a men who was heading towards his death – lunch!

But somehow Harry could not relate to his surroundings, he was still firmly locked into his finest year, 1942. For about a month or six weeks after the camel incident the 8th Army was still falling back and Harry and his ambulance were following it. Mid-July found him at Al Halfa. The fighting was fiercer than ever it had been before in the North African desert. Hundreds of tommies were being killed every day as the 8th Army retreated once again. Harry's mind was now on automatic recall, every tiny detail. He could see written clearly in gold letters '900 × 20 Dunlop'. He remembered thinking at the time why on earth were they still using civilian tyres and why didn't it have WD for War Department stamped on it like all the other machines of war. He smiled to himself. The British Army was still using track grips in the desert at that time. It took another hundred miles of retreat and a close inspection of captured Italian vehicles to teach the 8th Army that balloon tyres perform much better in sand. But Harry's ambulance was rigged out with Dunlop track grips. That reminded him of a pre-war visit he had made to Fort Dunlop from school. The only school outing that he had had and that when he was nearly sixteen. He remembered and smiled wanly to himself as the bus drove back from Birmingham with the school children in it gently holding the hand of the girl pupil sitting next to him. They could have made that tyre that very day that he had looked around the factory and then he thought of stories his uncles told him, from the First World War. The Ox and Bucks regiment, when they landed on the beaches of Gallipoli, swore to a man that there was more than one Taylor's mustard pot from Newport Pagnell lying on the beach. It made them feel better, more secure, and it made Harry feel better too, to think that there was a world outside where he was now, because propped against the tyre boasting the Dunlop markings on the back wheel of his ambulance, was a young Australian soldier who was dying.

Nights in the northern desert were always velvet soft. The blue dusk had turned to blackness now and the flicker of the chai tins, legendary amongst the 8th Army, who used to fill tins with sand and petrol and then light them to boil a mess tin up for tea. They gave a flickering light which joined the brilliant stars and the pale moon to illuminate the scene a little.

The huge rear doors of the ambulance were wide open and inside were the damaged bodies of men termed the 'walking wounded', several of them sitting on the lower bunks with field dressings around their heads and arms and bodies. One of the less wounded soldiers in the back was singing in a surprisingly clear intense treble voice *Waltzing Matilda*. Harry had little ear for music – in fact he always insisted he was tone deaf yet the purity of that voice on the desert air he would remember for ever. He couldn't remember why they had stopped half-way back to the front-line dressing station or why they were out so late but he did remember that a medical orderly sergeant who

71

was travelling with him at the time had allowed a badly wounded Aussie his last wish which was to be carried out, as he put it 'To die in the open, mate'. On the floor of the ambulance was the usual assortment of tin hats, boots, and even some of the Aussie felt bush hats which they had worn in the campaign a quarter of a century before but now they had a press button to keep up the brim so that they didn't get in the way when they sloped arms and shouldered their rifles. There was a cough from the wounded soldier, only a boy, he couldn't have been more than eighteen. The yellow field dressing wrapped around his chest was drenched in blood. More seriously Harry noticed the ominous trickle of blood coming from his mouth. The young boy felt it too and put his one good hand up to test what the dampness was. It was too dark for him to see but as he licked his hand he recognized the tell-tale taste of blood. 'Shit,' he said.

Harry bent over him. 'You'll be a' right,' he said, copying the famous Antipodean phrase of comfort. The wounded boy shook his head slightly.

'Nope' in a bigger drawl, 'but it don't matter.'

Harry replied quickly, 'Aw, come on, I've seen worse than you screwing a sister at base in a couple of days.'

The desert scene made a perfect cameo – a dramatic scene which Hollywood was to render to corn in the following decade but at that time and at that place it was a scene as precious as the desert air, as pure as the voice that sang in the back of the ambulance to accompany it. The dying soldier felt with huge effort into his battledress top pocket and produced a wedge of paybook, cigarette packet and a black and white photograph. Harry felt he was meant to look at it so he lit a match in the light.

Both Harry and the dying soldier looked at the picture and the boy said, quite quietly, quite distinctly, but still with a huge Australian accent, 'It don't matter you know, not with everything out there. I'm not even frightened and I don't feel sorry for myself,' and with a shallow last breath he handed the photograph to Harry who was still kneeling by him, 'and tell Til that it don't hurt.'

At the time of the death of the young soldier that night Harry was left tearless but now, fifty years later, tears welled down old Harry's cheek. But the tears he now wept were not tears of sadness but pride almost. He remembered a line in a book he had read recently when the hero, an old fossil like himself, the author claimed, had only to see a fucking flag flying and he would weep like a babe. 'That's me, all right,' said Harry but such sweet sorrow, so long ago, all sadness was swept away. God, he thought, most of the actors in that little scene would be dead of old age by now. The girl in the snap shot could not have been more than sixteen years old, wide-eyed, tight-sweater and wearing slacks, astride a bike with one foot on the ground on the path outside the door of a Sydney suburban semi. The snap of the dead Aussie soldier's girlfriend had haunted Harry, and inspired him throughout the rest of the war and well into civilian life. Even now he could imagine every detail of the picture down to the hollow letter H for Hercules – or was it Humber? – on the lamp bracket that turned with the steering wheel, sticking through the empty wicker carrier of a basket. He had done his duty and posted off a letter to the girl and returned the photo as soon as he got back to Alex but he could never put the memory out of his mind. He didn't even want to. It symbolized for him a faith he could never explain. Every time he saw a palm tree, an extra bright star, a lady's bike, even a wide-eyed girl, the blissful poignant memory of that night would come flooding back. 'Tell Tilda it don't hurt – Bloody hell.' He wiped the tears from his cheek and his vision cleared.

He could see a herd of cows that always seemed to wait until they saw traffic coming before the young herders steered them across the road. The girl was probably a grandmother by now, anyway, and her bike recycled. He smiled at his weak pun – all long, long ago.

Harry shook his head in disbelief – bloody good job he hadn't told that reminiscence to anybody before because he had missed the whole point – he had forgotten the significance till just now. As well as posting the letter to Tilda in Oz, he paid a RASC craftsman a half packet of Woodbines to get 'Tilda' written on the bonnet of his ambulance which he had been with now for over four months, in letters similar to those that were written on that other ambulance he had seen in Alex, 'KATY'. Many of his fellow Pom passengers had to ask, though few Aussies ever did. 'What does it mean then, mate?'

'You've heard of bloody waltzing *M*atilda I suppose – as in

Tank?' How many times in pride and in anger he had answered just that. 'Well, this is the 'Tilda bit.' He would swing the steering wheel from left to right on the open desert sand and say proudly, 'And my Tilda waltzes too.'

Despite the fact that the war in general and the North African campaign in particular couldn't have been going worse Tilda and Harry found themselves back in Alexandria; Tilda for major overhaul inspection at the base workshops, Harry for a little leave. He was astounded to read on 'standing orders' that he had been promoted to a Lance Corporal. Whether it was his public school accent or whether it was because he hadn't actually rolled his vehicle in the six months he had been with it, he never did know. Oddly, many years later when he was rummaging through some old letters which he had written to his aunt and which she had neatly filed, he came across one in particular which he had written from Alexandria at that time, and he was amazed at how proud he had apparently been at his tiny promotion. But the story about Tilda refusing to start, thus saving the convoy from the mined track, had got around. The army was badly in need of such morale boosters. Harry, of course, was delighted.

He was off to the beach with the platoon of other drivers, some thirty men in all, in baggy shorts, in the back of a Bedford QL troop carrier, similar to the Austin troop carriers he had been so busy welding two years previously. He looked across to the other side of the truck and noticed a newly, wet-behind-the-ears recruit with white knobbly knees. His legs were wide open and his baggy pants showing all, which in fact was a standing joke in the 8th Army. 'You want to cross your legs, lads,' said Harry. 'I can see all you haven't got.' The boy actually blushed and Harry immediately felt sorry for him. 'Oh, you needn't worry,' said an Aussie alongside, 'everybody can see Monty's every time he sits down.' There were endless stories about Monty's baggy pants. When the Torch Operation landed in North Africa and later when the Yanks got into trouble in the Kasserine Pass and the more experienced 8th Army under Monty rushed to their help, tempers were fairly frayed amongst the American and the British and Anzac troops. Over a few beers in the NAAFI or the P.X. a Yankee marine might ask one of Monty's men why it had taken them so long to knock out the over-extended Rommel, and suggested it was because Monty had no balls. As the Pom threw a punch at the Yank he would invariably say 'He's got balls all right, and that says I've seen them.' In fact by the autumn of '42 in UK – and Montgomery had only been appointed Commander-in-Chief, 8th Army, in the August – English children added another line or two or their nursery jingle. The plaintive notes of the songs of the children of the 8th Army, as they swung their arms and marched in file in the cold dark deadends of the walls formed by the lines of terraced miners' cottages, or on a hundred village greens or down a hundred town streets to school – young Diggers were too sophisticated – the song was the same, 'Hitler, he's only got one ball, Himmler has two, but very small, and poor old Goebbels has no balls at all' and then added, in a monotone, 'But General Monty has two like cannon balls.'

Innocent days in the dust, glorious over-simplication, with almost the same simplicity as the Spanish Civil War when black was black and white was white and there was no grey. It all depended on them, and they listened to Monty's naive peptalks about knocking the enemy for six with sheer and sincere delight. If a general had tried the same tactic in Vietnam he would have been laughed out of court by his men. The Allied troops knew that the Russians were taking a hammering around Stalingrad and wished them well, but they had absolutely no idea of the scale of things. After the war Harry learned that on average four or five Axis divisions faced four or five Allied divisions in the North African campaign up to El Alamein and even after the American Torch landings probably only twice as many, whereas at Stalingrad divisions were numbered by the hundred. The Axis had well over a hundred divisions engaged on the Eastern Front and eventually Stalin had nearly two hundred divisions to fight them back.

In fact the innocence didn't really disappear until 1945 when many men of the 8th Army found themselves in the British Army of the Rhine, consigned to bulldozing in the concentration camps. Himmler, with his small balls, was perhaps best laughed at for if one took him seriously civilization itself did not make sense. Every day, *every* day, he gassed more Jews, was responsible for more deliberate deaths on each day of the year than the total Axis and Allied killed during the ten days of the El Alamein offensive when the 8th Army broke out and sand dunes at Kidney Ridge were strewn with hunched dead bodies.

Harry was recalling a scene before El Alamein, when he went down to the beach. There were about two hundred of them down there, kicking a football around, swimming in or without their underpants, or just sitting on the shore, when there was a stir on the quay and Harry distinctly saw a Humber staff car drive up, followed by two more bearing the red plate with golden stars of generals, and he guessed it was big brass, top brass as they used to say. Every soldier knew there was a top brass party going on in Alex. The Auk was there, Churchill was there, Alanbrooke was there, Gort had just died in a plane crash, and Monty had replaced him. Everybody knew that things would be happening soon. Harry could hardly believe his eyes. A flabby, white body was running down to the sea wearing only a pair of bright blue underpants; Churchill was taking his famous dip.

Harry could think of no other place, no other time in history where he would rather have been. He was standing at the centre of the world's stage and Churchill stopped to talk to him!

Well, if not exactly to him personally – he later justified his exaggeration – then at least he was at the centre of the group to whom Churchill was speaking. Churchill enjoyed meeting fighting men and never failed to attempt to boost their morale. Harry distinctly remembered that, after mentioning the unfortunate recent death of General Gort in a plane crash the Prime Minister went on to explain what a good man he thought Montgomery would turn out to be. He ended by reminding them, that Generals can only plan battles, but that it was men like them, on whom Victory or Defeat depended.

A thousand years of fighting history stirred in Harry. He thought of Henry V, before Harfleur, he thought of Nelson dying below decks on the *Victory* and now Churchill, before El Alamein, talking to *him*. Churchill strode off purposefully, for a man of sixty-six, into the warm waters of the Mediterranean.

It was before the great November battle, whilst they were skirmishing around Tell el Eisa, which was always referred to as 'Tell Elisa' that the medical orderlies manoeuvred their shifts to ride with Harry and Tilda because of the stories that went around about the good luck ambulance. Harry had to admit to himself that out front in the cab he and the RAMC orderly were in one world, the brave world, exciting, romantic, even, and generally void of physical pain, and certainly without any thought of personal death, but just through the door behind him, into the back of the ambulance and that was another story. Do the spirits of lost souls haunt their last resting place on earth? Perhaps in a typical haunted manor house five hundred years old, said Harry to himself, as he tried to dismiss ghosts – but surely not an ambulance not yet three years old. Nevertheless, he often found the hairs on the back of his neck standing on end, because already in the less than half a year Tilda and himself had been together scores of soldiers had passed over or under or on, in the back of Tilda.

Harry couldn't remember the exact number of times that he had slammed the huge door shut on four stretcher cases very much alive, usually swearing and blaspheming and yet perhaps two short hours later, when they arrived at hospital, the same bodies were still, with glazed eyes. It was an eerie feeling. Harry thought of the hopes, the fears, the pain and suffering. The groans, the hysterics, the prayers, the despair that happened in Tilda. Harry remembered that when he used to go and park up amongst the other cars and trucks with their drivers, most of whom he knew at least casually, they would say 'Here comes 'Arry 'Ill and his bloody meat wagon' but this they said good-naturedly.

Once he found himself for a month in the company of ten similar army ambulances all attached to the New Zealanders and no less than four of them had had different crews because the drivers had been at least wounded and, in one case, killed and all by machine gun fire from German fighter planes. As he walked jauntily away across the sand to the NAAFI tent he heard one of the drivers say to another, 'About time old 'Arry had his turn in the bleeding back.'

He tried to sort out the days, fifty years on but they would not be sorted, they all merged. Very occasionally a female nurse would turn up. He was usually too busy being embarrassed because of all the 'fucking' and 'blinding' that they heard from the wounded men in the back to be able to make a pass. Occasionally these young girls would come out of the little door and sit beside him in the front. Usually, he remembered, there were tears in their eyes and Harry remembered that he was pleased about that but they would say, as they wiped the tear away, 'Sorry but . . . ' and Harry would answer 'For God's sake, man . . . er . . . lady . . . if you can't shed a tear for those poor bastards dying in the back, then when the hell can you?' and they would nod and often say, 'But why?' 'Dunno,' was his usual reply, 'but let's hope it's to save the world from a second Dark Age like Churchill says.'

He hadn't thought of that particular detail on that day ever – not for fifty years. There was a nurse in the front, that is what reminded him of that day. Unruly blonde hair, bursting out from under her cap, looking, he remembered with a smile not unlike Sheila Sims in the film of *Ice Cold in Alex*. Now he was reliving the scene as clearly as if it were yesterday and it worried him for at least a mile. It was often hard to remember what really happened years ago as opposed to what had been repeated over and over again, and perhaps exaggerated. Yet with this particular incident Harry was certain it had happened, just so, because he hadn't thought about it for fifty years.

It was usually stinking hot in the back of Tilda, yet the wounded invariably pulled blankets over themselves, fairly dirty ones at that. It seemed a comfort to the seriously wounded man to feel covered and warm. General issue of uniforms, tropical, for the use of, did not for the British at least, include the huge army greatcoat so typical of northern European campaigns. For once, the British quartermasters had the edge on the usually efficient Germans who had lumbered their Afrika Korps with a huge greatcoat across their knapsacks because somebody had said that it was cold at night in the desert. Whilst their soldiers were freezing at Stalingrad the Afrika Korps carried a useless greatcoat in their baggage. Yet somehow or other there had been just such a greatcoat left in the back of Tilda that day. Harry had assumed that it had come from a base hospital where he remembered some of the military police had been issued with them. Most macabre was the debris of dead infantry men that ended up on the floor of Tilda – gas masks, which hadn't been issued since early Tripoli days with Wavell, tin hats, of course, sometimes even rifles and Bren guns, boots, capes and billy cans.

A typical Australian voice shouted from the back, 'Hey driver, what's a bleeding monkey doing 'ere?' Harry turned round, he could afford to take his eyes temporarily off the wide stretch of desert, a thing he never did when he was on a road.

'What?' he said.

The Aussie accent continued, 'Didn't know they 'ad monkeys in Egypt.'

'They don't,' replied Harry, 'only in the bazaar.'

'Well, there's one here all right but he's . . . woops, sorry she's had her bleeding tail shot off.'

Harry remembered stopping the ambulance, glancing at the nurse sitting alongside him, and lifting his eyes towards the heavens asking for sympathy as they both squeezed through the little door into the rear compartment to see what the Aussie soldier's problem was. It couldn't have taken them more than two minutes but by the time they reached the figure in the greatcoat he was leaning forward, dead.

'Christ,' said Harry to the nurse, 'that's a bloody funny thing to hallucinate on – a monkey.' As Harry thought about that little incident he smiled and wondered where that nurse would be now.

☆   ☆   ☆

He was thinking about his great minefield experience. During the critical fifth day of Montgomery's main El Alamein offensive, November 10th, 1942. Harry and Tilda had been together for an unprecedented year. The scene was again a stylized one. Shells exploding all around causing cascades of sand. Tommies, still in First World War tin hats, which, unlike the American, or the German ones, left the neck vulnerable to shrapnel. Silhouettes advancing across the sand through the smoke with outmoded .303 rifles at the cant. The clank of track-laying vehicles in the background, the retreating Afrika Korps had hastily laid a minefield behind them. Rumour had it that the Germans were in headlong retreat but in this particular part of the battlefield near Kidney Ridge the troops realized it was as yet only a very strategic and possibly temporary withdrawal. For once that year Harry and Tilda weren't attached to Aussie or Anzac troops, they were attached to the Green Jackets. They knew it was a well-planned withdrawal, a trap even, because on either side a minefield that lay ahead of the column of advancing mechanized British troops with the infantry behind them, at the head of a sand blown valley were two, thirty foot high sand dunes. From behind the sand dunes mortar fire from the German encamped position was pouring down on the Green Jackets Brigade which had stopped because of the mines in front of them and more seriously there were two Tiger tanks new to the campaign firmly entrenched on either side of the valley on the dunes firing straight down at the Third Brigade. There was utter confusion in the British advance as ten newly supplied Grant tanks edged the infantry troops towards the minefield, all of them coming under heavy shell fire.

What makes an impulse? Harry's Kidney Ridge El Alamein impulsive action was a typical impulse. A hundred factors reached into his mind, facts that would take as many minutes to write, some of which went back a dozen years, some of which he was assessing with his eyes at that second. He saw himself opening up a linen bag, laced up to the neck, one Christmas Day morning in 1932 in his grandparents' house just outside Leighton Buzzard. Wrapping was all over the breakfast table and he really didn't know what was inside the bag till he pulled them out. A little wave of fear contorted the young boy's stomach. Immediately, because his proud father was watching him eagerly, the ten year old Henry acted his best, and he smiled as he tried on the boxing gloves and punched the air with them above the greasy plate of his Christmas breakfast.

Harry was as sad as you would expect a son to be when his father died shortly after that Christmas, but there was one side of his father's character that he didn't miss and that was the side that wanted him to be a champion boxer. Simultaneously there was a side of his own character that the boxing gloves had brought home to him. When it came to physical pain Harry realized that he had to admit, he was a coward. He could remember lying awake at night before boxing-match days at school. He could even remember trying to make a deal by paying the boy he was partnered against his Saturday sixpence if he didn't hit him too hard, he would lie and cheat without hesitation if it might save him from corporal punishment. It was the same with the pain of his twice-yearly visit to the dentist. He lay in a cold sweat the night before, terrified of the pain he would have to endure the next day. He remembered too, the glances that some of his infantry mates had given him when they learnt that he was an ambulance driver. He knew perfectly well that in a fluid front, like the North African campaign, where mines and machine gun bullets from fighter aircraft were the biggest killers, which he faced every day, he was probably in a more dangerous position than the infantry brigades, where, with any luck, they would only be engaged three or four times a year and never more than a fortnight at a time.

All these facts, like rays from a central point, converged on his mind at the moment of impulse. He actually decided in a flash of a second that he wouldn't mind carrying with him to his grave a complex of being a physical coward, but simultaneously he thought that if ever he was to have children he would hate the thought of them looking upon their father as a coward. The next conclusion he drew from much nearer, from his own eyes. He saw that the concentration of mortar fire that was surrounding them was getting nearer and nearer to Tilda who was in the front of the back-up of traffic facing the minefield with the conglomeration of armour behind her and he put the chances of being blown up by a high explosive shell at around only three to one against. Simultaneously with that conclusion he looked ahead at the minefield in the shallow valley which, unlike much of the territory over which they fought, sloped gently upwards. The particular patch was perhaps a mile and a half wide and three-quarters of a mile deep. He knew by past experience from driving amongst minefields for over a year now, nearly every day, that the Germans were very meticulous when they laid a minefield, invariably planting their mines at five metres apart. It was late afternoon and the sun was already at an angle of 45° behind them. Now every day for over a year he had been reading tracks like a Red Indian tracker – enemy tracks, friendly tracks, truck tracks, staff car tracks, tracks that got stuck, tracks in the sand, always tracks in the sand. It was vital to know which track was which. He knew exactly where to drive if one particular track sank in soft sand and because of this he seldom got stuck. Once he had watched a platoon of ANZAC sappers laying a minefield and it reminded him of an experiment the agricultural college in their village had recently carried out in fertilizing fields back home, with a tractor and a trailer laden with sacks of fertilizer. Every time the drilling machine required more fertilizer the two agricultural workers would jump off it and walk, usually diagonally, to where the trailer was parked. Mines were laid in the same way. The series of tracks that the truck carrying the mines laid was scuffed out by the Sappers but the herringbone footsteps of their returning to this mainline was not. What Harry now saw with that particular angle of the sun and the ensuing shading on the tracks was a herringbone pattern, and he guessed that the centre line of the herringbone was where the German truck had been and would therefore, most likely, be free of mines because it was very unlikely that the orderly Germans would think of placing a mine in their own tracks – two and a half metres left, two and a half metres right, that was the rule. The final thought that flooded in on Harry's intuition that second, Harry could truthfully say, were Churchill's words to him in Alexandria a few months before, 'Corporals win battles, generals only plan them.'

He remembered starting Tilda, there were naturally no wounded soldiers in the back at that stage of the offensive and the orderly had got out as had most of the passengers of the troop carriers in that confused little area. There was a Bren gun carrier between himself and the minefield and he remembered swinging around it and breaking into the field at exactly the place where the herringbone joined the barbed wire hastily strung up by the Sappers. He remembered the twang the barbed wire made when it snapped. He noticed for the first time a platoon of Royal Engineer sappers prodding away with bayonets advancing through the minefield at 100 yards an hour. He passed a second carrier with its track blown off; this had halted the advance. They were behind him now, then everything seemed to go silent. 'Fucking hell' he said to himself, 'I'm going to get stuck in the soft sand! I'm going to get stuck . . .' Tilda slowed and he revved up and slammed her into third gear, the engine revving loudly as he proceeded up the herringbone pattern, hopefully between the mines at around twenty-five miles per hour. The four minutes it took him to cross to the other side of that minefield were the four longest minutes of his life, concentrating like mad on the shadowy mark.

He was extremely elated and extremely excited as he realized that he was going to make it. The shelling behind had stopped and he was completely alone and, best of all, he realized that whatever else he had not been afraid. He had passed his own test. That he might have helped in some way with the battle was only a secondary cause of delight. 'No one can call me a coward now,' and he felt really good. He didn't quite know what to do next.

He pulled up and patted Tilda's steering wheel like a horseman with a Derby winner. 'Good girl,' he said, 'Good old girl, good girl.' He looked round and following him was a whole column of British armour, six Shermans and six Grants, he remembered, twenty or so troop carriers, Bren gun carriers, all crossing the minefield in Tilda's tracks.

With perfect precision four of the tanks wheeled right and four wheeled left to outflank the Tigers on the hill. He could even see the tiny dots of Germans with their hands up and it was the first time he had ever seen a German tank crew surrender. He could see them now the size of matchstick men, lifting the gun turret and coming out with their hands up. Much more usually British tanks would never get near a German one and if they did the Germans usually outpaced them. They could head out of range at up to forty miles per hour whereas the lumbering Allied tanks could only manage a maximum of thirty miles per hour be it a Sherman, Matilda or Grant.

He looked in Tilda's mirror and he saw three silver stars on a red background on the plate on the front of a Humber staff car which roared up and parked alongside him. As the subaltern jumped out he was wondering how he would modestly underplay his heroic act. He steadied himself for the congratulations, possibly a mention in dispatches; he smiled and put out his hand to shake the young officer's hand.

Then he saw that all was not well. The young lieutenant was fuming and it was the first time in that war that he had actually heard an officer swear. 'What the fucking hell do you think you were doing?' Harry's mouth dropped open. 'Eh? Who the fucking hell told you to do that?' Harry could see by the young officer's shoulder flashes that he was from Montgomery's headquarter staff and he then realized that Harry the minefield-breaker wasn't very popular.

'Now listen carefully soldier,' said the lieutenant, 'Major Harley sent a motorcycle ahead of you – right? Not many of us could see it of course, but you were following it, right? You've got that soldier? Because if you haven't there will be a court martial.'

'Oh, yes, yes, of course,' said Harry immediately realizing what the problem was. 'Yes, yes, I followed a motorbike all the way.'

'Right,' said the lieutenant, a little happier now. 'By the way, why the hell *did* you do it? A bit off your head, are you?'

'No sir,' Harry stood up straight, 'I'm not off my rocker; as a matter of fact Churchill told me to, sir.' All evening and all that night, the Green Jackets' armour passed through the gap. The breakthrough was at hand. At last Rommel was in full retreat. The Torch landings in North Africa took place soon after and the final assault on the defeated Afrika Korps began in earnest.

He and Tilda found themselves back amongst the Aussies again and word soon got around of their apparent indestructibility. First the camel, now the minefield story. Despite the wishes of the top brass, the truth came out because soldiers, even advancing soldiers, get killed and they need something to believe in and they all believed in the invincibility of Harry and Tilda as they shuffled the wounded soldiers from the mobile front to the rear dressing stations, all the way past Tobruk to Tripoli itself. They loved a legend.

Some weeks after his heroics he was sitting in the shade of Tilda's cab. His detachment was temporarily quartered on an old Italian airstrip on the coast somewhere west of Mersa Matruh and it was indicative of the great advance that a DC3 aircraft, instead of the fifteen cwt Bedford lorry, was now used to deliver the newspapers from Alexandria to the 8th Army. On the day in question not only had the plane delivered the Desert Rats' newssheet but actually a few precious copies of the UK Sundays had arrived. Harry was on the airstrip when they off-loaded them and was now sitting back with his feet on the steering wheel of Tilda smoking a Woodbine. It was one of the most pleasant memories of the war. He was reading Churchill's El Alamein oration. He learned how the victory bells had been rung across the wintery English countryside for the first time for nearly a hundred sad Sundays since before Dunkirk. Harry smiled to himself sitting there. 'The old bugger certainly has a way with words,' he said. 'This great victory,' he read, 'is not the end, it is not even the beginning of the end, but it is most certainly the end of the beginning.' Later Harry realized it was the last victorious battle of the British Empire. The Empire did not endure for a thousand years, hardly a thousand days, and there were other advances, many joint victories and Allied pushes, but never again did the British and its Commonwealth of Nations stand alone against the foe.

The DC3 lumbered down the runway and turned into wind for its take-off back to Alexandria. As it raced its engines, a blast of wind nearly carried the paper out of Harry's hands. Back on the Mombasa road a sheet of the *Daily Nation* flurried upwards as Harry's Corolla left a similar swirl of wind behind it as he raced towards the coast.

4

Surplus and Marriage

Out of Emali Harry knew that he would soon be passing Hunter's Lodge, and he had to start thinking whether he was going to stop for a cup of tea or not, one third of the way to the coast. At Emali also the Mombasa road crosses the single track railway line from Nairobi to Mombasa. From now on it lies to the east all the way to the coast. Sometimes it is so close that drivers on the road can wave to the engine drivers. Sometimes it strays two or three miles away to swing round a gentle hill but always it returns and never are you out of earshot of the friendly hoot of the good old EAR and H. 'No, no,' thought Harry, 'that's not right, East African Railways and Harbours, that was some time ago, and before that it was The Uganda Railway. It has still got UR written on some of the cutlery they use but now it is just plain KR.'

Harry raced over the bridge, at the same time remembering the days before the bridge was built when there had just been rumble strips to warn you of the level crossing ahead. He remembered, with a smile, a friend of his who still lived down at the coast, and with whom he used to enter car rallies. In fact it was in company with Spraggy that Harry had competed in two East African Safari rallies but on that crossing Spraggy was on his own going down to the coast, many years ago it was now, in a Singer Vogue at night. Along came the one train of the day, and carried Spraggy a clear three hundred yards. It wasn't hard to imagine what his Singer Vogue looked like after being rolled over and over by an express train, but the miracle was that Spraggy got out in one piece and lived to tell the tale. He had a scar or two, mind you.

There were many things around Emali to attract Harry's

attention; he noticed it was still the safari-ants' capital city. Normally such ants will build their castles of clay any distance from a hundred yards to half a mile apart, but for no reason that Harry could think of, just out of Emali there were literally hundreds of safari-ant chimneys – the legendary castles of clay, complete with the air ducts for cooling and the complicated hierarchy of division of labour that would put a modern totalitarian state to shame.

Harry soon forgot the ants. New thoughts were replacing the present, old memories came flooding back. After they had driven Rommel back, this time for good, to Tripoli, Harry was parted from Tilda. He had no idea what happened to her as he went on to Sicily and then the long, long haul from south to north Italy.

Before he knew where he was, the exhilarating days had passed, first VE day and then VJ day, then Clem Atlee arrived and the victors of the greatest war ever fought had to tighten their belts and pull up their socks and see the Empire dismantled. The utility logo replaced the Union Jack whilst the vanquished flourished. There was to be no crushing till the pips squeaked this time, no Treaty of Versailles, which might allow the defeated aggressor to resent their conquers. The Soviet Union who, with her twenty-four million dead, had really broken the Axis powers, was very nearly invaded by her allies, the United States, who had only lost one third of a million souls but somehow Patton was restrained and a fitful peace brought forth the Cold War and the nuclear bomb created a balance of terror. 'Bwana, bwana, cool it,' he heard his daughter's voice all the way from Australia. 'Why are you wasting time remembering things like those statistics that no one wants to know and even if they did want to know they would never know them from you because . . .' and then Harry joined in the conversation, 'because you are going to die before you can tell anyone, right?' 'OK' he said to himself, 'comfort, comfort: that's what I want.'

The Creed, the Creed, how does it go? I believe in the Holy Catholic Church, Holy Ghosts, rose again from the dead, third day, come on nobody in their right mind would believe in that. Heaven and hell. Right then, cool it. You saw Hell at Kidney Ridge, right? Yes, 14,000 pieces of hell, and as many bloody Krauts I dare say. Philosophy, try that, Aristotle. The logic of a guy going on a journey, anything going on a journey, for a beautiful, beautiful conclusion, which used to cheer you up. The conclusion that it is easy enough to arrive at a point and to say 'here you are' but logically *where* are you? That person arriving at that point must have been halfway to it at some stage, and a quarter way, at some other stage and an eighth of the way, a sixteenth of the way and a thirty-second of the way, and a sixty-fourth of the way, and so no way, says Aristotle, no way are you going to start from anywhere. Thus there is no such thing as nought, thus we are all a part of the infinite – 'QED,' said Harry to himself, 'so I'm not going to die because you can only die in time and there is no time.'

This relieved his fear not one iota. Next he tried to recall Priestley's *Rose and Crown*, that delightful little play where the Angel of Death walked into the public bar of the Rose and Crown to ask one of the customers to come with him. The customers included a variety of English men and women from the time that Priestley wrote about, and each had been complaining bitterly about their lot. Each was thoroughly dissatisfied, each was apparently thoroughly unhappy, and yet when Death's Angel called them they all, with one exception, thought of a thousand reasons why they had to remain where they were on the rotten old earth about which they had all been complaining so bitterly. Then up steps our hero who alone had not been bitching, who alone was thoroughly happy with life the way it was and who loved the world and all that was in it. Yet it is he who says to Death's Angel, 'OK, take me.' The others were naturally surprised as well as relieved, and the moral is in the last sentence of the one-act play, 'After all, if this life has been so good to me,' says he who has volunteered to die, 'I can see no reason why the next should not be equally good, perhaps more so.'

'Yes, yes,' said Harry to himself, 'that is all right in a play when you're middle-aged but it doesn't help to comfort you the day before you are going to die, and of course it's not any big deal to follow a supernatural proof of a continuance. I wouldn't mind volunteering to die if there was a tangible proof I was going to some place – but without that proof – no way.'

☆ ☆ ☆

The kaleidoscope came into focus again on the A6 north of

Bedford and south of Leicester at a little market town called Market Harborough which was once caught up in history when Oliver Cromwell garrisoned his army there ready for the nearby Battle of Naseby. After that the village walked into the wings of history and the villagers lived and loved and laughed amidst their soft Northampton stone and the rivers flowed silently. And then Market Harborough was to be remembered again for War Department Surplus Sales. In 1948 and 1949 thousands of ex-Army vehicles were driven or towed or low-loaded from as far south as London and as far north as Birmingham for the famous Market Harborough Army Surplus Sales. It was the Mecca in the immediately post-war years of the UK 'spivs', intelligent and enterprising young men from the cities, not liked by the more conservative countrymen. Both farmers and farm-labourers were highly suspicious of the London buyers that descended on Market Harborough, little realizing they were a prototype of the materialistic man of future decades.

He remembered, for example, his cousin Bill with whom he was living at the time, being given a watch, a Smith's watch, it had no especial significance, except, come to think of it, what ever has happened to the British watch industry? But Harry remembered now forty-seven years later, the black Roman numeral letters that surrounded it. But try to think how he felt that day, or any other day on the way to Market Harborough, and he found it much more difficult.

He vaguely remembered that despite the very restricted, rationed, cramped atmosphere where nobody travelled abroad – was it £10 or £20 that you were allowed to take out of the country? – and where most people were literally exhausted after five years of war – were clothes rationed three years after the war? He couldn't for the life of him remember. Definitely you could only get Utility clothes but despite such a background he remembered that he himself at that particular time was, on the face of it, happy and why shouldn't he be? He was young and healthy, considerably wealthier than most of his contemporaries, because of the money that his parents had left him. He had started a business for himself, delivering vegetables to the big houses in the district with his A.J.S. motorbike and sidecar. He remembered he had just put in an insulated compartment for the very first and only frozen food on the market – frozen peas. There were plenty of village girls at the village dances where, as he remembered, he was much in demand. A virile, young, well-off bachelor of twenty-six, even if no Clarke Gable to look at, was still quite a catch, yet despite all this he remembered feeling frustrated, not economically, not sexually, but 'stuck in a rut' best described how he felt. His ambitions were frustrated, which was all of his own making.

Nicky's voice again from Australia, rather sarcastically, 'It's not the gale, but the set of the sail, that makes the boat to go.' Harry answered in his mind, 'You're right, Nicky, of course, you're right, but I didn't know that then.' Back at the Market Harborough Surplus Sale Harry remembered he was pleased that it was muddy underfoot. He was wearing lace-up riding boots and breeches and one of those leather jackets with no sleeves that were also ex-army, and were so popular amongst the farming community just after the war. He remembered being pleased with the weather and the mud because he was dressed for it. It seemed right. The grass perimeter track of the old RAF bomber station was the centre of the sales area. Every vehicle had its lot number painted on its windscreen, if it had one, or written somewhere on its side if the windscreen was missing, which many were.

The spivs, the farmers, the happy little crowd followed the outrageous auctioneers. A few local gentry had brought their wives with them and they were obviously highly embarrassed at the language of the London auctioneers who were essentially an incredibly genial and humorous profession of men, and who were working very hard at the serious business of selling literally thousands of machines of war that were to be, figuratively speaking, beaten into ploughshares. All shapes and sizes of ex-army requirements were there – many army lorries, half-tracks were also for sale, Bren gun carriers by the dozen, which were bought mostly for their Ford V8 engines, huge Austin gantries, giant Scammells, motorbikes, bicycles by the score.

The scene was delightful in its geniality. 'Come on missus,' the auctioneer said to a raw-faced farmer's wife, wearing the inevitable scarf over her head, in the young Princess Elizabeth fashion. The auctioneer was selling a lot of six wheelbarrows. 'Don't bid any higher, for God's sake, lady, you'll get new ones for less than that down at Timothy Whites,' or to an ex-serviceman in a tank suit bidding for the Whites Half-Track, which he obviously hoped to use about the farm. The auction-eer, 'There you go, mate. You'll have to have it towed because I don't expect it will still start, but I can give you twenty more if you like.' Then to the crowd, 'He's going on to Moscow with them, you know,' and as a water carrier came under the hammer, 'I don't expect we will be needing them around here, not wiv all this bleeding rain. I haven't got the heart to go more than £10 – £10 do you say? £10? Ah, right you are. Yours for ten.' 'Now, what have we got here? Lot 105, Bedford, general purpose for the use of, troop carrying. Oh, very handy vehicle this, very handy vehicle this.'

He turned to his assistants – 'Just hop up and have a look inside, pull the canvas back and see what we've got there, will you Ernie? Make sure we are not defrauding His Majesty.' Then, to the crowd, 'Last sale we sold one with twenty first class motorcycle dispatch riders, for the use of, in the back, and no one knew they were there till it was too late. Truck and contents all went for £45.' To Ernie, 'All right, all clear? Now then, what am I bid, gentlemen? One QL Bedford. Who's going to start me? Did I hear £35, did I hear £35? Thank you, sir. £35, £35. £35, 6-6-6, give me 7-7-7, give me 8, give me 8, then £40, £40 there, thank you' and so on and so on his hard patter continued.

Harry was enjoying himself hugely. Looking back, he could now remember a warm feeling. The warm feeling of victory, no more fear of war and death. Of course there was the atom bomb but that somehow didn't seem as great a threat as the war had been. There were army surplus greatcoats, flying jackets, tank suits to keep out the cold winter, and as far as Harry was concerned, the Cold War. These were the sunlit plains of peace, he told himself. The bluebirds really were flying over the white cliffs of Dover and for most of the time there seemed to be blue skies with only an occasional sweet shower of rain.

It was late afternoon when Harry rounded a corner of the airfield's old perimeter track, following the little knot of people who in their turn were following the auctioneer. A huge Scammell had just been sold in excellent running order for £120. Harry looked past it and saw the next four lots, four identical army ambulances lined up behind a hangar which was now used as a hay barn. He spotted an extra interior light which he had rigged up in the driving compartment when he had been in the base workshops in Alexandria – at the same time that 'Tilda' had been written on the bonnet. A huge Austin gantry was parked so close to the other side that he couldn't get to the bonnet to rub off the grease but he had no need to – he knew what he would find written on it when he did. One of the huge rear doors was hanging off its hinge, all four tyres were flat, the seat next to the driver was missing altogether and there was a big yellow number, Lot 273, scrawled across two broken windscreens. Harry was surprised to see the wiper blades still in place. The wily auctioneer was completely mystified when two of his friends, London dealers he knew, had bought three of the four ambulances at a comfortable £55 a piece. Then the fourth one ran up to £75 before it was knocked down at £76 to a young man in a leather waistcoat tied up with string and lace-up motorcycle boots.

☆ ☆ ☆

Back on the Mombasa road, Hunter's Lodge flashed past. In the old days when the kids were young, everybody always either stopped coming back for tea, or going down for coffee at Hunter's Lodge. That was when it was still murram, but today with 100 miles per hour motorcars and tarmac, most of the few passenger cars that were still on the Mombasa road (and most people, Harry remembered, went by air to the coast) would drive straight past the old Hunter's Lodge and head for Mtito Andei, the half-way mark. Hunter's Lodge had therefore run down, a typical example of Africanization that would gladden the heart of the old colonialists that teemed out of Kenya at independence rather than submit to an African government. It wasn't too terrible when you come to think of it, though admittedly the cups were slightly grubby and there would probably be only hot milk served with the tea!

Harry then remembered, with a smile, another post-colonial food story. He had been on the Nile steamer at the time, which runs through the Mohammedan northern Sudan for week after week, and he remembered you could actually get eggs and bacon served on the Nile steamer then, ten years after Sudan became independent, and cold milk in the tea! Now here's Hunter's Lodge going over to African-style tea after – Harry had to think how long it was – nearly twenty-five years. Hunter's Lodge, he remembered, was named after Mr Hunter, not The Hunters, who did coincidentally frequent it in its early days. Those hunting types would probably spin in their graves if they could see the worst parts of Kenya today. The fastest growing birth rate in the world was the main problem with Kenya, and yet you still had ignorant parliamentarians standing up in Parliament in 1991 saying that the only hope for Kenya would be if she could double her population because Japan prospered with sixty million people, and Kenya still only had thirty million and that is why she wasn't as prosperous as the mighty Japan. A member of Parliament actually boasted eighty-four children when he died only about two or three years ago. The population explosion was the sad face of Kenya. Apart from that, and the metalled road, the diehards would not have been able to see much difference; there were more curio sellers, more trees had been cut down for charcoal but in the deep bush things hadn't altered too much. By the side of the road you could see the problems more easily – more goats, more bedraggled kids in rags and none in traditional dress.

On the day after Harry had successfully bid for the ex-Army ambulance in Market Harborough he took his A.J.S. motorcycle and side-car to collect his new possession. Cousin Bill went with him to drive the motorbike and side-car back, and they also brought along a girlfriend whom they both admired called Josie. She clasped him around the waist, sitting on the pillion, as Bill crouched over the battery in the side-car. It was slightly drier underfoot than the previous day had been but still cold. He wore a tank suit and Bill jokingly complained about the coldness around his feet where, as well as the battery, there was a footpump and a jerrican of petrol.

Harry went to a horse trough in the yard of the adjoining farm with an old can he found lying around, to fill Tilda's radiator as he had done so many times before. Then they made a cardboard funnel out of a discarded catalogue and poured in a jerrican of petrol. Amazingly all four tyres and inner tubes responded to the energetic foot pumping. Bill and himself did 300 pumps each while Josie had done 100, their faces all a picture of health on that cold, crisp autumn day so long ago.

At last all four tyres passed the kick test. The starting handle was still in its clip behind where the passenger seat should have been, the spare wheel behind the driver's seat, even the mica sidescreens were intact, not even cracked. They wired up the rear door with baler wire, fitted the rear battery, washed down the windscreen, dipped the oil and he turned over the engine with the starting handle with the engine off.

'Compression seems OK,' he said, mainly to Bill.

'That's a bloody wonder.'

A pre-war three-ton Bedford roared passed them splashing them a little, followed by a Humber staff car. Harry climbed into the cab, crossed his fingers to Josie and Bill who were outside watching him, switched on, pulled the choke, then pressed the starter as he had done thousands of times before. One revolution of the fly-wheel and she fired into life, then pushing the choke half in she ran at a steady 2,000 revs.

'Just like a bought one,' Harry exclaimed delightedly.

It was a very strange feeling driving Tilda home through the English leaf-strewn autumn lanes. His first impression was that somebody must have fitted a bigger engine, she seemed to go so fast. It was some time before he realized that this was caused by the inevitable hedgerows that they drove past, only ten feet away on either side which gave a relative impression of speed when compared to the nothingness of the Sahara desert through which Harry was so used to driving.

Now he felt confident that he could tackle the English Midlands and make a success of his vegetable business.

Signposts! He could write a book on signposts. He was looking in his side rear view mirror and neatly framed was a metal signpost saying EMI in capitals, followed by a small 12, which on a little metal post on the side of the Mombasa road told him that he had passed through Emali some twelve kilometres ago.

Signposts, milestones, his thoughts returned to a long finger-post of a signpost so popular in Britain before the war, but now only ruling over the more deserted areas, like the Norfolk Broads and the Yorkshire Moors.

'Husbands Bosworth 612'. The wording took up all three feet of fingerboard in neat black embossed lettering on the white background. He could not get the image of the fingerpost sign out of his mind, 'Husbands Bosworth 612'. Five weeks to the day since Harry had collected Tilda from Market Harborough the web of destiny had decreed that he should be halfway there again. Again, with his cousin Bill following on the motorcycle and side-car, but without Josie on this occasion. It was a beautiful day in early December, a watery sun shone out of a clearing sky. The week previously he had advertised his motorcycle for sale in the local rag. A phone call or two and the arrangements had been completed. There was a serious buyer at Husbands Bosworth and Harry and Bill were now delivering the motorcycle. Tilda had in the previous five weeks, had a coat of paint, headlight black-out hoods removed and bits and pieces of work done on her. The overhaul was by no means completed but at least she was roadworthy and running well and he had arranged the cab to his liking.

The six and a half miles to Husbands Bosworth were to change Harry's life. It had stopped raining and the sun was flickering through the leafless chestnut trees that lined the road. Harry remembered as clearly as if it had been yesterday. Because Tilda had no trafficators and flashing lights to indicate turns had not then been invented, he signalled with his hand that he was about to pull out to overtake a pair of cyclists that were ahead of him travelling two abreast. He needn't have troubled because he knew there was nothing behind him and as he pulled out to overtake he had a sudden tiny intuition that the rear door might swing open – but it didn't. Yet a strange mood of exaltation came over him. Perhaps, he thought, it was the result of the reunion with Tilda. Then about half a mile after overtaking the bikes he noticed that his cousin Bill was no longer behind him and at the same time Tilda started pulling badly to the left. It took Harry all of half a minute to realize that the left-hand front wheel must be losing air and going soft very quickly. He pulled off the road and onto the path on his left hand side to allow vehicles to pass him. He now guessed that Bill, following on the motorbike and side-car, had stopped at a village shop.

Harry was standing in front of Tilda with the jack in one hand when the two cyclists he had overtaken caught up with him. As they approached he sensed that something was very wrong by the angry movements, particularly from one of them, as she dismounted almost hurling her bike against the front of Tilda. She started angrily at Harry who just stood there with his mouth open.

'Do you know you just nearly killed us – do you?' shouted the first girl, obviously highly irate.

From a more relaxed Harry, 'Oh come on, I left you plenty of room.'

The first girl who wore spectacles faced him in anger, 'Yes, plenty of room, but did you know that your thing was hanging out.' Harry subconsciously looked down at his flies and the second girl smothered a guffaw of laughter. The first girl was still intensely angry. 'It's not funny. Look, that gate swinging at the back, not the door, that black thing, it could have easily thrown me off my bike.'

He looked behind him quickly to where the girl was pointing. 'Jesus H.' He walked to the back of Tilda and saw that the jerrican rack hinged fastener, the identical type he used to work on when he was welding army trucks in Coventry at the beginning of the war, had come undone and had swung open, adding at least two and a half feet to his nearside clearance. He was now really worried and remorseful. 'I say, old dear, I really am most awfully sorry.'

The irate girl, who was essentially incredibly good-natured, was completely disarmed when she realized that the driver was unaware of the bar protruding and smiled. 'Oh, well, then, that's all right.'

He looked more closely at the second girl. His mouth dropped again, and a strange thrill welled through him. Standing before him was the reality of his wartime vision of the original Tilda. Here in flesh and blood was the smiling wide-eyed girl of the photograph, complete with bicycle and basket. He knew, of course, that it couldn't have been the dead Aussie's girlfriend but he couldn't get over the likeness. He stood staring as if a thunderbolt had hit him. His eyes opened wide. 'Are you all right?' the second girl enquired as she propped her bike against Tilda and approached him. The face, the jaunty movements, the slacks, the smile, let alone the old-fashioned bike, with the string protecting female attire from catching in the rear wheel: Harry was absolutely enchanted.

'Can we help you?' said the vision.

'No,' he said, rather stupidly, 'Oh well, yes.' He realized that Bill was still a few minutes behind and he wanted to preserve the fleeting moment for ever. A psychologist would, of course, have said that the similarity of the cyclist to his war-time memory had made him hypersensitive. A less complicated explanation was what Harry always insisted – 'Love at first sight.'

He was still feeling elated, 'Hey, you don't half remind me of somebody,' he said, looking at the girl he now knew was called Jenny but it was the other girl who replied, 'You'll have to do better than that.'

'No, honestly, somebody . . . ' but it was too long a story to explain.

As they prepared to depart he managed to find a little sense and said, 'Do you live around here?'

Back came the answer, 'I do now, I've just moved down from Blackpool,' with a trace of pride as well as a trace of a Lancashire accent. Something in common at last.

'I was stationed at Blackpool.'

Again the first girl replied, rather sourly, 'Who wasn't? Come on, Jen,' she said and moved off. The other girl stood on one pedal of the bike and followed her, looking round only once to wave goodbye.

When the wheel was changed he replaced the jack and the wheelbrace under the driver's seat and snapped it shut. Bill noticing Harry was still a little strained, started off, 'Was it something that bint said?'

'No,' he replied, 'not that at all.'

As he got into the seat to start up he looked down at Bill and said 'You might keep up this time.'

To which Bill immediately replied, 'Good job for you I didn't or you wouldn't have seen those girls. Mind you, a lot of good seeing them does.'

Still dazed he repeated, 'Yes, a lot of good seeing them does.'

From an irritated Bill, 'Well, you can't screw them, not just like that. You're not in Port Said now, you know.'

'No,' he answered, still in a dream, 'not just like that.'

He jumped into Tilda, deciding to speed it up a bit, overtake the girls and make a date for once and for all, but all the remaining way to Husbands Bosworth there was no sign of them. 'They must have turned off,' he said sadly to himself and he realized that he could hardly turn around and go searching down every turning. Perhaps another day.

Harry had enjoyed his share of girlfriends in what he later called his *Cider With Rosie* phase, and he always imagined that one day it would probably be in the order of things that he would get married and have a family. Before the war he had considered himself too young for serious attachments and since the war, well, the girls who had crossed his path had plenty of sex appeal, were pleasant enough but somehow they didn't quite click. Now, though, Jenny of Husbands Bosworth had completely replaced his vision of Tilda of Sydney and he felt restless. His mind was not really on his work of selling vegetables, he could never remember any previous occasion when he had been so affected by the sight of a girl and slowly it dawned on him that possibly he was in love. Cousin Bill with whom he was staying at that time realized this long before he did.

'Why don't you go and look for her, you bloody fool?'

'Hm, I don't even know her surname; I don't know where she lives; proper Charlie I'd look, knocking on every door in Husbands Bosworth asking for Jenny.'

Two weeks later he was checking out the toolbox under the seat when he saw a hardback book. Absently he picked it up and read the title *Little Women*. Opening the fly he read in neat schoolgirl hand – 'This book belongs to Jennifer Ward, 6 Hill Street, Husbands Bosworth, Leicestershire, England.' So blind is love that he never noticed typed below – 'A fine of 1d. a day will be levied for every day late this book is returned.' In fact it was not until Simon was born, nine months after their marriage, that Jenny confessed to the plant.

When he recalled the early days of his married life he could not but help think of sex so for the next ten kilometres . . . . Caucasians of Harry's generation both male and female who reached puberty before the Second World War and got married after it have every excuse to be sexually 'hung up'. On the one hand, young males were warned that masturbation would lead to baldness and blindness and worse and young females were taught that only a harlot would lose her maidenhead even to a finger, before her husband was offered that ultimate sacrifice on her wedding night. On the other hand, the urgency of war romances, the wider distribution of mechanical birth controls, more commonly known as French letters and Dutch caps, and an awareness that most European industrial cities boasted twice as many prostitutes as bachelors, all heralded the permissive society.

As in any age there were many exceptions. He had been slightly surprised at Port Said when, given the opportunity of 'perfumed gardens' some of his contemporaries had visited them seven nights a week, four weeks of the month, for all the time they were stationed there but others had listened to the weekly pep talks, seen highly coloured pictures of the havoc venereal disease could cause if left untreated and had opted not to try it even once. Somewhere between these extremes lay the vast majority of those boys and girls of yesteryear. Snoggers all! He thought wistfully about those pre-silage, pre-baler, haystacks into which nut-sweet hay was harvested in June and July and which ricks would stay thatched all autumn until the winter when they were cut into with a hay knife like a giant cake. In all the many hayricks in the length and breadth of Britain, in the back of every Chevvy in every Levy in all the drive-ins of Oz, snogging was the vogue. Few of its disciples knew or cared that it had evolved from their parents 'spooning' nor that in the more permissive society of their children's puberty there would be no need to snog. The intensity of snogging varied from a French kiss and the squeeze on the outside of the inevitable brassiere to a joint series of huge climatic explosions that might be the envy of a latter-day pop king or queen.

He imagined a scene: the desperate booted farmhand still completely dressed in overcoat, shirt, flannel underpants, thick cord trousers, tearing away at his flies, tin buttons, often covered by verdigris from damp. After hours of kissing he throws his maiden down in the hay, she with equally thick flannel knickers forced aside, heavy serge skirt, rucked up to allow a dry, bulbous veined purple-headed penis to reach within a whisper of the entrance it must not enter. The girl often enough ecstatic under some huge army greatcoat could resist no longer and thrust upwards. The soft warm lubricated clitoris thus running the length of the tip of the penis was like striking a match and invariably resulted in semen exploding over pubic hairs to a gasp from the underneath partner. 'Now you've done it – I thought you had a thing on,' followed by a desperate handkerchief – no Kleenex in those days – mopping-up operation.

Strangely such sessions did not seem to lead to deep-rooted frustrations, often in fact both parties might agree that travelling hopefully had proved more satisfying than arriving. Harry even had, he thought with a smile, an ex-Army associate who always claimed he couldn't ejaculate unless he had his boots on! So Jenny had arrived at her wedding night a technical virgin but Harry soon learnt that when it came to sexual technique he was a non-starter.

Jenny was unusual in that for three weeks in a month although she would allow sex, it never really interested her, but for five days just before her period, he noticed invariably that when the moon was full, she turned into a veritable sex maniac. It was no coincidence that their honeymoon started the week of the full moon. It had taken them many a snogging session to learn this peculiar cycle of Jenny's. During their courtship he was, at one stage, a little concerned that his fiancée might be frigid, but he need not have concerned himself. Once the fear of pregnancy was gone, once it was full moon, it was Harry who tired first! Their honeymoon hotel room in the Isle of Man could have been the setting for a hundred dirty jokes. They didn't leave it for forty-eight hours, relying on room service to appease another, lesser appetite. *Time* magazine would later have put it, 'He seven times and she twenty-one times in the first forty-eight hours.' It augured well for married bliss and in fact for children, and sure enough Simon was born nine months to the day after the start of their honeymoon.

Even these days, twenty years after Jenny had died, he still felt stirrings when he saw a full moon. 'Mind you,' he insisted to himself, 'he wasn't past it yet.' Only last month his attractive Somali secretary aged around twenty-five had explained to him quite sincerely that girls like her, whose tribe had had a tradition of girls mating with much older men found young men gauche. In fact she urgently insisted that none of them would be turned on by any man under sixty. But he couldn't help equating such nomadic tribal traditions with all those dirty old patriarchs in the Old Testament; all of whom seemed to be bonking their daughters nightly. But that was unfair. Somali girls became particularly attractive to Harry at his three score years and twelve – 'You dirty old man,' he heard his daughter's voice again all the way from Australia but said kindly, as only Nicky could. He concluded that sex was no dirtier and no cleaner at eighty than at eighteen.

Harry braked as he dipped into a right-hander. His first baobab tree. How Nicky would have squealed with childish delight as she got her fifty cents for being the first to see a baobab tree when the family was motoring down to the coast for their summer holidays a hundred years ago. He remembered that before the tarmac was laid that very same deep bend he had just slowed to 100 clicks for used to be a treacherous lugger where in the 1967 East African Safari Rally his challenge had finally finished with an oil sump cracked open by a rock hidden under the sand of the river bed.

He tried to remember exactly for how long the fires of passion burned so strongly in Jenny. 'For some time,' he said to himself, 'it must have been for some time,' as he remembered an incident some seven or eight years after they were married when they were in a camp site in Algiers on their way overland. They had been sleeping in the back of Tilda all the way across Europe. The seven-year-old Simon had been sleeping with them. Most deliberately one morning on the North African campsite Jenny traipsed Simon through the pitched tents and caravans to where two young English children were playing. Having met the mother the previous evening she asked if she would be kind enough to look after Simon for the rest of the morning, as she had to go to the bank in Algiers to find out what had happened to a money transfer. He listened to all this, knowing better than to question her, but the plan didn't dawn on him until instead of catching the bus into Algiers she dragged him into the now empty rear compartment of Tilda forcing him to the ground and pulling his trousers down. Only then did he realize that the next night there would be a full moon over that beautiful city – the Paris of North Africa.

The five years of his life following his marriage, like Dickens' descriptions of those preceding the French Revolution, were for the Hills 'the best of times and the worst of times'. He was learning that this description fitted many periods of his life. Romantically and sexually fulfilled, disgustingly healthy, comfortably off financially, and within a year a boy child, Simon. If that didn't make you blissfully contented and sublimely happy what the hell would. 'No idea,' he replied to himself rather crossly, 'but something must have been not quite right or we wouldn't have packed up and left it all, would we?'

Harry had been reunited with Tilda for about a year before he was married. He had converted the back of Tilda by removing the four stretchers and replacing them with sloped vegetable racks. He had also worked up a fairly successful door-to-door round for himself, and as he opened the back doors of Tilda the villagers were tempted by the colourful display of vegetables. There were bright oranges, blooming plums, rosy apples, huge red tomatoes, greens galore, even the turnips polished to an ivory glow. Some ex-servicemen in the villages recognized the mobile shop for the ex-army ambulance it was, and to some it brought back memories that they would rather forget. Harry had painted her a dark green, though you could still see the outline of the huge red crosses on the sides. Nevertheless, she blended well into the leafy countryside and the new Elizabeth age dawned.

It had been arranged that after their marriage Harry and Jenny were to take over part of the old house behind Jenny's parents' grocery shop in Husbands Bosworth High Street and that Harry was to help Mr and Mrs Ward run the shop. This he did with a vengeance; he added groceries to the vegetables on display in the back of Tilda. He sold his first home round quite well and money was coming in nicely from the bigger and better Husbands Bosworth area. This allowed Harry and Jenny to tour the Highlands of Scotland with the one-year-old Simon in his carry cot in the back of Tilda and for the two-year-old Simon to cross the Channel for a summer holiday in northern France. It also allowed Harry and Jenny to indulge in their hobbies of following motorcycle racing on the Isle of Man and of following the early post-war British Grand Prix circuits when Castle Donington, Brands Hatch and Silverstone were still better known as wartime bomber command stations.

Sometimes they would leave the baby Simon with his grandparents and take a trip to London in Tilda for a West End theatre show or more likely to catch a new film at the Odeon, Leicester Square. In fact, the City and the West End, Hyde Park Corner and Knightsbridge all became very familiar to him. He remembered pointing out the Law Courts and the Old Bailey to Jenny. If anybody had told him then that the next time he would see them would be with his daughter who would by then be only slightly younger than his wife was at the time, and that he would be awaiting a trial there, he would never have believed them.

Harry flashed through Kibwezi thinking briefly about the time his young family had so enjoyed their weekend at Bushwackers' Camp some ten kilometres into the bush to his east. Nicky had seen her first lion there. 'Never mind that,' he said to himself, 'what went wrong with the UK?' He didn't really want to blame the UK for his shortcomings because he knew that was ridiculous. Obviously it was his fault. Later he would explain it by saying 'In the days of rationing if you wanted to expand, say, and start pig farming, you would be allowed as much ration of meal to coincide with the quantity of pigs that you sent the previous month to the bacon factory.' That was the gauge of your ration. A Catch-22 situation. Obviously you could send none until you had the ration. Then there was road transport. Harry, to supplement the greengroceries and the groceries, wanted to start a haulage business towing caravans but first one had to get an 'a' licence and there would be a board to enquire whether it was necessary or not, and the railways would automatically object, usually successfully, although the railways couldn't even get caravans through their tunnels.

In retrospect, and in all honesty Harry had to admit that many of his friends made a success of their lives; it was probably him and his attitude. Partly it was Kipling's fault. As a child at Leighton Buzzard after his parents had died his grandmother had found his father's old framed poem of *If* and she had it hung over the young Henry's bed in the same way that she would put manure on her roses to help them grow. It didn't do too badly in producing subconscious offshoots of imperialism. 'Making one heap of all your winnings and risking it in one turn to pitch and toss, fulfilling the unforgiven minute,' and all that jazz crept unnoticed into Harry's subconscious to cause an irritant to the blissful complacency in which he found himself. His seven-year sex itch was to come later. In the early years of married life a resentment crept in. A resentment against the limitations of life in post-war Britain.

He was not looking for fame or fortune nor did he think he might achieve either by emigrating. What he was really looking for was a wider horizon, Jenny too.

Simon had become inexorably bound to Tilda. The first word he said at eighteen months was a lisping 'Tilda' and by the time four years had passed he would sit on Harry's lap and change gear. The swell of contentment with each other, and discontent with their environment grew. Harry would remember until this day waiting at level crossing gates day after day with always the one narrow wiper of Tilda in the 'on' position wiping the eternal rain from the little windscreen. The inclement weather day after day seemed to help hatch the seeds of discontent which Kipling, and four years overseas during the war, had sown. Another irritant was a huge billboard on the opposite side of the street displaying a twenty foot by twenty foot picture of a slimy fried egg – Egg Board marketing efforts – 'Go to work on an egg'.

Dreary evenings trapped in their little room above the shop they spent listening to the early instalments of *The Archers* on a bakelite radio. A letter from an ex-army friend working on the Tanganyika Ground Nut scheme, and the dawning of the true significance of the revolution in retail purchasing which the newly-introduced supermarkets were to have on the village shop, were all vague memories now but at the time each was a spur to emigrate.

Soon they were actually discussing *how* to get to Africa as they still called East Africa. The obvious way of course was to fly. Both British Caledonian and BOAC had flights once a week, moreover it only took about twelve hours putting down for fuel in North Africa and there was talk of the new de Havilland Comet Jetliner being able to do the flight direct. For those who didn't want to fly there was a delightful voyage round the Cape, so appropriately called 'of Good Hope'. British India Lines sailed from Tilbury all the way to Mombasa once a month and offered a glorious holiday on the way. Then there was the unique but exciting possibility of driving overland and Harry was checking out the price of Land Rovers which had so recently become popular with the agriculturalists of England.

Overland particularly appealed to Harry because he was confident that he could handle the desert which the few authorities they could find said was the only difficult section. The authorities, they later discovered, had forgotten the mud of the Congo. The window looking out on to the street was wide open that springtime afternoon. 'All right then,' he declared, 'I'll go and see their local agent and get some brochures on the Land Rover then we'll write to the AA or something to see if they can give us a route. It shouldn't be too difficult.'

The wiring on Tilda's horn button was original and at the time sixteen years old; apparently old enough for it to short out, and from the street outside where she was parked, echoed into the sitting room the plaintive note of a shorting horn. 'Bleeeeee' it went. They all three looked at each other. 'Bleeeeeep' 'Well,' said Harry, 'Why not?'

Nearly at the halfway mark of Mtito Andei on his trip to the coast, he was still thinking, why did he leave England all those years ago? The first problem in answering that question was that when any young married couple with a small boy do anything it isn't why did *he* do such and such any more than it is why did *she* do such and such. Harry found his and Jenny's reason for emigrating were basically the same but with many complications. The reasons for Simon wanting to go were very simple. He learnt that it would mean at least three or four months, probably more, actually living in his beloved Tilda and if the journey was to hell itself it would *have* to be worth it in his mind. People later used to ask Simon when he had first learned to drive and quite seriously he would say he couldn't remember. He supposed it was on the journey out overland in Tilda but in effect when he thought about it there had never been a time that he could remember when he didn't know how to drive.

Harry had by then evolved a standard answer to the 'why did you leave England syndrome' which satisfied both the genuine questioners and critics alike. 'Oh, we were just fed up with socialist England, the weather and the washing up, you know.' Followed on that, from the more sincere visitors, 'You must have seen a lot of changes,' to which he would always reply, quite sincerely, 'Well, who hasn't? Take UK for example. They tell me the M1 flies right over my cousin's farm in Newport Pagnell,' but of course neither of them really meant the changes in the environment but the more subtle changes. Tarzan is dead might do. Occasionally if he was going on safari with some of the clients himself, in person, around the camp fire at night he would get more involved and explain the real changes that had happened in Kenya in the preceding thirty-five years.

'When I first came here you would get a tall, Luo African waiting at table diligently behind his bwana and I've known these bwanas wishing to make a point, turn round in their chair and point at the fezzed servant and include him in their conversation by saying, "This baboon here ... " Well, in my opinion such people deserved Mau Mau, a barbaric revolt that only took thirty-seven European lives which compared with the six million Jews that the civilized Teutons killed was nearly a non-starter, horror-wise.'

The point that he was trying to make to himself is that today he was on the Tourist Board with three Mzungus (white Europeans) and three Africans, all representing successful, tourist companies. More often than not he squirmed when the pompous, unbusinesslike, unprofessional Mzungus spoke, whereas he was tremendously impressed and counted amongst his friends the Africans on the same board. 'They are much more businesslike, much more aware of the problems that face the industry and have many better ideas of how to put things right. Mind you,' said Harry, 'I'm not saying all Afs are wonderful but then neither would they. These friends of mine, for example, would know only too well that there are some pretty dim idiots in Parliament, but a stupid person is not necessarily an evil person, and no race has a monopoly of stupidity – lack of education perhaps, different environment but that's something else isn't it?' Harry realized that he was allowing his mind to wander.

Why did he leave UK? The good old homeland. Inglenook fireplaces, white Christmases, thatched cottages, rolling downs, *Cider With Rosie*, the horse-drawn carts bringing back the harvest, those glorious summer evenings when yes, there were still hares about the corn and honey still for tea.

A friend from his distant youth every year sent Christmas greetings in the very best tradition of a Dickensian Christmas.

The Christmas cards were chosen with considerable thought. Phil could never understand how anybody could leave the tranquillity of his particular way of life for foreign climes. Where else could one possibly wish to retire except to a cottage down a lane within the sound of village cricket on a village green and skittles in a pub? He was genuinely sad that Harry refused to share such tranquillity and the appeal came not from a narrow-minded insular bigot but from one who had definitely been around a bit, who was in fact attacking with the artillery on the right flank the very day that he crossed the minefield at El Alamein. Views from such people demanded to be taken seriously. Phil was the most loyal of Englishmen, the most gentle of men, and had found sweet content and genuinely wished to share it. Lucky Phil, thought Harry, but then Phil had never experienced the call of the wild. Not so lucky Phil, he thought.

It certainly wasn't the call of the wild that precipitated the emigration of the Hills. In fact, the wild, he discovered, doesn't call until you try and leave it. The acacia thorn, the dust and the baobabs on the approaches to Mtito Andei couldn't have been further from the leafy lanes of England, the soft mountains of Mourne, but this royal throne of kings, this sceptred isle, complained the dying John of Gaunt 'is now bound in with shame'. So often used to conquering others it has made a shameful conquest of itself. Appropriate too as the proposition of a Young Conservative debate of the fifties. The British Commonwealth of Nations endured nearer a thousand days than a thousand years from *their* finest hour! He could not object to the efforts of a socialist Britain to change the greed motivation of capitalism. He could see that the extreme right was much more to be feared than the extreme left and the principle of 'to each according to his needs, from each according to his ability' was a noble, worthwhile goal. Whereas the monopolization of power by a handful at the top of the pyramid who would make it their business never to be replaced by the strata of humanity that made up the pyramid below them, was a terrifying thought.

In those days he was chipping the line a little to the left of centre, letting the chips fall where they may. He, Jenny and baby Simon and their dog could have been seen on the first march from Aldermaston.

It wasn't really a financial motivation that made them move out of Britain. They were 'comfortably off' as the saying for upper income bracket was then, but he and Jenny had seen a slide show presentation of the delights of settling in Kenya when they had been visiting the Royal Agricultural Show. In those days the Royal was not established at the same site every year but circulated. That particular year it was at Cambridge. The red combine, neatly slicing the cornfield, the young European girl on a horse overlooking the operation in the foreground, the backdrop of Mount Kenya itself, towering in the blue sky, was the image that they sought.

☆   ☆   ☆

With the wisdom of retrospect, he was now recalling an event from much later in his life. He had come to look on it as his 'Lay-by Parable'. His enlightenment then had been in the form of a sort of symbolic conclusion. It had occurred when he was visiting the UK as an old man attempting to 'sell Kenya' as he put it. This meant, in effect, teaching retail travel agents or more exactly their front counter girls, the majority of whom had never visited Kenya, how to market his safari holidays by extolling their virtues and Keyna's virtues against the competition!

He was parked in his new Hertz hire car in a lay-by on the A27 but in fact, and this was the cause of his sadness, – it could have been on almost any trunk road in Europe. Sadness, because of the concrete uniformity of the developed world. The inevitable embossed warning, not to discard rubbish, yet still the inevitable scrap of 'non bio-degradable' things flapping in the damp, caught on the rusty wire of a dilapidated fence.

The awful sameness, a menace even, as mobile boxes, large and small, snarled and screamed anonymously and meaninglessly passed him. White plastic garden furniture from Scotland, hurtled senselessly by on its way south to Spain, crossing around Lyons, with white plastic garden furniture from Spain hurtling senselessly north to Scotland.

Five tons of butter from New Zealand screamed past some of it on its way to mega-markets cut out of a Leicestershire grazing pasture, an acreage which had been better able to produce fine butter than any similar size of acreage on earth!

The turbulence from the giant turbo charged boxes buffeting his stationary little box, reminded him of the turbulence that the lumbering wide-bodied 747s always suffered when being carried on the air above the hot sands of North Africa when it met the cooler Mediterranean air, or how Simon's little Cessna used to jump around in the convectional currents at 500 feet above Lake Turkana. Nevertheless, he concluded in retrospect, it was less the idiotic urgency of the traffic, and more the awful isolation and loneliness that concerned Harry. One could rest on that lay-by for a life time, and no one would ever stop to pass the time of day.

The significance was in the comparison. Stop anywhere in Africa from Lagos to Mombasa, from Botswana to Chad, where the traffic density was one thousandth of the developed world's, and you will not be alone for long!

Significantly also, what little traffic there is, makes much more sense. An African District officer perhaps, off in a swirl of dust, with two traffic policemen in the back of the Land Rover, to investigate some minor disturbance, some understandable villainy of stock theft. A truck load of beer, the crate dancing dangerously to the rattles of a million corrugations, from the only brewery within a thousand miles, to quench some nomad's thirst in a Northern Frontier township.

It was not only the greater meaningfulness of the traffic, which pleased Harry, there was also the rugged beauty, layer on layer of distant rolling mountains, and Boran cattle grazing, the dusty thorn.

Nor was it the bone-warming sun, which made him enjoy the African lay-by – it was the humanity.

A distant impossible voice of his daughter . . . 'Oh, come on Bwana, you are not condoning the "give-me-one-shilling, urchins".'

Harry smiled and nodded to himself. He *was*!, when compared with the impersonal European lay-by. The truth dawned on him.

He knew that stop anywhere in Africa and children would appear from nowhere, first two, then a half a dozen, ragged smiling children with torn clothing.

A paradox indeed – simultaneously irritating because of their intrusion on your privacy, yet welcome for their obvious sincerity, greedy in their un-imaginative demands, yet generous with their friendship. Those soft brown eyes set in perfectly proportioned faces. An almost Christ-like simplicity. How could he deplore the loneliness of the European lay-by and reject such African friendship?

5

The Crossing

Harry was now back in his imagination at the Wards' shop in Husbands Bosworth High Street where the junk room and passages were filling with 900×20 tyres and mountains of overland equipment and in the lean-to in the builder's yard opposite could be seen the flash of electric welding and heard the clatter of hammering until late into the night. Both he and Jenny firmly believed that the joy people associate with messing about in boats can only be exceeded by the pleasure of kitting out an overland vehicle.

He had removed the Austin's petrol engine and replaced it with a Ford D – one of the first light diesel engines made. The engine mountings lined up and it dropped in the chassis a treat. The transmission lined up perfectly but to get at the injector pump for bleeding, the engine compartment side had to be hacked away and a new tin cover screwed on to the engine compartment inside the cab, and this modification always let in heat and dust, onto the driver's left leg.

The fact that diesel engines work at considerably fewer revolutions than petrol engines, and he had thought it unwise to mess around with higher gearing meant that Tilda's top speed was now forty-seven and a half miles per hour flat out. In pre-motorway days in Europe that was no great problem and in Africa where she spent the rest of her life, a good power-weight ratio and a good clearance made up for her lack of four-wheel drive and there were in any case very few tracks in Africa on which it was safe to exceed thirty miles per hour.

They fell into the usual novice's error of taking too much equipment. Half-shafts were allegedly necessary to protect the differential so Harry opted to take three spare half-shafts.

Actually, not one of them was ever used, then or later, for anything except a hammer ram to remove rusted-on tyre beads, from split rim wheels. Two clutch plates, though it was the thrust bearing that they actually required in Zaire, an injector pump that went rusty ten years later, having never been fitted even after they arrived in East Africa, gas cylinders for welding, huge spare batteries, chains, sand matting, all very heavy items. Two complete spring assemblies – for the front and rear suspension – whereas it would have been much more sensible just to carry an assortment of main leaves. He thought of how he had scoured the junk yards of Algiers after a second main leaf spring had snapped, and in the end drilling holes in the chassis with a hand drill under the midday Algiers sun so that the rear spring hanger could move forward to fit the main leaf which they had found in a scrapyard. Gas lights, gas stoves, gas fridges were also a mistake as replacement bottles, let alone with the correct regulator, were virtually impossible to get once they left Gibraltar. Useless also was a huge ex-naval surplus stock radio. About the only thing that *that* could pick up, said Jenny, was dust. As with love itself, no overlanders will ever take anybody's advice and generally speaking travelling hopefully is better than arriving.

'Good Lord, another new filling station just out of Mtito Andei.' That certainly wasn't there the last time he drove down. Then, for the second time that morning, a fierce jab at his heart started him sweating as terror took over again. 'Bloody old idiot, who cares about your preparations for your boring old trip thirty-seven years ago. Why aren't you thinking about seeing a doctor in Mombasa? No, no – no!' His Corolla purred forwards at 145 kilometres an hour towards the Indian Ocean, whilst in his mind a heavily laden Tilda emitting just a little too much black exhaust smoke, complete with her new diesel knock, was beating down to Dover in the May sunshine following the Roman's road the old A2. They rounded the last gentle bend that Tilda was ever to turn on English soil, and the white cliffs of Dover came into view, a glorious sight with white gulls, if not blue birds, wheeling over them. A poignant symbol of the best of Britain. Both he and Jenny experienced just a faint undercurrent of remorse in their tide of exaltation. An almost sub-conscious feeling that they were rejecting the beauty so perfectly explained by poets like Chesterton and Belloc, renouncing – betraying even, the blood of countless heroes down the centuries who had served under Drake and Nelson and Dowding. For young Simon not even one tiny regret, his pleasure was complete and simple – unadulterated, sheer delight.

Harry wondered why there were so many petrol tankers parked up in Mtito Andei when all the pundits said that Kenya's upcountry petrol requirements were now all pumped up the pipeline from the coastal refinery at Changamwe to the storage tanks in Nairobi. He knew that some of the Ruanda and Uganda companies who had to tank it onwards from Nairobi found it cheaper to tank it all the way from the coast but today there must be twenty tankers parked up on either side of the road just like the old days, outside the 'Day and Night' clubs which are East Africa's equivalent of English transport cafés.'

It was 'at this point in time' as computer salesmen insist on saying for 'now' that Harry remembered that he always kept a 'Personal Dictaphone' in the glove box for speaking office messages he thought of whilst driving to work. Holding it with his left hand it meant that he didn't have to stop to jot notes in writing on a pad. Because he was attempting to rationalize his thoughts he vaguely thought if he transferred them to tape it might help him sort them out if and when he arrived wherever he was going. Such self-spoken speeches seldom had a beginning and even less often an end, he would just switch off the dictaphone and carry on thinking to himself. He pressed 'Record' '. . . Does it matter more or less if one acquires knowledge, a piece as small as "Why those tankers are using the Mombasa road despite the pipe line" or as great as the reason for living. Does wisdom unshared die with you? What good is knowledge?' He found the old worry tugging at his mind. 'What am I? Why am I? From whence to whence, me and everything? It must matter. After Descartes "I think, therefore I am", of de Chardin "A pulse everlasting of the universe". Of his conclusions that size is relative, so is nothing, time is an illusion. Yet I know that soon my brain will cease to function and then I will not be. To drop off into the final sleep is a necessary degree of wakefulness. The unquestionable truth of paradox. Illness is necessary for health to relate to. Poverty so that there can be an excess called wealth. Unhappiness and suffering to create ecstasy, happiness and joy. In the same way death is a must for life itself . . . .' He switched off the little tape recorder.

A flash of philosophy broke in – '*ME* – Harry Hill, being a part of the inconceivable infinite dimension of time, must as a part of the whole be infinite.' Now a swift search through his education at the University of Experience of which he was so proud – 'ability to discern between right and wrong!' Education had hardly taught him how best to live, let alone how to die. Various religious dogmas, so sincerely and variously held by many of his friends, were all equally unacceptable to Harry's rational mind, particularly as to accept one was to offend another. A return of the intense fear, not of dying, but of being dead, brought him out in a cold sweat . . . .

Nicky, he remembered, had learnt to swim at a beautiful roadside lodge in the very village through which he was now passing. Now the lodge was overgrown and derelict through lack of trade. Rich people flew to the coast and for the poor ones, who still drove, the inevitable chai, the strong, sweet tea of Africa was a sufficient and affordable refreshment. Sad, but so what? You couldn't blame that change of fashion on the African government. He smiled; he was becoming obsessed with cold milk in tea, that had been his Hunter's Lodge observation. Then he remembered a conversation he had had a few days before with a cultured, well-travelled, well-educated African who claimed he actually preferred hot milk in his tea, and why not? Why, by the same token, should you have to put your knife and fork together when you finished your meal – continentals didn't. Why shouldn't you pick up a chicken leg and eat it in your fingers if you're allowed to pick up asparagus? Harry accelerated and he left Mtito Andei behind and flashed past the landing strip to the west of the road. 'Do you remember?' he said to himself, 'No, no, that came later – much later' and had he not heard someone say in any case Tsavo Inn was now being run by African Tours and Hotels – a first class tour company?

Tilda and the Hills were on the ferry leaving the soil of old England and heading for unknown Africa. They had taken Tilda on the cross-Channel ferry several times before. For five of Simon's seven years they had crossed to the continent so even for Simon the ferry was fairly commonplace. Now, seeing the white cliffs recede they were in a different mood altogether to when they first saw those same cliffs earlier that day. Now it really seemed no big deal. 'Flying to East Africa these days probably only takes a day, and I bet you it will get even quicker and even cheaper as the jet develops.' Jenny needed no reassurance. She and Simon were in the bows of the ship and every time there was an extra-large wave, the spray would splash over them and Simon would laugh outrageously.

Traversing France was a complete blank in Harry's memory. One thing he did remember was that as soon as they landed in Calais young Simon took up a position in the left-hand seat so that he could relay to his father whether or not it was safe to overtake, since they were in a right-hand drive vehicle and from now until Uganda they were going to have to keep right. An argument arose when Jenny put her thoughts firmly forward, that it was asking too much of a seven-year old to assess the speed of oncoming vehicles and she took up that task. 'Anyway' she said, 'he'd probably fall out.' Simon didn't mind in the least. It was just as good to be sitting in the middle on a little seat they had made and changing gear and watching the new world pass by, knowing when night fell he would actually be sleeping in the back.

It wasn't until southern Spain that very definite memories cropped up. Leaving Seville to the south, for example, they got hopelessly lost and couldn't find the main road out. In retrospect it was rather amusing. They found themselves going down a narrowing lane with dwellings on either side and the buildings getting closer and closer. On the roof rack of Tilda at that time were several trunks lashed down with canvas, the rack itself protruding maybe two or three inches over the side of the roof, and the luggage another six inches. When the lane got very narrow this protrusion actually slotted into an upstairs verandah. The result was that they couldn't drive forward, they couldn't drive backwards. A whole host of black bereted Spaniards dismounted from bicycles, or halted their donkeys in the lane ahead of Tilda, all giving advice, half of them shouting, 'left hand down' in Spanish and the other half shouting 'right hand down' in Spanish, as Harry, sweating, tried the hopeless task of releasing the stuck vehicle. Eventually, after much shouting and screaming he had to remove not only the cases but the roof rack itself, and all the geraniums, and all the flower pots, from the upstairs balcony and then with just a little scraping of the white-washed wall he managed to reverse out of the trap. His second memory of the trip was also in southern Spain. The balmy exotic perfection of the scent that fills the perfumed valleys, orange blossom in the spring, line after line, acre after acre, hill after hill, mile after mile, day after day, the orange orchards surrounded them. Harry found himself wondering why so many people opted to spend their entire lives in the damp, sulphurous, acrid stench of industrialized northern Europe, cowering beneath slag heaps and gasometers when the orange groves of southern Spain and the deserted Sierra Nevada were for the most part sparsely populated. Could the larger income from the northern factories provide as good a lifestyle, as was possible from so much less income in the south?

Harry remembered how those oranges features in the romantic colourful markets of north Africa, and much later in life, when he was back in UK for his trial and he found himself pushing a food trolley in a soul-killing supermarket, amid the melancholy of a shuffling, sad and frowning Britain doing its shopping, he would come across a shelf of oranges and they would take him straight back to the trip in Tilda, and southern Spain, and the thrill and the joy of the orange blossom scent.

Harry remembered too that in those days he used to get terrific pleasure when he discovered Jenny often thought the same as he did, whereas other people – the majority perhaps, might disagree. Bull-fighting was a good example. Neither of them enjoyed seeing the bull suffer but they surprised each other by both agreeing that they should revise their preconceived ideas that bull-fighting was wholly evil. Generation after generation, thousand upon thousand of humans have enjoyed, not the pain, but the traditional finesse, the exquisite excitement of the bull-fight, and the cost of such enjoyment was the death of a creature which would probably prefer to go down fighting rather than suffer the ignominy of a bullet in its

116

brain, which all the critics of the bull-fight would argue as being perfectly in order. He and Jenny did not become addicts of the ring, but at least understood better the stoic Spaniards' anger at the starry-eyed idealists of the anti-bloodsports leagues who had never seen a fight and were determined not only not to tolerate it themselves, but to attempt to prohibit others from enjoying their traditions. By the same logic the Spaniards said vegetarians should picket meat factories. Young Simon, however, did not appreciate the finer points of bull-fighting and in his young mind, for the rest of his life, he was to associate the Spanish race with brutality.

Just south of Mtito Andei on the Mombasa road there were, and probably still are, a string of potholes. These potholes are nothing like the huge, giant potholes in the road north from Nairobi to Uganda where the deformed road had potholes big enough to swallow half a Mini Minor and a sign saying Danger Road Deformed, but they were big enough to make him slow down to under the 100 kilometre per hour mark.

Looking in his mirror, behind him he noticed a twenty-ton Fiat articulated lorry catching up with him. He estimated it must be doing around 100 kilometres an hour as it roared past him like an express train. He pulled over into the side as the artic' cut in obviously to miss a pothole and swirled up dust as the back wheels left the tarmac, reminding Harry of the old days when it was murram all the way. Although it had been overcast, almost damp, there was still an incredible amount of dust and he had to slow down in order to see where he was going, or at least try. As the truck roared past something had tugged at another memory chord. the truck driver had slung a goatskin from his fuel tank to a mudguard stay and filled it up with water. The absorbent skin acted as an ideal cooler. He hadn't seen this for years. It reminded him of his first few days on the African continent with Jenny and Simon and Tilda. Parts of those early days were as forgotten as was his disembarking from the troopship at Port Said about which he recalled nothing, but he remembered those goat skins all right. It was just south of the most beautiful city he had ever seen in his life – French Algiers, the Paris of Africa, shiny white colonnades, side-walk cafés, a glorious waterfront and a glorious town.

It was beautiful Algiers that made him start thinking of third

117

world towns before and after their independence. It's a good job, he thought, that there were not many people in the world who had visited as many cities as he had in Africa, both before and then a generation after, their independence because a diehard colonial critic of 'independent Africa' would have a field day. Alas, there were no exceptions. All African colonial cities had been jewels in the crown, the pride of their colonizers. Clean, functional, beautiful, romantic with all facilities. In the early 80s Harry had visited many of these proud capitals again in the course of his final profession. Without exception they were run down, filthy, no garbage collection, few of the services working, none of the footpaths negotiable, and yet, in most cases, investment money for huge new ten or twenty storey hotels had been pouring in. Walk ten feet outside a five-star hotel, and you could fall into the sewers of the city where most of the manhole covers were missing. Algiers was a classic example of such degeneration. Decomposing and derelict – a shadow of its former graceful charm. Sleek motor boats actually used to take you skiing in Bangui, their wake lapping the neat stone walks and paths of the riverside cafés of the Ubangui River. Dubonnet, champagne and yesterday's copy of *Le Monde* were all freely available when he and Jenny and Simon and Tilda drove through.

Bangui revisited – weep ye children of the London School of Economics – fifteen years later it was well-known as the capital of the Black Emperor, who kept human heads in his refrigerator. Overlanders by-passed it as often as they could, taking a ferry over the Ubangui downstream or upstream because the stench of Bangui was too much to bear. Stanleyville and Elizabethville when Harry and Jenny first discovered them were sprayed with DDT every evening by aircraft. New potatoes were flown in from Paris weekly, cut civic lawns rolled down to their rivers which would have done credit to Cleopatra.

Dar es Salaam, the haven of peace had one of the most beautiful harbours in the world with fairy lights dancing in the tree-lined boulevards illuminating the soft night for mile after mile. The crisp white-washed towers of the Germanic cathedral hastily converted by eager Anglicans after the Protectorate was granted. The ingenuity of the settlers had been endless. Golf, cricket, badminton, baseball, football, billiards, tennis,

118

rugger and motor racing all flourished every Sunday. If you have got to live in a city, the old African hands used to say, you might as well live in Dar. Clean buses, cottage hospitals, efficient telephones, smart trains. Twenty years on and there are none of these things, which would have been fine if such material delights had been replaced by another culture or if they were romantically provided with ancient traditions like Cairo but they weren't. The vacuum left by the European withdrawal was filled only by filth, by mud when it rained, and dust when it didn't. A good definition of the Third World, Harry used to say, was a place in whose towns less than a third of the street lamps worked.

Nairobi, a once-green city in the sun was now a chaos without refuse collection. Lagos was the only African city that had little charm either before or after independence. They used to say of Lagos, even in those days, that it often took you longer to get from Lagos airport, twelve miles out of the city, to the city centre than it did to fly from London to Lagos. So many donkeys, so much filth, so many carts, so slow was the ride. Lusaka, Livingstone, Harare – the list continued with no redemption except that Harare had only had one decade of independence and was therefore considerably less collapsed than those which had had two decades. The diehard, 'told-you-so' ex-colonialist, possibly returning to the city of his colonial heyday after having left it for ten years or so changed the common phrase from they 'couldn't run a piss-up in a brewery' to 'they couldn't even run a bath'.

After a lifetime in independent black Africa Harry knew it wasn't quite as simple as that. Once, in Nairobi, at the United Kenya Club Sunday lunch a few years before Harry found himself sitting next to a young African from the Public Works Department whose job it was to replace the Keep Left islands in Nairobi city. After more than an hour's conversation he concluded that the young man was every bit as capable, honest and intelligent and able as his white counterpart would be, but the circumstances were against him. His superiors diverted the repair funds, not always to Swiss bank accounts but to vote-catching projects like schools. He mentioned one particular Keep Left island only some four miles from the Nairobi city centre which he had replaced already seven times that year and it was only October!

119

He knew that two wrongs don't make a right but it annoyed him intensely when the right-wing critics of independent Africa cited the run-down cities as proof of the lesser intelligence of the African race. 'OK,' he would say in argument, 'now I agree the Africans have lost the beauty of their cities, but what about the men of the English Midlands who between 1960 and 1970 lost the entire British motorcycle industry? Would you say they were basically less intelligent than the orientals who captured it?' 'Totally different situation', would come back the reply. 'I know, I know, they *are* different and you can't compare unalikes' he would have to agree, 'but the reasons, the causes for failure, and people's justification of them – they're the same'.

By the time the Hills arrived in Algiers Simon had persuaded his mother that he wouldn't fall out if he sat on the left-hand seat. He particularly enjoyed the occasions when Tilda was being driven in towns, which gave him the opportunity to hand signal and he at least, was pleased that there were thousands of miles of French colonies ahead of them where his hand signalling would be so necessary. There were several other English-speaking families staying at the camp sites in North Africa in those days and Simon got the nickname of 'The Trafficator Kid'. He smiled to himself as he remembered again how Jenny almost raped him one day in the Algerian campsite and how that night they so enjoyed watching the full moon dip into the Mediterranean. Jenny cooking exotic dishes, the inevitable laundry line going from the back doors to campsite fences, Harry nervously checking the tyres and the equipment as they realized that after the Atlas mountains would come the Sahara.

Those early overland days, sleeping in the back of Tilda every night, were some of the happiest in his life. The fridge failing in Algiers, his first fridge failure, Harry almost snorted to himself as he wondered whether more or less than a hundred fridges had failed him since? Then he remembered a slight antagonism. Of all the people, of all the villages that they were to pass on their journey, the villages of inland Algiers were the least friendly. He had not realized at the time that most of the north African countries had suffered three generations of Italian oppression, and an ex-army truck, driven by white people brought back unpleasant memories to the locals. This part of North Africa was a completely different experience for Harry from his North African campaign days. In those days there would always be movement, troop movement, a touch of danger in the air and friends everywhere. Now, he was enjoying the solitude of the desert and really appreciating the reliability of Tilda. In the 8th Army there had been no French Foreign Legionnaires, now they met many of them and Jenny was enjoying herself enormously.

In the English countryside in which he and Jenny had previously spent their married life together, the sexual rules never had to be taught or explained to anybody. One didn't have too much to worry about from other young men in the village. It was not in the nature of things for them to attempt to seduce young wives, that would make life too complicated, but with the dashing, romantic, Foreign Legionnaires, particularly the officer class that Harry now found himself surrounded by, it was a very different matter. He rather angrily thought that any females – huge, ancient, mother of six or whatever – were all fair game to legionnaires. They were perfect gentlemen – there would be no force used, but years of experience had taught these lonely males the shades of meaning in a glance from any female. They could read the signs all right, and with the attractive Jenny at the height of her sexuality he found himself constantly on the defensive. He suddenly realized that perhaps he had begun to take her for granted just a little. He was sure that she was completely 'faithful' but he was equally aware that she was enjoying tremendously being so highly prized by such an elite company of men.

Beau Geste-type forts were now beginning to appear. He remembered bits and pieces; two Foreign Legionnaires living in an oasis who used to walk about a mile every night with buckets of water and empty them out in troughs for the wild camels that wouldn't come anywhere near human habitation. He remembered crossing the Tropic of Cancer because of the signboard, which also heralded the Sahara proper. There are oases in the Sahara where, it is claimed by the inhabitants, that it had never rained in living memory within a hundred miles in every direction of the oases. The water flows down the subterranean hard rock for a hundred miles to form the oasis. It is always hot in the Sahara and May 1957 was so hot that often they couldn't bear their feet on the sand, even six hours after

121

the sun had gone down, well into the early hours of the morning.

If there had recently been a sandstorm, which meant that the sand was loose, tricks like lowering the pressure in their tyres, particularly the rear driving tyres to give more surface area, and tackling the sand in the early morning when there was allegedly dew on it, although it was absorbed instantly, were practices the Hills had already learned. Generally, although only two-wheel drive, because of the diesel engine which developed more power at low revs, Tilda was fairly good in the sand, but the problem with 'the crossing' as they later called it, was that they were much too heavily laden. They seemed to get stuck at the first sight of soft sand. The back wheels would only sink half a tyre's depth – may be some four or five inches and yet it would feel as if they were chained to a mountain. Harry would rev up the powerful diesel engine, let out the clutch in first gear, and because the back wheels wouldn't move, the engine, having strained all parts of the transmission, would finally stall. Out would come the shovels, the sandmats (or sand ladders as they were more often called) would be laid down and then revving like mad, Tilda would lurch onto the mats, travel the length of them, and sink in the sand again. As some of the soft sand stretched for 100 feet you might have to lay the sand ladders ten times or so to get across. Then Harry might find a little bit of hard going with a few specks of stones in the sand, like gravel, and he would be afraid to stop because he might get stuck so he would keep going while the going was good and look in the rear view mirrors to see Jenny and Simon struggling with one of the sand ladders which were left in the sand, carrying them across the desert at a temperature of 120° in the shade, of which there was none, and this was a sight that Harry would never forget.

Sweat dried before it had a chance to form and when he took his shirt off at night there would be a white ring of salt on the back of it. He expected any day the clutch to burn out or the differential to strip its teeth, or at the very least a half-shaft to break under such tremendous strain. Mirages became quite common. A stone on the distant horizon – the only thing protruding from the miles and miles of flat sand, catching the sun and reflecting a shadow, could be mistaken for almost anything you were expecting, like a complete oasis or even, once, Simon thought he saw a field of waving wheat but as one approached it would turn out to be a little rock, perhaps three inches by three inches. When, after two days' hard driving, an oasis *did* appear on the horizon none of them dare mention it in case it was just another mirage and the first thing they would do when they got level with a palm tree was, joking amongst themselves, jump out and hug it to prove it wasn't a mirage. Around mid-day Jenny would usually squeeze a sponge of water over Simon's head and by the time it reached his collar it had almost all evaporated. There were no roads through the Sahara in those days, just tracks of other vehicles which must have passed that way, sometimes months before, which had not yet been blown over by the endless shifting winds. The French administration in the Sahara at that time had placed marker beacons every ten kilometres along the route. This was usually an old oil drum filled with cement, and how eagerly would they watch out for these marker beacons. Every overlander has his own 'lowest ebb' story, often involving thirty or forty punters for whom one was liable, and usually a lack of water. Their lowest ebb by comparison was not too bad. They at least had plenty of water, they had no punters to worry about, but it certainly seemed bad enough at the time.

One morning, out of In Guezzam it had taken them twenty layings of the sand ladders to get some fifty kilometres. The track that they were following seemed to veer away from the main track but whereas the vehicles that had travelled on the main track had obviously had trouble, because you could see signs of where there had been digging, the particular track that veered away seemed to be hitting harder sand so they followed that one. Although there was no doubt that they were going in the right direction because they were some kilometres from the more popular route south there were no marker beacons. There had been nothing but sand in every direction for all the previous week. They were now about three quarters of the way through the worst of the Sahara, having done 1,500 miles and still had about 500 miles to go. Jenny was driving for a change because although it was incredibly hot they seemed to have got over the worst of the soft sand. Next to her on the little seat in the middle was Simon and on the outside seat for a change trying to catch a breath of air, was Harry.

Tilda's dynamo had ceased to function five days previously.

This was not too serious for a diesel engine because electricity is only needed to start it and light it if necessary, so theoretically one could carry on indefinitely provided one could start it with the charge left in the battery. However, by now the battery was getting flat, possibly from the heat, possibly from having started the engine five times for the last five mornings or possibly from a minor short. So at night Jenny would drive Tilda up onto two thick sleepers they carried with them for jacking purposes, and in the morning Tilda would roll off the sleepers with the clutch depressed. Jenny would lift the clutch just as the vehicle dropped off, in second gear, and the engine would burst into life just like a push start. It would have been quite impossible for even twenty people to push start her in that soft sand, let alone Harry and a seven-year old! It was therefore important to keep the engine running all day. Therefore when the oil gauge pipe fractured under the dash, and pumped boiling black engine oil all over the cab, they dare not stop the engine to stop the flow, in case they couldn't start the engine again. He recalled the scene: three figures covered in black boiling oil, himself attempting to hammer the copper pipe to stop the flow, which he eventually did, but not before they were all covered from head to foot in black engine oil. Having attempted to save their few clothes from being soaked in oil they were all three nearly naked. Being drenched in boiling oil was extremely painful but young Simon didn't bat an oil-covered eyelid as he held the spanners for his father.

They were just getting over this incident, tearing up a sheet which was in the sleeping compartment of Tilda and using, most sparingly, a little warm water and soap to try and remove the worst of the oil (this they were doing blatantly and nakedly in the middle of the vast Sahara) when, rolling lightly over the sands, coming towards them was a 2CV Citroen inside of which were two immaculately dressed Rhodesians. It was the first vehicle the Hills had seen in days. For ever after if anyone asked Harry's advice on the ideal vehicle for trans-Sahara work he would say without a doubt, the 2CV, because it is so incredibly light. The two Rhodesians, a man and a woman, gave the Hill trio time to drape sheets around themselves before offering Harry and Jenny an ice-cold beer from their cold box – the best beer Harry and Jenny had ever drunk in their lives, and an ice-cold Coke for Simon which started a life-long love affair with Coke for him. With smiles and waves the Citroen purred off as it if were on a London-to-Brighton run. The Hills got back into the oil-soaked driving compartment of Tilda and lurched south. Later in their lives, the Hills often laughed about that day when Tilda's engine was running all the time the Rhodesian couple were chatting and giving out beer. Whatever must they had looked like with torn white sheets draped round their oily naked bodies?

With the wisdom of retrospect Harry had often wondered why Tilda's oil-gauge pipe had broken just there. Presumably they would have met the Rhodesian couple anyway. When you see less than one vehicle a day it is customary to stop and pass the time of day with every fellow traveller. They never met the couple again, ships that pass in the night. Back on the Mombasa road, nearly thirty-five years later, Harry's eyes suddenly opened wide, and he grabbed for his tape recorder out of the glove box again. In a deliberately false deep voice he began, 'Being in full possession of my nuts and of sound mind I, Henry Hill, do solemnly state as follows: I have just recalled an incident that happened years ago which I have never thought of nor remembered before and which disproves, no not exactly disproves, but I'll place the facts before you and you can judge for yourself about predestination. When Jen and young Simon and I were somewhere south of Tam, covered from head to foot in engine oil in the middle of the Sahara desert in 1957 and the two Rhodesians in the 2CV came across us and gave us a beer, we asked them what the going was like ahead, and they said that they had had a spot of trouble about fifty clicks previously. "Nothing serious mind you" now *they* had been running to the east of the main track. They looked at Tilda and said, rather sarcastically, "I don't think you had better try that track. Try the west side, it can't be any worse . . .".'

He put the recorder away and started meditating about tracks. Sometimes he remembered where there was no wind and tyre tracks in the sand seemed to last for ever. Most overlanders had their own special variety of wheel track story. When the Hills had been staying in the Algerian campsite they had met a Swiss guy who had just crossed the Sahara from the south on a motorcycle and he had told them an incredible track story. One day as the Swiss boy was motorcycling along completely on his own, he suddenly noticed two giant wheel tracks going off at right angles to the main drag. Being curious the boy turned round to take a closer look and could see no sign of the tracks continuing either north or south, nor of them crossing from the other side of the track on which he had been travelling. They just started. Having plenty of time and fuel in hand, he pointed his motorcycle off the track and started following the giant new tracks that had come from nowhere and looked as if they must be going nowhere. They went on for mile after mile. It was quite eerie, two huge tracks of tyres wider than your average vehicle going from nowhere to nowhere, because the next habitation in that direction must have been five or six hundred miles away. Also, the more he followed them the more he began to think that they were made by two wheels, rather than four. It was unusual for a four-wheeled vehicle to leave only two tracks with no overlap. He had almost persuaded himself that it was some huge Loch Ness snake of the Sahara, when he came across an abandoned Italian fighter plane and although it was in fairly good condition he got the impression that it had been there for years and years. What it was doing over a thousand miles from the Italian war zone, where the pilot and the gunner had gone, for there were two empty seats in the fighter, or how the tracks had lasted for so long, because it was twelve years since Italian fighter planes had been operational anywhere in Africa, the Swiss motorcyclist couldn't begin to understand. Harry now believed every word of the motorcyclist's story.

Shortly after bidding farewell to the Rhodesians on the day the oil pipe fractured, they picked up a track which had been left by the twin rear wheels of what he had guessed to be an oil tanker. Most of the vehicles of the desert were either camel transporters or fuel tankers, in that particular part usually supplying Tamanrasset. Following those particular tyre marks they had not got stuck once and they dubbed them the 'good track' and when the tracks veered west about eighty kilometres later, remembering what the Rhodesians had said, they followed them. This driver, they concluded, obviously knew what he was doing and was avoiding the soft sand which now occurred along the more travelled track between the marker drums. Of course the oil tanker must have been going south; there was nowhere else to go, and so they were not too alarmed when they noticed that the line of drums was now out of sight on their left-hand side and what had caused him to grab at the mike of his dictaphone and describe exactly which track they had taken was because he suddenly realized a fact he hadn't realized before, and that was that as the 2CV came north on their track they would have been at least two kilometres from the line of drums. He now estimated he had been three clicks away from the other side, making a total distance from where the 2CV had travelled, of five kilometres from what they now saw.

Simon had been the first to notice it. 'Look Dad, isn't that a black car over there?' pointing into the distance. Harry gave his young son a very old-fashioned look remembering the illusions of his mirages and a black car from a black stone was an absolute classic so there was much discussion before they veered off to have a closer look. Sure enough the blur turned into what looked like a deserted Morris Minor. Simon was the first to jump out and have a look. Lying on the sand on their stomachs with their heads alone shaded under the car, were two bodies. 'Dad, quick, there's someone here.' Jenny was next out, Harry being slightly reluctant to leave Tilda ticking over without accelerating because the battery, he was only too aware, was still flat.

'Quick,' Jenny said, 'fetch the first aid box.' It was a frightening sight – a man and a woman with wide-open eyes that could see nothing, purple swollen lips, and black tongues hanging out of their parched mouths. They were both unconscious. Jenny squeezed her sponge of water over their faces whilst Harry who had put a wooden block on the accelerator to ensure that Tilda kept running poured the tepid water from the jerricans into their mouths and mixed up an eggcupful of brandy and water from the medicine chest. After what seemed an age, the terrible taut face of the man actually moved a little and he tried to close his eyes. The woman even lifted her head a little from the sand, shaking it from side to side in disbelief. Harry on the feet and Jenny on the arms dragged the two of them into a tiny patch of shade at the back of Tilda and Jenny kept applying cool water compresses from Tilda's sacred self-cooling canvas water bag which they never usually used till late afternoon.

After nearly half an hour the man recovered sufficiently to gasp out his story. The couple were an English ex-pat couple who had been in Nigeria for six months managing the Kano's Barclays Bank. That figured, Harry thought with a smile – bank managers and lift mechanics were always the last trades to be Africanized for obvious reasons. The previous weekend the couple had decided to explore the desert for themselves. The drive into the desert had been very tough going. The petrol-driven small horsepower and relatively heavy car was just about the worst vehicle for desert work. The bank manager was not stupid, and he knew that he had had engine failure because of vaporization during the day so he had started driving at night but that had proved really fatal because he had experienced the not uncommon 'desert disorientation' similar to flying in cloud without instruments. When they had got in a patch of soft sand the clutch had burnt out. They were in fact only six kilometres off the main track but they had no idea in which direction it was, and remembering the old adage to 'stay with your vehicle' they had done just that, which proved that advice to be correct once again. For the last thirty-six hours they had had nothing to drink, as even the rusty water in the radiator had leaked away through a leaking bottom hose and they had given up all hope of being rescued.

They were now safe in the back of Tilda, only some 200 miles out of the Tuareg wells at the end of the Sahara. Soon they were to see grass again, and thousands of camels and goats, and the two invalids in the back were well enough to take photographs of the nomads with their shining white camels and their dark blue robes, their jewelled dagger handles sticking out of jewelled scabbards.

They dropped off the couple at the front door of their house in the suburbs of Kano. By then the manager and his wife were quite well and were able to walk normally. As the woman walked to her front door she turned around to look at the side of Tilda and said, 'That's funny. Where have the red crosses gone? When I was regaining consciousness and opened my eyes in the desert back there, I saw a definite red cross in a white

128

circle – huge – on the side of Tilda – I know I did. Now I can hardly see it at all'. Harry replied, 'Just a trick of the sun I expect. She had got crosses on, but I painted them out years ago.' The wife was almost too gushing now for their liking, she had wanted with sincerity to kiss Simon goodbye but Simon had scowled, 'You ought to kiss Tilda, not me,' he said, 'after all she found you!'

Now at last in the garages of Kano they could fix the fractured oil pipe properly and repair the dynamo and relax with a glorious cold beer and eat in the Greek club.

The milestones, or more correctly kilometre irons, when he had last noticed them, were still reading to M/AD – an appropriate abbreviation for Mtito Andei he thought, with a smile. But now he noticed it was MBS and only 316 kilometres away. Near the horizon to his left was the unmistakable outline of the Yatta plateau, perhaps sixty or seventy miles away. Such a useful landmark to the light aircraft flying between the coast and the capital. The skies were still overcast but the wide horizons of Kenya were, despite the gloom, working a trace of their magic of old.

He told himself that he felt as well now as on all the other occasions he had driven down to the coast, so why must this be his last safari? Then he remembered the bathroom floor that morning and the ghost story from Julie and the picture of Oliver's twins' playhouse. Was he escaping after all, he asked himself, with a ray of hope. No – he was heading in some direction to some rendezvous – and that thought strangely cheered him. That implied an entity beside his lonely death. 'That's OK,' he said to himself, 'California here I come, right back where I started from' – a distant jingle from a long-forgotten tune but somehow that feeling of following – of being led like the character in the *Rose and Crown* – eased the terror of the unknown, and that thought, together with the timelessness of the Yatta plateau, cheered him slightly on his way.

When Harry tried to put together the part of his life that

included the experiences of his overland trip, from after crossing the Sahara, to before arriving in Kenya he found his memory more muddled than usual. CAR – Central African Republic, Congo and the Ruwenzoris all blurred into one. It was not until Uganda that his vision cleared a little.

The first month in Kenya – that he would never forget. That had been second only to his 8th Army days for excitement and terror. More terrible in some ways because it was his loved ones and not himself who were at risk.

In the jungle of the French Equatorial African countries certain scenes were now coming into focus. There were the rumours of human flesh for sale in Bangui market which, even to this day, Harry had never discovered were true or not.

In Zaire there were the countless times they had had to remove Tilda's battery and drain a jerrican of diesel from her tanks in order to get various river ferries working. Listening to stories of overlanders of the eighties, things hadn't changed very much in Zaire, even today he decided. If any overlander today asked advice from the grandfather of the overlanders, as he styled himself these days, he would still rather over-dramatically insist that a 2CV Citroen was best, not only for the sands of the Sahara, but for the black cotton mud of the mudhole that is Zaire. Deux Chevaux are so light that they can be carried literally knee high by a band of twenty or thirty men whereas heavy agricultural tractors with spiked wheels that churn themselves into the mud have been known to be irrecoverable until the dry season arrives.

Tilda was at her worst in mud. Two-wheel drive, no tyre chains and too much weight. Some days they only did about ten kilometres, digging, digging, digging. Harry wondered if the *barrières de pluie* were still functioning. That was a system where the Belgian authorities would close the road if it had rained ahead, in order to stop vehicles from churning it up, but even in those days a few francs would often get the barrier lifted. Heavy trucks would churn up the muddy roads which had no foundations, like a disk plough going over a field of stubble.

In Harry's old Langata bathroom, there hangs a predominantly orange and black coloured photograph that captures the thrill, the adventure of crossing those Congo rivers. Against the giant red ball of the sun as it sinks into the two-mile wide

Ubangui are highlighted the silhouettes of two boatmen, paddling across, overshadowed by the massive banks over two hundred feet high. Jenny took the photograph from a ferry and it turned out to be a classic.

With a stagnant, rotten river smell, humid atmosphere, and black bodies glistening with sweat, the little strip of the village had grown up around the clearing where the ferry docked, with towering green shaded forests clawed down to either shore. Only a half mile of this giant forest has been cleared and broken to allow the tiny settlement. With the rich soil somehow indecently exposed, in this arboreal territory, cultivation looks obscene, like a knife wound would in the flesh of those shiny black bodies, nevertheless there is a feeling of arriving. Generation after generation of riverine people have lived hereabouts and proudly call it home. A civilization complete in itself and not dependent on the blankets, the rusty cans of corned beef and the red plastic bowls or even the dilapidated inboard engine of the ferry, that the superimposed western civilization has brought. That, and the corrugated iron that made up the shacks that house these tiny products of civilization.

Both he and Jenny felt that such things had eroded, rather than improved the lifestyle of these riverside people. Then there was the only other civilizing factor: the corrugated iron mission school with the gaps in its tin walls instead of windows, a mud floor and axe-hewn seats from the copious logs, and run by a dedicated Jesuit priest. Whether that smattering of knowledge had enhanced or destroyed the happiness of the children who lived there God alone knew. Neither Jenny nor himself would venture an opinion on that subject but Simon was more certain, 'Dad, do you mean these kids actually have to go to school as well as live in a place like this? That's not fair Dad.' An imagined voice from his daughter Nicky in Oz, again, 'Remember the journalist bit, bwana.' Nicky had called her father bwana ever since she first learned to speak. She had caught the habit from Simon who started calling his father 'bwana' as soon as he learnt the word, on his arrival in Kenya.

The journalist bit – he smiled to himself. When he was in the UK for the trial years later the old friend he was staying with dug out some copies of the *Northampton Chronicle* and *Echo* which somehow or other had syndicated the story he had sent to his local rag. On re-reading them he was embarrassed by his early naivety. 'Dateline, Stanleyville', it read. 'The Belgians are doing a good job in the Congo, educating the native Africans for the responsibility that will force them into civilization when they become an independent nation and an independent nation I am sure they will become. It will be a peaceful transition and it will come whatever the diehards say. If not in this generation then most certainly in the next.'

In fact it came five short years later. The Belgians had almost criminally and definitely deliberately, neglected to teach any African anything. It was reliably reported that on independence there were only two qualified African doctors in a country twice as big as France! As for peaceful transition, it was a bloodbath. He thought to himself what exciting days those were before the Prime Minister of the UK, Harold Macmillan, when visiting South Africa a few years later, was to coin the phrase 'the wind of change' which was to blow right up the continent from the Drakensberg in the south to the Atlas mountains in the north. When the Hills drove to Africa only a handful of the fifty states were independent. Today, he thought, for better or for worse, and mostly for worse, they were all independent.

Mixed up around that time he remembered crossing the equator and their entry into the southern hemisphere. Everybody, including in their case a Dutch couple overlanding in a Volkswagen Beetle, stopped at the equator sign to take photographs. It is always cold at 6,000 feet in the Ruwenzori Mountains, often wet and windy and this anomaly always appealed to the many amateur photographers whose photographs show pictures of well-wrapped up passengers and whose titles invariably read 'On the equator'. The more experienced overlanders do not stop – the Tropic of Cancer sign rotting sun-bleached in the Sahara to the north and the Tropic of Capricorn sign in the Kalahari to the south are also both 'old hat' to them.

Harry's thoughts about their 'crossing' was suddenly put out of his mind by another memory. It was an idea much later that his twelve-year old daughter had while she was staying with a schoolfriend during the 'summer' holidays at Nanyuki in Kenya. It was during the pogo stick craze. Her friend's farm at which she was staying lay sprawled across the Equator on the foothills of Mount Kenya. One glorious November morning as the sun tinted the icy tips of Mount Kenya a celestial pink to herald what sick men and women later called 'Another fucking lovely day in Paradise' Nicky and her friend were trudging down the farm track to the road at the bottom where the sign clearly stated 'The Equator' with a red line dividing a painted map of Africa neatly in half. They both had pogo sticks over their shoulders and it was six-fifteen in the morning. From then until eleven thirty the same morning they jumped on their pogo sticks, literally jumping from one side of the Equator to the other, averaging 2,000 jumps per hour to a total of five hours with five-minute breaks every half hour. They totalled 9,650 jumps across the line, then Nicky's friend's big brother drove down in the Land Rover and took them back to the farm for a huge breakfast, and since it was before mid-day and since it was the first food they had had to eat that day, they claimed it could be called breakfast. Nicky then wrote to the editor of the *Guinness Book of Records* claiming the record for having crossed the equator 9,650 times before breakfast. She never got a reply to the letter but it gave the whole family considerable enjoyment and even to this day Harry would smile when visitors enquired if they were going to cross the equator on their safari but that of course was much later.

Uganda, geographically the blessed prelude to the majesty that is Kenya, is cursed politically. Poor old Uganda, which all the experts including a twenty-five year old Churchill, had said would lead the East African community in triumph. So friendly were her natives, so rich her soil, so ancient her kingdoms. Once Uganda was freed of the fetters of the British Protectorate, said the starry-eyed world of 1957, she would blossom forth in peace and plenty and the mighty shout of 'Freedom' would herald a new and glorious age. Sitting in his car Harry shook his head, not once but often. The most tragic actor in the tragedy that is independent Africa, is Uganda. The very waters of her Lake Victoria were to turn red with blood as a maniac performed his genocide, and Britain flew him in a VC10 full of whisky once a month.

Uganda was to know no peace even after the expulsion of the tyrant, warring tribes constantly fought each other, until she who should have been the greatest of the East African trio was the least.

☆   ☆   ☆

Like all private overlanders he and Jenny had a list of 'useful contact addresses'. Nebulous strands from associates of people who might be able to help, not friends of friends so much as acquaintances of acquaintances. Over the following thirty years he was to have his fill of such nebulous associations when at six o'clock in the morning the phone would ring, 'Hi, is that Mr Hill? This is so-and-so, so-and-so said I should give you a ring when I got to Nairobi. I'm stuck at Nairobi Airport' – pregnant pause – 'and I wondered if . . .' but that first time in East Africa he had not yet been plagued by 'the takers' and he naively thought the addresses would welcome them. Fortunately, in his case, the majority of them did. One such address led him via a left-wing firebrand from the next village of Husbands Bosworth whom he had occasionally met at village hops, to a friend of his called Doris Kabaka who apparently had been at the London School of Economics with his neighbour and who was now back at Makerere University in Kampala. 'You must look her up when you get there . . . .' Another address they had was from Jenny's parents who, during the war, had been neighbours to some Lancashire farmers and when, after the war, there was talk of a new road, called a motorway, being planned which would bisect their farm. They had taken off to East Africa lock, stock and barrel or, as the Wards put it, cow, heifer and milking parlour. Jenny could just remember, as a very small child, going for walks amongst the Singleton herd of Friesians and now she was soon to find the same herd, the same people, in the Aberdare foothills in Kenya; the Harrisons from Lancashire had settled in Kenya. The first contact letter however led to Doris Kabaka who turned out to be an attractive African girl about twenty-five years old.

During all their trips they had avoided hitch-hikers like the plague. To begin with, there was not much room for them across the front of Tilda and they didn't know what they would

134

get up to if they put them in the back! In fact, they had almost decided not to go out of their way to look for this Doris woman at Makerere University because they selfishly thought it would be of little use to them and she would be bound to want a lift – which she did. As it happened, the weaver was at work again. They were having trouble finding a campsite in Kampala, and as they were driving to the outskirts they happened to pass the entrance to Makerere University. 'Shall we?' Harry looked at Jenny.

'Oh, all right,' she nodded, 'why not?'

So they swung Tilda up the drive, young Simon perked up hopefully, 'I bet they'll have a swimming pool, Dad.'

Jenny added, 'Yes, and it will be nice to talk to a local. We really must find Ken's friend from the LSE.'

'Yuk,' said Harry who could not accept the LSE even then.

Before they knew where they were, there she was sitting in the front of Tilda on an ice box they had taken out of the back because there was not any room on the seats. She had wanted a lift to Nairobi and she was such a cheerful soul that they couldn't find it in themselves to refuse.

Two addresses as large as life itself, the Lancashire farmers, as Harry was to remember the Harrisons, and Dory, as they all soon called Doris like Simon did from the start. He made her his special friend. Who can doubt the web of destiny must have a weaver as the African girl is transported down one of the strands of the web by Tilda through the green banana fronds and past the bright red soil, over Rippon Falls perhaps to dance her Kismet in Kenya's Aberdare Forests – the very womb of Mau Mau?

So big an impression did Dory make on them all that when he was trying to recall those days he completely forgot that it was in Queen Elizabeth National Park or QE Park as everybody called it, that they saw their first game proper – their first lion that is. They had seen their first elephant in the herds round Putnam's Camp where most overlanders watched the unsuccessful efforts of the Belgians to train the African elephant to work like their Indian cousins and where always the same racial joke was made about the failure. 'Well, what do you expect? It's an African elephant?'

Dory took over Simon's seat which he had been using lately which was a drop seat like a London taxi which was fixed to the back of the adjoining door into the rear of Tilda. This left the main passenger seat on which so many nurses had sat in the past with Jenny sitting on it. Looking through Tilda's narrow split windscreen at the row of four faces any observers who were likely to observe both black and white would probably only note the unusual sight of an African girl travelling in the company of Europeans, but on closer inspection the observers would also have to agree that they were a particularly impressive-looking quartet; for a start there were no knobbly white knees. Nearly half a year on the road, much of it in the tropics had ensured that Jenny, Simon and himself were sunburnt to a uniform and healthy-looking dark brown, from their foreheads to their ankles.

Doris Kabaka's ebony black skin had a most attractive softness. Harry had never thought much about skins before, let alone their colour. The Arabs in North African were usually draped all over in loose-fitting cloth, but now next to him he found himself glancing down at the shapeliest of bare black legs and whilst being fairly platonic about it, he found that that leg disappearing into the whitest and shortest of shorts that Dory wore attracted him rather than repelled him. Dory's black skin came in for comments from both Jenny and himself. One day Jenny, when she was eulogizing over Dory's good looks said, 'God, Dory, you are lucky. You've got a perfect black peach complexion, half the girls in our village would give their right hands for that'. Dory found this hard to believe as just about every other friend she had would secretly have given their right hand to have had Jenny's colouring.

One night while they were having their evening meal on the camp stools they were discussing the subject of skin again. 'Present company excepted, of course,' Harry said, rather pompously, 'whites as a general rule do have rather a grotty complexion.'

'Pasty, pimply, pale and pink,' put in Doris, with a wink at Jenny – a sentence she had obviously often heard before.

'Right,' agreed Harry, 'present company excepted' he added again, noticing a rather peculiar look from Jenny. Jenny, at that time, was exuding the sexuality of an outdoor glamour girl. There was an added firmness to her figure, and that, together with her new confidence and an obvious satisfaction with life, had made her look a little taller than her already above-average five feet nine. Her hair, once critically described by her mother as mouse-brown, was, after months of sunlight, almost golden. Her steely blue eyes showed to their very best advantage in a tanned face. Add her perfectly proportioned nose, and generous mouth and there was little wonder that Harry was always counting his blessings and was extremely proud of her. In the UK she was referred to as a 'pretty girl', now 'beautiful woman' was a more accurate description. When they were alone he used to say 'Jen, you know you look like a film star these days – what is it?' and she would smile happily.

Harry had started growing a beard the day they drove down to Dover. By now it was neatly trimmed to a surprisingly smart half-an-inch in length all the way from one ear to the other with just a hint of ginger in it. Unlike most overlanders who invariably grow a beard and shave it off as soon as they complete the trip, usually in Nairobi, his was to stay with him for the rest of his life. The 'growth' as Jenny carefully called it, having not yet decided whether she liked it or not, did something for his receding chin, but seemed to accentuate his already large Hills' family nose. Dory had the classical features of the ancient empire of Upper Egypt. She was tall as well; in fact she was the same height as Jenny. Her hair was swept back or what little of it there was. 'Don't laugh', she confided in Jenny one night, 'I've never had a hair-cut in my life. It has taken me all my life to grow that little pony tail.' The two girls were the same age and were soon swopping intimacies and obviously enjoying each other's company tremendously. Dory had a high forehead and prominent cheekbones. Together they made a very striking pair and Harry was, in the terminology of the day, 'highly chuffed' to be in their company. These were 'first impression' days for Harry and suddenly he found himself being classified as a 'liberal wog-lover' by the right-wing European community in Entebbe for example. He noticed that it was usually the mature white wives that scowled on seeing the black girl sitting alongside him, even the most reactionary of males couldn't hide the fact that both girls were full of sex appeal.

As for young Simon, well, most young children have a natural charm and Simon was an excellent example. Golden long hair, more suited to the seventies than the fifties, but Jenny hadn't got around to a barber's shop yet. A genuine smile of interest more often than not across his well-proportioned face and more than once Jenny had confided in Harry, 'God help the girls in another ten years. Simon will charm the pants off all of them'. Dory was interested in the workings of Tilda and her equipment, and Simon enjoyed every second of showing her around. 'Which tap is your drinking water from? Which shovel to take with you on the night walk?' Simon, of course, knew every nut and bolt on Tilda. He had been driving her during the easy flat desert sections. Harry was particularly proud to notice that Simon had even mastered the gear shift which, for a seven-year old, was quite an achievement since British Military three-ton Austin gearboxes did not have a synchromesh. Harry smiled to himself, remembering the sight of Simon with two cushions stuffed behind his back, and then because the pedals were so hot in the desert, he would put his sandals back on because, like the hundreds of young Caucasian Kenya children he was shortly to meet, none wore shoes when they need not. Their feet became as tough as rhino skin. Strangely most African children only went barefoot until their parents could afford a pair of shoes for them and then they took them off as little as the European kids put theirs on. That, and the African girls desperately trying to lighten their skins and the European girls desperately trying to get sunburnt were the first idiosyncrasies they noticed in the glorious cloud-cuckoo-land they were now entering called Kenya. Those idiosyncrasies, he thought, they soon learnt to tolerate. What he couldn't tolerate was present-day Kenya where the electricity supply would fail fifty times a year, where you met more people who had been robbed than had not, a city where on one occasion a Mini Minor actually had to be towed out of a pothole and saddest of all where hundreds of thousands of university degree students flooded the job market with only ten per cent of them getting a job.

As they crossed Uganda they had perhaps become just a little blasé, or at least travel-blunted, when it came to the appreciation of magnificent scenery. They had seen so much, so many dramatic escarpment roads, winding through so many a mountain range, so many silver sheets of lakes, in so many valleys, yellow deserts, green forests, sombre mountains, and because there was no super-dramatic scenery they found Uganda just a little boring.

Many years later when Harry and his son drove south from Nairobi to Cape Town he would yearn for the green gentle slopes which were Uganda, as he discovered that Northern Rhodesia, or Zambia as it is now, was a truly boring country and much of Southern Rhodesia equally so. Although the Zims made up in interest what their country lacked in scenery.

Dory was an ideal travelling companion and her knowledge of Swahili assisted them to such an extent that they wondered how ever they had managed without her. Simon proudly showed her off when they went shopping. In the pre-Dory days it had been quite difficult to explain that they wanted margarine, not butter, or toothpaste, not toothpowder, and toilet paper, of course. Harry smiled at the amount of times they had to enact that one, in order to get it down from a high shelf in some forlorn tin shack of a shop. Wicks for paraffin lamps were another item they found extremely hard to describe, but now Dory was doing it all for them, easily, pleasantly. Shopping became fun. One bright sunny morning five and a half months since they set off from Husbands Bosworth, a grand tune could be heard coming from the cab of Tilda as they all sang in unison, 'One more border, one more border to cross' to the tune of 'One More River' – Kenya's.

Never before could Harry remember being so happy for so long as during his first months in Kenya. Jenny in a slightly less extroverted fashion was also extremely pleased with life and proud of having arrived at their destination. Simon couldn't have been any happier than he had been every day since they had left home, for him there was just the faint cloud on the horizon that perhaps they would soon be at their destination and then what? The last frontier implied an end, and school, and staying put, and a routine. Naturally, as a seven-year old, he couldn't explain all this but he thought it, especially just before he went to sleep. In fact he caught his mother by surprise one night when he asked in a completely innocent voice, 'Mum, would it be all right, if I was a sailor when I grow up?'

'A sailor, dear, what ever gave you that idea? You've only sailed on the Channel in your life.'

'I know – but well, sailors in big ships, oil tankers and things, they must always be going somewhere – I'd like that.'

Jenny gave him her full-scale Madonna smile, Jenny looked

ethereally beautiful when she smiled like that. 'All right, darling,' she whispered, 'you be a sailor.'

6

The Gun Fight at the Harrisons' Corral

Lord Delamare, who gave his life and most of his family fortunes in various attempts at farming in Kenya before and after the First World War, first entered Kenya from Somali on horseback. He instantly fell in love with the country. So it is with overlanders today who can find nothing wrong with Kenya and very much right with it. Their exuberance was heightened by the plenty, coming so suddenly after there had been such scarcity. Starting with the second imperative, fresh eggs, fresh oranges, fresh shrimps, oysters, fresh fruit of every kind you can imagine – strawberries, raspberries, even, and probably several you can't imagine. Harry and Jenny, although they had been fruitmongering for many years had never even seen an avocado in those days, before tons were flown to Amsterdam every night. In Kenya they were rotting on the trees. Fresh asparagus, paw-paw, pineapple, mangoes, broccoli, lobster, Malindi smoked fish as good as Yarmouth bloaters. Prime beef and tender Molo lamb. When it comes to food Kenyans can out-Texan Texans with their hyperbole.

All this after months and months of deprivation, because from the Mediterranean coast to East Africa a tin of peas is probably the only vegetable that you would taste – that, and for the fruit the banana. But the second imperative is only a start. In Kenya they found totally unexpectedly a profusion of such sports as polo, hockey, cricket, golf, rugger, squash and played with such enthusiasm in such perfect surroundings. Then there was horse racing, motor racing, repertory theatre, and amateur musicals, the like of which had to be seen to be believed. There was an almost personal pride of all Kenyan expats and Europeans alike, as the Black Kenyans dominated the

Olympic Games track events. At the time they arrived in Nairobi, for first night cinema performances, people still actually dressed for the occasion. Beer and cigarettes were at a quarter of the price of Europe and twice as good.

Add to all these little treats the delightful atmosphere, the glorious clean, spectacular scenery, the snow-capped mountains, the lakes, the forests, the valleys, the game of the plains grazing eternally, the waving fields of wheat, the vast horizons, the blue skies, and the coral reef. Even the development was welcome. In the UK Harry used to wince every time a by-pass cut through a moorland or every time pylons desecrated a hillside. Here in Kenya when there was development there was so much space that one felt happy that a small piece of the wild had been tamed.

The social atmosphere as well – everybody they met seemed to welcome them. In the UK they had felt that to do anything was to compete. Here just about everybody wanted your endeavours to succeed – jobs galore, good pay, servants, company cars, glorious gardens. Another strange and unexpected advantage of emigration was that somehow one found it easy to distance oneself from the outside world's crises and problems and yet involve oneself in the world's good news – the moon landings, for example, were enjoyed on Nairobi TV instantaneously with Washington. The naturally optimistic Harry was naturally optimistic when surrounded by such a congenial atmosphere and he had no doubts that it was a paradise they had entered. Now thirty-five years later, he had his doubts. It was perhaps then the best of times all right, but it was also the worst of times. The 'Cherry Orchard' days, beautiful flowers, but rotten at the roots. Like the French aristocracy 200 years before them, the Kenya settlers had been sitting on a powder keg and it had just ignited.

After some 150 evening meals sitting on folding canvas stools round a small table, usually between the two large rear doors of Tilda that were left open for easy access to the stove and sink, the work routine was down to a fine art. The quality of the food was constant.

It said much for Dory's character that she slid into the

142

intimate pattern so easily and was so completely accepted.

One night during their second week in Kenya the scene was typical. It was a perfect evening, the sun setting as it does every night in that latitude between six thirty pm and six forty-five pm with the short tropical dusk, gas lights ready but not yet necessary. A perfect temperature, almost balmy, with the evening scents and the birds calling as they picked their branches for the night. Then the cicadas and crickets would start their din. All present and correct.

Harry, Simon and Dory sitting expectantly as Jenny steps professionally and expertly down the steep step in the rear of Tilda on which so many a wounded soldier had sat, efficiently and effortlessly placing a plate of steak and mash in front of each of them. She then goes back to get a steaming saucepan of brussels sprouts.

On this occasion there was also a mangy half-starved dog, the same sort of dog as is found all over the third world, called in Swahili, a Shenzi, a very useful word which is also used to perfectly describe inferior work, inferior objects or even an inferior person. Looking so unhealthy and appreciating the possibility that it might be rabid he tried half-heartedly to shoo it away and it cowered in the background, its head between its front paws with the bones of its haunches showing clearly. He was delighted at the small, sweet, tender brussels sprouts which they had just been served, and he recalled an incident that happened just a month or two before they left England. Harry and Simon had gone with Tilda to fetch two tons of brussels sprouts from Biggleswade. He had a friend there and he heard the market was depressed, ideal for Harry who had been trying wholesaling on the Leicester market. Typically, of his trading efforts in the UK the low price for brussels sprouts reached Leicester at the same time as Harry's brussels sprouts did, but the joke was that he had been teasing young Simon when he had asked exactly where they came from by saying, 'Brussels of course, where else do you think sprouts come from'. Then, when his schoolteacher asked him the day following his truancy where he had been he proudly replied, 'Brussels'.

Simon, Harry was pleased to note, was enjoying his food in general but liked vegetables the least. 'Wonderful, wonderful vegetables,' he said proudly and deliberately pompously, 'anybody who doesn't agree that they melt in your mouth and are

143

perfection, will have to do the washing up,' he said with a wicked grin, knowing that Simon was not too fond of them, but Simon had the last laugh. He couldn't restrain his giggles. Dory had quietly got up from the table with her plate empty, except for the brussels sprouts, which she had unobtrusively placed at the feet of the Shenzi dog and was now bending down trying not to be noticed to recover the plate and Harry could hear her whispering, 'Well, go on, eat them up, you silly idiot'.

Then the sun set completely and the lights were lit. Three beers and a Coke were brought out of the fridge. Harry inhaled his new 'Clipper' brand cigarette enjoying becoming addicted to them as much as he had been to Players. God was in His Heaven and all was well with the world.

Two whole weeks in the magnificent glorious White Highlands of Kenya but then even the optimistic Harry had to agree that the best of times came suddenly to an end and soon would come a terror to all their breasts. Soon Harry's mouth was to be so dry with fear that he couldn't speak. Soon, was to be the worst of times indeed. Yet thirty-four years later he had to admit that, in a way too difficult to explain even to Nicky, just as the black smoke and tumbling walls of the Blitz, and like the creeping barrage from howitzers that rendered the night asunder before El Alamein, so roaring up a Kenyan track in the moonlight with Sten gun blazing from Tilda's cab, held too, an awful pleasure.

All Kenya farmers who lived in the Aberdare Highlands and farmed their foothills will assure you that when it comes to a comparison with Scotland, Scotland is the second best. There is moss, there is heather, icy mountain streams, there are sand grouse, there is peat, the similarity cannot be avoided and the little streams feed the feeder river that tumbles over Thompson's Falls and round the falls had sprung a little market town devoted to the settlers of the White Highlands of that area.

The Hills' second contact, the Harrisons, the ex-Lancashire farmers, lived here. Morale was high, Tilda was purring away like a kitten and all her crew were ready for a stay in a genuine up-country farm with all the rustic delights that that entailed, horse riding, tennis probably, swimming in the mountain streams, and glorious walks in glorious countryside.

Many situations in real life in Europe, as in bedroom farce plays, start and end with the opening and shutting of doors. When overlanding, and in East Africa in general, it is different. Usually the characters you are looking for or departing from, are first and last observed outside their houses. The memsahib could well be seen in her garden and the bwana instructing his labour in the yard. The European children of the farms usually enter the scene on horseback, new characters appear usually at the end of the inevitable drive, even in a Nairobi suburb it is usually outside the house that it all happens. No slamming of a door to end the scene in Kenya, there you leave behind the friends, still waving their farewells in a faint haze of exhaust as you drive away, and so it was as the Hills and Doris Kabaka drove up the Harrisons' drive in Tilda. There was no name board at the end of the drive and they were therefore uncertain that they were on the correct track. The first sign of life they met was a Ferguson tractor coming towards them pulling a trailer and in the trailer must have been nearly a hundred labourers. Such mundane sights as these still amazed the greenhorns. But Dory quite nonchalantly took the opportunity to ask the tractor driver if the Harrisons were at home and if in fact they were on the right farm. She called to the tractor driver in her fluent Swahili, '*Mwenyewe – Harrisons iko hapa?*' to which he cheerfully shouted back, '*Hapana, lakini wale mama wazee wawili iko*'. From this useful conversation Doris explained to the others that they were on the right drive, it was the right farm, but Mr and Mrs Harrison were away, but the two elderly ladies who looked after the farm were there of course.

So it was that Harry and Jenny and Simon and Dory first met two of the most incredible people they would have the pleasure of meeting in all their lives. The two elderly Miss Watsons, Daise and Fran, or '*Mama Wazee*' as the tractor driver had referred to them, were in their most typical of poses as they arrived.

The Watson sisters were both in their seventies but were as sprightly as forty year olds with an intelligence which stood out amongst their contemporaries. The Harrisons' farm, on the rolling foothills of the Aberdares, was in the most beautiful setting that any of the visitors had ever seen, and the old brick-built Elizabethan timbered mansion of a farmhouse was worthy of the setting. Despite being built amongst some of the finest building timber in the world, like cedar and Meru oak, some of the beams for the building, it was alleged, had been specially imported from the UK before the First World War.

The purple mountains climbed away behind the farm. At the end of the giant valley, sweeping down to join the Great Rift Valley itself well sprinkled with acacia trees and whistling thorn, could be seen the snow-capped peaks of Mount Kenya, some seventy miles away. As they approached the house they saw the low walled sunken rose garden in front of it giving a riot of colour which would have done credit to any summer garden at a desirable residence in Marlow on Thames – and such a fragrance. Highlighted to perfection by being set amid the very epitome of Kenya's vast horizons. The two Watson sisters seemed completely worthy of the unforgettable scene. Each wore a straw hat, and calf-length skirts, and each had an ivory-handled Colt revolver tucked into belts around their waists. Side arms were still worn by most up-country settlers in Kenya in 1957. Some settlers thought that the Mau Mau was finished. Deden Kimathi was awaiting the gallows in Kimiti prison just outside Nairobi and the RAF were bombing the forests around Mount Kenya daily to burn out the handful of defeated gangs that still tenuously stuck to the mountainsides. Others were not quite so sure. The security forces were at their height and every village the whole length and breadth of the White Highlands boasted a police post with sandbagged windows.

The two elderly sisters were gardening, or as near to gardening as Kenya settlers ever get. Each was standing behind a kneeling shamba boy, '*Ta fanya nini na he musigi saga?*' – 'What shall I do with this one memsahib?' asked one of the boys holding up a broken rose bush to the elderly lady behind him. Fran Watson was already framing a rude reply, to tell the garden boy just what to do with the broken plant. He never got an answer because she turned round to see the four passengers alighting from the front of Tilda which was by now neatly parked in the huge swept grass area at the end of the drive, which obviously served as a car park.

Harry was rather surprised to see that there were no other vehicles there. Tilda was in the shade of the one object which belied the perfection of the scene; the goon tower. In common with most remote White Highland farms, even towards the end of the Mau Mau emergency, these towers which had been erected at the beginning of the emergency were still very much in use, looking like prisoner of war towers manned by a loyal Askari all night long, often boasting two 'Very light' rockets to be fired to alert neighbours or the security forces in the event of trouble in the form of a Mau Mau raid. In Indian file the four visitors approached the two old ladies. What they never dreamt was that they were walking in on a living legend.

The Watson 'girls' were older than Kenya Colony itself. Their story was the story of the British Empire in south, central and east Africa. Their father, the late Major Alan Watson, along with two lieutenants, two sergeants of arms and thirty-seven troopers, all mounted, had been, as the Boers always put it, 'massacred to a man by the treacherous Matabele in 1892'.

Chief Lobengula would have described the scene rather differently. He would have said, 'That lunatic Jameson whose raid the previous year had almost set the continent on fire, had persuaded the major, who did not require much persuading, to cross the border with a troop of forty-two mounted horse to capture a chief whose territory they had invaded. The chief would insist that the 'massacre' occurred when warriors loyal to the Ris household, numbering hundreds, set upon the invaders and with severe loss of life on both sides, it being a question of attacking on foot with spears against the mounted men with rifles, the Matabele managed to defeat them, thus saving their chief's life'.

Like all history, the truth of how the good major met his death so long ago is probably somewhere between these two views. What is certain is that the ill-fated major left behind in the Cape Town Barracks Officers' Quarters an eligible widow with two little daughters, one aged five and the other six. The legend continues by telling how the girls got the 3,000-odd miles from Cape Town to northern Kenya's town of Eldoret in an ox cart with their mother and stepfather and two more baby siblings in tow. The story says that they had little money and less resources but tremendous determination. Fran herself would love to explain how she could remember being laid out spread-eagle on a table with a sheet of canvas beneath her and how her mother would run round with a chalk mark down her arms, down her body, round her legs, and up the other side and this would be the pattern for one side of a coarse canvas coat she would be given to wear to keep out the cold rains of the Kenyan Highlands.

Before the First World War Fran and Daise were respectively associated with, in the fullest meaning of the word, two of the greatest characters of the century, Teddy Roosevelt and Winston Churchill, both of whom visited up-country British East Africa around the time that the two Miss Watsons were at their most beautiful and fancy free and footloose. But such stories were inevitable with two such glamorous girls living so wild a life.

Apparently only some two or three years previous to the Hills meeting them, a very British District Officer complete with pith helmet was on his knees begging forgiveness from Daise, she having just learned of a Somali mistress the officer favoured a day's ride north. 'Believe me, Daise, you have no cause to be jealous . . . .'

'Jealous, you bloody old fool, jealous! – it's not that emotion that is turning me orf. It's fear – fear of the clap that's holding me back.'

Each sister always had a perpetual untipped cigarette in their mouths, the smoke from which had stained both their greying hair yellow in front. Their voices were as clipped as that of a huntswoman from the English shires.

Not unkindly Fran held out her hand to the visitors saying, at the same time, 'Harrisons have gone orf I'm afraid, orf to a wedding and polo and such like. They said they'd be back today but I doubt it. Still, I expect you must be tired. Go in and sit down. I'll get Sampson to get you some tea.' As the little troop entered the huge French windows opening into a large and well-furnished sitting room they could hear Daise shout '*Sampson lete chai ngini*'.

Then Fran's eye caught sight of a bottle of JB whisky which Harry always found worked wonders at borders and the like. This bottle was the last of a crate of two dozen which he had started out with. 'You're very welcome to stay if you like, you know. Plenty of room. It would be company for us too.' Then, and not in the least unkindly way, Fran looked at Dory and Simon and said, 'I expect the ayah would like to take the young man and have their tea in the kitchen' raising her voice at the end of the sentence to make it a cross between a question

148

and an order.

He and Jenny's mouth dropped open and embarrassment showed on their faces. Dory was much more prepared. She had had more experience and she and Simon rose perfectly to the occasion. 'OK. See you later then,' Dory said, tugging at Simon's coat sleeve as she left the room with Simon in tow and departed to the depths of the kitchen. Simon later found himself in a huge bedroom which belonged to the son of the house, who was only slightly older than himself and was away at boarding school at Gilgil, some forty miles away. His bows and arrows, bicycles, and water skis were everywhere, along with a huge bed and piles and piles of comics – a perfect paradise indeed, and all the fun of reading in bed by a hissing pressure light. The potential quarters for Dory, the ayah, weren't quite so splendid. In fact one look at the little hut where she was meant to be sleeping, and she opted to stay in the back of Tilda which she knew she would have to herself as all the Hills would obviously be sleeping in the big house.

Over tea Harry and Jenny learnt more details of the facts that the Harrisons, the original Lancashire Harrisons who had immigrated complete with their cattle just after the war, were away as the sisters had originally told them, at a neighbouring farm where there was a polo match and a wedding combined. 'Bloody great piss up. Shouldn't wonder if they are not back tomorrow night either,' said Daise as she became more familiar. After a cucumber sandwich tea had been served and cleared away by red-fezzed Sampson in a white kanzu it was suggested that Simon might like to have his supper. Tradition had it that children ate high tea and did not attend their elders' dinner parties, thus was enacted the most amusing scene, Simon playing the part to perfection. Around six o'clock, sitting up in solitary state at the end of the high tea table, Dory entered from the kitchen with beans on toast for him. She was acting the part of an ayah, with a flourish of her right hand as she majestically set the plate in front of the young Simon. 'Tea, m'lord'. 'Yes, and hurry up' replied the laughing Simon curtly, enjoying the act tremendously. Then Dory scuttled out, dragging her feet in a most amusing fashion across the tiled floor.

During the evening meal proper, as it was referred to, Simon was in his huge bed upstairs. Dory had withdrawn to Tilda and Harry and Jenny were eagerly learning more from the two

Watson sisters. Apparently the sisters were staying at the Harrisons and had been for over eighteen months now, ever since the guest house that they had owned and managed about ten miles away had been burnt down by the Mau Mau. That had sounded a pretty horrific night, but strangely as the elderly ladies had run out of the burning house they had not been molested and had been allowed to escape. In fact they ran, in their nightgowns, all of three miles to the nearest police post. That was a year and a half ago by now and the Harrisons had apparently got so used to them being around that neither they nor the farmers wished to part. Harry was later to learn that this sort of mutual set-up with friends for life was typical of Kenyan settlers. The Hills retired to bed that evening weary but happy and slept the sleep of the just.

They were finishing breakfast the next morning – Simon was allowed to join them for breakfast, though Dory was not – when a Land Rover swung into the farmhouse car park and parked beside Tilda. Peter Harrison had rushed back to make sure all was well on his farm. He was still slightly 'hung over' from the night before, and in a terrific hurry as he had to be back for the first chukka of his polo match in less than an hour. His reaction to the four unexpected visitors was also typical of that kind of settler. He was genuinely pleased to see them but of course they must not be allowed to interrupt or alter his plans. The obvious thing was for them to join in. 'Great, super. I know what. All of you come over to Lloyd's place.' 'No, no, he won't mind – they have got this bloody great wedding going on and nobody knows who's who anyway. They would love to see you.'

After a little thought both Harry and Jenny saw no reason why they should not accept the invitation. They were enjoying being organized for a change. It was agreed that young Simon and his 'ayah' should stay put in the big house with the Watsons whilst his mother and father went off to the party, it was all rather rushed and they did not even have time to change. Leaving Simon behind was just as well, Harry realized, because he felt sure that the black girl would not be welcome at the Kenya society wedding of the year. Not at the front door anyway. Before any of them really knew what was happening Peter had them all organized and he was ushering Harry and Jenny into his Land Rover.

'Bye Daise, bye Fran, be good – don't do anything I wouldn't. Take young Simon riding if you like. Sagana is about the best nag left here. OK. See you.' As he drove down the drive in the Land Rover he turned to Harry and Jenny and said with all genuineness, 'I really am glad to see you. Sorry it's such a rush.' And he really was glad to see them, in those days any new white face was an ally, an automatic ally for the beleaguered settlers. As Jenny looked back and saw Tilda parked there she had just the slightest qualms about leaving Simon and Tilda for the first time in so many months, but as they mixed with the polo-wedding guests where the champagne flowed like water, she soon forgot her misgivings.

Back at the Harrisons' farm Dory and Simon had had a perfect day. Simon had ridden a little before, bare-backed, in the field opposite the shop that he used to live above, in England, he told Dory, but was not an expert. Dory was the same standard, having ridden her brother's horses on occasion in Kampala but again was not really into horses. They had ridden for miles and miles in the glorious countryside, both enjoying themselves tremendously. As they rode leisurely back to the house on horses both were healthily tired. The two sisters had seen them off that morning. They were surprised to find that the ayah rode.

'I've never known an ayah to ride before, have you Daise?'

'No, can't say I have' replied Daise, 'but I don't see why not. Get them out of our hair anyway.' She continued, absent-mindedly, 'Not a bad kid, as kids go. Fancy him remembering all those places he has seen. You know we really must have a look round one day. We've been stuck here for long enough. I'd love to see Egypt before I die,' ended Daise, just a little sorry for herself.

'Bloody old fool,' replied Fran, 'you know you wouldn't go anywhere if you had the chance and anyway we're needed here.'

Now that the 'ayah' and Simon were back from their successful day's riding and the Tanganyika boiler had been stoked up, it only remained for Simon to have his bath, his high tea and spend his second night in the big bedroom. Dory ate comfortably and adequately in the kitchen with Sampson and then went out for her second night in Tilda.

It was eleven o'clock in the evening, Saturday August 12th,

151

1957. The star-strewn night was perfect with a crescent moon casting silver shadows across the farmhouse and its outbuildings; young Simon was fast asleep in his huge bed and Dory curled up comfortably asleep in the bottom bunk of Tilda. The Watson sisters were both reading in bed by the light of the pressure lights which together with the oil lights and candles illuminated everything. There was no electricity in most up-country farms in those days.

In the still of the night there was a blood-curdling scream as the watchman in the tower thudded to the ground thirty feet below with an arrow literally in one side of his neck and out the other. He had not died in vain. Fran and Daise in their separate rooms each hearing the scream moved in unison. Each hurled their book away, and leapt up grabbing a rifle from the sides of their beds and then collected another one and ammunition. Both ran out into the passage. Fran ran to the end of the passage where there was a little low alcove overlooking the front of the house. Within forty seconds of the scream she had shot six rounds off out of the upstairs window and two bodies lay dead in the rose garden. Some half-dozen more bodies retreated behind the rose garden wall to get out of the deadly line of fire. As Fran continued firing and holding down the attacking Mau Mau terrorists or freedom fighters, as they were later to be known, she shouted over her shoulder from her kneeling position at the open window, 'Daise you cover the back door, right? I shouldn't think they will go for the side French windows; I hope not.'

Daise was kneeling down already with her .303 Lee-Enfield at an upstairs window which covered the back door, and firing at shadows as they too retreated into the bushes. Not two minutes had passed since the death of the watchman. Simon was awakened by the noise of the shooting and was standing in the passage in his blue and white striped pyjamas looking at the old ladies firing from either end of the landing. A muffled crash, followed by tinkling glass was clearly heard. Fran and Daise spread out equidistant along the upstairs passage.

'Shit,' exclaimed Fran, still in the kneeling position. Then, seeing the boy standing in the passage, 'Listen, boy, they're at the side door now, below your room. We can't move from where we are or they will be through the front or through the back. Quick, boy, go and loose a few rounds out of your

152

bedroom window will you? That'll scare them off,' and she thrust a smaller .22 repeating rifle into the hands of Simon who was now standing behind her. Simon had handled Harry's air gun in the UK so he knew at least where the trigger was. He was also used to doing what he was told so he trotted back into his bedroom, knocked out a pane of glass, as he had seen done in cowboy films and quickly fired three shots in quick succession out of the window, across the yard in the direction of the dining room French window below. He thought he saw two figures run back into the farmyard about a hundred feet away from the door. 'Good on you, boy' shouted Daise from the passage.

For five minutes which seemed more like five hours, each of the upstairs marksmen fired any time any of them even imagined they saw a movement. Simon was by now used to his new role which he took very seriously. The two old ladies were certainly not showing any sign of fear, even if they felt it. On the contrary, they seemed to be enjoying themselves tremendously. 'Got plenty of ammo down there, Daise?' shouted Fran from the other end of the passage.

'Enough to hold these fellows down,' replied Daise. Then, in a voice of enquiry, 'Think the boy's OK?'

'Yes, he seems all right. Can you see anybody moving down there?'

'Nope.'

It was some seven minutes after the start of the attack that Simon heard a sound outside his window that both cheered and terrified him. It was Tilda's starter motor turning and turning but the engine not starting.

Dory had had the most terrifying time of her young life. She had been awakened by the scream of the falling Askari, from her deep sleep in the back of Tilda, tired after her day's ride. For a whole minute she sat up in the back of Tilda on the bunk bed and then moved no further. Whose side was she on? As the cousin of the ancient black ruler of a neighbouring African state, also attempting to rid themselves of British rule, she must be in sympathy with the Kenyan freedom fighters who were her spiritual brothers. They also were attempting to dislodge the stranglehold of the white settlers' rule. What sympathy could she have for a family that naturally and with supreme condescension relegated her, a black cousin of an African

153

prince, to their kitchen for no other reason than that she was black? If black is fighting white and for freedom, she told herself, she had no choice. She must side with her brother freedom fighters. It also struck her that to resist the freedom fighters and attempt to help the outnumbered whites was certain death.

Then she thought of young Simon whom, in the short week or two she had known him, she had grown tremendously fond of. He was the most super kid she had ever met and with the Mau Mau at the door they would very soon be severing his curly haired head from his body, with one swipe of their razor-sharp pangas. That was standard practice. Even as Dory weighed her loyalties she knew what she had to do and that there was really no choice. She knew that even if she had rushed out of Tilda with her hands up shouting 'Comrade' to the twenty or so Mau Mau who had the farm surrounded they would assume her to be the loyal servant of the white owners and would shoot her dead. But that had been the lesser consideration, the major consideration was the fact that she knew that the two old ladies and Simon, inside the house, would not rise up and murder Africans in cold blood under any circumstances. She had to be on the side of restraint and civilization. She had to achieve her Uhuru peacefully. She owed that much to her many friends at the London School of Economics.

She realized that the telephone line to the house would have been cut, she realized too that the watchman would not have had time to fire the warning rockets. She knew also that the household did not have one of the precious few portable radios of the time. No one, she realized, knew of this Mau Mau attack and she must therefore get word to the security forces.

Tilda didn't have an ignition key as such because she had been converted to diesel but Harry still used a little knurled switch that came through the main light switch as it did on all pre-war Austins, as a means of getting current to the starter motor, or switching current off from the starter motor. She pulled the starter lever after carefully switching on and the engine turned over very fast. Simon, just inside the window, knew exactly why Tilda's engine was not starting. It was because the engine pull stop had been left in its extended position. He shouted with all his strength out of the window,

'Push in the engine stop, Dory.'

Dory later swore that she never heard his instruction but almost instantly the engine started and Harry later assumed that the vibration must have caused the engine stop to return of its own accord. In any event the engine burst into life. Two terrorists were dispatched to deal with what seemed to be the noisy and terrifyingly slow departure of the vehicle. Dory, clenching her teeth, slammed Tilda's gear shift from first to second with a crunch so loud that Simon heard it upstairs and muttered to himself that old joke between them – 'Women drivers!' Tilda roared down the drive, going flat out in third, with only the side lights on.

'Who the devil's taking that vehicle?' Daise shouted as she heard the vehicle depart.

Simon from his window heard the question. 'It's Tilda and Dory going for help,' he shouted back, between shot.

'Tilda who? Dory who?' Slowly the realization dawned on Fran. 'Good God, boy – you don't mean to say that that ayah of yours can drive as well as ride?'

Dory's sense of direction was surprisingly good, she remembered seeing a police post about three miles down the road before they had turned left into the drive when they had approached the house two days before. Ten minutes after the attack had started Dory drove into the police post, and within three minutes ten police Askaris had fallen in and jumped onto a Land Rover. A corporal left behind got in touch with the Lloyds' farm some thirty miles away where the Harrisons and Harry and Jenny were.

As those four roared back horrified and fearful to the farm, they screamed into the police post to collect some rifles and Sten guns. It was then that Harry and Jenny saw the hulk of Tilda shining in the moonlight in front of the police post.

Desperately Harry pulled a still-trembling Dory from the driving seat. 'Christ Almighty, woman,' screamed Harry, 'you haven't left Simon there have you?'

'He was inside and I was outside,' she blurted out in exasperation.

Without another word Peter Harrison roared off with his wife and his guns in their Land Rover, and Harry rather roughly moved Dory from the driving seat and turned Tilda round and with Jenny hanging out of the other side headed off after them back to the farm. Dory was now in the back of Tilda. By the time they arrived at the farm the other two vehicles and fifteen armed men had arrived.

It was all over, bar the shouting, as Harry drove Tilda down the drive, Jenny to the left side firing off shots and Harry with a Sten gun he had been given by the police across his lap also firing blindly as he drove, more for effect than to shoot anything. Jenny prayed as she had never prayed before, 'Just Simon, that's all,' she asked. She would do anything for God for the rest of her life, anything, suffer anything, if only her son were alive, please God. The dead watchman was still at the foot of the tower. Tilda roared to a stop between the body and the two Land Rovers already in the car park.

The front room seemed to be full of people. It was twenty-five long minutes since the first security forces had arrived. Harry and Jenny hurled themselves into the room through the open French windows. It was an amazing sight. The loyal Kikuyu forces in the light of the pressure lights were standing round sipping tea from mugs. The old ladies had laid down their arms and the first thing they had done was to put on the kettle on the wood stove which was still smouldering in the kitchen. In no time this had brewed up a cup of tea for those who had rescued them. Sampson was hiding in his quarters and it was the first time for many years that the sisters had had to make their own tea. Congratulations were everywhere. Somebody was pumping up a pressure light. Jenny propelled herself at Simon who was standing a little apart still in his pyjamas with a .22 gun at his side. Tears flowed as she embraced him. Chatter, laughter, rejoicing, mugs of tea all round, Daise embraced the Regiment captain, Dory embraced the loyal Kikuyu policeman, Harry was shaking hands with everybody and everybody was slapping each other on the back. Tears of joy welled down Dory's cheeks.

Then up piped Simon, 'Come on Dory, I suppose you and me aren't allowed to drink this here,' he said lifting his mug. 'Let's go to the kitchen, Dory.' This said with the wicked grin of a seven-year-old. But Jenny was hugging him and Harry was hugging him, the sisters were hugging each other. Everybody seemed to be hugging everybody else.

Harry still smiled to himself thirty-five years later. That had been a night to remember all right. Now for the first time, he wondered – did Dory push that engine stop in? Or did it slip in by itself? It had certainly never done that before, if it had then. The Watson sisters passed out of the Hills' life shortly after but they left behind them an infectious courage that inspired Harry to his dying day. It was then remembered by the up-country settlers that when the farm the Harrisons now owned was being built by the original owners who had arrived by ox cart from the Transvaal in 1906, it had then, and for some years after, been called 'The Corral' because during the building of the farm house the Boer Trekkers had 'outspanned'. Thus, naturally, one of the last Mau Mau incidents of the Emergency was dubbed 'The Gunfight at the Harrisons' Corral'.

The aftermath was also significant. Rumour had it that the Mau Mau general in charge of the gang held court under a fig tree in the forest the next day and all his returning troops were shot. They had taken the oath to fight like demons, and two old women and a child had defeated them. They were not fit to live. The dead Askari's family was so generously compensated by Peter Harrison that his descendants own two four-storey hotels in Nyahururu Falls and one of his grandsons is an assistant Minister of Agriculture.

Shortly after the Mau Mau incident at Harrisons' Corral, Nyasaland, Northern Rhodesia and Southern Rhodesia, with pomp and circumstance for the best of administrative reasons, were to be federated. For less good reasons the new Boer-orientated Republic of South Africa was allowed to contribute towards an additional monument to be erected by Rhodes's lonely grave on a mountain top at Matapos, an ugly stone block of a monument with a copper frieze to be dedicated 'to all brave men'. There were pictures in bas-relief on all four sides, of the forty-one troopers led by Major Alan Watson who were massacred by the Matabele so many years before. The major's surviving daughters, together with dignitaries from the federation, including the guest of honour, D.F. Malan, the architect of apartheid, from South Africa, were duly invited and they all laboriously climbed the hill to Cecil Rhodes's grave less than an hour's run by Land Rover out of the busy city of Bulawayo.

The unveiling of the obelisk completed, Daise Watson was invited to say a few words. Recording speech was a cumbrous job in those days but somebody had lumbered up the hill with an old tape-recorder and somebody later had managed to smuggle a copy of the tape to a liberal Capetonian lady. Daise held the microphone firm in her grasp. She had been working on her speech for many days and it was word perfect: 'Mr President, ladies and gentlemen, thank you all for inviting my sister and me here today to honour my father's death, but much as I wish to honour him and the brave men who died alongside him so long ago I refuse to be associated with your efforts to imply that those who killed him were treacherous and inferior. I know better than most how glorious my father's death was. It was as glorious as the death of the horsemen of the Light Brigade at the Crimea. We honour the Light Brigade, but do we condemn the Russian Artillery that massacred them? Why therefore must we condemn the soldiers that killed my father as he attacked them? But I *will* give you a toast, ladies and gentlemen, on behalf of my father, to all brave men, both black and white.' There was a deathly silence as she finished speaking. The little crowd gathered on the mountain top did not know how to handle this betrayal; their mouths dropped open but that was only the half of it. Fran grasped the microphone from her sister and piped up (now Fran's speech had *not* been prepared, she was impetuous and simultaneously embarrassed and pleased with her sister's bombshell) 'And why only brave men? What about brave women? I'll tell you something that some of you might not know. It's what my mother told me a long time ago. "Fran" she said, "if ever anybody wants to know if Uncle Cecil was a homosexual you can tell them from me he wasn't".' A gasp went around the crowd. 'Mind you,' Fran continued, 'as far as I can remember, and I only knew him as a little girl, he was a pretty cold fish, and didn't really enjoy sex at all. He couldn't stand us girls anywhere near him, so as Daise and myself are every bit as brave as some of those troops of my father's who didn't have much choice but to die, how about you burying Daise and me up here alongside Cecil when we croak? That'll teach him! He could never bear to have females near him while he lived, and a little proximity now he's dead wouldn't go amiss.'

By now the group at the monument was in complete disarray. Some of the British who were there, and who were still resentful of the Boer's take-over of South Africa, were cheering Fran on. 'Good old Fran, you tell 'em.'

There were no more speeches and they all trooped off down the hill. One old Colonel Blimp was heard to say, 'Do you know, I think old Rhodes would have liked that. Probably didn't want that hideous thing overlooking his grave anyway, whatever it is dedicated to – wogs, dogs, that idiot Watson, or women.'

☆   ☆   ☆

Harry couldn't remember whether he had passed Voi or not. He would never have forgotten such a thing in the old days when he drove his giant car transporters backwards and forwards between Mombasa and Nairobi but these days it was different. Voi was bypassed now so it was easy to miss. He braked hard and forced his mind back to the present. Now, for a few seconds, a new fear crossed his mind, another type of terror. He thought to himself that not only was he driving down to his appointment with death, in the form of a heart attack most likely, but it seemed he was losing his grip on reality as well. He was going barmy, seeing things, that couldn't be, not in 1991. What had caused him to think he was seeing things was that there, nonchalantly tearing away at the bark of a baobab tree on the left hand side of the deserted Mombasa road were no less than six elephants. Two huge matriarchal cows and four young, approximately half the size of their mothers or aunts. What worried Harry was, that it must have been well over ten years since he had seen eleys on the Mombasa road. One just didn't any more. Then he thought of what he had seen in the last fifteen or so minutes and remembered also that all the petrol tankers had been parked up, a common enough sight ten years ago before they built the pipe-line – but today? A time warp? He was dead already. These were definitely eley, not vague shadows of elephants, like the ones he used to see at night when he was dog tired in the Coronation Safari Rally for example: they were the famous night blindness 'visions'.

'I suppose these *could* be real,' he said to himself. Harry had been chatting to Richard Leakey at the tourist meeting in Nairobi the week before and Leakey had been full of the increasing elephant herds of Tsavo, and not a little proud of his own efforts in encouraging their return. 'OK, so they're real,' he said to himself. How many times had he driven past that baobab tree and seen not only elephants but rhino at the side of the road around here and lion also.

This was the 'Lions of Tsavo' country about which the story by the same name had been written – a most thrilling and true Victorian cliffhanger from darkest Africa which had filled the daily papers a century before. It did make exciting reading, even today, thought Harry. How many sick workers did they get? About thirty if he remembered correctly. Lions jumped clean over the barricade into the hospital tent, for the sick coolies who were working on the track-laying of the lunatic railway line.

There were the huge rings of thorn which the Indian labourers had built right round the hospital tents in their attempt to keep the lions out. Most nights for a month the lions would raid the hospital for their meal – on occasions two or even three sick men were taken by the man-eaters. No one seemed able to stop them despite the fact that professional hunters were called in. Harry smiled sadly; perhaps the lions knew what the white man's 'iron snake' was to do to their traditional hunting grounds. Perhaps they knew that white man's medicine would cause the population of Kenya to increase from around half a million in those days to thirty million a century later, that these hordes would plant their crops, and there would be no place for lions in that environment. On balance Harry found himself on the side of the lion.

He directed his thoughts comfortably back to Jenny's and Simon's early days in Kenya. Some thoughts were out of focus, but others were in perfect perspective. Happy days, in love with Kenya, in love with his wife, delighted with the welcome Kenyans gave them and proud of his son. They only saw Dory for a year or two on and off. She married a UK Labour MP's son, as far as he could remember – Foot or Cripps or some such. Her poor old uncle, the Kabaka of Uganda climbed his palace wall one night to start his retreat to London, leaving behind the only civilization East Africa had known before the coming of the white man and leaving it to a generation of genocide no less. They never saw the Watson sisters again either. Simon Hill took his place amongst the White Tribe of Kenya's folklore along with old Grogen who fifty years previously had walked from Cape to Cairo to prove his love of his fiancée Gertrude and Meinertzhagen who by his presence suppressed 10,000 Nandi tribesmen who were in a just revolt with the help of only a hundred Masai spearsmen; and Ian Henderson, Mau Mau – hunter par excellence.

The attitude of the boys and staff at the Gilgil boarding school to which Simon was sent was still locked into the Tom Brown mentality. Ninety per cent of the boys were much older than Simon, mainly European, with just a handful of Asians and even two aspiring African students. This could well have meant a hard time for the wet-behind-the-ears Pom who had just arrived, and hadn't even seen the Indian Ocean. However, the legend of Simon holding off the Mau Mau with the help of two old women created an aura of respect and Simon had sense enough to build on this convenient 'in'. 'How many Mau Mau did you shoot Si?' 'Definitely one, and winged more.' Well, he justified his little white lie, he might have done!

After the first year Simon decided he liked school, but he loved the holidays more. Riding down to Mombasa in his father's huge car transporters was for him sheer delight. Nicky was already in her own nursery during his second holidays but until she was toddling and talking he didn't have much to do with her. Neither did Jenny, come to that, who had found herself an interesting job in public relations in Nairobi.

Ayahs were wonderful African women who often turned into nannies every bit as sincere as the great Victorian nannies of England. The starry-eyed idealists condemned all who used such cheap labour of exploitation, but the reality was the labourers were delighted with their way of life, the children were delighted with them, and the mothers were delighted also. And, as Harry used to say to Jenny's parents when they came over for a visit, 'We don't actually horse-whip them you know'.

He realized in retrospect that his views of the time when Simon and Nicky were growing up were looked at through rose-coloured spectacles or tinted windscreens, a phrase the young Nicky had coined. Kenya was kind to the Hills. His first job in Nairobi was with his old army acquaintance, Guy Shaw, originally from the groundnut scheme in Tanganyika; it was he who had written to the Hills in UK suggesting they come to Nairobi. Harry and Guy remained the best of friends until Guy died, and after that Simon and Guy's son Oliver were close but

161

the actual job Harry started did not last long. Harry found himself overseeing about fifty African workers who spent their days drilling and riveting and bonding replacement brake linings for Kenya's fast-growing vehicle population. Guy soon realized that Harry was under-extended and because the actual job wouldn't stand any more salary he replaced him with an African. He was scooped up by the Ford Motor Company tractor division, and two years later he was Sales Director earning a salary and enjoying a lifestyle that few, if any, of his contemporaries in UK exceeded.

It was not the material well being alone that made Kenya appeal to the Hills, it went deeper than that.

Anybody spending their life amongst that infinite variety of people could not fail to be enchanted. There were Greek Coffee farmers for example, all rich as Croesus, all owning Mercedes, the value of each of which would take even their middle-income workers over two hundred years to earn. The Bohemian Italians continued the pre-war, 'Happy Valley' tradition in their splendid Naivasha lakeside homes. People from Scandinavia brought their socialist ideology which, invariably, eventually floundered against the rocks of emergent African greed. There were highly cultured Poles, unreasonably bitter about their treatment by former British foreign policy and unreasonably forgiving of their treatment by former German foreign policy.

Americans struggled with their 110-volt appliances on the 230-volt grid in Kenya. The Dutch, the Boers, the Swiss, the French and the Israel nationals were all represented. Then there were the Hindu, the Muslims and the Sikhs whose grandfathers came over from the sub-continent of India to lay the East Africa Railway track. Ismails boasted photographs of their Aga Khan, a respectful inch or two lower than the President. Seychelle, proud Somali nomads, and a million coastal Arabs – descendants of Sinbad the Sailor who used to trade in gold from distant Sofala still sailing proudly in their great lateen-sailed Dhows.

All thriving in a sea of Bantu.

Harry often found himself wondering why the West (the person who held the purse strings) were not more appreciative of the pragmatic Moi who tried so hard to stop disintegration, and why they blindly called for democracy.

Democracy, Harry decided, was impractical in such a context.

'Democracy,' he would scoff. 'It was a democracy that elected Hitler . . . .'

7

Tilda Pulls It Off Again and Again

His thoughts raced on. The years glided past, Christmases at the coast with the kids on Kenya's endless deserted white sands, scraping oysters off the rocks, swimming, goggling, fishing, water-skiing, paragliding, mini-sailing, all were second nature to the European children. They could ride horses, ride motor-bikes, and swim like fish. Ten-year old Simon won a cup for motor-cycle scrambling. Then there was the riding of push bikes round the deserted lanes that separated the jacaranda-leaf-strewn gardens, weekend safaris in the Masai Mara or Tsavo before the tourist boom of the seventies began to crowd out the residents from those most beautiful areas on earth.

Sometimes the Hills camped on Guy's plot at the coast, sometimes they stayed with friends who owned a coast hotel. At the coast, on up-country farms or in the huge Nairobi subur-ban gardens – all had their delights. By any standards Kenya of the sixties was a perfect place in which to bring up children.

Those Nairobi suburban gardens, and those up-country farms! For almost a century spawning such sensitive children of literature of the White Tribe, from Elspeth Huxley playing under those Flame Trees at Thika to Kuki Gallmann's boy hunting his snakes on the Laikipia. Such heroines as Beryl Markham, first to fly the Atlantic solo 'West with the Night'. The literary achievements of the White Tribe are out of all proportion to their numbers.

He, Harry had insisted that 'Change is the spur of evolution' when confronted with the opinions of the extreme environmen-talists, of whom there were hundreds. Harry always quoted this 'change is the spur' argument when the conservationists pro-duced their statistics to show the impending exhaustion of many of the earth's resources necessary to support life. He would infuriate the earnest pessimists by suggesting, 'That's it! – That's good! – just in the same way the old ice ages forced mankind to new inventiveness like the invention of fire and cloth. So too, necessity being the mother of invention, the exhausting of the earth's resources will drive humanity to explore the stars'. The environmentalists would reply scornfully, 'So after ruining Mother Earth – you think what's left of humanity should ruin the rest of the universe!' 'Yes,' would reply the equally adamant optimist Harry, 'change is inevitable – change *is* progress – Those guys in the bountiful tropics who have a wild banana drop in their laps every time they get hungry admittedly won't harm the environment, but they will *never* get anywhere either'.

Trite as Stevenson's dictum had become, it did not lessen its truth . . . .

'To travel hopefully' he was convinced was 'a better thing than to arrive' and equally true the often forgotten second line which summed up his philosophy, 'And the true success is to labour.' 'Bwana?' a questioning tone from a distant Nicky followed 'who are you lecturing to?' 'No one in particular' replied Harry to himself, 'Just getting it off my chest – that's all.'

Nairobi's smog, rhino horn, and elephant tusk – poaching, the crowded game parks, the population explosion – were all still un-dreamt of by most, and each day for Simon and Nicky was another perfect day in paradise! . . . .

Harry considered himself extremely fortunate to have had the blessing of that environment in which to rear his children. All such children felt completely committed to the country in which they were born.

It was in fact the later efforts of these tireless, efficient, fun-loving children that helped guide Kenya through her first years of independence. They accepted with no chips on their shoulders old Jomo's call of 'Harambee', Harambee being the national motto coined from the phrase of 'one, two, three, heave' or 'Harambee' – all pull together whatever the colour of your skin. Say 'Harambee' and build a nation!

As Christmas at the coast rounded off the years so the Nairobi show was a traditional set piece not to be missed. The Royal Nairobi Show, as it was then, when all the bwanas, not only from the farming community but from the industries and the motor distribution agents in the capital would traipse to the permanent site of the Royal Nairobi Agricultural Show and their secretaries would say, when anybody was stupid enough to ring up for them at work, 'Bwana's at the 'chow.' The Kikuyu girl secretaries were unable to handle the delicate pronunciation of 'show' and 'gone to the choo', 'choo' being Swahili for lavatory, invariably caused amusement.

Perhaps, though Harry, it was only the seasons that he really missed, the seasons of Europe. An eternal summer was slightly lacking as one grew older. He would have to concede that to Phil, who worshipped English village life, the next time he saw him. Next time? 'Remember this bloody morning will you? Heart attack! – death! You won't be seeing Phil again and there won't be any next bloody time this side of the pearly bloody gates! God, what a euphemism – pearly gates, six foot under with maggots gnawing at your eyeballs, pearly fucking gates, perhaps I wouldn't mind if I had been in pain, in agony for a year. Perhaps then I could have looked upon it as a happy release. Perhaps I wouldn't have minded if I had been going over the top with my old uncles dying in the company of thousands of men, but I don't *want* to die.'

There was another story from those days that Harry recalled with a smile. It was during the last sad days of the professional white hunters of Kenya. Sad, not for hunting's demise, but because latterly, anticipating collapse, the calibre of the clients decreased as the calibre of their guns increased. Incidences of machine gun massacres of plains game, not all for the pot, and shooting the big five from the safety of hunting cars, began to circulate in the New Stanley Long Bar. It was therefore with some trepidation that Harry greeted Stan Granger-Smith, one of his neighbours, and one, as Stan himself often jestingly said, of the 'oldest' white hunters in the business. Stan always used International trucks for his hunting cars so there was no mistaking who it was when he pulled into the Hills' drive and got out and approached the verandah. The usual formalities – 'What's your poison?' The usual comments of the sun being down so a Sundowner was called for.

Settling comfortably into a wicker chair on the verandah Stan explained the reason for his visit. Short of breath, he was at that time suffering from angina from which he was to die some three years later and in typically short sentences he began his request. 'Short of a gary. Wondered if you would lend me Tilda, hunting trip, not for clients of course, just the watu and the tack, few boxes of ammo, wouldn't be too hard on her, perhaps a bit of firewood and water collection.' Because Tilda was not then required for anything else, and because Stan was a very congenial neighbour always helping out when necessary, Harry agreed with a slight reluctance, because although he thoroughly approved of Stan himself he wasn't quite so sure about the hunting scene, killing for trophies.

Harry was due down at Mombasa during most of the time that the vehicle was required so it was decided that Jenny would take Tilda out on safari during the week she had off from her job in Nairobi and Nicky was to stay with friends. Simon was at boarding school. Out in the bush in Hunting Block 9, Tilda, driven by Jenny, climbed through a lugger; two camp boys jumped out while she was still moving and started looking in the dried-up river bed for choice pieces of firewood for the evening's camp fire. They must have been some three or four miles from the camp and this was the traditional area for firewood collection. Slowing to a walking pace over the rock-strewn track, dipping towards an even bigger lugger Tilda started to misfire. Jenny looked heavenwards with raised eyebrows. Tilda rolled lumpily over a few more small boulders and came to a halt at the top of a gentle slope. Having all the time in the world and thinking it might get better if left alone Jenny decided that it was as good a place as any to collect firewood. She climbed down from Tilda, sent the two boys to look for more dead wood, and sat down under the shade of a thorn tree, pulled a cardboard box of 100 Clipper cigarettes from her handbag and lit up looking for all the world like a TV advertisement.

At this time in the Masai Mara game reserve which borders on Block 9 there was a young American girl to whom a City and Guilds-type organization from Tennessee had given a grant to study the behaviour patterns of black-maned male lions of the Masai Mara. There was also one particular female lion that the girl had named 'Broken Jaw'. The girl had been camped amongst the pride for almost a year and she had got to know personally most of the predators in that area. A missed zebra kill and a well placed kick from the escaping zebra at a water hole had broken this particular lioness's jaw some six months previously, and she had since had a litter of four healthy cubs now at the peak of their playfulness around twelve weeks old. The jaw had partially healed enabling her to hunt successfully, with the occasional help of other females in the pride, but the wound gave a lop-sided look to her face. The girl often drove her Land Rover right up to Broken Jaw to check that all was well with her and her playful kittens, especially when Broken Jaw wandered into the hunting block adjacent to the reserve. This particular lion had therefore become relatively used to the sight of vehicles, though nothing like as familiar as her grandchildren were to become, with the mini-bus invasion of the eighties.

The lioness was out on an early morning hunt with another female in the pride walking gently, both sensing rather than hearing a vehicle downwind, but so used had Broken Jaw become to vehicles that she didn't even look round. She heard an explosion, followed instantly by the sound of a second one, then a searing pain as the .303 bullet entered her left shoulder. Still able to run, both animals bounded off in opposite directions.

Stan insisted that the blasé Texan who had fired the shot accompany him with one gun-bearer, to follow the spoor of the wounded lion. 'It's open country, Stan,' the Texan drawled. 'Couldn't we follow with the jeep?' Stan gave him a look that said it all. They left the vehicle behind and started off into the bush fulfilling the most ancient duty of sporting hunters, to put a wounded prey out of its misery. The lioness instinctively knew that both retreat and rest were necessary. She set off at a fairly fast pace back towards her pride, then some instinct made her veer away from her cubs – wild animals seldom lead danger towards their young. After about three hours she had walked in a huge arc and found herself badly in need of rest. She was lying low in the dense cover in the bottom of a lugger when she heard the noise of hunters approaching. It had been easy for them to track her by following the trail of blood. She wearily stumbled up once more, climbed the bank of the lugger and trotted slowly along the top.

Jenny had got into the habit of leaving Tilda's huge back doors open when she was on firewood runs so that the long branches could lie on the floor and stick out of the rear. The stretchers had been removed. The lion topped the lugger and noticed some 400 or 500 yards away three people in a little group. Nearer the wounded lioness saw what looked like an empty hut with open doors. She loped down the slope and jumped into the back of Tilda, crouching amongst the firewood as she laid down on her side to try to lick her wound. She looked rather like a giant cat in a giant kennel. Jenny and the camp boys had not noticed the lioness jump into the back of Tilda but they now saw three figures approaching over the hilltop, crouched in a hunting position, their guns at the ready.

'Jambo Jenny' Stan called out, 'how is it going?'

'Oh great,' Jenny rather absentmindedly replied, not expecting to have seen them. 'How are you? Got your simba yet?'

'No, not yet,' Stan said panting a little, 'she is leading us quite a chase, we must have been after her for three hours now. You haven't seen her, have you? We saw her spoor disappear just at the top of the lugger there.'

Jenny shook her head, 'I haven't seen anything.'

'OK, she must have been going down stream, do you know I think they know it's impossible for us to track 'em in water.' The hunters took off down the almost dry river bed, away from Jenny and the two boys – and away from Tilda. Jenny returned the fifty yards or so towards Tilda. As she approached she was surprised to notice Tilda's body rocking on her rear springs. She was even more surprised to see a lioness jump out of the back and take off down the track. Being in complete sympathy with the wounded female Jenny never mentioned this to either of the two camp boys who soon rejoined the vehicle with armfuls of firewood, nor to the rest of the hunting team back in camp that night.

When she was retelling the story to Harry after the end of the safari Harry said, 'Yeh, but I thought you said Tilda had packed up'. 'Good Lord' replied Jenny, 'that's right – she had, but went like a bomb when I started her up to return to camp with the firewood.' 'That figures,' was all Harry said.

☆   ☆   ☆

The Indian coolies when they were laying the tracks for the lunatic line at the turn of the century called the area through which Harry was now driving the Taru desert. There is not much to distinguish it. You enter it by degrees, there is little that lets you know exactly where you are. Harry seemed to remember that in the old days round about there the 'Mombasa 100 miles' signpost stuck up. Around about there too, was a signpost put up by the Rotarians, a reference to the longest straight line pram-push, the only reference to Kenya in the *Guinness Book of Records,* to commemorate the occasion when a Nairobi rugby team had relayed a pram-push in twenty-four hours and got as far as Harry had from Nairobi.

Harry was thinking about the Chyulus though by now the Chyulu Hills were behind him, a sinister black line across a sinister grey thundercloud to the north-east. Perhaps it was a little stream of orange water flowing across the tarmac that jolted his memory. There must have been rain in the hills, he thought, although it was not actually raining on the Mombasa road. It was in the Chyulus that the 'Great Confirmation' as he and Jenny called it, occurred. As he recalled that delightful day, one of the most pleasurable days of his life, he found himself generalizing again. He was thinking that most lifetimes have a decade that is what the liver of the lifetime thinks about when looking back on his or her life. The 'most fulfilling' part would be the best way to describe it. Harry decided that he definitely had had such a decade.

His childhood seemed, in retrospect, to have had little impact on his life as a whole; even the war years, exciting as they were, and his vegetable round and the shop at Husbands Bosworth were vague. As for his last twenty years, they were absolutely as anticipated and certainly not epic, but the sixties! Those were the days! At the beginning of that decade Nicky had been two years old, and Simon ten. Harry remembered how they welcomed the decade in. Just the four of them, he and Jenny and the two kids in a freak thunderstorm on the first peak of the Ngong Hills only some twenty-five miles out of Nairobi. Rain lashed against the windscreen of the Humber Snipe which Harry was using at the time. Harry remembered that he had given the silencer a knock on a protruding rock and it was now blowing badly as he climbed the rock-strewn track to the top of the hills. A quarter of an hour before they had passed the overgrown grave of Dennis Finch-Hatton. Finch-Hatton – nothing could have been further from Harry's mind at the present than Finch-Hatton and yet he realized that at that very moment he was passing the spot where Dennis Finch-Hatton had crashed in his aircraft those many years before and Karen had insisted that the body be transported 200 miles to the Ngong Hills for burial in sight of Karen's house like a lesser Livingstone.

By the time Harry passed Finch-Hatton's grave that New Year's Eve, 1959, it was almost obliterated by undergrowth. The old Baroness von Blixen was still alive but many miles away in Denmark, too far away to attend to it, and nobody else cared enough. The red murram track cut out of the side of the hill passed through high banks, then as the Humber reached the top, the Hills suddenly saw spread out before them the lights of Nairobi, 3,000 feet below like so many tangled pearl necklaces thrown haphazardly into a pile on the 5,000 foot plateau on which Nairobi was built. The ten-year old Simon was still very much awake, even at eleven fifty-seven pm, his baby sister was curled up on the green leather of the sumptuous rear seat, her head on the padded arm rest. By the magic hour Simon had procured four champagne glasses – typical Simon, thought Harry, other kids might have remembered to bring cups but not Simon, even at that age he must do the thing properly – and Harry poured out champagne whilst Jenny woke up Nicky for the occasion.

He pictured the scene on the rain-swept 8,000 feet Ngong Hills towering above Nairobi, a shining new Humber car and the Hill family together and alone lit by the light of the interior light. He had rather unimaginatively raised his glass and tapped the other three. 'Here's to the sixties'. They all sipped, as *Pomp and Circumstance* the winning bid of 'Ring in your Choice' blared out of the car radio across the deserted hills. 'May *we* grow closer together still', echoed a moist-eyed Jenny. 'God, you couldn't get much happier than that,' thought Harry in retrospect. Enough cash to do most things you wanted to, perfect health, two super kids, a beautiful loving wife and a brand new country about to be born, change in the air, peace and plenty. He remembered the green-lit walnut dash of that Humber and that brought him back to the present as he studied intensely the fuel gauge on the Corolla. A popular disc jockey of the time – Harry couldn't remember his name – had once made the profound philosophical observation that the first half of a car's fuel, as shown by the gauge, always lasted longer than the last half. Life, too, thought Harry. After twenty years of running mainly diesel engines Harry could never bring himself to say 'petrol gauge' but always 'fuel gauge' and now the Corolla's gauge was on half. Did that mean it wasn't working? Did that mean he was only half way? Many thoughts crossed his mind, putting in more fuel was not an immediate one.

Now all of a minute later he was wondering, 'Why didn't I think of refuelling? Because when I arrive, whenever I arrive, and the fuel gauge reads E my life will be over – that's why. I must not fill up. Bloody fool,' he said to himself, 'even if it was death's hour glass you are only half way through your real life. Don't be silly, another seventy years, that's just not possible. I'm halfway through my recollections.' A cold shudder visibly shook Harry.

As Harry sat welcoming in the new decade neither he nor anyone else in the motor industry dreamt that they were ushering in the end of an era. An era that had led to that green monster, the Humber Snipe, in which they were sitting, roads that led from Birmingham and Coventry, Cowley and Derby, from Brooklands via superb Climax engines and too-good-to-produce Javelin Jowett engines, the HRD motorcycle, the best in the world.

This mighty industrial Goliath was soon to be conquered by an Oriental David, whose industrial power, at that time, was best known for tin toys.

In the early sixties they visited Addis Ababa one year, down to Salisbury the next. One year they shipped the car across to Karachi and drove through the Sind Desert into Kashmir, over the Khyber Pass, into Turkey where they flew back to their beloved Kenya, shipping the car back unaccompanied, from Istanbul. On another occasion in the early sixties they found themselves flying out of Tel Aviv a week before the Six Day War. And always they returned more convinced than ever that all that the rest of the world had to offer could not compare with the joys of Kenya in the sixties. Because it seemed to fit in well with his work, apart from his two-month holiday, he also had the time and the resources to enter the East African Safari

Rally on two occasions. He drove a Volkswagen which in those early days was fast enough to win, but he never completed the course, getting time-barred both times, but for the rest of his life he was connected with the organization of the Rally.

He noticed a Kenya Railways goods train passing on its way northwards over an iron bridge some half a mile to his left. It must have been in that very part of the Mombasa road that he had had one of his last breakdowns with the motor vehicle trade, before he changed to the tourist trade. He remembered looking at that bridge as he lay under one of his vehicles changing a broken crank. If his life had taught him anything, if he could claim to be an authority on any one subject, he had to admit that it was a subject that he would rather forget. Why couldn't he have been an expert on East African bird life, for example, or Greek philosophy or medieval literature? That would have fascination but reluctantly all Harry could really claim to be an expert on was breakdowns. It was so unromantic, so mundane. The internal combustion engine, their transmission systems and the breakdowns therein. He could think of no part of a motor vehicle from a single cylinder motor cycle to a juggernaut, that hadn't at one time or another broken on him. He then did a little quick calculation. He supposed, over his lifetime, he must have personally owned some 200-odd vehicles and then he could think of at least ten times when a crankshaft, for example, had broken. The first time in UK, on the vintage Alfa-Romeo which his wife's parents had given them for a wedding present – the sale of which for £47 when they left for Africa being one of his larger financial misjudgements. The last occasion, not six months ago, when a Mercedes 911 tourist truck he was running carrying some economy tourists had a broken crank, after only 20,000 kilometres of operation. Now that means, he said, ten vehicles out of 200, that is five per cent. Surely there couldn't be another person in the world for whom five per cent of the vehicles they had owned had all suffered the worst thing that could happen to a motor vehicle – a broken crankshaft?

Statistics, statistics – they mean nothing. The whole modern world is run on them, computers are fed with them, economics and politics rely on them, but they mean absolutely nothing. Good God, I mean, believe statistics and you've got to believe that every tenth male you meet in the United Kingdom is a child molester, every fifth woman you meet from eight to eighty has just finished masturbating, if you listen to statistics . . . . He said to himself sarcastically, 'I quote, of the 2,003 housewives interviewed, 90.8% claimed to have . . . .' What about the most incredible one of all – '. . . within a decade AIDS will have saved black Africa from itself, by reducing the population by fifty per cent?'

A whole kaleidoscope of life in Kenya in the sixties flashed across Harry's mind. The growing Nairobi, the skyscrapers just beginning to appear, a city described disparagingly by the American visitors as half the size of New York's cemetery and twice as dead, but a city feeling its way with African participation, with the beginning of the tourist boom, with a confidence and with a tolerance of which Harry was proud.

The Shifta's skirmishes on the Northern Frontier District when both Idi Amin and the Somalis got hold of hundred-year-old maps which made a nonsense of the modern demarcation lines and showed Somali and Ugandan borders 200 miles into Kenya and the new National Governments being prepared to die for the colonial frontiers which each nation had so criticized at one time or another – over it all old Jomo Kenyatta dominated the political scene, leaving no room for lesser politicians. Jomo ruled supreme. Even the climate seemed perfect in those far off days. There were still Europeans on the White Highlands farms which were backwaters of delight. There were not too many people about, the population explosion hadn't really got under way, the diehard critics had all travelled to the south, leaving tolerant Europeans who wanted to follow Jomo's call. Again he recalled the motto of the new nation, 'Harambee', 'All pull together' – whatever the colour of your skin, whatever your religion, say 'Haramb*ee*' and build a nation.

It was not until the end of that glorious decade that the clouds appeared. Unemployment, over-population were still in the future. 'And the personal clouds?' he said to himself. The personal clouds – when did they arrive? Jenny was still extremely attractive. He, in his mid-forties, on occasion considered her a little too attractive. A thousand tiny spears had of course been hurled by each. He recalled her saying, 'Why are you so obsessed with cars? We haven't been down to the coast for months. You know Nicky would love it.' This, when Jenny

174

learnt that he had just taken on a voluntary job at one of the checkpoints in that Easter's East African Safari Rally. 'You're like a whole bunch of those cloth-capped pre-Sunday lunch lounge bar Englishmen talking about MGs. Surely you could give it a miss for one year? Well, I'm not spending *my* Easter up all night on some bloody escarpment in the rain. I mean, if you hadn't done it all, it would be different but it's going backwards just running a checkpoint.'

Much to the dismay and, in some cases, disgust of the ever-growing religious, particularly Christian church-type religious lobby in Kenya, Easter in Kenya in the sixties was given over almost entirely to the Coronation Safari Rally. This rally, later to be called the East African Safari Rally, and still later for a while the Marlboro Safari Rally, originated as its name implies, at the time of the coronation of Queen Elizabeth II when nine stalwarts from Kenya, Tanganyika, as it was then, and Uganda, all jumped in their cars, raced to each other's capital, got the signature of the mayors of Dar-es-Salaam, Entebbe and Nairobi and the first one to return to their starting point with the other two signatures was the winner. By the sixties, however, it was fairly sophisticated and fairly well-known and a source of pride for the whole of the White Tribe of Kenya that no overseas entrant had yet won first position in the four-day event. All the menfolk connected with the motor trade in Nairobi took their wives or girlfriends to some distant escarpment to man a checkpoint over Easter if they were not actually competing or if they were not actually helping a competitor.

He remembered a tight section on the Rally in the Chyulu Hills. It was raining, as always, and a crowd of Africans appeared from nowhere. The crowd swayed against the ropes that kept it back from the track up which the entrants would soon roar in their safari cars, stopping at the gas-lit table to check in at the checkpoint and have their route cards stamped. He often wondered how it was that these hundreds of Africans, obviously extremely poor, living on very little, many of them unable to read, were always so fascinated with the rally in which it was very unlikely any of them would be able to afford to compete. Yet they cheered like mad as 'Simba' Joginder Singh screamed through the checkpoints.

It was excitement and they enjoyed being a part of it. He

remembered the conversation that year as night descended. There had been no cars through and they were in radio communication with the previous checkpoint. All the talk had been of how Joginder Singh had left a tow hook down and torn up the loose planks across a bridge making it impassable. It started to tip down, a real storm brewing. The Africans, many of them already drenched, held their programmes over their short-haired heads. There were four organizers at the checkpoint which included himself and a young lady school teacher who was helping him, by the name of Wendy. Wendy was cheeky and young and curly and round and shallow and sexy and fun and it slowly dawned on him that possibly she had contrived to find herself in the position which she now did. There were two tents pitched for four 'officials'. The other two at the checkpoint were male associates of his in the motor trade who had just taken on an agency by a funny sounding Japanese name – 'Datsum' he had thought at the time. Fifteen years later he thought of how those very cars – Nissan, Datsuns – would roar through that very checkpoint accounting for up to fifty per cent of the entrants and invariably having two or three in the first six places.

On this particular night it was Peugeot and Volkswagen and, a poor third, British Ford, and DKWs and Fiats. It came crackling over the relatively primitive radio of the mid-sixties that vehicles were entering Checkpoint 30 but the clerk of the course had decided to omit section 32 over the worst part of the Chyulus because of a stretch of impassable black cotton as a result of the sudden downpour. The clerk of the course's car was even at that moment bogged down on its axles. A disappointed crowd on hearing the news that the vehicles wouldn't after all be passing that checkpoint started to disappear as silently as they had arrived. Half an hour after receiving the message there was only a little knot of Africans and the four Europeans, all in padded top coats – no one in Africa owned a mackintosh as such. It was still raining fairly heavily and hissing against the Tilly lamp on the table.

Wendy put her arm through his and looked up at him with an impish grin. He thought about his family: Simon who was staying with friends up-country and who would in fact also be assisting the manning of a checkpoint and helping with the Safari Rally the following day in Nairobi. Then he thought

176

about Jenny who had gone down to the coast with Nicky. He remembered now how much his mind dwelt on Jenny. For all the sixteen years of his married life, incredible as it may sound, he had been faithful to his wife and she, he automatically assumed, to him. There was low cloud in the Chyulus that night, almost a fog but there hanging just above the tent was a watery full moon. He had smiled to himself, wondering even more intently what Jenny was up to. As he had walked towards the tent with Wendy he had thought that one act of physical adultery would probably make little difference to his marriage. But in retrospect when he realized how shortly afterwards Jenny's life was to end so tragically, he fervently wished for her all that life could give. He would not have minded in the least had she experienced some fling which might have pleased her.

They must have been half-way from the table to the tent when suddenly one of the helpers at the table shouted, 'Good God, that looks like a light beam of a vehicle coming round the escarpment, doesn't it? You're sure they did say this section was shut?' Harry picked up the binoculars that were slung round his shoulders, put them to his eyes and peered towards the wet escarpment where the other route controllers were pointing and sure enough there was a the beam of a headlight. 'Good God,' said Harry, dropping the binoculars, 'that's a car all right. How the hell did it get through the black cotton? Old Tony wouldn't have shut the section if it had been passable.'

Then, from one of the other men on the checkpoint. 'Perhaps it's one of the service cars that doesn't know.'

'Well, it could be,' said Harry, very knowingly, 'but I don't think so because even four-wheel drive wouldn't get through that black cotton at the bottom there. I know it well when it's wet.'

The headlight beam kept appearing and disappearing as it rounded the hairpins of the escarpment.

☆   ☆   ☆

The hardest thing, Jenny decided, had not been the drive but the little betrayal she felt when parting with Nicky. Nicky, she told herself, would be much happier playing in the swimming pool of the next door neighbour – a girl of about her own age – overlooked by that mother and the two ayahs in sunny

Nairobi. Much happier than bumping around in the back of Tilda on a wild goose chase to try and catch up with the rally and perhaps meet her father. That had been the hard bit. Following the route in Tilda had been fairly simple until it came on to rain but even then Jenny didn't find it impossibly difficult. She didn't drive Tilda much these days but the trusty old vehicle had started first go and was running well. The rain lashed down with the wiper arm clearing about a foot of the windscreen of the teeming rain. It was black all around and black ahead and the stony escarpment road looked black in the yellow headlights. There was a nasty stretch at the bottom of the escarpment. She gunned the engine through it with Tilda flat out in third and was quite surprised to pass what appeared to be a deserted car as she got on the firm ground again and started to climb.

The Tilly paraffin pressure light was still standing on the table and the headlights of Tilda illuminated the two men and Harry and Wendy side by side across the track looking straight at the oncoming vehicle as it roared out of the night. Jenny passed the table and pulled off the road just before the men and Wendy. Tilda slithered to a stop just in front of the second tent. Harry's surprise turned to pride as Jenny jumped out of the driving seat of Tilda and embraced him. As he noticed the hazy outline of the full moon over Jenny's shoulder his feelings turned to sensuality and ended in sheer delight. Words were unnecessary after hasty introductions all round. The two lovers slid with almost indelicate haste into the waiting tent. Harry looked proudly at Jenny, amazed how attractive she looked after so tough a drive. She, with a smile, murmured a line of poetry which Harry did not quite hear.

'What's that?'

'Only a line of a poem I remembered from school,' replied Jenny, 'I'll come to thee by moonlight though hell should bar the way.'

Ask a serious motorcyclist what makes two wheels more exciting than four and he or she will answer 'minimum contact'. The Hills found it harder to describe the delight of sleeping under canvas in a thunderstorm in the remote African bush, but it was the same sentiment. A storm lashing a skyscraper or a dam and you are against the elements. Lightning illuminating the African night, sheltered by a few strands of flax and beeswax – that was different; you are a part of it, not against it but with it, a gene of early man pulsing down the centuries from the pleasure those forebears of ours enjoyed from the security of a cave.

Wendy ended up sleeping in the back of Tilda as Harry and a re-united Jenny commandeered the tent, and for the rest of his life Harry would always say 'There's nothing like a tent, nothing like a tent, for making love in.' How Harry's old army ambulance had managed to sail through a section of the rally which had been considered impassable to some of the finest men and machines in the world was a subject Nairobi motoring circles talked about over many a flagon of Tusker beer for many a month to come.

It must have been a few years before the great rally 'confirmation' that thirteen-year old Simon said, out of the blue when the Hills were driving down to Mombasa for their 'summer' holidays, 'Bwana, is there a God?'

He remembered, happily now, that for a whole hour he had had the opportunity of gently implanting his views to his attentive son. Most of what he had said was way over the head of the four-year old Nicky, and Jenny, as usual when the conversation got really serious, was listening without comment. How he answered the question he could not now recall. The main thing he remembered with delight in retrospect, was that it was asked at all. He assumed he must have given the reply which at that time was all he could think of. Dogmatic gods definitely not; gods sitting on clouds – no; but purpose and reason rather than chaos and accident – most definitely yes.

So the happy decade rolled by and before they knew it Simon was asking if he could have flying lessons. Kenya was a perfect country in which to learn to fly and it seemed no time at all until a proud seventeen-year old Simon obtained his pilot's licence, much to the pride of his mother and father, particularly as he achieved it after only thirty-four hours flying instead of the usual, now mandatory, forty hours. A born flyer, his instructor insisted, and his instructor was no fool, no greenhorn. He, Harry, was delighted to find out that the instructor, a man of about his own age, had roots going back to Biggin

Hill. There wasn't much that impressed him in those days, but praise for his son from a Battle of Britain pilot, that was praise indeed. He thought to himself, It's all very well having a son who is a brilliant flyer and a daughter who is a brilliant horsewoman come to that, but what about himself? Just a bloody expert on breakdowns.

'No, No' Harry said to himself, 'that's not quite fair.' And then he remembered Brian. Brian had been a friend who he seemed to remember had been around all his life. Actually, he now recalled, Brian was the headmaster who had first employed Wendy of the Rally confirmation fame, when she had turned up in Kenya many years ago.

Three years after Kenya's independence Brian uprooted his lifestyle by the roots – wife, three-year old, three-month old, two boys if he remembered rightly, washing machine – one of the first in Kenya – they always used to tease him about that washing machine. Who needed a mechanical one to break down when there were so many human ones, they used to say. Anyway, old Brian piled the whole family and all his furniture in the back of a Peugeot 203 pick-up and drove down to Salisbury. He stayed there some ten or twelve years and then after UDI failed, he uprooted again and took the family to Windhoek, where he was given another headmastership. When Namibia got its independence a couple of years ago old Brian moved down to Johannesburg and believe it or not Harry had just learnt the other day that Brian was now the headmaster of a school in Cape Town and during one of Harry's illicit trips 'down south' as they euphemistically called a trip to South Africa, he recalled Brian with his back to the fire in the Arbutus Club, Cape Town, pontificating to a whole roomful of curious whites. 'Now I personally have lived through three independences in my thirty years in Africa . . . .' He had a captive audience for his expertise. As he had said his farewells to Brian that time, he couldn't help adding, 'I expect you'll be teaching in the Antarctic by the next time we meet'.

As well as breakdowns he must also be an authority on racialism. A scene came into focus that said it all. Only about a couple of years ago, three at the most, in the upstairs bar in the New Stanley Hotel in the heart of Nairobi, a Saturday lunchtime. Probably one of the most crowded places in all Africa, about the only decent hotel bar in Nairobi that had a

180

predominance of Wananchi, a political word for the African proletariat, and only a sprinkling of tourists. He found himself sitting in unusual company, an unusual situation come to that, for his latter years, drinking with some fairly hard drinkers, some six of them around a table. It was a noisy place and most people there seemed to be there with the one purpose of getting drunk. People were crowding round the bar, it horrified Harry to realize that one actually had to push to get a drink. The last time he had pushed at a bar for a drink, except in theatre intervals, must have been in his army days. But it wasn't his round and he was sitting comfortably. He felt sure he could manage to call one of the hard-working waiters when it was his turn. Most of the customers looked as if they had already downed two or three pints or more and were not going to have a more solid lunch. A scene peculiar to the third world; whereas in the developed world most of the drink and drive regulations had cleared such scenes. Harry was not particularly at ease with the company in which he found himself – all much younger than himself for a start, all the other five men he estimated were between thirty and forty years. They were all in the safari business. Harry had arranged to meet one of them when he had agreed to purchase a Range Rover from him which had been purchased by the present owner for a film crew job some six months before and which he now no longer required.

The carpeted floor was blotched with stains, the beer glasses were thick and still wet from washing up, the beer not as baridi – the famous call in Swahili for 'cold' – as he would have wished. He then recalled the old days at the Long Bar at the New Stanley downstairs. A totally different atmosphere. No Africans or Asians for a start. Not because they weren't allowed in the Long Bar which continued to operate at least ten years into independent Kenya, but because they would not have enjoyed the 'clubby' atmosphere of the old Long Bar. You couldn't call that sort of exclusion 'racialist' because a white tourist would have felt equally uncomfortable in that atmosphere. 'Oh dear,' thought Harry, 'there's only the Muthaisa Club left.' In the back of his mind Nicky was saying: 'Stop wandering – describe the scene which you are so proud of.'

The Meru white rhinos had just been massacred, right? Yes, that was it. Sitting opposite him was a character whom he was not particularly fond of, he didn't know him well, he had perhaps met him once or twice before at the Kenya Association of Tour Operators' quarterly luncheons. He was very Germanic with a typical German accent when he spoke English which was obviously not very frequently. He had been in Kenya for about five years, if he recalled correctly. There you are, said another part of him, you are jealous of him, aren't you? Jealous because he's got more vehicles in five years than you have picked up in forty. Don't be silly, I'm not jealous. I just don't like him very much, that's all. He wore his hair cropped in a typical German fashion, and a safari jacket not unlike his own, and an open shirt. One of the other five who were drinking at the table had mentioned that he had been in Meru the previous week just after the massacre of the five white rhino. 'God, you should have seen old "Jerogi" run.' A click click with his finger and thumb to indicate running.

Somebody else interrupted, 'How many of them were there?'

The instant reply, 'Three or four, I think, they took off like bloody rabbits.'

Harry was not famous for his tolerance but he found that particular conversation nauseating so he asked, 'What were they armed with?'

'Who?' said the German opposite.

'Both,' he replied.

The third member of the party who hadn't spoken before said, 'Well, if you can believe the papers Jerogi had two 303s and no ammunition and the poachers had two AK automatics and 200 rounds. Harry concluded his point triumphantly, 'Well, I think I would have bloody well run then.' This annoyed the German, and he cut in 'Even if zey had been armed to ze hilt zey would still haf run. No guts these niggers. Look at the Mau Mau – filthy dirty people. How can you sit zer and say zey're civilized?' Now Harry was really riled. 'You were here in Mau Mau, Harry,' pressed home the German, 'you know how zey would cut ze children's heads off and stick them on a gate post?'

'Yes,' replied Harry, 'I know, thirty-nine of them.'

'Well,' said the German, 'zer you are. Acht, ze make me sick, drinking and eating afterbirth. Well, it's obvious. Look how long zey hav come out of ze bush. Cannibals. You can't expect

182

zem to act differently.'

He remembered standing up and talking straight to the German, 'Hans, Fritz, or whatever's your name? Say this after me slowly. "They are not civilized like us Germans. They have not got our great cultural background. They are savages".'

A little surprised the German repeated it, word for word, 'They are not civilized like ze Germans. Zey have not culture. Zey are savages.'

'And how many people did they kill,' went on Harry, 'how many people did they kill for their independence? Thirty-nine Europeans and 10,000 loyal Africans.'

The German repeated it, and then added, angrily, 'Vat's all zis about?'

'I just wanted to get the figures straight,' said Harry.

'So,' said the German.

'So, six million wasn't it? With your great cultural background, six million! God, Fritz, it's you that makes me sick,' and he walked out.

'Zat's different,' spluttered Fritz to Harry's departing back.

'Yes,' he had said with his parting shot, 'very, very different. That wasn't to throw off the yoke of oppression; that was to please the whim of a madman.' He never did buy that Range Rover.

Harry now searched those more distant days with equal enjoyment looking for any meaning to his and to all life! That last thought cheered him slightly, search for a meaning, a reason for *your* life, and it is doubtful if you will find any, say, meaning for *ALL* life and logic demands, there must be some reason for life in general, yet your life is a part of all life so there must equally obviously be meaning to it. He combed the 'summer months' of his youth, just before the Second World War searching for a clue.

His formative years seemed to have been encompassed by English Norman market towns and villages, with double-barrelled names and single-steepled churches from Leighton Buzzard of his grandparents, to Husbands Bosworth of his in-laws and Newport Pagnell for cousins. An uncle or aunt or two were in Newton Blossomville, Houghton Regis, even Milton

Keynes before its metamorphosis.

He smiled to himself as he fondly remembered a dozen village halls that housed those village hops. Built with dull Maston Valley bricks in Wesley's time. The ugly empty chairs that ringed the dusty boards. His mother's generations vital 'flapping' had slowed to a jerky fox-trotting. The sudden plunge into darkness for the 'last waltz' – an embryo of Disco technique yet to come. To justify what seemed in retrospect, a stilted image, he would tell his daughter – much later 'We did at least touch each other in those days; not just cavort in front or behind each other, like you guys do'; but, such 'old hat' justification could not recall the sheer delight of sweet romance – those village queens, 'Good God – they must have been older than sweet sixteen!'

Such innocence in his imagination, over half a century of recalling the best and forgetting the flaws, turned memories into beautiful girls, all of them.

Most of them were then still linked in some way to the land. When golden evening's harvest called for hands, they would stook, or pitch sheaves of corn, whilst their young sisters helped their mothers glean the stubble; Rosies all.

Partners taken for the last waltz in Husbands Bosworth, boys as innocent as the lambs they tended, girls the embodiment of true romance. Challenging the sensuality of even that Last Tango in Paris.

Then full throttle for those five freezing cold miles, carrying the gentle partner of that last waltz, triumphant on the pillion home. Leather helmeted and side valved AJS echoing through the bible-black unlit sometimes cobbled streets, to the bungalow beside the pub, where she lived and loved and waxed more beautiful each day.

Those characters that brought those horse-drawn harvests home to the yeoman farmers' rick yards, in the days just before the Second World War, were, he concluded later, amongst the most reliable, sound, lovable people to be found anywhere in the whole world. Most would then be wearing cloth caps, braces and waistcoats, most would be heavy smokers of pipes, or hand-rolled cigarettes. All would grumble profusely from sheer habit, but all of them enjoyed their work and envied no one, and automatically took a pride in their craftsmanship, even it was so mundane a job as tying down a waggon load of

184

sheaves with a waggoners hitch knot. It was unthinkable that even one sheaf would ever fall off *their* loads, and he smiled to himself as he thought of the debris on the Third World's roads from insecure loads.

Those pre-war farm workers had probably visited London only once or twice in their lives, although it was only two hours away by train, and since the time when many of the elder ones had returned from Picardy, twenty years before, none had been abroad nor drunk a glass of wine.

Excepting perhaps a bi-monthly sip from the communion chalice for the more devout.

They never dreamt either that some of their children would commute daily to that once-distant city they so infrequently visited. That, he reflected, may show an improvement over the years in the reliability and comfort of the motor car but did not really bring an improvement in the quality of life. On the contrary to spend four hours of each day on a polluted motorway and another eight in an air-conditioned hi-rise was a questionable improvement on their father's eight hours behind a horse-drawn plough.

'Where you are and 'ommoks on it gal,' the old rick-builders would proudly explain to one of the young girls who would be helping them, exactly where to place the sheaf which another labourer had just pitched up to her on top of the growing rick from off the horse-drawn wagon below. Those ricks, although they only had to last from early autumn to late spring, would have walls as straight as a house. Those characters that made up the cast of the set of his early youth, were the antithesis of sophistication, but Harry decided that they were that much the better people for being so.

'So what?' he said half angrily to himself as he concluded his review of three generations of the lifestyles of villagers in the home counties, by realizing that many of the grandchildren of his contemporaries would complete the circle, and would spend most of their working lives in the village again, as computer screens made a physical presence elsewhere unnecessary.

'That's about lifestyles – not death styles!' He almost resented the comfort which those contemporaries of his, enjoyed in their cosy little hamlets, still obtaining it from the pill – the same pill that eased the agony of the eighteen-year old

Lady Jane Grey, the night before her execution.

He could not believe that mumbo-jumbo of dogma, and knew that the pill, like 'black magic' was worthless without belief in it. To Harry the New Testament was a beautiful record, of beautiful hear-say, of a beautiful man, with a beautiful philosophy; martyrs only proved stubborn natures, not a continuity of existence!

The older generation of farm labourers that made up the sort of people by whom Harry was surrounded as a boy were far from 'refined' by most standards. Their boisterous jokes were crude. In his mind's eye, as he drove along the Mombasa road, he could see a scene coming into focus. May Day 1935, a cloth-capped waist-coated red-cheeked farm worker with a stubbled chin and laughing blue eyes was doing a burlesque of a dance, lifting his corduroy-trousered knees up high and clowning away on the midden. In a loud but tolerable tenor voice he was singing 'Hoorah – Hooray the first of May! Outdoor fucking starts today!' Ribald of course, but in the great pastoral Shakespearean tradition, not in the least unkind.

Unlike their traditional enemies across the Rhine, the English proletariat would never allow anybody to con them into accepting genocide – not at any price. Their children might eagerly learn how to blanket-bomb German cities, but that was very different, that seemed the only way at the time of attempting to stop the aggressor. They would never labour for a 'final solution' which after all ultimately depended on manpower.

Later his few German associates might protest their innocence, saying they were anti-Nazi. 'Yes,' he would reply 'so was everybody! – There wasn't one Nazi in Hamburg when I got there with the 8th Army in '45' he scowled. 'They knew what was going on all right; they hated in the plural – that was their problem.'

He was a little annoyed that his own resentment at a whole race, had taken his mind off the joyous days of rick-building, so long ago.

'I resent them – I don't hate them,' he justified himself.

He had been searching for a meaning to life – and found none, but he did find reassurance. All his life it seemed he had been blessed with a glorious environment in which to live it. He certainly didn't despise his roots, but he didn't miss them

186

either, he felt pride and pleasure that his children were perhaps even more blessed with *their* roots.

The stark majesty of Kenya. Her vast horizons, the eternal game grazing the plains, unchanged since the dawn of man. The purple black mountains or her Northern Frontier district rolling range after range for ever. There you *had* to feel at peace, there you found an affinity with the infinite, such feelings as had induced Harry much earlier, to write and stage a *Son et Lumière*, set up for his clients up there in the remote deserts of Northern Kenya.

The glint of her inland lakes nestling in her highland-rifted valleys; the whitest sand in all the world lined her coral sea-shores. The dawn chorus of ten thousand songbirds in her gardens; even the masses of tribes in her markets, the problems of her future, still exude a colourful vibrance that cannot be denied, and with Lake Paradise on Marsabit Mountain for his own special watering hole, protected by presidential decree, the largest pachyderm of them all, Ahmed the Giant Elephant walked free.

A blessed place to live and a . . . 'Bullshit Bwana.' Nicky interrupted his train of thought again, although of course she wasn't present . . .'You always used to say it didn't matter where you died – you were just going to say – "and a meaningful place to die", weren't you?' He nodded ruefully, he supposed he was, – 'Do you remember that essay you wrote for Simon after Uncle Guy died at Mount Kenya Safari Club?'

'Yes,' he conceded as his thoughts rambled on, 'but, you must admit that life-wise, of all the eras of history, famed as most of them are for pestilence or war, and of all the places on earth, most of which are synonymous with famine and want – *we* have been lucky, – peace and plenty surrounds us all the days of our lives'. The optimist waxed lyrical.

He could never understand the prophets of Doom and Despair. Occasionally, he found himself thinking such pessimists only painted their world so black, to try to lessen the sorrow of their inevitable and eventual departure from it. His final emotion after the 'Review of his Roots' as Nicky would have phrased it, was that a small part of the sheer terror of his imminent death, was replaced by an awful sadness.

His huge fear that he was living his last day was coming slightly more under control. The panic action of jumping in his car and driving he knew not where, to do he knew not what, was settling down to an almost unbearable physical pain in his stomach – fear, but not irrational fear. This pain he knew would be with him until he died. The minor fears and hopes, like when he feared that time was turned back, about half an hour ago when he had seen the elephants outside Mtito Andei and all those petrol tankers just to the north were totally forgotten.

His obsession with his Corolla's fuel gauge was also dying down as he sped south still in the scrub desert south of Voi. He must concentrate, he told himself, he must recall all Tilda's idiosyncrasies, add them up in his mind to prove something, to comfort him. 'How the hell' he asked himself, 'could a £75 Army surplus vehicle prove immortality?' Or convince him that his life had a purpose. How the hell could it? It couldn't, that was obvious. Anyway, even if it could, over the last twenty years without Tilda, what of them?

Simon had driven Tilda back from that huge crater into which that idiot Oliver had driven her and left her all night. It must have been late 1968 and eighteen-year old Simon had been flying two years and Nicky was nearly ten. With Simon getting his PPL and with the acquisition of half a share in an aeroplane and a willing pilot in their son, a whole new world had opened up for Harry and Jenny. At least once a month the Hills would take off to a remote part of East Africa to which they had never been before. Lodwar, even a weekend in Tanzania's Selous, allegedly the largest game reserve in the world, was all within the range of Simon and his Cessna. Their world shrank delightfully. The two days it used to take them to do their favourite safari up to Eastern Turkana could now be done in a two-and-a-half-hour flight. Simon took to flying like a duck to water, or rather like a swallow to the sky. His meticulous mind (probably a reaction to his father's rather erratic one) together with a fairly high intelligence – meant that you could not lose him within five hundred miles of Nairobi. This was partly because of the seventeen years of travel which he had done in East Africa before he started to fly. All who flew with him were at ease, a confidence usually only enjoyed with those pilots with

188

very much more experience.

In the early days of Simon's first solo cross-country flight, Jenny had been concerned. Their Langata home was in the flight path for descent to the air strip at which they kept the plane and the sight of Simon 1,000 feet overhead in his little blue and white Alpha Tango became commonplace. With the familiarity grew not a contempt but a confidence in Jenny that all would always be well. The fraternity of the light aircraft men and women of Kenya in those days and indeed, of these days, was an inspiring camaraderie of serious young people who worked hard and played hard. Not one of them would bend the rules, like taking alcohol before a flight, but most of them would celebrate hard at the weekends.

Harry's reminiscences came into focus again. One hot morning in November 1968 in their home at Langata Simon had been back home from Fort Worth for a week after successfully completing a Commercial Pilots' Licence course. He addressed his father, 'Bwana.' Harry could tell from the tone of the long 'a' in bwana that his son was about to ask him a favour which he anticipated he might not be able to grant.

'Bwana, could Oliver borrow Tilda this weekend?'

Immediately from Harry, 'What's wrong with his *gari?*'

Simon replied, rather dolefully, knowing that it would do his case no good, 'He bent it coming back from the coast last weekend, didn't he? You remember.'

'Good God, he writes his own car off and then he wants ours.'

'I know it looks like that but he only wants it to go up to the Ngongs to set out control points for a four-wheel drive rally he's helping organize.'

Rather sulkily from Harry, 'Well, Tilda's not even four-wheel drive.'

Sarcastically from Simon, who must have heard his father say it a hundred times, 'It's not four-wheel drive that counts, it's power-weight ratio and clearance, isn't it, bwana?'

Rather reluctantly Harry gave in to his son's persuasions and so it was arranged that Oliver would borrow Tilda that weekend.

Any pilot, however experienced, will tell you the same thing. That most light aircraft accidents start hours before the impact, that you 'collect' things going wrong, and it is the airmen's and women's job to have the courage to say, 'Stop, enough' before the combined gremlins triumph in disaster.

The first gremlin in Simon's case happened in the Masai Mara game reserve. The African driver of the Land Rover that was bringing Simon's client to the airstrip made the first mistake. He should not have attempted to cross the wet lugger without walking ahead and checking it out, but he was already running late so he chose to chance it. Possibly due to pressure from the American Newsweek photographer and his new-found girlfriend whom he was taking to meet the flight out, the photographer had his own reasons to be in a hurry. He was doing an article on the wildebeest migration which was scheduled for a fortnight's time's edition and it was very important that he should catch the PanAm flight that was leaving Jomo Kenyatta that night for Europe and onwards to the States. The Land Rover bogged down some four miles from the strip. The driver volunteered to carry the heavy camera equipment. The next unfortunate circumstance was that the photographer had recently met an extremely attractive young American freelance journalist at the lodge where he had been staying and it seemed the most natural thing in the world to allow her to take up one of the free seats on his special charter flight back to Nairobi.

By the time the three of them had walked from the stuck Land Rover to the strip where Simon was waiting for them it was already dusk. The vital and critical sixty minutes Simon had in fact been waiting should have been employed in flying back. 'Sorry, sir,' Simon said, trying to find a confidence he didn't have, 'we'll have to stay here for the night. I'll take off at first light but we haven't got time to get back to Nairobi now.'

'Like hell you will, son, we've still got forty-five minutes' daylight. I wasn't born yesterday you know and you're not the only pilot around here.'

'I know sir, but that leaves no margin for . . . .'

'Now, look, where the hell do you suppose we are going to stay here? There are four of us, right? The vehicle we came in is stuck, we can't get back to the lodge. For God's sake start up and let's get the hell out of here while there is still time.' Simon was only eighteen and he had only 220 hours under his belt; he was thinking to himself, 'You're right' and he had to admit that Wilson did have runway lights that were always on for two hours after dusk but he hadn't got his instrument rating . . . but then with three-quarters of an hour you would just do it if you were quick.

'OK,' he said, 'get in.' Then it dawned on him that the girl would be coming, as she climbed in. He had originally assumed that she would be waiting with the African driver until the vehicle was unstuck. 'Good God, she's not coming.'

'It's a bloody four seater I hired, didn't I?'

'Yes, but you've got a lot of equipment.'

'Look here, sonny, I've told you once I'm not a fool. I've been flying for more days than you've had hot dinners. Now what are you worried about? There's plenty of daylight, plenty of lift.'

Simon was busy doing sums. The runway was at an altitude of 3,500 feet, which meant a ten per cent loss of power before he started. It was fairly thick grass. There had been a slight shower of rain that afternoon and it was still damp. The thorn trees at the end of the strip seemed to have doubled in their height while he looked. The third gremlin was a huge black cumulo-nimbus thundercloud with its head some 30,000 feet in the sky above them. But there was a comfortable 1,000 feet below it. Simon's plane was in perfect condition, only half-full fuel tanks, the three of them and the equipment were well within limits. With perhaps another year's experience he might have had sufficient confidence to discount his client. With eighteen years and 220 hours he still felt he had something to prove and he hadn't quite enough sense to realize that there were too many gremlins lined up against him. 'Clear start!' He shouted the words before starting the engine despite the fact that there was no one to hear him on the empty grass strip.

He got off, just, and cleared the thorn trees at the end of the strip by all of ten feet. Turning towards the Loita Hills and Nairobi a huge red ball of a sun slid down into the earth behind him. The anvil headed black cloud which he could see from the Mara strip refused to move. He knew that to go over it he would need a turbocharger and pressurization come to that. It must be at least 25,000 feet. Circumnavigating it to left or to right would add at least twenty-five minutes to the flight which meant that although he would have enough fuel he would not be over Wilson until well after sundown and, well, the lights might be on but yet again they might not. To add to his problems an evening mist was rolling over the Ngong Hills beneath the base of the nimbus cloud's anvil-shaped head. Nevertheless it seemed to Simon that there was still a comfortable 200 or 300 feet which he could 'sneak through'.

Wisps of cloud flashed past the cockpit windows. Simon gripped the controls and prayed he was not flying into the terror of all uninstrumented light plane pilots – the indescribable disorientation of complete lack of vision. His prayers were answered; he could still see patches of ground, despite the mist. His air speed increased a little as he put the nose down to underfly the black thunderclouds. There was blackness behind him and just an eerie grey light ahead of him but no matter, another five minutes and he should have Wilson in sight. He relaxed slightly, unharassed. There was slight turbulence and they would be landing shortly so he turned round to his two passengers who were sitting behind him and enquired with a smile, 'Safety belt tight? – Christ!' Then to himself 'Oh my God'. At least he reacted correctly. Fully forward with the throttle, stick back and right and climb. A light shone out of the murk about a hundred yards ahead almost exactly level with him. It must be an oncoming plane. It all happened in a second – the longest second of his life. That second started with Simon believing that a head-on collision with an oncoming plane was unavoidable – and ended with him laughing outright as the Cessna lifted sharply upwards and banked right and as the light flashed by beneath the rigid undercart it was the photographer client in the rear shouting, 'What the fuck was that?' that made Simon guffaw, reminding him of the Mayor of Hirahima joke.

There was not much weight of fuel and the machine reacted magnificently. That the light was on the ground and not in the air never occurred to Simon at that moment, nor to his passengers ever. Simon estimated later that they cleared the highest peak of the Ngong Hills by about six feet or the height of one of the many bushes. They must have been down at bush level, but no one would ever know. The crisis passed and in another two minutes they were flying down the slopes on the other side to the lights of the Ngong village and beyond them, Nairobi. The air was suddenly as clear as a bell as they flew out of the cloud. Three minutes later they were over the Monastery for 'Monastery Finals' and shortly after that did a perfect landing at Wilson. The lights were on and there was enough light from the dying daylight to put down safely in any event. His passengers phoned up for a taxi, Simon tied down his Cessna to the two weights which were always used for that purpose. He then grabbed his old Morris Minor from the car park. About all that he used it for was getting him and the other owner, Oliver, backwards and forwards from their houses in Langata to the airport.

As he entered the living room Simon saw Oliver standing there. 'Hello, you're back early. I thought you would still be sorting out your handicapping for your rally.'

'That's right I just called in to tell the bwana. I'm afraid I've got Tilda stuck right on top of the bloody Ngongs. But don't worry, she'll get out all right with a pull. I'll get a tractor laid on and there's no harm done. I mean she just went down. I couldn't help it. I had to abandon her and walk all the way back.' Simon closed his eyes. In a flash it dawned on him. He knew Oliver wouldn't have left the headlights blazing. Tilda would have had to arrange that for herself.

'Left her pointing towards Mara I suppose?'

Oliver looked at him mysteriously, half turning, waving his left hand and right hand as he found his bearings. 'Yeah, why?'

Simon never answered the question, just said, 'Thought so.'

The next day Oliver and Simon hired a tractor and drove up the Ngong Hills to bring Tilda back out of the hole. Simon wasn't surprised when he found the battery was flat because the headlights had been on. Too flat in fact to start the engine. But being a diesel they gave it a quick tug with the tractor and she roared into life.

'Bloody old thing can't be charging,' said Oliver knowingly.

'No,' said Simon. He would never tell Oliver about what he later called 'The Light of the Ngongs' but that evening around the fire in their Langata house he told his mother, father and sister.

'Good Lord, Simon,' his mother said, 'what an incredibly lucky thing that Oliver took Tilda up there in the first place.'

'And left her lights on,' added Nicky knowingly. Harry said very little at the time but in retrospect it was that incident more than any other Tilda coincidence, that made him think the most.

'I mean,' he said to his daughter much later, 'I mean even if Tilda does attract supernatural powers like a sort of a haunted house or some such, no one would believe us. So why make ourselves look silly bragging about it?'

8

Death and Suicide

Harry, now some twenty minutes out of Voi, allowed himself
the luxury of remembering some non-Tilda-related incidents,
at least as far as he knew, he thought to himself with a smile,
they were non-Tilda. What a close-knit, understanding, loving
family they had been. Simon at nineteen had looked like a
Greek god with his long, blond curly hair and wide-set blue
eyes and Nicky, as she approached twelve, was losing her
puppy fat in the start of a figure which looked as if it might one
day become as attractive as her mother's. But it was the little
things that Harry had been so proud of. He couldn't resist
recalling a tiny incident.

Nicky had been doing her Christmas shopping in Nairobi
soon after the light in the Ngongs affair and being a thoughtful
girl she remembered him saying, 'I must get a cover sheet made
for Alpha Tango's dash, the sun's cracking the leather'. When
she was in a motorists' supermarket in Nairobi and saw a rolled
tin screen with two rubber suckers to stick it to the windscreen
of a motor car, she thought that would do ideally for a
Christmas present for her brother. Christmas morning and
Simon immediately realized that the rolled tin screen would be
impossible to use in the plane because of its magnetic attraction
so close to the compass but he did not wish to hurt his young
sister's feelings by telling her. He went out and brought a cloth
screen of similar proportions and the next day said to Nicky,
'Hey, Nick, you know that screen you bought me for Christmas, well, it was just a couple of inches too big and by a great
deal of luck there's a guy who has just flown in from Tanzania
who had one just right for me so we did a swop. I hope you
don't mind.' Harry thought over this example of loving

thoughtfulness so typical of the Hills' happy family.

There was little to distract him on the hundred-mile stretch of road south of Voi towards the coast – a good surface and always the semi-desert scrub on either side. Not much traffic, few bends and always the railway track parallel to the road which seemed to slide slyly towards it and then peel off again. The backs of concrete signalmen's boxes, a lonely baobab tree, a bare patch of desert without any scrub, and then the inevitable charcoal burners who would place on the side of the road that sack which was their reward for rape – a sooty bag of charcoal propped up for sale and stuffed up with grass at the neck.

As Harry tore along he was glad that there were few distractions. He was on ninety-nine per cent automatic now. And he conjured up, with morbid relish, that day of his life more than twenty years before a day which he would never forget. A wet September evening, 1969.

☆   ☆   ☆

It was interesting, Harry thought, to note that his time in Kenya had coincided neatly with the world's long-haul transport revolution. In the fifties most of those going on leave from Kenya to Europe would be seen off at the restaurant bar in Nairobi's railway station. That would be followed for them by an overnight journey in the train to Mombasa, possibly one night in the old Mombasa town hotels of the Castle or the Manor, still standing, and still not bad hotels Harry thought, with a little touch of pleasure. Setting sail for between two and three weeks depending on how much of your passage was spent in Durban and the Cape. Well within three weeks you would be in Tilbury Docks under the Port of London's authority. How sadly, how suddenly did those monarchs of the sea sail into history. No more would you be driving through a foggy London dock area, turn a bend or cross a bridge and see the prow of *SS Kenya* positively exuding the sun of the tropics and the happiness of all who sailed in her. Before the Hills arrived in Kenya both before and for a short time after the Second World War, there had been the most pleasant of all transport of delight – the Sunderland flying boat – seven days from the Solent to the Cape, setting down for exotic night stops like a giant pelican in such romantic waters as Capri, Luxor, Khartoum, Naivasha, the Rift Valley lakes and finally False Bay in the shelter of Table Mountain.

Today all of the travellers to Kenya are dropped off at Jomo Kenyatta International Airport where there is only a grubby bar for the wayfarer's friends and eight and a quarter hours with their knees around their necks for the wayfarers to Europe. However did those clever PR people coin the 'jet set' image.

In 1969 the new Jomo Kenyatta International Airport for Nairobi had not been opened, one was still using the old Embakasi Airport. The tourist invasion had not really got under way. There were perhaps two or three 120-seaters every other night, not five 400-seaters every night, non-stop to Europe, like there are today.

It had been arranged that Oliver – the same Oliver that had left Tilda stranded on the Ngong Hills the previous year – was to accompany Jenny and Simon to London and Nicky and Harry would remain behind. Jenny, particularly, was bursting with pride. Simon had just won himself a flying commission with the RAF and was off to Cranwell and Jenny thought she would take the opportunity to do a little pre-Christmas shopping and introduce her son to the few remaining ageing relatives she had still alive in the UK. Simon was as much looking forward to the winter in Europe as he was to Cranwell. Apart from the mountain passes in the Alps he had never seen falling snow and was hoping against hope there would be a white Christmas. Jenny had a spinster aunt who lived in a little cottage near Oxford and it was with her that Simon intended spending his holidays.

Harry remembered it as if it were yesterday instead of over twenty years ago. Oliver turned up at the airport that evening in a Hilton Hotel company car as his job was training in hotel management at that time. It was a Hillman Super Minx. The car had three keys – one, a master key which turned on the ignition and opened all four doors and the boot lock. A second key, invariably supplied, only operated the ignition and the steering lock and a third key was supplied to open the doors and the boot.

Oliver was leaving his company car parked at Nairobi Airport for the night to be collected by a Hilton company driver the following morning. He had left one of the three keys on his desk in his Nairobi office for the driver to collect the following morning and had taken one key with him. Such a little thing to remember for years like ducks on a pond. Such a little thing. At the time Harry didn't even know about the key mix-up, he just thought the boot lock of Oliver's car must have jammed. In fact he and Jenny and Simon arrived on the scene in the car park just as a heavy tyre lever had been found to supplement the jack handle with which Oliver was attempting to prise open the boot in order to get his suitcase out. They hammered, they banged, they prised, they levered and such was the strength of that boot that only the corners turned up like a stale sandwich, with nothing like enough room to even get a hand in, let alone to pull a case out. Oliver knew that the longer he tried to open the boot the less time he would have to rush back home and get the third and correct key, open the boot, release his suitcase, bring the car back to the airport and catch his flight. It would be touch and go. It was a calculated risk. With a hasty explanation Oliver drove out of the airport car park at knots per hour. He missed his flight by five minutes. In fact the next he saw, and in fact the last he saw, was the graceful VC 10 climbing over the Mombasa road some 400 feet above his car. He told Harry later that he thought he had seen Simons face at an illuminated window but Harry doubted it.

Off into the damp soft night flew Jenny and Simon. The VC 10, one of the most majestic of aircraft, climbed perfectly over the Ngong Hills, her red signal light could be seen by Nicky and Harry from the ground after the mighty roar of her engines had melted into the night. With a little sadness Harry and Nicky wandered out of the Kwaheri bar and into the car park. Strangely, because the Hills had not been using her very much at that time Tilda *had* been used to bring the Hills to the airport. As they drove home a little sadly, Nicky said to her father, 'What a good job Tilda's back doors didn't jam shut like Oliver's boot did.'

'Poor old Oliver,' replied Harry, 'it could be days before he can get another flight. What an anticlimax!'

It must have been around that time that Harry and Nicky were driving home in Tilda that the weaver of the web of destiny was busily at work on an exquisitely fine piece of weaving, nearly 2,000 miles north of Nairobi in Ethiopia.

An empty trolley train of three mini-flat cars had been towed by a Ferguson tractor across the aerodrome at Addis Ababa. A load of special nitrogenous fertilizer in hessian sacks for a United Nations agricultural project at Marbella had just been loaded onto a waiting cargo plane and now the trolley train was bouncing back across the runway to the airport terminal buildings. Nobody could really blame that tractor driver, nor his mate perched on the mudguard, that the weaver of the web of destiny chose him. It was common practice to hook the two sack-loading hooks which they had been using into the body bar of the first trailer. Possibly they should have noticed that one was missing but they knew their next job would be handling passengers' luggage loading the international flight that was due to land there later that evening and as that wouldn't need sack hooks one was not missed – oh, the exquisite timing of that weaver!

A little jolt as the tractor driver decelerated his hand throttle in order to light his cigarette then the little acceleration and then the middle trolley nudged gently against the front trolley and one loading hook fell to the ground, point side up. How many millions to one that it should be in the exact path of the front wheel of an East African Airways VC 10 which passed it by a hundred feet on landing, which passed it again on taxi-ing out but which was to be exactly in the right place at the end of the take-off run which would be rolling out in four hours time.

Two thousand miles south of Addis Ababa International Airport Harry was fast asleep. It was three o'clock in the morning when the bell of the phone by his bed startled him awake with that urgent peal, which the eighties had tamed into a discreet purr. Somehow even as he reached out to grab the receiver he knew it was a disaster. An associate of his at air traffic control who had actually passed a few words with him that evening in the airport Kwaheri lounge was on the other end of the phone. He asked did he have anyone on that flight because seeing him at the airport .... . He had just got a jumbled message on a radio-phone relayed from a ham whom he knew in Lodwar that flight EC 614 from Nairobi had had a serious accident on take-off from Addis where it had stopped for a scheduled refuelling stop. There were apparently very few survivors from the 124 passengers and eleven crew that had been on board. Not unusually Addis phones were down and the East African Airways telex was also inoperable. Messages were coming in every half-hour by the Lufthansa telex in Embakasi. He rushed into Nicky's room to wake her up. He was a little surprised to see that she still slept with her teddy bear. Come to think of it he couldn't remember the last occasion when he had actually seen her in bed.

That night drive from Langata to Embakasi in Tilda was, in retrospect, a little blurred but the next scene was in perfect focus again. The many heads of the seething crowd round the Lufthansa telex at the airport. Somehow or other they managed to push to the front and they could read the message as it came in.

'Oh God, oh God, how could there be so many people amongst the 124 passengers whose surname, like Jenny and Simon's, began with H.' The list was in alphabetical order. 'First reports, unofficial' the telex snapped out. There was nothing so informal as a telex. 'Survivors list follows . . . Repeat. Surviving passengers as follows . . . Angel, T. Mrs,' the carriage returns with a snap, and 'Ball, B. Master,' it returns again and under that, 'Ball, C. Miss, Belitti, D. Master, Block, J. Miss.' The minutes that followed as the list and the telex crept through the alphabet seemed like hours to Harry as he waited. At last the Hs snapped out. 'Hamilton, J. Miss, Harrys, K. Mrs, Harrys, L. Mr.' There was even, he remembered, an H – i, but it turned out to be Hindrick E. Miss, Liz Hindrick, Nicky's friend going back to school in UK. Lucky Liz, but there was no Hill – either Mrs J. or Mr S. On went the telex, 'Ingles, A. Master, King, D. Miss.' With awfully finality the telex message stopped with the words 'flight deck survivor, Flight Engineer Clarke.' Then it started off again. 'Identified killed, Macdonald, Captain, in command, First Officer Preston' and five of the seven cabin crew's names followed. 'There are approximately seventy-five unidentified bodies. Transmission ends. Karl, Captain, Lufthansa, Ethiopia.'

An awful heaviness swept over Harry. Figures rushed through his head. 114 passengers, ten crew, total 124 on board. The alphabetical list of survivors totalled thirty-nine, another seventy-five estimated dead, still ten unaccounted for. Harry knew in his heart that the eleven to one against shot of either Jenny or Simon being amongst those ten was a poor bet but even if he had known that they had been dead he would still have welcomed the diversion of the flight that he and Nicky got two hours later as soon as it was light. They took off with a friend in a twin Beechcraft nine-seater. He found it helpful to be doing something, as if the four and a half hours it took to fly to Addis was 'doing something'. A nightmare of course but better than the same amount of time spent by that awful telex machine.

The wreck of the VC 10 was clearly visible as they came into land. It had broken in two before catching on fire and had finally come to rest about 300 yards beyond the end of the main runway in a flat field where it had apparently collided with a four-foot high concrete lighting plinth which at over 100 knots on impact had pitched its nose down. The aircraft had rolled over, broken in two, before it had exploded like an atom bomb. He found himself wondering how anybody could have survived that. A hospital nurse with a Scots accent was in charge and it was she who looked after Nicky whilst her father was suffering the most awful agony of doing the most terrible job he had ever had to do in all his life. The fourteenth in line blanket-covered corpse was Jenny's and a tiny consolation next to it was the body of Simon. By then he knew that it would be the dead bodies of his wife and son that he would see, because there was a list pinned up in the airport restaurant rather like a golf club fixture list, listing the survivors most of whom had been hospitalized and the name 'Hills' was not amongst them.

Unkindly it was a perfect day in Addis that September afternoon. Nicky sat on Harry's lap in the front seat of the Beechcraft when they flew back to Nairobi. The nine passenger seats had been removed and six bodies in body bags had been placed in the little aircraft to be flown back to Nairobi. Harry shuddered on learning that a stack of plastic body bags has to be held at all international airports. Harry didn't ever know if Jenny and Simon were amongst the bodies on board. Two DC 3s from Nairobi were being flown up to return the rest of the bodies to Nairobi and one of them landed just as the Beechcraft was taking off.

A terrible numbness, then a little determination that in Nicky he would make sure that all the hopes of Jenny and Simon would be fulfilled. All Nicky could say on the way back was, 'Why Memsahib and Simon? They weren't bad people.' Harry remembered searching desperately for a scrap of comfort as they flew back at 10,000 feet over the Rift Valley laid out like a carpet below them. Lake Turkana, two million years, what was two deaths? What was a lifetime to that which had seen it all?

Then another thought crossed his mind and would not go away. Tilda had taken them to the airport faultlessly. Now what about the lock problem on the vehicle that had taken Oliver which had prevented his catching the flight and had thus saved his life? Why had Tilda not interceded? Why had she not? 'You bloody fool,' he said to himself in the plane. 'Why should she; how could she?' Then he thought back to all the Tilda intercessions right up to the light on the Ngongs the year before. Why on earth had Tilda saved Simon from death for only eighteen months? Why? He remembered being angry with himself for smiling up there as he overflew the Rift Valley with the bodies behind him with a sobbing Nicky on his lap. 'Fucking fiend,' he said to himself. 'Well, Jenny would have laughed,' he smiled. 'What are you smiling at? I'm smiling at my optimism,' he told himself firmly. If Tilda who had so often helped in the past had failed to help yesterday there must be a reason, and if there was a reason – that's great. Everything fits into place – it must have been meant or Tilda would have stopped it.

Stories and rumours built up like thunderclouds around the disaster. There were at that time about 40,000 Europeans living in Kenya, and one of the nice things was that on average one would know between an eighth and a quarter of them. Which meant that wherever you went, whether it was the coast or up country or a restaurant in Nairobi there was a fairly good chance you would meet someone you at least knew by sight. Jenny and Harry used to joke that there was no chance in Kenya for a secret dirty weekend with anybody. You only had to pull up at a filling station halfway to Mombasa to find you knew the guy in the car filling up in front of you. Harry smiled to himself, 'Oh, this is my cousin, she's come over from the UK to stay with us and Kathy wasn't feeling very well, a bit under the weather you know this weekend, so I . . . .' 'Oh, I see,' would reply Jenny with a smile. The infidelity and adultery of acquaintances was of no particular interest to either of them. But now knowing that most people you met would know of your bereavement gave a sort of warmth and helped a little, better than being in lonely London, thought Harry.

It turned out that over half the casualties were children returning to the UK for the Christmas term at school and no less than fifteen of them had lived in either Langata or Karen. It reminded Harry of what his uncles used to tell him about villages in Oxfordshire and Buckinghamshire during the First World War after the Ox and Bucks infantry regiment had been engaged on the Somme. A lot of people were in mourning that month. It helped a little. Eventually the rumours subsided and what was accepted as the truth emerged in *Newsweek*.

Two of the flight deck crew were killed and the third seriously injured with bad concussion causing loss of memory immediately prior to the accident. It was established, however, that the Flight Engineer had calculated and displayed the all important V1 and V2 cards, the former showing a figure of ninety knots, the latter 140 knots. The V1 figure meaning it was recommended the pilot in command aborts take-off if any fault occurs up to the speed indicated. The V2 computed figure means the pilots should only abort up to this figure in extreme emergencies – and once being exceeded an abortive take-off is prohibited. Captain Macdonald's speed was estimated to be five knots under V2 when the sack hook picked up on the nose wheel causing it to burst. Now by that time in take-off it is not absolutely vital to have an intact nose wheel. The plane would have taken off with the burst tyre. Whether it would have landed safely is another question but the point was that in that split second all the captain could tell was that he knew he had a serious fault with the undercarriage and this card indicated there was just enough runway left in which to abort take-off. Everybody, with no exception, agreed completely that he carried out the correct procedure. There is a reverse thrust on the VC 10 and spoilers but they only marginally slowed the forward movement of the 150 tons travelling at over 150 miles per hour as it hurtled down the runway. Its stopping power mainly depending on the brakes applied with all the skill you could muster to achieve maximum slowing. The survivors all recalled that the plane slowed instantly as the throttles were shut and the reverse thrust levers pulled back: they remembered being thrown forward with the sudden deceleration but then suddenly the braking power seemed to be taken off and they rolled forward free and fast. An abortive take-off should have been relatively safe and relatively easy. The surviving Flight Engineer, although seriously injured, lived to confirm that the brakes had been working perfectly whilst taxi-ing and indeed whilst landing a mere three-quarters of an hour before the disaster, but on all those occasions, it materialized, they had only been used to a maximum of fifty per cent of their potential. When a hundred per cent pressure was applied, just like a burst in a hydraulic braking system of a motor car when the foot goes flat down to the floor, there were no brakes. The plane had perhaps slowed to something like a hundred knots when it hit the obstacle. There was an unconfirmed report that the pilot forced his way out of the emergency exit of the cockpit, where the second in command was dead and the engineer unconscious, and had rushed straight into the fiery furnace of the rest of the broken fuselage some 100 feet away in a futile attempt to save his passengers. Captain Ian Macdonald's body was certainly little else but a charred mound and yet there had been no fire in the cockpit which seemed to imply that the story was true. Nairobi, Nairobbery and Rumourville.

The crash was the subject of much speculation. Had not that very VC 10 of East African Airways been in for a brake overhaul just before the fatal flight? Had not the job been done by Africans? Could not a student have put the brake rubbers the wrong way around which could have meant a hundred per cent correct operation until an emergency, when the brake pedal would have gone right through, right down to the floor of the cockpit. Or had the sack hook broken a hydraulic pipe as well as burst the front wheel tyre?

No one would ever know. On balance Harry thought the anti-African rumour was probably not true, but it was a typical sort of rumour that the diehards would put around. True or false it made no difference to his awful void.

In the following twenty years of his life there was not a week that went by that he did not think of that awful tragedy. But then he remembered a new fear that he had at that time. A fear that the tragedy would in some way damage Nicky's mind. Was she not behaving strangely? That month following the tragedy of the VC 10 at Addis would be remembered by all the

Europeans.

Michaela Denis, whose husband Armand had recently died, was proudly known to most white Kenyans as the pioneer of a wildlife series on the BBC 'telly'. It was said that she was going a little kinky in her old age, she refused to cut trees down because she could hear them screaming, for example; that sort of thing. She held a special séance for the grieving of Langata and, of course, Harry had to attend it. It may have helped some but it certainly didn't help him. Had it not been so awful, so truly awful, he might have laughed.

He remembered sitting in the garden and Nicky sitting there too, just staring. From the verandah they could see where Tilda was parked up and it comforted them both a little to look at Tilda. Harry recalled all the incidents in Tilda's life for Nicky's benefit. It helped a little to be near that old vehicle which Jenny and Simon had so much enjoyed.

Harry had the remains of his wife and son cremated and Oliver flew Harry and Nicky up to Lake Rudolf, over Ol Donyo Nyiro. Oliver banked steeply and Harry emptied the two small urns of ashes out of the cockpit window. Jenny had most seriously asked for such an end when they had been visiting the lake only three months previously. Harry was to have much to do with that part of Kenya for the rest of his life – when Jenny made her wish it was not a morbid occasion but at the end of a wonderful day. Simon had flown the whole family to an airstrip the army had made, in a secret valley of the lofty mountain range – they had then climbed on foot another thousand feet with two lightweight tents and sleeping bags and a frying pan and a bag of four choice 'T-bone' steaks, to camp above a mountain stream which gushed out of a rock face at the head of a grassy glade. There were elephant and buffalo spoor in abundance but the shy reed buck and kudu were the only animals they saw. Probably, Harry estimated, they were the first white people to sleep in that mountain glade and the number of white visitors to the mountain at that height was probably less than a score. No white man had even seen the mountain till 1888 when Teleki and von Hohnel stumbled past with a hundred thirsty porters. From then for the next fifty years only those names belonging to the expedition they led had seen that mountain such as Neumann the gentle recluse who massacred more elephants than anybody, Donaldson

Smith from Philadelphia, Willby Harrison and Austin for the Brits and an Italian or two.

Leaving Voi Harry smiled, well, he supposed, one day he might be remembered for putting that part of the world well and truly on the map. Harry Hill's Safaris started the legendary Turkana Bus – but that was years later. 'The most perfect place I have ever seen,' was Jenny's excited description, 'promise me you'll scatter my ashes here when I'm gone, Harry.' Harry smiled and nodded. One just didn't argue with Jenny when she was in that sort of mood. He didn't even add the usual ageing husband and wife comforting suggestion 'And more likely you – me!'

☆ ☆ ☆

The White Tribe of Kenya was a little prejudiced, he decided. Not prejudiced against Africans; generally speaking, with one or two major exceptions, they liked the Africans, possibly in a slightly paternally despotic way but a genuine affinity nevertheless. Surprisingly enough, again with one or two exceptions, which only went to prove the rule, the admiration was mutual. No, the post-independence White Tribe of Kenya was prejudiced against its own race: against many white two-year wonders, originally hailing from the UK but latterly more frequently from that other ex-British colony, that dreamt the American dream, as Harry invariably found himself describing citizens of the US of A.

The two-year wonders usually consisted of one working male between the age of thirty and forty and a non-working wife with two young children. The prejudice, Harry said to himself, was unfounded.

Their other problem was with their workforce, which had determined, and always would determine, to work for only a strictly limited number of days per month, because they found days off far easier to come by than an increase in pay. All employers knew that it was common practice for their labourers to bury at least one mother, one grandmother and two brothers two or three times each year, taking perhaps seven to ten days off for the ensuing and often mythical wake.

Four-year wonders were not completely accepted but if they stayed for a third contract then they were fully integrated. If ever an out-of-work African university graduate dared to suggest in a letter to an editor of one of the three daily rags that just possibly he might be capable of teaching at the kindergarten – that had just obtained a fourth work permit for an unqualified English girl – then the White Tribe would forget their pro-African tolerance and gang up on the out-of-work intellectual African.

'Remember old Jimmy running the City Hall before independence? Ten Afs do his job today at three or four times his salary each, and look at what a balls-up they make of it.' Tales of unsuitable Africanization from traffic light repairers who failed so dismally, to bank managers who often absconded with the till were legion.

The problem was that he was using his daughter as a sort of therapy for himself, not for her benefit as such, and his constant over-attention wasn't really helping the poor girl. She was becoming totally dependent on her father. This was a triumph for him he felt, and he didn't realize that it was no help for her. She had been totally extrovert but now she was becoming introverted. A tomboy par excellence, now she would not stray very far from her father's side and was always holding his hand. The tragic loss they had both sustained was throwing them together but the absolute dependence on each other was good for neither. Paul and Rita could see what was wrong at a glance and were, during those months, trying to get Nicky to go to parties with kids of her own age but seldom would she go without her father. There was a look of terror in her eyes if she inadvertently crossed the road leaving her father on the kerb. Any minor reprimand or criticism would bring a flood of tears.

Just for something to do and to indulge his daughter who had loved swimming, Harry had a swimming pool built at the Langata house but Nicky wouldn't even venture into this on her own. 'Poor kid,' said Rita, 'Harry's smothering her but how the hell can we tell him that?'

'Poor Harry,' added Paul, 'you can't blame him really.'

☆   ☆   ☆

It was March, March 1970, six months after the Addis crash. Paul and Rita had insisted that Harry and Nicky came on safari with them for a change, and he had agreed. That was

207

one of the first years for many a year that Harry wasn't involved in the East African Safari Rally. Instead, Good Friday found Harry and Nicky and Tilda in the middle of the NFD, as Kenya's Northern Frontier District was referred to. They were less than an hour's drive from Ol Donyo Nyiro, the mountain Jenny had loved so much and over which her and Simon's ashes were scattered. Today, twenty years later, Eastern Turkana had become Harry's home-from-home but he never guessed at the future involvement that March afternoon in 1970. Harry used to tell his tourists much later that Eastern Turkana was a desert enjoying only seven inches of rainfall a year. That could be missed in three or four years running but when it did come 'it will all come on top of us' he used to say, 'all in one night so be prepared to dig'. A slight exaggeration but it was not uncommon for four inches of rain to fall in twenty-four hours in those huge electric storms.

The safarites were in the Matthews range of mountains passing one of the remote tracks that led across the Milgis lugga, the biggest non-river in the world. The Milgis lugga, although it extended for nearly a hundred miles, seldom had water in it, perhaps for two or three months of the year after the rains it might have a trickle. When that dried up eleys would probe downwards for a foot or two and turn their trunks into an incredible borehole pump. The look in the elephants' eyes of perfect contentment as they squirted the dirt off their backs with the cool water beneath the sand of the Milgis was a sight that he would remember with fondness for ever. Perhaps two or three days after the elephants had plodded on, the nomadic tribesmen would come down with their camels and dig three or four feet for the water under the sand. But for ninety-nine per cent of the time the Milgis lugga, like many another lugga that criss-crossed these deserts, was completely dry. The average height of the banks on either side was something like fifty feet, the width was never less than a hundred yards, and often up to a mile with always rounded boulders down in the bed of the river, and sand; in fact the perfect river in every respect except that it had no water in it. On occasion for two days every seven years it might fill to its fifty foot brim but how so small a flow could gouge out this non-river for so many miles, was one of the mysteries that was beyond his understanding.

The Public Works department of Kenya Colony twenty-five years before, when Kenya was at war with Italian-controlled Ethiopia, had built a causeway across the centre of the huge river bed where the track crossed it. This was over half a mile wide at that place. Consequently there was a very steep firm earth track descending into the lugga. Then some 300 yards of powdery sand, then the 300 yards of concrete causeway across the centre rocky section, seven feet wide and sticking up above the river bed two or three feet, then another 300 yards of soft sand before the sharp ascent out of the lugga and back on to the track.

In those days when Harry and Nicky and Tilda arrived, the track had some two or three vehicles a month crossing it. The odd resident on a safari into the interior with his Land Rover, the Italian Catholic Mission Land Rover, heading to Maralal for supplies once a month and perhaps a District Officer off to settle some remote argument. The causeway of the Milgis lugga, however, did afford a crossing for many camels as the nomads came south in endless pursuit of the sparse grazing. Lightning all around, and yet no rain falling was one of the eeriest feelings that Nicky had ever experienced. She cowered against her father, physically frightened. She looked out to the right to see the gigantic Barsaloi barrage, a huge mountain range rising 10,000 feet from the 2,000 feet floor of the Rift Valley to the east and the Great Ol Donyo Nyiro massif to the west, 'their mountain' where the elephants still grazed the wooded peaks; the mighty mountain ranges of the desert with their heads in the clouds. The scene was so very typical of Jenny's dreamland Northern Frontier District – rounded rocks of all shapes and sizes stretching for ever to the distant vast horizons. Sometimes the rocks were small, sometimes they were veritable mountains but always they were rounded lava rocks. Stunted acacia trees hugged the banks in a desperate effort to refresh their twisted exposed roots.

The ancients of the Orient, Harry had heard, enjoyed a rock garden. Harry could understand that. Here was a rock world. Some rocks were piled so perfectly on each other that Teleki, who finally put the area on Victorian maps of 1888, had a chronicler who insisted that a Zanj-type civilization must have existed there. He was so certain because the rocks placed on top of one another to form their endless walls could not have been an act of nature and must have been an act of man like a giant stone cairn grave. Sadly one or two modern expeditions had disproved this romantic theory. It still required only a small amount of poetic licence to believe that giants built the walls as volcanoes belched fire over the land in those distant days of dinosaurs and crocodiles when red hot stones were strewn around.

Once every seven years or so the rain would come and the day after the rain, as far as the eye could see, the majesty of the carpet of wild flowers. Another mystery for Harry was how those seeds could survive for so long without water and then burst forth in such abundance so quickly.

Lightning sparked all around like a shorting high-tension electric cable and thunder shook the very ground and yet, where they stood, it was still as bone-dry as Pharaoh's tomb. Tilda, with Harry driving and a petulant Nicky sitting on her hands alongside, arrived at the lugga around three o'clock in the afternoon. Rita and Paul were somewhere behind in their petrol Peugeot pick-up converted to a camping van. The four of them had had a picnic lunch together two hours back but now, as there was no sign of them, Harry decided to cross the dry lugga. The soft sand at the bottom of the steep hill in the bed of the lugga made Tilda grunt a little as Harry gunned across in second gear up onto the raised causeway and in no time at all he had climbed the hill the other side and pulled on Tilda's engine stop to wait for the other two in the party.

It was then that it happened. A sight that Harry afterwards said had to be seen to be believed. Literally a wall of water six foot high swirling down from the Barsaloi Hills, an incredible sight travelling at about the speed a man could run, anybody or anything that was in its way must have been carried before it. Harry thought he caught the glimpse of camel legs being swirled around at the head of the water; there were certainly many trees and many huge branches heading that giant bore. Within five minutes the head of water had carried on completely out of sight leaving behind it swirling reddish brown waters already up to the level of the causeway fast spreading outwards over the sand. There was now a river and to Harry's alarm it was rising fast. Afterwards everybody told him it was only to be expected with rain in the hills and didn't he know that it always happened and hadn't they been carried away by just such a bore of water? Wise after the event. What was worrying Harry at that particular moment was the fact that if Rita and Paul didn't arrive soon, very soon, the water would be too high for them to cross and their little party would be parted for God knows how long. Then, about five minutes later just as he was getting desperate, when the water hadn't actually risen very much above the level of the causeway, he saw the pick-up descending the other bank. A sigh of relief and Nicky gave one rare smile and waved. Harry remembered that particularly. Nicky didn't smile much in those days, let alone wave.

The pick-up had crossed the concrete causeway; there was only about nine inches of water covering it, then it drove into the 300 yards of sand and then, half-way across that, about 150 yards from the climb out the pick-up stopped, bogged down, back wheels screaming, sinking lower. Rita got out, knee deep in water which was rising fast and gave a half-hearted push. Knowing the water was rising about a foot every quarter of an hour and that it would be too late if they didn't act quickly, Harry started up Tilda, backed her down the slope into the sand, reversed the 150 yards through the swirling water, tied on the rope to the front of Paul's pick-up, dropped Tilda into first gear and, as he knew she would, pulled the pick-up out with no trouble at all. 'Cor, good old Tilda.' A flicker of enthusiasm from Nicky – the first flicker Harry had seen in the six sad months since Jenny and Simon's death.

It turned out that Paul's pick-up had got stuck because the water had flowed on into the fan, the fan had thrown it over the spark plugs which had shorted out and caused the engine to stop. Both vehicles were now at the top of the slope and he and Paul busily dried out the leads to the distributor of the Peugeot with their handkerchiefs. Still not a drop of rain and still the river behind them rising fast. By now the causeway had completely disappeared in the flood.

At about half past five that evening the Peugeot was roughly dried out and had just started and Paul and Rita shot off at high revs to dry it out completely indicating that they would meet them further down the track. Harry turned round to climb back into Tilda and Nicky went around the other side to climb back in. Just as she was halfway in she looked across the river and shouted, 'Hey, bwana, whatever's that? There, look.'

'Good God,' said Harry and he reached in to get out his binoculars which he always kept between the seats. A Volkswagen Combi van was descending the slope the other side of the giant swirling river and heading straight into it. Even if they got through the sand, which was extremely unlikely and on to the concrete causeway which was already under water, the flow of water against the low-sided van would mean inevitably that they would be swept away. He ran to the back of Tilda waving his arms furiously in an attempt to try and dissuade them shouting uselessly, 'No way; don't come; stop.' The van's occupants, over half a mile away certainly couldn't hear them and didn't even appear to see them.

By now the river must have been all of ten foot high in the middle and rising and he felt sure that by night it would be up to the top of its banks at fifty feet. He couldn't believe his eyes. Incredibly the van traversed the two or three hundred yards of sand with the water up to its doors and then started across what he assumed to be the causeway. It was towards the middle of the causeway when another mini-bore about two foot high came downstream carrying huge logs before it. How it happened, why it was there they could not imagine. The trunk of some uprooted palm tree, without a head and without a branch, looking for all the world like a manufactured telegraph pole pitching down the turbulent river, broke the window of the Volkswagen van like a spear. The van stopped halfway across the causeway. They knew that if he left them there within minutes they would be swept off the causeway and drowned in the ever-rising river. He was considering whether Tilda would make it back across the sand flat which now had some four feet of water swirling over it. But it was not in his nature to do nothing in an emergency. He backed down the hill for the second time in half an hour. Tilda descended in reverse, Nicky hanging out the side looking backwards at the toppling Volkswagen with what appeared to be a giant spear stuck through the front door window. How they weren't washed away backing out in the turbulent boiling water Harry never knew. The adrenalin was high. Nicky was behaving strangely, shouting at the top of her voice, 'Come on, Tilda, come on.' They were only about twenty feet from the front of the half-submerged van when they had a problem.

He knew that he would have to get out to secure the tow

rope to the front of the van and that if he took his foot off the accelerator Tilda would stop and all would be finished and he knew that Nicky? – he looked at Nicky – Nicky didn't even need asking. She jumped across just like the Nicky of old.

'Nicky, you sit here and keep your foot down,' shouted Harry against the roar of the raging current. 'I'll try and get out the back and fix the rope.' Nicky sat proudly at the steering wheel, her foot right down on the accelerator, the bubbles coming out of Tilda's submerged exhaust pipe like an outboard motor. The last words her father spoke to her before he disappeared from her view were 'Keep your foot down hard'.

He never remembered quite how he managed to secure that rope. He noticed that the driver of the Combi had been pinned against the seat by the huge log that had entered the window and had jammed the door on the other side. There was a woman and child behind the wet windscreen, both screaming and crying and pushing and tugging desperately at the door which would not open and which he knew would not open now because it was more than half covered by the flowing river. He had secured the rope to the front of the van and was holding it as the current tried to sweep him downstream as he edged back towards Tilda.

Then, like all accidents, it all happened at once. It was a jumble. The river had dislodged the van from the causeway swinging it downstream. The rope became taut and knocked Harry clean over. The next second it gave a huge tug at Tilda and one wheel came off the causeway. Harry was hanging on by the skin of his teeth to the rope halfway between the floating Combi and Tilda but the current was such that he couldn't edge himself forward. Nicky sitting in the driving seat of Tilda with her foot hard down saw it all as she looked over her shoulder behind her. Harry would remember for ever that scene, although from his position clasping the rope for fear of being swept downstream he couldn't really see very much.

Nicky was inspired, inspired by finding herself in a situation similar to which her beloved brother had been in so often. She knew that everybody's life depended on her and Tilda. She had loved her brother and watched his every movement, especially where driving Tilda was concerned. Just like her father in the minefield so many years before at El Alamein sitting in that very same seat, his twelve-year old daughter overcame the fear and despondency that had been dragging her down since her mother's and brother's deaths. They weren't dead really. She distinctly heard Simon's voice for example, 'Shove it in gear, Nicky'. She had to virtually stand on the clutch in order to get it depressed sufficiently then she pushed the gear lever forward and engaged first gear. With the engine still revving fast under her, right foot on the accelerator, she eased her small left foot off the clutch like she had seen her father and mother and brother do, so often before.

Harry heard the exhaust increase in tempo as it bubbled out in front of him and he knew that Tilda was moving forward. The engine revs died down, despite the fact that Nicky's foot was hard down on the accelerator. The huge dead weight of the van was almost too much for Tilda and slowly the revs increased as the back wheels started to turn, be it ever so slowly, pulling the dead weight and Harry towards the bank.

Nicky could just see over the steering wheel from her somewhat extended position with both feet forward under it clasping the wheel like mad. She knew, before Harry even, that things were going to be all right. Triumphantly Tilda and Nicky lurched across the sand pulling Harry and the Combi to safety. Then, as if to confirm her new-found confidence, Nicky drove on up the bank on the other side.

Harry could now walk again on the shallow edge of the flood and he watched in amazement as Tilda, driven by his daughter, pulled the Combi out of the water and that too climbed the bank. Large as life, or even larger than life, like a trucker on a state highway, Nicky slipped Tilda into neutral, hauled on the handbrake, pulled the engine stop and jumped out of the cab.

Harry pulled the log out of the window of the van which was now firmly on dry land, releasing the driver and the door. None of them was badly hurt and they all, when they saw Nicky, could hardly believe how small the person had been who had driven them to safety.

Rita and Paul had, as all bush drivers would have done, waited for twenty minutes then turned round and retraced their track to find out why Tilda was not following as planned. They were parked at the top of the steep descent to the lugga. By the time of their return the Milgis lugga had at least fifteen feet of water in it, a swirling muddy torrent which was nearly halfway up the banks. Uprooted trees flowed past like as many matchsticks split from a box. Harry jumped in Tilda after they had blocked the back wheels of the mini-bus with one of the many stones that lay around to stop it rolling backwards. Tilda had been finding it hard going pulling the sodden mini-bus up the forty-five degree gradient so Harry decided to turn her round so that he could engage reverse gear to complete the pulling of the van up the hill.

The excitement, the triumph, the pride, the praise the mini-bus occupants showered on to the girl, and a new affinity for Tilda had all worked their therapy treatment. An excited and transformed Nicky was sitting in front of the Peugeot with Paul and Rita. A laughing, exuberant and confident Nicky which gladdened their hearts.

They all saw Harry park Tilda pointing downhill on the left hand side of the track. They saw him jump out and start to fix the rope onto the front of the Combi.

A 'twang' from a snapped cable echoed up the lugga. Harry looked up and knew at once that the handbrake cable had snapped on Tilda. Not a unique occurrence. Tilda rolled forward, the engine started as any diesel engine would under the circumstances. She seemed to be accelerating as she entered the river and moved about a hundred feet across the sand. Harry might just have been able to jump in the cab but most of the six spectators thought he would not have made it; in any case he didn't even try. At about 150 yards out the torrent picked up Tilda like a matchbox and carried her downstream at a fast running pace. The last Harry saw of her was one of the rear doors bursting open. Then she seemed to be sucked under the water.

They all spent the night camped by the torrential lugga. Next morning, although the Milgis was still very high, about ten feet from the top of its banks, it did seem to be slowly subsiding. They decided to end their safari there and Nicky and Harry returned home in the back of Paul's camper. Harry didn't even have to tell Nicky what he was thinking. 'It was suicide, wasn't it bwana?' And just as Harry didn't really make his usual effort to stop Tilda from entering the flooded river, so he didn't really make a very great effort to find her. Of course the loss of a vehicle is generally no great cause for despair if there is no loss of life but nevertheless knowing some of Tilda's history Paul and Rita could not quite understand why Harry and his daughter did not seem upset just a little.

9

Life Begins to End at Forty

'Right,' said Harry to himself, as he approached Mariakani, 'I know you've got twenty years of your life to go, but nothing happened after Tilda's suicide, nothing really. They went fast though, those last twenty years.' Good God, he thought, it has taken me from just out of Nairobi to within sixty kilometres of Mombasa to recall the twenty years of my life from my marriage, to Tilda's suicide, and now there's another whole twenty years of nothing. Just an old man getting old from fifty to seventy with no family. Some time slightly less than halfway through those last twenty years Nicky had found herself the ideal husband and taken herself off to Australia. Harry received at least one letter a month from Nicky and her husband begging him to retire to Aussie with them. Somehow Harry had always left it for another year. He had been over to see them once or twice but he couldn't yet bring himself to leave his beloved East Africa for ever. The roots seemed to grow stronger as the flower became less beautiful.

Just as at the beginning of his journey he didn't really know what he was doing and felt that he was not fully in control of his actions, so now, towards the end of his journey he found himself feeling that he had to turn left, compelled to drive eastward. The track through Tsavo park to Malindi was well behind him, as he purred slowly into Mariakani village, indicated left as he nearly bottomed on the giant speed bumps, and swung left off the tarmac onto the sandy, gravelly road. Two miles out of the village the hump in the middle was such that it showed that few saloon cars had been down that track recently – just a few vehicles with high clearance. The ridge of sand on occasions scraped on the front suspension of Harry's squat Corolla. He slowed from his average of over a hundred kilometres per hour to something like a maximum of fifty kilometres per hour. The atmosphere compared to that of the main trunk road was startlingly different. The twentieth century was left behind, instead there were timeless palm trees, sand, and little grassy hillocks.

Some five miles out of Mariakani Harry pulled over to the side of the deserted road and stopped the engine. 'Jesus H,' he said to himself, 'what's this? The last pee stop?' The pee stop was one of the first novel ideas that Harry's many economy clients learnt about when they went on safari with his company. Boys to the left hand side of the bus, girls to the right.

The car had only been stationary for about two or three minutes. He had only left the main Mombasa road five minutes before and yet Harry already felt more relaxed. He didn't find the desperate necessity to think so eagerly about the past in order to forget the future. Could he be learning how to die? 'Perish the thought,' he said to himself, but for the first time allowing himself to talk to himself slightly more objectively.

The end of Tilda had been more of a triumph than a disaster. Harry had immediately felt that she rightly belonged to his past, a past filled with happy memories; she belonged in the past part of his life so he mourned her not at all. Tilda's sudden disappearance seemed to heighten Nicky's memorable achievement, not detract from it. Nicky's spirits soared. It was like throwing a crutch away. People are grateful to crutches for the help they give them but certainly do not mourn their being no longer necessary. Tilda, they both subconsciously thought, had served her purpose, had seen a perfect 'out' and had taken it.

As he walked back from his pee stop and got in the car again he started thinking for a change about his surroundings, possibly because his new gleaming car now seemed out of place in those timeless surroundings. Mariakani, like most Kenya towns, had started life as a tribal village in this instance of the Giriama tribe. The settlement had enjoyed for many centuries a quality of life both tranquil and enviable. Being only three or four days' march from the coast, and enjoying an altitude of two thousand feet above sea level, the climate was perfect. Situated at the southern end of the Taru Desert it became a 'first and last' outpost for slavers' caravans. For centuries it had been synonymous with cool, whispering palms and sweet well water. It was the border town between the great unknown interior of the dark continent, and the Sultan of Zanzibar's Arab coastal settlements and with this strange mixture of pagan African and converted Mohammedans, for centuries it had been a village of peace. These days some of the women still opted for the yashmak of purdah but Harry felt that this was less from religious zeal than to heighten their sexual appeal; more wore it on high days and holidays. There was one mosque to teach the Islamic faith and two churches – Evangelical and Catholic – attempted to persuade the villagers to follow the Carpenter's rather than the Camel Herder's philosophy. In the old days very few of the inhabitants ever saw the endless waters of the Indian Ocean some fifty miles away and even today with buses hurtling through the village every half hour, quite a few of the old and even more of the inhabitants under twelve years old had never actually visited Mombasa – the city which dominated their life.

When Simon and Nicky were young and they passed this village towards the end of their drive to the coast for their holidays, Harry would inevitably explain to them, to the minor irritation of Jenny who had heard the story many times, how Mariakani got its name – he hadn't thought this thought for twenty-five years. The village was not called Mariakani till the middle of the nineteenth century. In those days the British Empire comfortably dominated the Indian Ocean, and her Royal Naval ships of the line blockaded the Arab dhow-borne slave trade from the mainland to Zanzibar. It was therefore surprising, to say the least, that a whole cargo of bales of cloth, never seen opened before by the villagers and which had been transported the four days' march into the interior on the heads of porters, had originated from the hold of an American and not a British trading ship. The American vessel had almost accidentally found itself in nearby Port Reitz harbour.

Harry imagined the scene of a century and a half ago: porters dumping their heavy loads of bales outside the chief's house and starting to chatter excitedly amongst themselves as they saw the bundles of ivory elephant tusks laid out before them with just one or two choice female slaves, for which, with the Royal Navy around, it was not worth risking trading more than one or two as temporary concubines for the Yankee officers. These they could sell when they returned to their home port in the States.

There were probably very few people around that knew, and still less who cared about, the origins of the name of the little township. The men who had first traded with the village were Americans, shortened, or rather lengthened, to Americanies – 'Mariakani'. The traders had given their nationality's name not only to the little village, which had first traded with them, but also to the cloth itself. The Swahili name for a bale of trading cloth so popular with the slave traders had been known as 'Mariakani', a word which today still means any sort of cloth suitable for making clothes from.

Five minutes out of the busy little town, it was already tranquil. In the town, on the main road, there was vitality right enough but squalor too. The men consumed more alcohol than food and the explosion of children were a part of the way towards being undernourished. The village typically had given up its ancient civilization of the gourd and yashmak and traded it, or rather had pressed upon it, the worst of western civilization. Red plastic bowls, transistor radios and bottles of beer. A freedom of sorts, but with little hope. The population explosion meant every generation was getting poorer than the previous one and the land itself was being fragmented. Things were not yet as bad as the poor of the Indian sub-continent because for another generation it was still possible to retreat from the virtually non-existent pavements of such settlements to the relative security of their grandparents' shamba but even there there was little to do except to sit and drink.

On and off all that morning Harry had been speaking into his dictaphone which he had found in the glove box toward the start of his safari. Now he was absent-mindedly groping around among the tapes and to his surprise he came across a bigger tape that would actually fit his car's tape deck. He settled back in the seat of the car and shut his eyes. The words he had anticipated didn't come out. For a moment he couldn't understand this and then he remembered the jottings which he had dictated himself onto that tape. It must have been years ago – to answer one of Simon's difficult questions. To start with Harry squirmed a little on hearing his own slightly whining still UK Midland-accented voice. Odd villagers walked past but unlike the up-country Africans these tranquil coastal people respected one's privacy and wandered on without even turning their heads. Nevertheless, Harry found himself turning down the volume of his quadraphonic sound in order not to disturb anyone. A strange feeling hearing what he had written so long ago.

☆   ☆   ☆

The tape spoke out – Imagine a close-cropped emerald green lawn studded with peacocks stretching mile upon mile until it merged with the very foothills of the snow-capped mountain of God astride the equator. A club waiter in an immaculate uniform whispering across this deserted lawn majestically bearing afternoon tea and cakes on a highly polished platter.

As a bonus to perfection behind the crystal peak where the eternal purple mountains rolled, fold after fold to the Ethiopian border, the African sun hangs high in the cloudless sky. Best of all, the certainty that when the sun eventually sinks behind the mountain's peak a perfect honeydew melon of a hunter's moon will replace it with a new and different magic.

No man has a right to be sad in such a setting but the setting is really of no consequence, and it must be the same if you slurp your tepid coffee from an unwashed saucer, arms cramped between the sour-breathed humanity in some Puerto Rican city café where your horizons are confined to a fly-blown ceiling, your senses drowned in an electrical blare of music and outside forever, the horizons blocked with hideous soulless towering buildings; or in some British transport café, where tired unsmiling eyes look right through you and sexless tight lips say 'What's yours dearie?' and is the spoon still tied with string? Anyway, it makes no odds, just more cause for sadness.

Hiding shamefully between last month's *Vogue* and this quarter's *Swara* on the glass-topped coffee table by his side, so inappropriately lay that substitute for philosophical thought, the *Readers Digest*. 'Life begins at forty?' a typical article – feeble, wishful thinking from those whose life has already passed. *Readers Digest* nonsense – in reality the decade to the fifties hurtles by unproductively, like an express train and then ... movement, walking, climbing mountains, once a sheer delight becomes a nightmare. Another ache, another pain, another sense diminished. Eyes demand spectacles as the telephone directory blurs up. (Last year you blamed the printers.) Cheeses lose their flavour. You resign yourself to knowing that leftover little cough from last winter's 'flu will never now clear up. What pitiful wisps of hair are left, turn grey faster. It dawns on you at last that it's not the teenage kids who want to go out every night that are odd, it's you, for wanting to stay in. Long-dead uncles bring home despair, 'You're not going out again tonight?' they used to say to *you*. And motorbikes are dangerous now. Pastry after seven, calls for mints after eight, or else another restless night fighting with indigestion. You, who once could eat whole pies, steak and kidney pudding, Bedfordshire clangers without thought of their digestion. Now you puff up slopes, you gasp on hills, forget names and shrill uninteresting memories into uninterested ears. You become terrified of any twitch around the chest, intoxicated on a pint of ale, weak-bladdered, yellow-livered. Awake at night at the slightest sound and find yourself unable to sleep again, where once a shot gun would not stir you. Toenails grow in as life dies out. You even slip when grasping out at the bath and saddest of all, your appetites die down like spent camp fires at dawn, grotesque signals of approaching death. Your once-proud member shrinks from the world, and vibrant pubic hairs turn grey. In the still of a sleepless night you search for characters who blossomed in their dotage. Of course, there is good old Winnie who saved the world at sixty-four. The odd Sheikh who pumps out kids at ninety, but with the dawn, another one of the few left, gone, – reality prevails. They are exceptions that prove the rule. Who, over fifty years of age can logically do aught but put on a brave face to try to save themselves from pity.

The magazine that dared to insult him by pretending that life began at forty slipped from the man's lap. He was dreaming now of those dear distant days beyond recall when life was fun in summer weather. Of the cake of life, try as anyone would to deny it, very few crumbs remained. God, he thought to himself, oh God, if only that cake were larger. Symbolically the red disk of the sun began to sink with greater speed towards extinction behind the mountain range with all the speed of an equatorial sunset.

With the dusk more shattering despair, more melancholy. Huge waves of self-pity settled on the old man's head and

222

nothing would cheer him. Oh God, if only the cake was twice the size. God of reason wherever you are. Make it bigger . . . if you can. I don't want to die . . . why can't the span of life be longer. I beg you make the cake of life a little bigger for me, miserable insignificant nothing that I am. Pity my anguish. Dropping subconsciously into seventeenth century English of his childhood from the King James I version . . . 'Help me thou O Lord, that madest me. Please anything. I beggeth you bigger' he sobbed. 'I will lift up mine eyes unto the hills', more sobs.

Then a voice incongruously loud and with a cocky accent above the heart-rending sobs seemed to speak both out of the distant mountain and just in his ear. With a modern classless English accent and just perhaps a trace of Scouse, or was it New Zeal? Sounding like a well-tuned CB crackling on the silent night. 'Cool it, cool it. You'll be a'right. No trubs. Twice as long, did you say? How about three times as long?' 'Don't mock me, sir.' 'I'm not – four times if you like. A hundred.' A doubtful question to this, 'You want my soul?' 'No way'. 'What then?' 'Nothing.' Very doubtfully, 'You mean that at no cost will you allow me to live four times as long as I would if I hadn't asked?' 'Right. Five – six times if you like.' 'There's a catch – it can't . . . you can't, not a hundred times as long. I just said I wanted the cake of life to be twice as long didn't I?' Briskly, 'twice, three times, ten, a hundred. You name it.' A pause. The old man gets up from is chair, takes in his breath and says with finality 'Four.' – 'OK. No catch. You've got it.'

And he had. With the regularity of a powerful compressor inflating a huge balloon before the old man's very eyes it happened. The little cake on his plate grew from two inches to four inches across. The plate became equally big to accommodate it. The table became bigger to accommodate the plate. The ground, the thorn tree, all grew before his eyes. Amazed, he glanced at his watch. The space between the second hand doubled, even the ticks grew louder and slower. The cake was now nearly four times the size. The cake, the table, the field, the mountains, the crescent moon of course. 'Christ!' he exclaimed, everything, everything was four times its size and then with a sort of a click nothing grew any more. The old man looked at his hands. They were huge. A smile of delight on his face froze. The cake was bigger, the world was bigger, the man was bigger. An angry, loud, long drawn out shout from the old man sitting in the chair – 'Bastard!' 'Now what's wrong? Four times not enough? Are you not now in exactly the position that you begged for? Is not your life four times as big, four times as long?' 'But for Christ's sake, there is no difference.' 'Ah,' said the voice after a pause, 'What you really meant was that you wanted everything else to stay the same but just you to have longer. Is that it? Is that what you want? Everybody else to die, just you to carry on?' 'Well, no, not exactly,' thoughtfully, 'how about some long, some short' with a satisfied smile, 'just so that I can feel I am living longer relatively speaking.' 'Strewth, you don't want much' CB voice thoughtfully and puzzled, 'some long, some short.' Brightly from the CB voice, 'Hey man, wait a bit, we do that already don't we?'

Somewhere between the mountain and the man, the giant video screen appeared to go with the CB voice. On the screen appeared a postage stamp of a front garden of a semi-detached in Watford where he had been spending a memorable night a hundred years before. Then he recognized what was a black-trousered backside that had appeared on the screen and pushed open the latch of the little gate leading up the tiny path to the front door. The old man guessed he was seeing all this from the next door house because he could see it quite clearly. Another black-trousered figure followed the first and between them was a stretcher with a little boy on it covered by a blanket. But he could see under the blanket. An awful bruised face of the dead six-year old brought bleeding back home from the carnage of a fog-bound by-pass. The old man, seeing all this on the video screen frowned a little, remembering how the incident had saddened his day but for the life of him he still could not see the significance. That picture faded out and another one, more flickering, the old man thought, came on. A glorious sunny morning about half an hour's motoring out of Gravelines. The old man had completely forgotten his days in the Signals with the British Expeditionary Force in June 1940 and there it was – a fifteen cwt Morris commercial van in convoy. He was looking into the back of it from the front of a similar one. Seven of his platoon mates were in there. He remembered it now as it played on the screen. He was cupping his hands against the breeze lighting a Woodbine on the front facing seat, and as he glanced up he realized that it was at that exact minute when a mortar had landed in the pick-up ahead. Seven of his friends with whom he had been chatting half an hour before were now mangled corpses and they, now, fifty years dead. He even saw and heard a bugler. 'They shall not grow old . . . .' The picture faded. The screen disappeared and the hill returned. The CB voice was not there any more. It didn't have to be. He heard it clearly enough without it speaking. 'Some long, some short, is that what you want? Is that what you want? Hey man, we do that already . . . .'

A sacred ibis roosted on a nearby bush. The old man felt complete. It's perfect; it cannot be bettered; I shall not want; I am complete. An infinite part of an infinite whole. There can be no more. There is no more. It is complete and I am it.

The wine waiter slid towards the body slumped over the table. He gently shook the bent shoulder but the old man did not move.

The tape came to an end and there was just the hissing sound as the blank played on in Harry's tape-recorder in his smart new car. He felt quite lost without it.

'Some long some short!' reminisced Harry. 'More and more true in Kenya, with every day that passes!' He remembered having read recently that one is twenty times as likely to be involved in a serious motor accident in Kenya than you would by anywhere in Europe. Fewer and fewer of his contemporaries were dying of old age. Add to these shocking road accident statistics, the premature deaths, from cerebral malaria, deaths in light aircraft accidents, drowning in sudden storms in lakes and seas, dying by the hand of an armed robber, snake bites, buffalo maulings, each event claiming only a tiny proportion, they contributed to a whole of alarming proportions. Only last month, Harry recalled, one of his up-country camp boys – a waiter at Harry Hills' Turkana camp on the shores of Lake Turkana, was cut clean in two pieces by a crocodile, whilst he had been swimming in the lake!

Violent death took a much higher toll in Kenya than ever it did in Europe. Horrifying as the statistics were they held a strange consolation, a paradox that appealed to Harry and he suspected to many others though few would admit to the appeal. In an old folks' home in Europe, for example, death was of course inevitable, but also what was almost as depressing was that there in Europe – death was also predictable, whereas, it was slightly less predictable in Kenya where one could not help but live a shade more dangerously.

Another entry on the credit side of dying in Kenya, was that although life was cherished as dearly as anywhere in the world, as Kenya's recent best-seller *I Dreamed of Africa* had gone to great lengths to explain, death amid the eternal mountains of East Africa seemed preferable to death in Europe. To die as part of a changeless primaeval vastness, eternally renewed, seems just a shade less meaningless than being spruced up in a North London parlour of remembrance, before being squeezed into a narrow gap along side the tailback on the North Circular Road, where daily, hurriedly, shamefully, seemingly with embarrassment, they would plant strange corpses row upon row.

For as long as he could remember Harry had been fascinated with the philosophers' 'Why?' as well as the cosmologists' 'How?' His old friend Paul had recently lent him Stephen Hawking's popular book, *A Brief History of Time*. He found himself as usual simultaneously impressed with the brilliant minds of the theoretical physicists, and irritated that his untutored mind could accept the concept of 'infinity', whereas those much better-informed minds could not. 'Take a jelly fish' – he was rethinking his old arguments – 'A jelly fish, a rat, a chimp, Aristotle, Einstein, and any seven-year old school child of a hundred years hence – plot a graph of their "knowledge" and it would rise fairly consistently across the page – superimpose a "wisdom" line to the same scale and how would *that* look?'

Once upon a time, a well-meaning schoolteacher attempted to describe 'eternity' to her class.

'Imagine, a lofty mountain,' she began – 'towering high above her sister peaks – imagine a little blue bird landing on the hard granite rocky surface, to sharpen her beak.' She would pause then for effect and continue, 'once every thousand years! – Now when this sharpening process has worn away, the whole mountain we could say that – then, a second of eternity would have passed!'

'NONSENSE!' an incensed Harry shouted into his dictaphone. 'Ignorant, dangerous, totally misleading bloody nonsense! You couldn't find a better example of the ignorance of "finite thinkers". Infinite thinkers like himself could so clearly see that by mention of the finite 'second" in the analogy, it completely contradicted what the story was meant to portray.

Teaching people to think finitude when the good-intentioned teacher was trying to describe the opposite. Harry could see so clearly, that when the 'time' came that the blue bird had worn away the mountain, then there must be exactly as much time left as there was on the first day it sharpened its beak.

Harry put down the little dictaphone to put two hands on the steering wheel as a large orange-coloured Mercedes fifteen-ton truck swinging a ten-ton trailer appeared out of a dip in the road. By the time the diesel fumes from its badly-adjusted injection pump had worked their way up the Corolla's 'fresh air' ducting, it was a ball of black smoke in Harry's rear-view mirror.

Almost without thinking, Harry spoke into the mike again. 'Now that charming elderly lady teacher – when you get over sixty yourself it's "elderly", not "old" – with her "beak-sharpening" analogy can easily be forgiven for her finite gaffe, but what of today's quantum mechanics?', Harry deliberately omitting the word 'thinkers' implying the word 'mechanics' meant labourers as in motor mechanics, instead of the name of an incredibly sophisticated and ingenious theory, the life's work of many brilliant men and women. 'What of their "quarks" and "string theories?" Were they not, in the dimension of space/mass, thinking as finitely, as his old childhood teacher had been, in the dimension of time?'

'The theoretical physicists are searching for the ultimate building block of the universe. With painstaking diligence they come up with hypothetic theories – on the smaller and smaller particle, or alternating pulse-wave. "It", the smallest "thing" that *they* could imagine, was now too small for light waves to see.'

It seemed obvious to him that all the predictions were subtle examples of finite thinking. Whereas what must be 'down there' in infinite terms was as many galaxies in the nucleus, an infinite number of solar systems, and an infinite number of earths. As many earths in fact as necessary to accommodate as many alternate possible situations of matter on each. As many

227

to accommodate all the infinite number of earths inhabited by people exactly the same as you and me and identical copies up to the next different strand of the weaver's web which you or I choose. Millions upon millions of rooms like the one you are in now in a neutron and in each atom in each of those other worlds.

He assumed that the sum total of human knowledge might answer – 'We can prove *that* is nonsense – with nothing travelling faster than light . . . .' His instant reply – 'What about human imagination *that* travels faster than light'. He would argue 'Even the keen minds of the scientist, the astronomical combinations of computerized mathematics – could not conceive a "nought", could not contemplate "NOTHING".' Harry therefore felt that because the world *was* infinite, his theory was at least as likely to be right as any other, after all a child could confound the finite thinkers 'And before *that* Daddy? . . .'

Then it was Nicky's turn – 'Oh come on Bwana! I've never heard that bit before – There *can't* be – that's *impossible* – a different earth, lots of galaxies and earths in an atom – with everything we know happening somewhere only slightly different! – In an atom! – That's daft!' Harry replied indignantly to the distant criticism – 'why?'

'There isn't room silly.'

'Sorry *sana*,' replied Harry. 'Infinitely small and infinitely big or just plain "Infinity" has to mean there is an infinite amount of room.'

A now laughing Nicky replied but not unkindly. 'They should give you a Nobel prize for that Bwana – what are you going to call your law?'

He replied to himself – 'Harry H-I-L-L *H*arry's, *I*nfinite *L*ogical *L*aw.'

Harry was quite pleased with himself thinking of that HILL name, he had never thought of that before. He swerved to miss a flattened bird of prey lying forlornly at the side of the sandy road, wings still twitching, killed by the truck and trailer no doubt. Harry could not be sorry for it, 'it will still be alive somewhere no doubt,' he said to himself, 'according to the Harry HILL Law! Not just somewhere,' he corrected himself, 'but in many places, shouldn't wonder.' After all, the chances leading to the two masses of the twenty-five tons of Mercedes and the thirty pounds of African Kite coming together to change the state of one of them considerably and the other not at all, were high to say the least!'

It almost seemed as if the spinner of the web was not quite ready for him. If he did play the other side of the tape, the whole Son et Lumière he had written, that would take an hour yet he knew that he was now only an hour from the coast just through the villages. Now so near to the 'Empty' on the fuel gauge, so near to seeing Tilda revived, reborn like she was in the photograph that Oliver had shown him only yesterday. Now it seemed it might not be going to happen. His breathing was almost normal, no pain, just a fear, and compared to the terror with which he had viewed death that morning in Nairobi even that dull fear seemed to be abating. The weather was still overcast, but it looked like it might be a pleasant evening as the wind sprang up from the sea and swept the clouds inland, and a clearer sky followed. By now the equatorial sun was sinking fast and as he slowly approached the first village off the Mombasa road, Kaloleni, he tried once more to sort out his current thoughts. Were they the same now as they had been when he had written that little story for Simon?

He tried really hard to bring the rest of his life into focus. He was conscious of the fact that his motive for recall seemed to have changed slightly, from distracting his imagination from the finality of his own imminent death, to rethinking his life. Until this morning, Harry had concurred with the cynic's descriptions of faith as 'believing that which you know cannot be true'.

Now, clutching at every available straw, he was searching for some confirmation of the rationality of faith. Magellan! There was a man, who had faith. All the collected knowledge of all humanity at that time, would confirm beyond any possible doubt that the world was flat. Otherwise, how could those unfortunates underneath, prevent themselves from falling off? Yet, faith alone in his believe that it was round, set him off sailing round the world.

Everything seemed to have fallen in on the approaching-fifty-year old Harry and his daughter entering her teens in the early seventies. First, the VC 10 crash and the death of Simon and Jenny, then huge financial problems for the first time in his life. The fact that Harry seemed to be heading towards being a 'poor white' at that time didn't seem to affect his enjoyment of life. He had a little nest-egg stored away overseas for Nicky's education and he appeared to be almost enjoying his tragic role at this unfortunate time. 'It's only money,' he said to himself, and he really meant it. The loss of material possessions and what they could buy compared to the loss of dear ones was absolutely nothing. He had lost so much that by comparison his present financial cash losses seemed totally unimportant. Looking back over fifteen years he could see those days in a fresh light. It had obviously been a case of the doom complex. The 'fear and be slain' psychology at work.

The first disaster for Harry was a boon for the rest of the Tribe, the tarmacing of the Mombasa road. Every one of the two million Asians in Kenya seemed to be buying a truck for themselves and getting in on the act of Haulage Contracting. The influx meant that profits that used to be earned from freight dropped to zero and this had knocked Harry's hitherto successful transport business for six.

In the first decade of Kenya's independence as the African clerks took over the Customs and Excise collection, as well as corruption, there were many amusing incidents. WARN, the well-known manufacturer of vehicles winches from the United States of America had invoiced Harry for two new winches he had ordered. The invoice for these new winches read 'By Warn Brothers of Minnesota, Two Warn winches' followed by the dollar value. Everybody knew, especially the African clerk in the Mombasa Customs Office that it was prohibited to import 'second-hand' machinery like two 'Worn' winches and so these were thus duly returned to the States: to add insult to injury Harry was billed with their return flight!

The ultimate pride and joy of Harry's transport business was undoubtedly the Super Mac truck tractor unit that he had just purchased, probably the most expensive vehicle on the roads of East Africa at that time. It had been assembled in the States because they did not do a kit but the joke this time was that for customs collection categories they had to be imported in their stripped-down state, so having been assembled like a normal truck it was stripped down, shipped as a cab, chassis, axles and engine. Somehow or other it was all put together correctly at assembly in Mombasa and it did look a magnificent machine. Harry drove it down to Mombasa the first two or three times himself. When Nicky had a week off from her boarding school at St Mary's in Limara she rode down with her father. It was a year after Tilda's demise and Nicky enjoyed tremendously sleeping on the stretcher at the back of the huge cab behind the driving seat. The truck, the like of which today can only be seen in Australia or the USA highways had a chromium exhaust poking skywards from the back of the cab, an air cleaner alongside that, the size of a small car, and sixteen forward gears.

Harry had managed to nail the contract for bringing up all the iron necessary for reinforcing the highest building in black Africa, all twenty-seven storeys of pre-cast structure that was being built in Nairobi at that time: twisted reinforcing rods, twenty tons at a time. Two months old doing its fifth trip down to the coast, the chrome still gleaming, Harry decided to run the truck down empty to pick up a load of the heavy iron rods that were wanted in a hurry. That is where N'Jerogi comes on the scene. N'Jerogi is a favourite name that the White Tribe of Kenya use to describe their African Joe Bloggs. It is N'Jerogi that rolled Harry's truck on a not very tight corner on the way down to Mombasa – there just aren't any tight corners on the way to Mombasa – and thus wrote the value of the finest machine in Kenya down by ninety per cent.

Such not uncommon disasters are exactly what you insure for. But here, another N'Jerogi had appeared on the scene, and he has had a brainwave. Just one week's input into the bank account that his brain wave caused to be opened, he realizes will exceed his annual salary by ten or twenty times. This N'Jerogi worked at Mill and Co, the famous reliable old Muzungu insurance company in Nairobi. For a whole two months dozens of cheques which should have been encashed by the Kenyan National Insurance Company had not been reaching their right destination. The typed-out windscreen stickers assuring their owners that their vehicles were insured appeared, even the Certificate of Insurance appeared, even the correct registration number added to the fleet list appeared, and the receipt for the premium payment.

An honest branch manager of an honest bank run by an honest Muzungu was actually quite impressed to receive regular payments into the account of an enterprising Kikuyu who had just started a company called 'Milletcops' – just what the government wanted, a middle class of Africans to stabilize the country. It was a fairly easy job for the N'Jerogi in Mill and Co to amend some of the cheques for Mill and Co to 'Millet-cops', his new fake company, and fraudulently encash the premiums. The long and short of it was that Harry received not a penny insurance on the value of his beloved new tractor unit which he estimated at that time would be worth at least a thousand or possibly a two thousand acre corn farm on the foothills of Mount Kenya. To add insult to injury the turn-boy – do they call them that in Europe, he wondered? – the driver's mate, spent two months in hospital and successfully sued Harry for five years' salary, a sum which also came out of Harry's pocket being covered by the same bogus invalid insurance.

Another financial and intrinsic value problem related to Harry's income was that when he had bought his home in Langata thirty years before it had been the last piece of development and you could see clearly and ride a horse without obstruction even as far as Mount Kilimanjaro 180 miles away. Now the two huge arms of the expanding Nairobi slum outskirts with nightclubs and loud discos were engulfing the property and reducing its value. Harry was not completely broke but the great insurance swindle was enough to make him alter his career again.

Typically impetuous, he mortgaged the house, sold off what assets in the way of trucks that he had and started afresh in the tourist industry which he correctly anticipated was the boom industry of the future as far as Kenya was concerned. The younger teenaged Nicky now heard of back packing punters, and itineraries, airport collections and pax as the exciting and expanding world of Kenya tourism flooded into their lives.

Koinage Street on a late Friday afternoon in March 1971. The long rains were very much in evidence. The quarter of a million workers, men and women, boys and girls, mainly black, splashed out of the city on foot skirting the edge of Nairobi's industrial area, to their homes which for the most part were walking distance away. Walking distance, that is, for a people whose nomadic grandparents had probably walked twenty miles most days of their lives. The heads of those fortunate enough to enjoy a home on one of the many fast-mushrooming high-density low-cost housing estates would probably have a highly-coloured umbrella over it to keep off the worst of the torrential downpour. The heads of the less-affluent would have to make do with a plastic bag or even a sheet of discarded cardboard. The latter seemed more successful in ensuring a torrent of water poured on the back of the dirty-shirted body below than in keeping its owner's head dry.

Another quarter of a million were fighting rather than queuing for a space on one of the huge buses which usually had written on them Harry remembered, 'Licensed to carry 64 seated, 102 standing'. When these buses lurched from the bus stops and joined the queues of traffic they would creep into the traffic which was stationary, packed nose to tail from Nairobi's southern suburb, Nairobi South, to its northern one of Muthiga and from Westlands to Eastleigh. The traffic was static, mostly belching black diesel smoke. One solid honking mass. An occasional Matatu would hurl itself in deliberate defiance past the two lanes of stationary traffic, hooting madly across the centre line to block one of the two continuous lines of traffic coming the other way and cause an even worse jam than before. And all the time the long rains tip down that give Nairobi as much rain in five short weeks as Manchester receives in a year. Roads quickly flood as inadequate drainage fails to cope with the downpour. Sewers erupt covering the dainty wet shoes of the office girls scurrying home in toilet paper and worse. Everyone is in a hurry. The sky is a steely grey, tempers are raw. Nairobi is not a city designed for the wet.

In Koinage Street lights are beginning to come on illuminating the endless identical curio shops. Every other shop in Nairobi is an African Art Gallery, the remainder are banks, photostat shops, travel agents, chemists and a score of multi-storeyed, mega-bedded, pod-lifted five-starred hotels clawing their way upwards above the high plateau. The wiser shopkeepers even get out their candles because they know that as a rule at this time of year first comes the thunder, then the rain, and then the power failures. As water gets into the inefficiently-installed underground supply lines the nightwatchmen squeeze their army-overcoated bodies more deeply into the shop front doorways. Some fail in their attempt to find something dry enough to burn to keep off the coming night's chill but some succeed and to the carbon monoxide belched out by ten thousand exhausts is added the acrid smell of charcoal burning.

As darkness falls the suburbanites have dispersed to their suburbs leaving the streets to the Hogarthian type of characters – the balaclavaed ex-army overcoated nightwatchmen, the thieves, the beggars, the pimps, the prostitutes and an occasional simpleton who has given up the fight to keep dry and is now shouting wildly as he walks down the swilling gutters shoeless and half trouserless, a huge pendulous penis clearly visible as it hangs down the torn short trouser leg which once contained it. Sadly quite sexless, clearly indicating not obscenity but extreme poverty.

Against this macabre setting the bright lights of Harry Hills' Safari ground-floor shop in contrast cast shafts of warm yellow light onto a cleaned brushed pavement in front of it. A beacon of prosperity in a sea of squalor. If, by contrast to the wet, drab Nairobi, the exterior of Harry's shop looked inviting, the interior was the more so, dry and bright and clean and cheerful. Any client pushing open the glass door on that ambivalent atmosphere of warmth and welcome must have felt like Mole as he entered Badger's snug house leaving behind the cold Wild Wood. By that time of night there were no customers as such. The surrounding shops had locked up and gone home three hours previously. Harry's shop alone was open and behind each of the three business-like desks surrounded by travel brochures were Harry's three attractive sales girls. Actually only the two Kikuyu girls were pukka travel agents and tours sale ladies, the third, slightly younger, and of Somali origin, was Harry's secretary but he always insisted that she sat out front with her typewriter when she wasn't actually taking dictation or working in Harry's office to make a more impressive front, as he put it. Their neat dress could not have been more different to that of those without in the wet streets. All three girls wore a neat brown blazer with HH enclosed by a tent-like triangle on the breast pocket and neatly pleated brown skirts to match. Although it was late and they guessed that they would not have much evening left by the time they got home, as always they were in great spirits. Harry always boasted that an African sales girl or secretary was amongst the friendliest, sincerest and most efficient to be found anywhere in the world, with the added virtue of enthusiasm not found in the more jaded western work force.

Behind a glass partition in the Nairobi travel office was a

safari-suited Harry now nearly fifty-years old, sitting at a black leather desk, the thirteen-year old Nicky, blue-jeaned and white-shirted was lounging against it. Behind Harry was a superb blown-up photograph by Mohammed Amin, six feet by ten feet of the South Island in his beloved Lake Turkana with a matchbox-size truck parked by the shore. Harry was chatting to Nicky about their current problem. Since Harry had decided the previous year to put all his eggs in the tourist basket they had had plenty of problems. It had seemed a good idea at the time, thought Harry, after the transport disaster and Harry had mortgaged his Langata house and had broken into the little nest-egg that he had put away for Nicky's secondary education. Harry told himself that an investment in the tourist industry would, in any case, be the best way to attempt to get the money overseas where it would be needed to educate Nicky. As in tax avoidance, as opposed to tax evasion, it was half-way legal to withhold a small percentage of the tourist income by starting a limited company in Jersey and the tourists would pay the Jersey account, ninety per cent of which was then transferred to the Kenyan account and ten per cent remained. However, it wasn't working out quite like that and Harry found himself having to bring over a hundred per cent of his earnings in order to stop, or at least to attempt to staunch, the flow of cash outwards.

His other and rather naive reason for entering the tourist industry was that he fondly imagined he would be able to spend not only his time, but Nicky's also, in Kenya's great wild life reserves that he so loved. He had overlooked the fact that in order to accrue the income you had actually to deal with people. There were many glorious exceptions, in fact already in eleven months' trading he had made many friends for life, but overall he had to agreed that people en masse on economy holidays were, to say the least, selfish. A voice from an imaginary Nicky again, 'Assholes you mean, don't you?' 'Well, yes, I suppose so.' At that time and particularly when they had just started in the cut and thrust of the Kenya safari world Harry and Nicky's futures did seem to be in the hands of assholes. Contracts were the life blood of the safari industry and with much investment of cash, many long hours and much hard work Harry had landed one or two good ones but it only wanted one jaundiced client to get diarrhoea and claim it was food poisoning to completely upset the apple cart and cause a cancelled contract.

Harry, like all the other operators, came across that dreadful breed, that unspeakable vermin, 'the professional rebate hunter' who would check all holiday brochures until they found a likely package to suit their perfidious purpose. They would then take a photograph of one mosquito in one of Harry's tents for example and send it to the UK agent demanding a rebate because 'it says in the brochure that the tents are mosquito-proof'. The worst of it was that the Trades Description Act being balanced so heavily in favour of the consumer that at best the poor long-suffering operator had to give back the price of a safari and at the worst, ten times that amount for negligence. American clients, in particular, were bad in this respect, being brought up as they were with the strangulating evil of the American legal system which had already strangled their light aircraft industry and killed off every roadside Good Samaritan. Harry had once seen an American law firm advertising on television under the banner 'Can't you think of something you could sue someone for?' Hence the burning of the, if not midnight, then at least evening light, oil in Harry's Nairobi office that November evening.

Harry had been operating a tourist firm of his own for eleven months and he had been targeting the economy safari market or, as he proudly put it, 'the bottom end' and that lunchtime he had had a radio call from his Masai Mara camp that one of the trucks had been stuck in bottomless black cotton mud all the previous night with eighteen clients on board. By the time he got the phone call the crew had apparently dug the truck out and had called in the camp for a late breakfast. Harry, on discovering that it was only some three miles from camp where they were stuck, wondered why The General, as the Hills' most experienced driver was known, hadn't marched them back to camp. He also wondered how he had managed to get stuck on a main road, especially with a four-wheel drive and as he knew there would be chains for the rear wheels in that sort of weather. All he could do from his end in Nairobi, was to make sure of a really good welcome when the safari eventually arrived back. He had bought six bottles of champagne and some glasses to go with it. He had kept the office open in order to welcome them back and he had arranged on the radiophone that they would do an extra four hours' game running that morning in order to make up for the time they spent on board the truck the previous night.

They had apparently seen lots of game so he was keeping his fingers crossed and hoping there wouldn't be too many complaints. It was nearly nine o'clock. The three girls out front still smart as new pins, were laughing and chatting and planning how to please the General, who was very popular with the girls in the office. It was because of the General's character that Harry wasn't really too worried. Not only was the man a brilliant showman and a very knowledgeable safari leader and one of the best bush mechanics in all Kenya but he also had a way with clients and could usually get them on his side even if things did go wrong. He was, as Harry laughingly said, a late developer. Way back in the hunting days before the Second World War the General was a gun bearer and wasn't even allowed to talk to the big white hunters' clients whose guns the General bore. Nobody quite knows how he got the name the General because it was agreed that he hadn't been anywhere near the Army. Harry guessed it was an abbreviation of 'General Factotum', the euphemism the hunters used to use for camp boys. However, with more than thirty years' experience of driving gombies, as they called the early RL Bedfords, through the bush of East Africa from Somalia to Tanzania the General now made the perfect safari leader in independent Kenya. Some of the few diehards who were left criticized Harry for lifting him out of his station but most were more philosophical. 'Good God, I never thought you would make a leader out of the old General.'

Harry immediately recognized the knock of his Mercedes safari truck as it pulled up at the kerb outside the office. It was still raining, though not quite as heavily as it had been a few hours earlier and although he had only been operating for less than a year the whole staff always looked forward to the return of a safari, rushing out of the door waving, asking everybody how it was. Often there would be enthusiastic hugs and kisses all round, cheers for the General and lots of back-slapping as the dusty but happy clients dumped their haversacks and newly-purchased artefacts on the floor of the office. This evening, however, it was different. Silently, one by one, they descended the steps and trooped into the office eighteen

237

bedraggled clients.

Whatever else Harry was, he was not a snob. J.B. Priestley had had a Yorkshire accent and Harry admired him as one of the greater intellects of his day. However, when a Yorkshire accent comes whining from a whingeing Pom it grates, to say the least. It materialized that the Staff Sergeant Wallace and Lieutenant Clifton were the self-appointed spokesmen for the irate group. They, *of course*, were not acting in their own interests but in the interests of the regimental British Army Welfare Fund donated to by the Nuffield Foundation, a funding that had allowed them to take the economy safari while on a six weeks' posting in Northern Kenya.

From Sergeant Wallace in the whining Yorkshire accent, 'Don't touch it lads, don't touch it'. Then to Harry, who was beaming behind one of the desks, 'You don't think you are going to buy us off with that, do you?' nodding towards the champagne.

'Buy who off? What off?'

'Us off!'

'Well, as a matter of fact I've got a package here for a day's safari refund for all of you. That's what we normally do in these circumstances. I mean you didn't really, actually, miss anything did you?'

'Miss anything! It's lucky for you that we're not all dead, I'll tell you that.'

'Hang on a bit,' said Harry. He waved to the General at the back of the group. The General walked through the crowd back into Harry's office. From Harry when they were out of earshot, 'What the hell happened, General?'

'It's those two army guys, bwana. I've never known anything like it.'

Harry said, 'How come you got stuck anyway. Didn't you have chains?' in a hushed voice so the clients wouldn't hear over the glass partition.

The General also started whispering, 'Yes, but the bloody things came off . . . I walked back and looked . . . .'

'Come on, General.'

'It's true, no sign. They could have been buried in the mud. I walked back three miles looking.'

'OK, so why didn't you walk them into camp.'

'Because the bloody British Army wouldn't let me.'

238

'How's that?' said Harry.

'That young lieutenant chappy said we all had to stay put.'

'Well, I suppose his technique is right. Did you have the reserve tents with you?'

'Yes, but they wouldn't even get out of the truck into them when we put them up.'

'Christ,' said Harry.

'And we managed to get a fire going when we found the reserve kettle, a drop of water and made them a cup of tea, then I walked to camp for blankets and stuff for 'em.'

'OK, I think I've got it now.'

Harry walked out of his office to the front again to face eighteen glowering clients and particularly their two spokesmen, Staff Sergeant Wallace and Lieutenant Clifton.

'Come here, let me show you.' The Staff Sergeant trooped out to the truck and pointed at the rear tyres. Harry followed. The particular tyres had their corners off, as is inevitable when chains have been put on them. Harry knew that they were new on the trip before and had probably only done about one thousand of their ten thousand mile expectancy. 'How can you send us out with tyres like that? It's not right. It's negligence, that's what it is. That's why we got stuck – not a bit of tread on them, look.'

'You got stuck because you lost the chains.'

'Aye, that's what General says.'

'Well, it's true.'

'How come we lost both and how come he couldn't see 'em? I'll tell you, these tyres, negligence. Lions all round, all night in the truck. No radiophone. Don't call that a holiday do you? Some of the women couldn't even get out to relieve themselves. It's not decent.'

'But, but . . . these things happen. I mean what can I do about it?'

'I'll tell you what you can do about it. And if you do you won't hear any more about it.'

Harry looked up at the implied threat of blackmail. 'What do you mean, won't hear any more about it?'

From a cold, calculating Lieutenant Clifton, 'Well, let's put it this way. We paid hard-earned money for that seven days' holiday. It nearly killed us through your negligence. Now either you give us all back every penny we paid or else I'll make sure that you will be a broken man. I will write to the Ministry. I will write to all your agents telling about this . . . .'

Harry had learnt one thing. One couldn't give in to blackmail. 'I'm sorry you feel that way about it, sir. I've tried to explain. It wasn't our fault. Just one of those things.'

'You mean you are not giving us our money back?' said the horrified sergeant.

'That's right, I'm not, especially now that you've threatened because you have implied that you will exaggerate this unfortunate incident out of all proportion in order to punish me for not giving you money. That's blackmail, you know.'

Coldly they turned. Harry withdrew to the rear office. Three very quiet girls were joined by the two helpers off the truck. The girls were using the three phones to ring up for taxis to get the clients back to their hotels.

Nicky was standing alongside Harry's secretary. 'You all look quite clean,' said Nicky trying to be friendly and helpful.

'Clean,' snorted the Staff Sergeant. 'I'll tell you what will be cleaned. You will be cleaned out.' He lowered his voice, 'The Lieutenant has a plan if you don't pay up – we're going to take your Dad to the fucking cleaners.'

One or two of the clients away from the two main troublemakers reluctantly admitted that they had seen a fantastic amount of game but all added, 'But it's not really good enough, you know, sending just one vehicle out in conditions like that, especially with tyres like that.' There seemed little doubt that they were united against Harry Hills' Safaris Ltd.

The front office that wet evening was no longer a symbol of cheerfulness. All were shattered. All three girls took the unjust criticism personally. So used were they to congratulations all round when safaris came back that they just couldn't understand why the eighteen clients were so unfriendly, antagonistic and downright miserable. The joke prepared for the General was left uncracked. The champagne uncorked. For a week Harry asked himself where he had gone wrong. He thought he could handle people. What else could he have done? The two ring-leaders having had their 'compensation plus' plans abort departed, reminding Harry that he wasn't dealing with ignorant wogs this time and he would see what happened when he tried to rip off the British Army. 'Just you wait and see.' Harry didn't have to wait very long to see.

10

The Road to the Cleaners

Five weeks later, on his fiftieth birthday, in fact, the mail Harry received was hardly conducive to a happy birthday. It was a large brown envelope locally posted from a fellow tour operator whom Harry had been seeing quite a lot of lately, an African guy running another touring company, who also happened to be chairman of the Kenyan Tour Operators' Association Ethics Committee. The covering letter from him read:

'Dear Harry,

Thought you ought to see this. The enclosed arrived with the UK mail this morning. Why don't we have lunch? It sounds like very bad news and I see they have sent a copy to everyone, including the Ministry so we're going to have to work fairly fast if we are to help you.

Best, Sam.'

The attached was three sheets of closely typed foolscap. It was addressed to the Permanent Secretary of the Kenyan Ministry of Tourism and copies to Kenyan Tour Operators' Association, the one he was reading now, and ten others. The ten others were, in fact, every one of Harry's overseas agents that had been supplying him with clients since he had started the company and in their order of importance.

It was hard for Harry to believe that anyone could write such preposterous lies and, worst still, half-lies. For a long time he could not guess how a copy had gone to the very ten people in the world where it would do him most harm. The very first on the list was the Swiss-based Condi International. If they took this seriously that would be sixty per cent of his turnover lost. It was Rose, his young Somali secretary who remembered that on the day of the disaster she had had out on her desk the routine letter which she had been typing to the Kenya Treasury which companies had to do every six months, giving the names and addresses of overseas operators who had sent overseas foreign exchange for tourists during the past month. 'Of course,' said Harry, 'that's it. Though we would have a hell of a job to prove these bastards stole it. They would probably say they had got the list from the Treasury or something like that. But, of course, that's it. That's where the bastards got our vital statistics from. That's how they will manage to cut our windpipe clean in two.' Even twenty years later Harry could remember most of the letter by heart.

'Dear Permanent Secretary,

We feel it is our duty to protect other potential unfortunate clients who might otherwise be conned into taking a safari with Harry Hill's Safaris Ltd of Box 4801, Nairobi. We have reason to believe that by doing so they would be endangering their lives due to the negligent treatment the above company meter out to their clients. My friend, Lieutenant Clifton and myself and sixteen other unfortunate passengers who will testify if necessary, bought a safari off the said company from March 10th to March 17th last . . .' and so it goes on . . . 'other unfortunate victims, lucky we weren't killed, don't put the blame on the driver, put it squarely on the organizers, gross negligence, etc . . . .' Detailed problems 'old lorry with a leaking canvas, herded on like cattle, half-an-hour out of Nairobi, engine boiling, get to Samburu, see another one of Harry Hill's safari trucks, had a quick word with twenty-four poor English schoolchildren who were not looking forward to facing a night in camp with no blankets, no sheets and no sleeping bags. Typical negligence. On to Nakuru, where on the way a huge spare wheel became free of its carrier which was in the passenger compartment and rolled about all over the place, nearly broke a passenger's arm. That morning, vehicle failed to start until the driver pumped out at least a gallon of diesel oil onto the grass in the Lake Nakuru Park. When asked, did he know that he was ruining the environment he replied "It will go away". Get to the Mara reasonably uneventfully (though I think here it must be mentioned that the Ministry of Works should do something to repair the awful state the roads are in.) Next morning we all had to push the truck to start it at all. Driver refused to radio Nairobi for another one ... but this was only the beginning of the problems. Out on a game run that afternoon it started to rain, driver about to return to camp when we persuaded him to continue looking for game because we had not yet seen a rhino or leopard so driver puts on chains, we slither all over the road and at 1700 hours get hopelessly bogged down. Driver makes it worse by revving, can't find chains, walks a mile back to look for them, still can't find them. They are definitely not on the wheels at this time. Seven o'clock, dark, two mini-buses had passed about an hour ago but now driver tells us park gates are shut and there will be no more traffic. He suggests that we walk the three miles to camp but on being asked by me whether this was allowed or not, he replied that it was not allowed. All passengers, therefore, stayed in the very damp truck whilst driver walked to camp .... At 2100 hours driver and camp boy return, not with a vehicle but with a kettle, some tea and a pile of blankets which are already wet. He informs us that the radio in camp is not working because the battery is flat and therefore he cannot send a message. He also informs us there is no vehicle either in his camp or any other camp and on asking him what we are to do he suggests that we make a cup of tea, get out the reserve big tent and sleep where we are. This we refuse to do. At nine o'clock the following morning we finally get unstuck but all might have been trampled to death by elephants or eaten by lions, etc., etc. Gross negligence on Harry Hill's Safaris part and it is our clear duty to warn all other possible clients who might use them.

Signed Staff Sergeant Wallace,
Royal Army Pioneer Corps,
Bordon, Hants.'

'Jesus H, Christ,' said Harry only half to himself as he put the letter down. 'That's it, curtains for all of us. The rotten cunt.' His secretary heard him and pretended not to. 'Well, that's it,' said Harry. 'Hundred per cent black ministry – can't help but take the side of the white complainant, especially when he is British Army against a fellow white.'

The following week the die was cast. Condi International in Zurich even sent out their sales agent who Harry had met a year before to arrange their contract. The young crew-cut fire-fighter was the essence of politeness. 'Listen Harry, I know you're OK. I know your outfit is OK, but just supposing, supposing one tiny thing happened, a road accident or some-thing, and one of our clients was hurt, and then the legal eagles got wind of this letter. Where would we be then? No, sorry, Harry, perhaps when it's all blown over.'

Harry was flabbergasted. His mind went back to the Kipling poem his grandmother had put over his bed when he was a child, probably the same Christmas as he got those awful boxing gloves. 'If you can make one heap of all your winnings and lose it all on one turn of pitch and toss'.

Yeah, I know but I've done that twice. I'm getting too old to start again.

'Of course,' said the crew-cut Swiss, 'if you can prove it was libel . . . .'

Events propelled Harry forward. He found he had very little choice in the matter. Although his African friend Sam in the Kenyan Tour Operators' Association managed to talk a little sense to the Permanent Secretary and the Ministry miracu-lously didn't revoke his licence, he found that seventy per cent of his turnover was gone. It would cost him every farthing he had left to fight. It would take eighteen months before the case came up. Worse, it would have to be done in the United

Kingdom, the place of residence of those he intended to sue. Worst of all he found himself suing not Staff Sergeant Wallace but the Welfare Department of the British Army Overseas backed by the Nuffield organization, but his lawyer assured him that this was a blessing in disguise because in the event of their winning the Welfare would be able to pay up with costs. Whereas it was extremely unlikely that Sergeant Wallace would have that sort of money, but it meant that Harry's lawyer was fighting one of the greats. Money was no object to the defence.

Harry Hill's Safaris Ltd in Nairobi was struggling on, hardly managing to take enough to pay the salaries, let alone rent, while Harry Hill and his daughter Nicky, eighteen months later, found themselves in the West End of London looking for the Old Bailey. Nicky was fifteen and despite the fact that she knew she would have severe financial problems if they lost, was excited, thrilled and enjoying life tremendously; Harry somewhat less so. 'Risk it on one turn of pitch and toss,' he kept saying. 'You can say that again.' What it boiled down to was if they lost the libel suit paying the costs alone would mean that Harry would have to stay in UK and go on the dole. If, on the other hand, they won he would be a fairly rich man for the rest of his life and the expense of Nicky going to St Margaret's, so cherished by Jenny, would be comfortably within the financial range. Nicky had hardly yet got used to the travel jargon of whingeing Poms, airport collections, of paxes, of ETAs, the Mara triangle and the cat in the car park, when suddenly she found herself surrounded by a new jargon – the legal talk.

Despite the awful legal battle that loomed over them in that spring of 1972, both Harry and Nicky were enjoying life. Harry particularly enjoyed showing his daughter sights so well known to him and Jenny nearly twenty years before but which, of course, Nicky had never seen. Nicky, in the three years since her mother's death, had blossomed into a strikingly beautiful girl. Her tight curls of blonde hair covered a well-shaped head, her mother's wide-apart blue eyes, an almost too-large mouth, and a nose that just had to turn up at the end to give a touch of cheekiness. But it was her constant enthusiasm, her endless exuberance and interest that never failed to amaze her father. Occasionally Harry found himself calling her Jenny by mistake.

One weekend when they had the weekend off from legal briefings they both hired bikes to pedal round Cambridge and tears came into Harry's eyes when he looked up and saw the image of Jenny the same as when he had first seen her on a bike outside Husbands Bosworth the time when he had nearly knocked her off her bike – then he hastily had to assure Nicky that his moist eyes were not from sadness but from joy. Punting on the Cam Nicky exclaimed with a wicked grin, 'And don't think I don't know that I mustn't say "I can't punt" quickly.' Harry laughed outright, relieved of the very thing that he had been embarrassed and inhibited about.

During the three years that they had been flung close together by fate Harry realized what a wonderful daughter he had, but it wasn't until that day on the Cam that he realized that he was blessed above all men with a daughter who really cared for her father.

The court was smaller than he had anticipated and so used was he to seeing the Stars and Stripes rolled beside the judge as on American television, that he was actually surprised not to see the Union Jack somewhere and where was the gavel? All sober judges had to have a gavel and how inappropriate was that French sentence for the chief motto of an empire 'Honi soit qui mal y pense'. Its sentiments might have been successful in stopping foppish courtiers around four hundred years ago from calling King Henry VIII a dirty old man but seemed singularly inappropriate for bolstering the morale of the innocent in front of the formidable Queen's Bench and, as Nicky pointed out, the whole massive wooden coat of arms suspended over the judge could not have been dusted for months. Then there was the unpleasantness of actually having to face Staff Sergeant Wallace and Lieutenant Clifton, both of them dressed in their newest of dress uniforms, but what got Harry most of all was the fact that his counsel and his accused's counsel were actually joking with each other.

Harry felt as helpless as a body on an operating theatre table. The law was about to operate. He felt totally anaesthetized. Physically the courts couldn't have changed very much since Dombey and Son presented their case. Harry fervently hoped that the law wasn't still an ass but Harry and Nicky then had the difficult problem of trying not to ingratiate themselves with the jurors by smiling at them. On the other hand they didn't want to appear rude and not look them straight in the face. After the end of the first day, after six hours in the confined space, everybody seemed to know everybody. Nicky had already irrevocably nicknamed both the barristers. Their enemy, as she insisted on saying, who was defending Messrs Wallace and Clifton, did have a fairly large hooked nose and wore a black gown and from Nicky's perspective he seemed to swoop down from the rafters of the Old Bailey in an effort to kill his prey. Thus he, of course, was Mr Hawk. Their own counsel, therefore, became Mr Owl, although his likeness to that bird was not quite so striking but there were two haughty cocked eyebrows which swept up from brown eyes that certainly gave a brief indication of an owl. The trial came at a time when nothing unusual was happening in the world. The massacre in Vietnam was already stale news. So both Harry and Nicky were thrilled to bits to find at least half a page coverage of the first day's arguments in the pages of *The Guardian*. The arguments swayed back and forth like the winds that bent the doum palms on the shores of their beloved distant Lake Turkana. First, from off the lake and then from off the land. First, seeming to the complete advantage of Her Majesty's Services and their Welfare Fund, and then equally in favour of Harry Hill's Safaris Ltd.

The report in the daily papers and the fair sprinkling of visitors in the public gallery surprised Harry because it was certainly no bloody murder trial. In fact, had not Harry had so high a stake in the outcome of the proceedings he himself would have been rather bored. During the opening stages of the trial the briefs unspilled with meticulous, and to Harry's mind, unnecessary detail. The Hawk started the defence of the two soldiers by producing and reading the three foolscap pages of the complaints which Lieutenant Clifton and Sergeant Wallace had circulated to Harry's ten overseas agents: stating the unroadworthiness of the vehicle, the negligent fashion in which it was operated, the fact that the spare wheel stowed in the passengers compartment in the rear came adrift and nearly broke one of the client's arms, that fact that it boiled on a hill going north the first day before they even got to a game park, and entered Samburu after dark, having to set up their tents in the dark, the fact that next day they found some, as they put it, more people on a Hill's Safari, this time children from England, who were shivering because they had had no sleeping bags supplied the previous night, another typical indication of the company's gross neglect and on and on with every minor detail of stale bread, monotonous food, too many meat loaves, leaking canvas, balding tyres until they came to the crux of their argument. To the event which really underlined the company's incompetence. And which, to protect future clients from such danger, Messrs Wallace and Clifton had written their letter which Harry claimed was libellous. Some three miles from their camp in a high density game area of the Masai Mara game reserve round about five o'clock in the evening they became stuck in bottomless black cotton and had to spend the night on board the vehicle with no food, hardly daring to leave it even to relieve themselves because of the close proximity of lions which were clearly heard roaring for most of the sleepless night.

Mr Hawk, for the defence of the soldiers and to prove there was no libellous statement but a true one, had also produced fourteen affidavits from the fellow travellers, all of whom appeared, from where they wrote, to agree with the criticisms. It turned out easy for Mr Hawk to show the jury that every single one of the complaints levelled was absolutely true because Harry had to agree that it was. Mr Owl attempted to show that although it was true, it was not necessarily negligent or dangerous behaviour on his client's part. Therefore to state that there was danger that was not there *was* libellous. Mr Owl did not have much trouble in persuading the jury that as a result of the twelve letters written by the two disappointed soldiers his client, Harry, had undoubtedly suffered serious financial loss. Mr Owl read the jury extracts from a letter from Harry's Swiss agent which ended by saying that they regretted that in view of such serious warnings against using Harry they felt they would be unable to risk sending him any more clients and therefore would he please consider all safaris which he had arranged for that company cancelled. Mr Owl went on to show that that contract alone was worth some £35,000 of turnover for the next year which now would not materialize directly resulting from the letter. A more light-hearted but equally damaging quote from a note which Harry's west coast of the States agent had sent him, date line LA, 'Christ, Harry, what did you do to those two creeps? Give them the clap or have them circumcised? I'm afraid we'll have to hold fire till the dust settles. You know what our Yankee law men are like. If anything did happen after receiving a warning like that, but don't worry – give it a year.'

One of Harry's lowest ebbs was when Mr Hawk actually produced a boy who had been on the safari two years before whom Sergeant Wallace had mentioned he had seen shivering in the cold Samburu morning because they had been given no sleeping bags by Harry's company. The boy was about Nicky's age. He had been thirteen when he was on the safari and now he was fifteen. Round faced and bursting-buttoned-blazered the boy stood in the witness box. The Hawk swooped. 'Were you on safari in Samburu game park two years ago and were you with a group of other boys from your school in a truck that was owned and operated and had the name Harry Hill's Safaris written on the side?'

'Yes sir, that's right, sir.'

The Hawk was obviously enjoying himself. 'And did you hear your master in charge of the safari mention to some people on another truck that passed you that you had had an uncomfortable night because the organizers had forgotten to supply you with sleeping bags?'

'That's right, sir,' nodded the blazered boy.

'Thank you, you may step down.'

Real Perry Mason stuff. The Hawk came as near to beaming as ever his face could. It seemed to say, 'There's negligence for you. Poor little English boys freezing to death at six thousand feet because of this disorganized man's gross negligence.' He didn't actually say it. He didn't have to. The message had got across.

Then Mr Owl seemed to shake his feathers and said to the judge, 'May I have a word with the last witness, My Lord?'

'Proceed,' said the judge.

'Now, Master Belton, cast your mind back to that night on safari that we have just been talking about. Were you cold that night?'

'No sir.'

The Owl's eyebrows rose up, 'Why not?'

'Because our driver got some blankets from somewhere.'

The Owl nodded and produced a neatly folded piece of paper with a big heading, 'Advice to Clients' written across it.

'Have you see this before, Master Belton?' It was put right under the nose of the boy.

'Yes, sir, yes sir. It came round the school before we actually went on safari.'

'I see,' said the Owl. 'Will you please read paragraph twenty-five.'

The boy reads, 'All passengers on economy safaris must bring their own sleeping bags. If this proves difficult we will rent them one but an order must be put in for this twenty-four hours before the departure of the safari.'

The Owl was now enjoying himself hugely. 'And you were given that before the safari?'

'Er, yes, yes, I suppose so.'

'And you read it?'

'Yes.'

'So,' said the Owl finally, 'even though you were so stupid as to disregard a very clear instruction, thanks to the brilliant organization of my client you did not suffer.' Harry noticed that that caused a bit of a flutter which he felt must be in his favour amongst the jurors. Despite the fact that the proceedings were proceeding at a snail's pace Harry began to feel fairly optimistic again.

The first day's hearing was over and they were an hour into the second day which turned out to be the last day. The drone of conversation had lulled Harry into a somnambulant state. Although every word of the argument was vital to his success or failure the monotonous dreary tone, the heat of the Indian summer and perhaps also the two pints of draught bitter with which he had swilled down his ploughman's lunch were causing him to feel drowsy. He had been reluctant to forego the beer because as every member of the White Tribe of Kenya knows, bitter, together with a decent chocolate biscuit and fresh kippers, are some of the few delights that are unavailable in Kenya and were therefore the staple diet of many ex-pats on home leave, along with Mars bars and Marmite, both of which were astronomically priced in the republic, when they were available.

Harry snapped back to full alert as a well-dressed, dapper little gentleman in his late forties in a pin-striped suit moved towards the witness box. 'Christ Almighty,' Harry whispered to his counsel, 'that's the London Rolon man. We're dead men.' Paul Stopps was in charge of the West End office of Rolon Hotels Kenya Ltd. Harry recognized him from occasional Tour Operators Association meetings in Nairobi at which he had turned up. Harry's concern was that up until then he felt that his case was going well. The arguments at worst had been equal. Neither the Kenyan government nor Rolon worked, thank God, like the Mafia, but as everybody knew, Rolon was firmly established in the Third World and the line between capitalism and corruption was extremely faint.

Incredibly the new witness had not been talking for long when Harry realized that what he was saying by his standards was absolutely true. Up until then Harry had subconsciously thought, Right will win. The jury must see we are telling the truth. What was now making matters worse was that Harry had to admit to himself that Rolon and Stopps were not against him for economic reasons. His share of the market would be a drop in the ocean. They really did want to tell the truth, as they saw it. Mr Stopps was in the box. The Hawk ruffled his feathers, 'Ladies and gentlemen of the jury' he started in the traditional fashion, 'you have listened to arguments from both sides about this case but Mr Hill has never denied that our clients along with sixteen others had to spend a night in a dangerous situation. The question is whether this was an ordinary circumstance or an extraordinary circumstance. Mr Hill has brushed it off, having said that it was certainly not the first time, no harm came to them and it was a fairly common occurrence. Well, such dangerous situations may well be fairly common occurrences to those negligent operators. Mr Hill, you will remember, has been in business for less than two years, has taken something less than three hundred clients on safari during those two years.' Then the Hawk slowed, 'And, has, to quote Mr Hill's own words, "caused his clients to be left in a game park, in a truck, overnight on more than one occasion". In the middle of a wild life preserve, mark you, when it is prohibited to put one foot outside the vehicle. More than one occasion; two perhaps or three. Now assuming that he takes, as he would be the first to agree, fifteen or sixteen people in each one of his buses let us say, at the very least, some forty of his three hundred clients have been subjected to such treatment. That, as a percentage, I think you will find works out at an incredible fifteen per cent at risk for their very life. He doesn't deny it, except to say it is normal. Normal? Well, we'll see. Now, if it was normal we would have no case. But if we can say, members of the jury, that it is abnormal then . . . .'

'Mr Stopps, you are I believe currently stationed in London and were for two years the manager of Rolon, Kenya Ltd. Is that right?'

'Operations Manager, that is right sir.'

'Now, during the two years preceding the safari in question, that will be for the years of 1972 and 1973, would you be good enough to tell us very approximately how many clients your company took to the Masai Mara game reserve, in total, during that period.'

'Er, I should imagine it would be around four thousand sir. The total company turnover of clients that year was somewhere in the region of eight thousand and I believe half of them went to the coast and the other half went on safari and any of those that went on safari would, of necessity, according to our itineraries, have spent some time in the Mara.'

'Thank you, Mr Stopps. Four thousand. Now of these four thousand can you remember how many had to spend a night in their vehicles in the game park because of getting stuck or breaking down or whatever?'

Immediately Mr Stopps beamed 'None, sir.' Harry groaned. But the Hawk was not going to leave it there.

'And why do you suppose that was, Mr Stopps.'

'Well, a number of reasons. Firstly, of course, our vehicles are always renewed every two years which means they are always in first class condition and, of course, they all have a shortwave radio which means that if they do get stuck then they can get in touch with the lodge to which they are going and they will send out an emergency vehicle to bring them in.'

'Thank you, Mr Stopps. Thank you.' The point was very well made and of course was absolutely truthful.

Harry touched Nicky on the knee. 'Dole for me and Watford Secondary for you, old dear.'

Nicky looked very sad. Harry was so confounded by his truthful combination that he didn't notice that the Owl was on his feet again this time with a huge red bound leather gold inlaid lettered law volume in his hand. As Mr Owl walked across the floor with the book in his left hand he patted Nicky on the shoulder and whispered, 'Cheer up. It might never happen.'

Both words and actions were most out of character for this serious advocate. Harry felt that the Owl actually had an air of enjoyment about him. The time-honoured words again from the Owl. 'Ladies and gentlemen of the jury, with his Lordship's permission I am about to quote from a judgement in this very court some seventy years ago, Chief Justice Hollis of Oscar Wilde fame presiding.'

The judge nods. The Owl opens up his red leather bound law book. 'Carruthers versus Kent,' he commences. Then turning to the judge and addressing him almost in confidence, 'Er, in this case, my Lord, Carruthers had taken out a libel suit against Kent to compensate for the loss of his good name which Kent had caused when he published in the *Gloucester Gazette*, which incidentally he owned, an article. Now,' the Owl turned to the jury again, 'Kent's counsel all those years ago did a fairly good job of showing that Carruthers was indeed, if not an alcoholic, at least well on the way to being one. Then, after an adjournment, Carruthers's counsel produced a letter which had been written to him by Kent. Parts of this letter are written in this book for the interest of all and sundry. "It is earnestly requested by the owners of this journal that you do forfeit your standing for the Liberal party for the seat of Stroud at the forthcoming General Election because, as has been explained, we wish to put forward our own candidate and unless you concede to this demand my paper will do its utmost to frustrate your ambitions".' The Owl looked up with a beam on his face. 'He who was libelled had therefore been proved to have been threatened by the libeller. The learned judge is quite clear, quite clear, in such circumstances. If it can be clearly shown that the libeller had used the alleged libel not to serve the community at large but to carry out a previous threat then there can be no case for justification.' The Owl was almost Churchillian in his final submission.

Everybody, including the judge and Harry, looked a little vacant. The Owl was enjoying himself tremendously. 'Miss Nicola Hill to the witness box please.' Just fifteen years of age Nicky stood proudly and demurely. To her father she was the most beautiful girl in the world and he was bursting with pride. A fifteen-year old girl of any tribe is an anomaly to the dust and decorum of a court of law. With Nicky there was an infectious freshness, an innocence that cried out not to be hurt. She represented almost a symbol of purity, of endeavour, of all that was best in humanity. This is not, of course, to say that Nicky was all or any of those things. But she certainly seemed to radiate that ambivalence amongst the solemnity of the Queen's Bench.

The old Owl rolled his eyes around the court once more. 'If malice and the desire to injure can be proven the libel will not therefore be justified. Nicky, please repeat for us as exactly as you can remember, the words spoken to you by the defendant, Staff Sergeant Wallace, in your father's Nairobi office that evening in 1974 when the safari we have heard so much about returned. The exact words, now mind.'

Nicky then remembered straight away one of the first questions that the lawyers had put to them when they first met some week previously. She therefore had the words to hand. A slight pause and a blush coloured Nicky's cheeks. Harry frowned.

'Exactly now, mind,' repeated the Owl.

Nicky took a deep breath. 'Tell your old man if he doesn't give us back a good rebate we will take him to the fucking cleaners.'

There was a visible gasp as the court held its breath. Staff Sergeant Wallace's head across the courtroom visibly shrank into his shoulders. The Owl rose to the peak of his performance as he flung out an arm accusingly in the Staff Sergeant's direction. 'Did you sir, say that?'

Perhaps it was because the sergeant had a fifteen-year old daughter himself, perhaps who knows. It might even have been as the ever-optimistic Harry later said, 'No man is all bad'. Whatever the reason the sergeant nodded and mumbled, 'Yes.'

Pandemonium broke loose. The gavel which had not been used before was hammered furiously. It was all over bar the shouting.

A short ten minutes later the judge announced a foregone conclusion. 'Mr Harry Hill is awarded £50,000 damages and costs.' Nicky could never remember being so happy. The pin-striped Stopps slid up to Harry, 'Pop round and see us in Regent Street now you are here, Harry old chap. Let's have some of your brochures.' He was just idiot enough to give him some too, thought his daughter, and he was.

☆   ☆   ☆

The days in Britain after winning the court case were heady days indeed for Nicky and Harry. Harry tried to fill in some gaps which Nicky had in her historic education by a lightning visit to Husbands Bosworth which in essence had not altered in twenty years, and on a broader scale by trips down the Thames. Nicky had always been a fan of Lady Jane Grey so a visit to the Tower was a must.

They were staying in a comfortable hotel behind the Cromwell Road and it was in the residents' lounge there that discussions about their future between the two of them were constantly taking place. What to do with their lives. Harry determined to be unprejudiced. £50,000 in the early seventies, together with what he could scrape up in Kenya, was a very sizeable sum and could set anybody up for life, a good life, just about anywhere in the world. The rain lashed down onto the hotel window and Harry stared out. He noticed that the line of houses he was absentmindedly looking at ended abruptly and then maybe a hundred feet later started again, making way for a rather unnatural but very beautiful garden.

With a smile he turned to Nicky. 'Do you know what that gap is? That's a bomb site.' Then he remembered that he had been a hundred miles north in Coventry when that bomb fell. And then he realized how little of the world Nicky had seen and then, being a very impulsive person, he said 'Right. Let's get a couple of tickets and look at the Virgin Islands, the Bahamas and Bermuda. I've never been there. They say land is very cheap. How about it, eh?'

'Why not?' said the very mature Nicky.

The whole trip had only taken them two weeks and they were now back in the hotel room discussing whether to invest their futures in the UK, the States, Aussie, South Africa or where. 'How about New Zeal?' said Harry.

'No,' said Nicky firmly, 'we are African people, bwana. I will go to St Margaret's to please Mum, but then I want to learn to fly like Simon and carry on in Kenya.' Harry knew that she was voicing his feelings and there was no more argument.

It was typical of Nicky to say 'to please Mum' just as if she was still alive. There was no chip on her shoulder, no hangups now, just a healthy love for the past. It was typical of her also to want to fulfil one of Jenny's dreams to send her daughter to a boarding school Jenny had played hockey against as a girl, just after the war. Rather ridiculously Jenny had fallen in love with the permanence of the school, the aristocratic upper-class look of it and it had been her dream to send Nicky there. Actually, though Nicky never even told her father, it was really rather a pretentious school but Nicky made the best of it.

The years flew past. Nicky got her Private Pilot's licence on her seventeenth birthday after forty hours solo, an achievement only slightly less than Simon's. However, she did not do quite so well with her A levels. Harry found it hard to accept the fact that Nicky was not an academic. This failure turned Harry completely against British and Kenyan educational systems. His argument was just a little prejudiced: it went like this, 'a brilliant girl like my daughter fails – and every one of those boring, ugly, bespectacled, Asian girls that you see being driven all over Nairobi, sitting on the back seat of Peugeot station wagons on a Sunday afternoon amongst a family of ten, they succeeded in their A levels – well then,' concluded Harry, 'there must be something wrong with the system. You need a bloody parrot's memory, that's all. That's what education has come to. Not discerning between right and wrong. No thinking for yourself. Just memorizing lots of bloody unimportant nonsense,' he used to add, getting more indignant as the years passed.

For the two and a half years that Nicky helped her father with his tourist business after she left school these were vintage years indeed for Harry. The tourist boom in Kenya was just about to begin. Harry's company had established itself and with the increasing number of tourists arriving things really stared to take off. It was a very pleasant way of life. In those days both Harry and Nicky would go on safari themselves, meet an endless stream of fascinating people and just keep their fingers crossed that they would get no more Sergeant Wallaces or Lieutenant Cliftons. And they didn't.

Harry's clients often asked him why he didn't write a book about his experiences and he thought to himself that there could be a few laughs reminiscing along that line, more than on this morbid bloody death business you are thinking about now. A few laughs in Harry Hill's memoirs – that would sell. He tried desperately to think of an amusing incident and the best he could come up with was the time he was taking some VIPs, the French Ambassador and his friends, in two Toyota Land Cruisers across the Chabi Desert. Nicky was also driving, just behind him, and out of his dust. They hadn't seen another vehicle since they left Loiyangalani the morning of the previous day. In those days it was very unusual to see any traffic after leaving what they called Piccadilly Circus which was a desert crossroads, both other tracks only leading to nomad wells. In fact the nearest vehicle would probably be in Marsabit over a hundred miles away. That part of Kenya, east of Marsabit, and north of Mount Kulal, was the nearest Kenya scenery got to being a typical sand-dune desert like a smaller version of the Sahara. The total arid area was, in fact, nearly as big as the Sahara but the typical flat sand part was relatively small, perhaps one hundred and fifty miles across.

Right in the middle of this section ahead of them they saw a tiny dot. The dot turned out to be an American tourist complete with blue rinse hair and an imitation leopard skin belted bush hat.

She flagged them down, stuck her hand in Harry's window and said in a slow perfect Big Apple accent, 'Now would you be going to Mar-say-bit please?' The incredible thing was not that she had been left behind from another safari the previous day which presumably only had around fourteen or fifteen people in it which was the average capacity of the trucks that passed that way, and no one had missed her, and the safari had gone on and left her alone the whole night in the desert with no water and no company. It was that this daughter of the American dream who had spent the last forty of her sixty years in New York city suddenly reverted back completely naturally to the Wild West heritage of her great-great-grandmother. She didn't get hysterics, or shout or scream or even ask for water. She didn't even mention the fact that she had spent the night in the open desert but just calmly flagged down a vehicle that couldn't be going anywhere else except Marsabit and say, 'Excuse me, but would you be going to Mar-say-bit?' remembering also where her safari was heading.

Even now, many years later, Harry chuckled to himself, but

those years had rolled past with tremendous speed and then suddenly Nicky was gone. The Australian who swept the twenty-year old Kenyan girl off her feet was not your typical Aussie. He was short, stocky, and called Antony. He had never been in the outback. He had come out to Kenya with his Sydney rugby football club. They didn't get anything like the amount of games they wanted but nevertheless Nicky met him when he was playing against her local sports club in a Nairobi suburb. Nicky at the time was the Chairlady of the welcoming committee. So great was his infatuation with Nicky that when the rest of the team flew home he remained behind. Three months later Antony took Nicky home to Sydney to get married. Harry flew out for the wedding some two months after that and despite the fact that he had come to depend on her so much in his business, he surprised himself by thoroughly approving of the match and the move by Nicky to Aussie. He knew that Antony was absolutely sincere when he assured Harry that he would be only too welcome to spend the rest of his days with his daughter and himself in Australia should he so wish.

Harry looked upon the whole thing as a sort of an insurance. Nicky and any grandchildren that might follow could come to Kenya for a month or two and 'should anything happen' with which words all the Europeans always prefaced their remarks, and had done ever since Lancaster House (the name given to the London conference which 'gave' Kenya her Independence). Should anything happen like a coup d'etat or a bloody revolution to throw out the whites then his dotage could be spent comfortably in Oz. Harry knew that wherever she was Nicky would always belong to Kenya, would always love Kenya. Yet he also knew that she would never be a 'Whenwe' and that she would enter one hundred per cent into the life of her adopted home.

This love which the White Tribe at that time felt for their homeland was an unrequited love. In the early days of settlement the British government didn't want the embarrassment of settlers, then there was the horror of Mau Mau. From independence to Jomo's death there were the halcyon days of Harambee when everyone was accepted by Jomo and his government pulling together to build a nation. Then slowly there started to be talk of indigenization, instead of Africanization, implying the wealth of the republic would be reserved for the indigenous, a euphemism for the black population and the white citizens, or non-indigenous, who had until then been treated so fairly, were gradually feeling that they were not wanted again. But despite all this, particularly the sons and daughters of the White Tribe of Kenya in the seventies and eighties were passionately fond of the land where they were born. Harry found himself trying to think why this was and he decided it was probably deep primaeval feelings of a warm association with the land which is the cradle of mankind.

Harry sat up. He decided to play the tape of the Son et Lumière that he had written for their up-country camps. Their camps were on the shores, or rather two days' march away from the shores of Eastern Lake Turkana in a little secret valley where they had built a lodge.

11

Son et Lumière Interlude

Welcome to Harry Hill's Safari's Kurungu Camp. Those of
you who have arrived today from Maralal over the Great Rift
Valley's Lesiolo escarpment will not need reminding exactly
how remote this Horr valley is, but even you may be surprised
to learn that *that* was the developed quarter! The wilderness is
all around you. To the west the lava fields stretch endlessly, to
the east the Kasuti desert, to the north Kubifora and Richard
Leakey's excavations on Lake Turkana. In this wild country
you could travel the distance from the Canadian border to
Mexico, from Portugal to England and find no towns, no
tarmac, just a nomad or two with their camel trains. In front
the backdrop to our set, the nine thousand feet of Ol Donyo
Nyiro, behind Mount Mara. Here, the black-maned lion, king
of the beasts still rules supreme. This mountain stream is the
only water between here and the Jade Sea and little has
changed in this remote part of Kenya since our story took
place. Originally we considered setting tonight's *son et lumière* in
that even more perfect place, a half a mile from here with its
waterfall, its waist-deep pool where frolicked Gret and Eve but
on reflection we decided to bring the show to our camp's
restaurant verandah and leave the rock pools to the terrapins
and the hammercops.

Roll back the centuries, let time unfurl
and join with us in sliding down the years
to a past so distant, so remote
that you can scarcely hope to find in it
affinity with anything you know.
One million years ago tonight, right on

this site there came into mankind a light
which all the terrors, all the fears of years
to come could never quench nor extradite
which burns still in our hearts and shows us we
have cause to hope. There's meaning yet and time
enough for us to grow and for us to sow
such genes as Gret's one million years ago.
But if the fourth dimension's hard to grasp
the other three must help you comprehend.
Unchanged the lake where all our heroes lived,
unchanged this valley where the act takes place.
But better still be tuned to cosmic time.
Look up, my friends and see the stars of heaven
galaxy on galaxy for ever.
The infinite makes nonsense of our scale.
Let's see the action as it really was.
Turn back our faulty clock and share with us.
This place has magic yet. So if you can
join in the scene. The set – 'The Dawn of Man'.
One million years ago and three days' lope
to north of here there lived a tribe of man,
alike yet unalike their thousand brothers who
through millenia foraged north,
and south across the fertile plains.
Ever since that ere more distant age-old
ramapithecus had left the trees.
In the shape and size and form of brain in fact
we think that differed only slightly from us.
The mighty difference lay in mind,
free from most guiles and jealousies and hates.
Our tribe, the troop we are meeting with tonight,
unlike the rest of gatherers who roamed
eternally without a base called home,
had come so deeply to depend on fish
gathered so easily from out the lake
they paused a thousand years or so
and built a pile of lava rocks
to stop the winds which then as now did gale
back and forth across the foam-flecked waters
of the giant sea.
They had taken palm fronds too and twisted them

together giving a shade to cool them from the everlasting sun.
They had put up too a fence of thorn to
shield them from the lions of the dusk
and here within this ring fence they called home
a hundred generations of them had
both lived and bred and died in a stability
that made them differ from their fellow gatherers
who roamed always onwards and never knew a base.
But by and large between our hundred who preferred a home
and those who wandered there was no cause for enmity nor
strife,
togetherness with them a way of life.
Of course in many ways they were the same,
the fifty grunted words they had evolved
were shared by all the tribes who roamed the lake
being carried by some to e'en more distant shores.
Their hand axes, the symbol of a man,
more oft killed hippos than the dreaded lion
and crocodiles, of course, to prove their strength.
But in truth the greatest tie between
true gatherers and our lake homestead men
was great evolution's call to bond
in unity their ultimate protection.
As it was with Greece a million years ahead
their stability gave them time to think
and when mankind pauses after he has climbed a hill
the very choirs of heaven catch their breath
and are aghast to see what he will do.
What will he now invent?
Or now create, a beauty to delight the angels
and the sons of man and so it was this night.
Hope filled the air as all the men and women
of the tribe harkened as their chief held forth.
Remember all that crocodile they had killed,
the way their womenfolk had used the skin
to be a store to put their water in,
thus saving them some fifty steps of red-hot sand
by using water stored inside the skin?
Out spoke, or rather more by gesture clear, their
chief and all the folks agreed with him.
Instead of a hunt this moon why should they not explore?

Explore! The gatherers' hearts beat loud.
A chosen band of half their full-grown men
would make an expedition to the lands unknown
and here is the point for thoughtfulness all round
and take with them water preserved in
the crocodile skins their women used.
For the first time now in living memory
men took their water with them.
The group, hand-axes, and a water store,
the very stars within their grasp that night.
Savour the moment well.
A group of men like us, hung in eternity,
like us plan to set out on the morrow morn
towards this very valley where we sit this night.

Of the twenty-odd chosen men to go
on that great journey of discovery
only a few could even boast a name
none knew their father's or had
any special bond with mothers
once they had left the breast
so names were only given to the best
of every generation and our hero
answered to the call of Gret.
And most men thought that when the old chief
had climbed the hill to join his bones with those that went
before,
Gret, so lithe of limb, so helpful to the troop
would lead them next, the heir apparent to their little realm,
but to us this day a greater claim to fame,
for from his clean and ungirthed loins, my friends, we did
descend.

There is no length of time on cosmic scale,
one million years and his and our tomorrows
take up a similar space in pools of time.
One atom of his genes causes us to be the sons of man.
Both and equally we share time in the infinite.
Sleep well, young Gret. Your journey leads us on a pace
a stumbling footstep to the throne of grace.
A hunters' moon hung over the jet-black lake
as did the twenty-one pre-chosen men

depart their home and set off to explore
the vast unknown; the land beyond the fringe
of settlements around the friendly lake.
Children from their home camp did follow them
a mile or two and then with haste returned.
Eleven of the intrepid men had clasped
in their grip their very best hand axe
and the other ten proudly but clumsily held
their brand-new invention wrapped up with care:
the skins that held their precious water.
Like latter-day children on a holiday
they eagerly climbed the treacherous slopes
towards the mystic mountain none had seen behind
yet all their lives it towered above.
One last look back. Their tiny settlement
no bigger than a hand beside the lake.
Up lava beds until they reached a foreign plateau
baked in noonday sun.
Here did the frontiers of their new worlds begin.
The barren scorching wastes went on and on.
Instinct and legend told of men of yore
who had wandered off and never more returned.
A touch of pleasing fear ran through the troop.
Gret felt with pride the water in the skin
lap reassuringly against his naked side,
confirming him there was no real cause to fear
the unknown desert as it stretched beyond
the farthest sight even their keen eyes could see.
Man's enemies, the cats, were limited to hunting grounds
with water within reach and as the sun did set
that distant night, imagine them with heads on stones asleep,
the only living thing to see within those vast horizons
that we still respect. Two full hot days have passed
and on the noon of that exciting third
with nuts, dried fish and water running low
a tuft of grass and then a thorn, and then
they saw not far the desert's end
beneath a mountain high a fig and berry-bearing tree
and last of all by eve, the magic sound – water!

The chief did call a halt 'Now stay close up'

for in such paradise he knew lurked ill.
For here must live the enemies of man
waiting to strike if they were not close-grouped.
The paramount rule, the over-riding law,
with axes in a ring we are supreme
can vanquish any foe but a gatherer
on his own is easy prey, won't live a day.

So in a knot of unity they climbed
the little hill that bound the chattering stream.
Gret in his excitement leads a pace
and is the first to see a sight so strange,
so awe-inspiring and unexpected.
The troop's hairs bristle as a man for there,
playing in the cool stream carelessly
were half a dozen human females spread.
With muttered terrors speedily they flee
but not before one glances up at Gret
and in a second's stillness looks at him.
A look that sets his very soul on fire.
Confused, the group of twenty-one discuss
with grunts and gestures what they now must do.

To capture fellow man is quite taboo.
Besides, their camp has for an age gone by
an equilibrium they can't improve.
Their brief was to explore and not to raid
and so their chief does call a halt. They'll find
the limits of the wastes another time.
Perhaps they would return to meet these men -- not yet.
Now, to fill their skins, gather more food and return
with news of what they had all seen
and they adopt the safety once again.
A ring of men against a world unknown.
To sleep the desert side of that great mystery.
Next morn a final gather of the fruit,
replenishment for the scorching journey home.
Sunrise on that fourth day did see them all
stripping the trees of nut and flower and fruit.
Then came the signal to return to camp. A call
so clear no word was needed for it.

A group reflex that instantly compelled the troop
to change direction like the wind.
An irresistible impulse from each to all
a long-since dead primaeval call.
A telepathetic reflex we don't use
but still today this impulse lingers yet
and makes us catch each other's yawns we see.
A million years ago that much more strong,
how could poor Gret resist this mighty call?
An instinct built by nature through the years
to protect the gatherers from their common foe.

It sometimes happened that an errant youth
with a still undeveloped sense might miss
this signal to return engrossed deep in a feast
of mulberries. Then a man, irate and dominant,
would leave the troop, run back to fetch the youth
and bundle him away from danger to the moving pack.
On some occasions, too, a broken limb
or hair snagged in acacia's thorny bough
might mean such extra over-riding force
was necessary then to aid the youth
to gain the safety of the troop.
But on this day, a mystery formed deep
within the minds of those that saw Gret stay.
The chief himself walked up to Gret and used
the few words that his simple brain commands,
authority, persuasion, each he tried
and finally resorted to a tug
but still Gret stood as rooted to the ground.
There was no precedent to deal with this behaviour.
He was neither maimed nor sick
and so with many a sad and backward glance
the troop retraced their steps towards night's camp.
The chief himself had claimed Gret's water bag
and given him his axe. A last kind sign
and twenty men began their journey back
heading for distant home and one remained.
Gret watched the men dissolve into the bush,
fully aware that with his brothers gone
his life expectancy must count in days

but in his mind there was no room for fear.

His heart and mind and body were on fire,
a new emotion coursing through his veins.
Could this new hurt which only she could heal,
could this new fire which only she could quench,
be in her too?
Gret's great brow furrowed, searching for past experience
to show him how to act but no help came to him.
Poor Gret. To us his problem is as old as time itself
but he created it in pristine freshness at the dawn of man.
The problem crowding out his brain was this:
at home, beside the lake he had mated oft
with all the females as they came in season
as naturally as he would drink when thirst craved slaking
with the waters from the spring.
To mate was natural. That, all men knew,
by day or by night and any mate would do
but now the difference and now the same.
He neither knew nor cared were she on heat.
He wanted just to be with her alone –
to touch, to hold and follow blindly
for all his days to come.
Rest, in her arms.
To learn her different ways and teach her his.
To follow her along the mountain tracks.
To watch the sun rise in its majesty
with her, and see her drenched in soft moonlight,
sharing his all, his life, himself, with her.
How could this be when all his brothers,
his chief and every single soul he knew
had never known such feeling as he felt?
Instinctively he feared they could not be
shared by the girl with that one searching look
yet were they not, then life itself must end
for none but she could now make life worthwhile.

As in a dream he climbed the little hill
for all the time that passed since first he saw
the girl she had been foremost in his mind.
Thus, when he saw her standing 'neath a bough

alone beside his dear sweet mountain stream
senses first told him this was but a dream.
Her eyes looked up and carried him to heaven.
Certain he was that any life he would miss
could not exceed in sheer delight this day.
What deity or power it was that made her arms outstretch
we'll never need to know.
Suffice to see them standing by this stream under Ol Donyo
Nyiro's peak.
Love face to face, mankind's first sweet embrace.
A sacred union whose hopes and fears
endured you will agree one million years.

For two full moons they lived their loving ways
here in this valley and amongst these hills
made sweeter still by knowledge of the fear
they lived on borrowed time.
For both did know instinctively that neither
one nor two could survive alone for long without their troop.
With every step the fear of sudden death
heightened their love of every second spent
in terror of the fangs and tooth and claws.
And yet our love-struck Gret refused to share
his girl, his love, with any other man,
refused to meet her tribe who lived nearby
and even if he did he guessed full well
rejection still or being put to death
would be his lot for troops of men he knew
did learn as children the survival rule –
to keep out strangers from their ancient bands.
Very occasionally a wandering child, orphaned or lost,
or even now and again, an older person might
be welcomed in but virile males
a change too great to take and Gret guessed too
the girl could never now return two outcasts of convention.

More oft than not in early man's first days
the females of the tribe had not a name
but now Gret found himself longing to call her name
and with a charming thought he chose the time of day,
of life he had met her first. His Eve.

For could not those Semitics a million years ahead
have echoes in their legends
of the first woman who alone could claim
the noble title of mankind's first wife.
But cared they not as joyously they ran
or walked or loved or lay in their sweet home
and in this very stream they cooled themselves
by playing in the noonday sun just there.
Perhaps the most idyllic love
that earth has ever blessed her children with.

But evolution would not have it so.
The vulnerable must be the meat and drink
of any predator that preyed nearby
and one night when the stars hung out the sky
in just the order they shine tonight
a mighty savage black-maned king of beasts
leaped out the bush to seize an easy feast.
For Gret the end was mercifully quick.
He never really woke from that last sleep
blissful within the arms of she he loved.
For Eve a lion's claw's scratch which quickly healed
but something new and something terrible,
a wound there had never been before that night
a wound to stay with her throughout her life.

How tenderly she took his few remains,
scratched out a shallow grave to keep them safe
and as she looked down onto the mound of stones
she had piled to keep the scavengers at bay
came over her a feeling, not quite fear,
ran down her cheek, a drop, mankind's first tear.

And so, my friends, this story never ends.
Strangely her troop accepted her again
and Gret's child roamed this valley and these hills.
How we would love to think that child of Gret's
shone forth a light that was by man acclaimed
the best, the gentlest soul alive that age
but evolution does not work that way.
Gret's child is no different to the rest.

But hold, a greater miracle you'll see
as age after age nurtures, protects and cherishes
a single gene that's growing yet. A tide unleased,
a seed was sown that day that spread o'er all the world
that man did tread, laps yet the eternal shores of time
and down to this day cheers hearts like yours and mine.
Whene'er your senses fear that death will be
a senseless grain of cosmic dust no more
think on this night when Gret died blissfully
and even your most commonsense will see
who died one million years ago tonight
still lives when e're we see love at first sight.

The mighty opening chords of Strauss's *Also spräch Zarathustra* echoed across the palm trees. Harry was now well aware of the fact that just about every advertising film in Western Europe and the States had used that same theme until it had become commonplace and corny. But when he chose it ten years previously, when he had written the script, he had never then heard it played apart from as the overture to Kubrick's epic *2001: a space odyssey*.

12

Enter the Angel

He returned to the present – a pleasant enough evening under the coastal palms. As the tape finished the ensuing silence seemed compounded. Had the 'infinity plug' he had played from himself to himself helped him to come to terms with 'non-existence'? 'No,' he corrected himself, 'not "non-existence". That is too finite an expression. Just "death" will suffice.' Well had it? Then thoughts crowded in: a kaleidoscope of thought, a fast-forward whirl of thoughts: he found himself thinking that the *son et lumière* script had helped a little – like replacing the comfort he missed from not living amongst ancient buildings as fortunate Europeans do. Then the memory of his and Jenny's time spent in *his* cradle of mankind – 'I will lift up mine eyes unto the hills from whence cometh my help.'

He decided he was a nomad at heart, their gods lived in mountains. Were not Jenny and Simon dust on that same mountain 'where frolicked Gret and Eve'? Yes, he said to himself, his old script had helped a little.

'No, God, I am *not* asking for it – but we've all got to go sometime.' He decided it had been the background music on the tape which had altered his mood slightly – he had chosen light classics which had been Jenny's favourites.

'Wait a bit – wait a bit – what do you mean "had been". Past tense – they still "are", present tense, her favourites, are they not? So what? So that proves a continuance.' Then, with a smile at what Jenny would have said to so weak an argument he added, 'All right, a bloody small one!' But you only need a pinpoint of light in the dark curtain at the end of the corridor – one tiny pinpoint like anybody having seen a ghost or a time wharp – just one pinpoint of light proves beyond doubt there is

271

light unlimited on the other side. It was a pity, he thought, that they had found at last those World War Two fighter planes which had disappeared so dramatically in the Bermuda Triangle.

Absent-mindedly he returned the tape to the glove box where it lay amongst unsung Kenya's very own Roger Whittaker and Elton John which had belonged to Nicky. Despite the fact that overall he was pleased with Nicky's marriage and subsequent departure for Australia, it had left a big void in his life. For exactly one week.

He had returned from Aussie picking up the Kenya Airways flight to Nairobi from Bombay where Qantas had dropped him the previous Friday, so he had now been home exactly one week. The action in his yard at the back of his Langata house on Friday nights had evolved over the last decade to typify his life and he was pleased to note that his African managers had run the show smoothly in his absence.

Strangely it often seemed to rain on Friday evenings and the raindrops would hiss on the glass of the four 250-watt floodlights which illuminated the yard. Always there were over a dozen Africans at work, their muscles bulging beneath their singlet vests as they unloaded and reloaded the Turkana buses. The routine had, over the years, become a very smooth operation. Some of the team had been doing it most Fridays for the previous ten years. A hive of activity, each of the team knowing their job, and performing it both willingly and well. Between most safaris there was a week free to clean and reload the equipment, but not in the height of the season when there could be a double back-to-back turnround of the Turkana bus.

On such Friday nights two or even three huge Turkana buses would arrive back in Nairobi from their one week's safari to Lake Turkana, their passengers would be dropped off at the Nairobi office, the very same room in fact where Staff Sergeant Wallace had, all those years ago, told Nicky that he was going to take her father to the fucking cleaners. The trucks would then drive the fifteen kilometres out to his house for the equipment to be unloaded, cleaned, repaired and reloaded. Because they had just returned from a really tough thousand-mile trip and because they were about to start another one the next day, on occasions his mechanics would work all night renewing a clutch, or half the night changing a broken rear spring main leaf. But more usually they would arrive in the yard just as it was getting dark at around seven o'clock and would be washed ready and loaded, oiled and greased by ten o'clock.

It was a scene of African labour at its very best. All were conscientious, efficient and cheerful and not a little proud of their association with one of Kenya's most successful safari operations. The truck drivers would drive off in the company pick-up to their homes, some of them living as far as thirty miles away, and the ground crew would take over, preparing the vehicles for the next day with a trace of the same sort of pride in their work that the Battle of Britain ground crews had given to their servicing and re-arming endeavours nearly fifty years before. The drivers would always pull into the yard at six-thirty sharp the next morning ready for their next thousand-mile, seven-day trip. In the ten years Harry had been operating their safaris not one of them had ever been late once. In fact, in some ways he agreed to himself in retrospect, the African labour force was superior to the European. Whenever they had to lift a spare engine in or off a truck chassis, for example a huge six-cylinder diesel weighing half a ton and covered in oil, it would be cheerfully lifted right out and into the back of a pick-up by a score of willing hands.

He was proud also of the relationship that existed between himself and his staff. He counted the older members who had been with him for ten years and some for over twenty years, since his road transport days, as amongst his best friends and as each of his fifty-odd staff probably supported at least ten, and more likely twenty, dependants, Harry knew that there were probably a thousand mouths dependent on the successful operation of his company.

He liked too, of course, the fact that the profit from the company allowed him to do more or less what he liked. Business class flights to Europe and the States once or twice a year had been standard for Harry for the last few years, nominally to travel fairs to sell safaris but more usually just to have a holiday. Most of Harry's visitors these days, especially at night, were business-related and Harry never dreamt that

273

the visitor he was about to receive that Friday night would change his life.

He had been recalling his passionate month with Amina, when unexpectedly and un-announced, her daughter drove up his drive. Harry would never forget Amina, but on the other hand, he probably had not thought of her consciously for a year or more.

For a whole out-of-character erotic month, just six months after his wife's death, Amina had literally taken Harry into her ample bosom. He always thought of her as having stepped out of a Renoir canvas. Rounded and pink, but as well as a large, well-covered form she possessed a very lively mind, and an exceptional artistic ability. Her Naivasha Lakeside home was a gallery of sculptures, in various stages of completion, mostly of her aquiline-nosed friends. She seemed to style herself after a heroine of a Greek tragedy. Her late husband, one felt, just had to have died tragically, which he had, drowning in the lake at the bottom of their garden. Harry later confided to his closest friends, that all through the lightning love affair he felt she coveted his friendship because he was at the time a tragic figure himself.

It was a wholly physical association as far as both were concerned, she being much too emotional and melodramatic for Harry, with his stiff upper lip and suet pudding-solid character. Nevertheless, he could never forget Amina! This was partly because she was only the second person he had slept with in the last twenty or more years, the other being his late wife.

'I've been as faithful as a fucking Dik-dik,' Harry used to shout to his wife, when they were having one of their rare arguments. A reference to the tiny antelope that 'mates for life'. Even if one partner is killed the other will not take another partner.

He had first met Amina a year or two before the Addis disaster, Simon and Amina's eighteen-year old daughter had seemed at one stage very keen on each other. Then to Harry's and Jenny's horror, and Simon's relief, the girl took off and married a much older man at very short notice.

Later, Nicky had become friendly with the younger sister whom she had met at one of Kuki Gallman's wakes for her tragically-killed son and husband. 'Bet Amina was there too,' said Harry, sourly when Nicky was telling her father all about it, 'Wakes are right up her mother's street!' Fortunately for Harry's enjoyment of the next five years of his life, his daughter had found a more lasting relationship with Amina's daughter of about her own age, than either Harry had with her mother, or Simon with her sister.

Amina's youngest daughter had been involved for over a year with a Pirelli-sponsored Zaire expedition led by yet another colourful Italian character, who very like G.K. Chesterton's Donkey in his poem of that name, also had 'one far fierce hour – and sweet – thorns about his head and palms before his feet'. His unique and only claim to fame was being chosen to act Christ in *Ben Hur*!

As he watched the turnaround of the Turkana buses, he heard the sound of a vehicle approaching. He recognized the sound of the engine as that made by a VW combi mini-bus. That meant it would be at least five years old since Volkswagen had not made the air-cooled engine in their vans for years. Never in wildest imagination did he imagine anything or any person could capture his love and attention so completely as the passenger in the van. He walked towards the driver's window.

'Hi, Mr Hill,' shouted the girl as he approached the window. 'Is Nicky about?' He sensed from the tone of the voice that there was more urgency in the request than just for the friends to meet.

'Sorry, dear. Nicky and her husband left for good, for Aussie about . . . it'll be five weeks ago.'

'What! You're kidding. She can't have.'

'She can't have, but she did. She couldn't but she could – not a bad bloke,' he admitted grudgingly. From the girl came a desperate long drawn-out 'Mama Mia'.

'Why, what's the problem?'

'Well, it's a long story but briefly this,' she replied as she pointed to a large wooden box on the passenger seat. Harry noticed that the box had air holes drilled in the top. As he watched the lid seemed to raise itself, and two neat, small, black hands with very long fingers reached out, clasped the side of the box and the inquisitive, frowning face of a ten-month old female chimpanzee appeared from under the lid. There was no crescendo of music, the world didn't stop still, Harry's workers carried on working, the girl carried on pointing to the box smiling at the appealing face and he was slightly surprised but certainly not flabbergasted.

An instant and complete love affair then ensued between the ten-month old chimp and the fifty-eight year old human. Until he had Ruzizi thrust upon him he had probably not seen a chimp above once or twice even in a zoo in his whole life, and never in their natural state, because chimpanzees are not indigenous to Kenya.

All his friends immediately called it a frustrated grandparent complex, but generally speaking he was not silly about pets. He had always had four or five dogs around him, as did most Langata households, as night guards which he couldn't even tell apart, let alone know their names (thoughtfully given by Nicky) except the biggest, which he called Big Boy. Cats he tolerated but were no big deal.

Nicky's girlfriend had, it turned out, personally saved the baby chimp from certain death when she came across it in an export crate virtually labelled 'Chicago for vivisection' standing on a bush landing strip in the middle of Zaire. There were several other bigger chimps but Nicky's friend realized she could hardly save them all, but the baby she couldn't resist. She bribed the African who was looking after them on the lonely airstrip to make it look as if one chimp had broken out of its cage and the girl had driven virtually non-stop the two thousand muddy miles back to Kenya.

'What was the drive like?' he asked her. He was still interested in the Trans-African routes.

'Well, the first forty-eight hours to the Ugandan border weren't too good.' A typical understatement that endeared Harry to the obviously incredibly capable girl. Only people who had driven Trans-Africa could appreciate the sort of experiences she had been having for the past three days. Roads in south-western Zaire are non-existent most of the time, yet she, typically of most born and bred Kenyan drivers, considered the drive no big deal. Harry considered that nine out of ten drivers of any age from the tarmac developed world who tackled that drive would still have been bogged down in mud, or wondering what to do about a car with no front suspension, broken down beside one of a million deep dusty holes in the thousand-mile-long stony track.

Some idea of the distances African travellers cover, can be appreciated by an amusing incident, with nine-year old Nicky when the Hills were on holiday, one glorious summer, travelling across Dartmoor. When Nicky read the sign ... 'Next petrol, thirty miles!' she thought that it was good news that you are fast approaching help! Whereas, she found it very hard to believe that it was in fact a warning – help was a long way off by European standards of distance.

The other occurrence which children on holiday in Europe could never understand is white men labouring – 'Look Bwana, there are white men working on the road!'

The Kenyan Italian girl was already overdue back at work at the Milan Travel Agency where she had been learning how to sell safaris, before she joined the expedition, and she had been banking on Nicky to take the illegal immigrant off her hands. With Nicky she knew the chimp would be spoilt to death. And so it was that Ruzizi, named after the river near which the girl had found her, entered Harry's life. He later discovered that 'Ruzizi' does in fact mean 'The River' in many different African dialects. The girl assured him that Ruzizi was absolutely no trouble. 'You'll love her,' she added with a tiny sob and drove off down the drive in her Combi.

He carried the box with the baby primate in it into his Langata house office and gingerly lifted the lid. Immediately the hairy creature flung its arms around his neck, grasping under the arms with her feet. It was a characteristically platonic, but passionate embrace that was so typical of Ruzizi.

Of the myriad of friends and of foes, of lovely and of unlovely creatures and people who had crossed his long life, Ruzizi stood out as unique. Completely lovely. God made *man* in his image so other primates have another god. He soon discovered she had none of the malice and subterfuge of homo sapiens. Whilst fickle to a degree, she did not know how to be malicious or disloyal. Premeditated evil was not programmed in her genetic make-up, nor come to that premeditated anything. She lived for each wonderful instant, she played non-stop through every waking hour.

For the next six short years there was no other word for it – they loved each other dearly. She, a chimpanzee from Zaire, and he a lonely widower of Kenya. The relationship that developed is hard to describe. Not many people have had the privilege of being possessed of a chimp and therefore most people automatically assume it is similar in degree, at any rate, to owning and loving any other pet like a dog or a cat. But this is not the case and Harry soon realized that the void of the missing Nicky might well be filled by the chimp. After living together for a year or so they had no need to talk to each other. Each immediately recognized each other's expression. As Harry thought back on Ruzizi he realized that he could quite easily be accused of mawkishness, yet mawkish he knew he was not. He therefore grabbed one of the blank tapes from the glove box, shoved it into the machine and absent-mindedly started dictating as he sat there less than an hour's drive from the sea.

☆　　☆　　☆

Now that Harry had stopped travelling and was just sitting stationary in his car he found that he could give to the task of recollection the added concentration of that small part of his mind which he had previously reserved for driving rather than recalling his past.

He made a supreme effort to make some sense of his life now that he was so certain that it was about to end. For some reason Harry felt that it was very important to him that he recall in detail those few years of his life which he had spent in the company of Ruzizi.

He had to overcome a mental resistance because he still had no time for people who go overboard about dogs or cats and he knew it would be difficult to justify even to himself, his fascination and his fondness for the chimp. He pressed the 'Record' button and started in an exaggeratedly sarcastic proud tone of voice: 'Famed as I am locally for exaggeration, more commonly called bullshit, I suspect that some might doubt the complete truth of what I am about to record and suspect a slight exaggeration but there is none. I am merely recalling exactly how Ruzizi behaved after she had been with me in Langata for a year or two.' Harry flicked the dictaphone to 'Off' for a few seconds whilst he said aloud to himself, 'And so someone, some day might better understand "The Miracle",' then he flicked the button to 'Record'.

☆　　☆　　☆

'I feel it is important you get to know Ruzizi so I crave your tolerance, ladies and gentlemen, for a small piece of description. Her day began by her most devoted and faithful friend-cum-servant, the shamba, bringing to her a huge mug of tea. Shamba, in Swahili, means loosely translated, vegetable patch, the garden, the man who looks after the garden, the gardener. Chomba, the shamba, always brought her tea in the morning in a huge tin mug. From the second day she arrived in my life at Langata she had slept in a cage. The cage was to keep the leopards out rather than her in. I had been told that many baby chimps in their natural state, when sleeping in a tree with their parents, are often taken by leopards. The chimps have a characteristic of sleeping very soundly and are literally taken in their sleep. Because Ruzizi was a proper Houdini when it came to getting out of cages and undoing knots, in the early days she had a collar round her neck with a heavy strong nylon cord attached to it. The other end of the cord, some ten foot away, might be padlocked to an immovable object because were one to tie it within minutes it would be undone – there was no knot that Ruzizi couldn't undo. The cord was only to restrict her movements by night but she came to really enjoy the ten foot of trailing rope and upon occasions I would leave it on and she could climb to the top of one of the tallest trees on the plot, well over a hundred foot, and literally abseil down with the rope deliberately hooked in branches by her in an incredible fashion.

I looked upon her cage as her room, rather than a cage. I had built it about six foot square in the branch of a tree just outside the side doors of the house clearly visible from my bedroom window so I would stand at my bedroom window in the morning and look out and see the hairy arms come out of the cage, pushing the tarpaulin that covered her exit aside to grab the mug of tea. If it wasn't sweet enough it would be poured onto the ground in a most disdainful fashion and shrill screams would follow until a second cup was brought that was sweet enough. The little breakfast was concluded by a long thin finger scraping any undiluted sugar from the bottom of the mug. That always seemed to be the best part of the drink and the process of drinking the tea and scraping out the sugar would usually take about half an hour.

Although the shamba boy always unlocked her as he gave

her the tea Ruzizi never seemed in any hurry to leave her house, particularly on wet days, when she would have a lie-in for at least an hour. But following that, the mornings from about nine o'clock were invariably her most creative time, undoing any knot in rope or string and I mean absolutely *any*. Then she would descend from her 'room' to the sand pit under it and chip away at a brick with a harder stone or build huge mounds in her sand pit or fill a bucket with a shovel. Often in the morning one of the dogs would visit her in the pit and they would play for hours religiously pulling ears and tails and skin, the dog using his mouth and Ruzizi her hands and feet. It was small puppies that Ruzizi loved best in all the world. Anything small was a pleasure to her and a small warm furry animal seemed to excite her deepest maternal instincts. She would lay back and if there were a litter of puppies around she would take one or two of them from the non-protesting mother into her house and lying back put one under each of her armpits. There was no attempt to feed them at virtually non-existent breasts but she enjoyed the wet nuzzle of their cool noses where she had no covering hair under her arms. She would often carry them up a tree and the mother bitch was never worried and only on one occasion did she drop one some twenty foot and then she swooped hurriedly and guiltily down to pick it up, apparently relieved when she discovered it wasn't hurt. She picked it up and put it down to see if it could stand.

One of her other morning intelligence tests that she often gave herself was to pull a key ring with ten or a dozen keys out of the shamba's trouser pocket and then with an intensely concentrated look sort through them one by one until she invariably came up with the one that fitted her padlock which she would then insert and open the lock and hand the key ring back to Chomba. Saws, hammers, nails and wood were all littered on the ground below her tree house. If you started off hammering a nail into the block of wood she would take hold of the hammer and continue doing so, hitting the nail at least once in every three swipes. One most significant and impressive thing she did very early on, quite untaught, was when she was about eighteen-months old and enjoying her first coastal holiday. Paul and Rita had asked me down to stay at their coast house and because there were several other families there Ruzizi and I were sleeping on the floor of the upstairs verandah. Ruzizi usually went out like a light round about six o'clock. Nobody had to tell her to go to bed; she would just wander off to her mattress and fall asleep at once, having been superactive all day, but nevertheless at that time it was found advisable to padlock her length of rope which ended up at her collar round one of the wooden stays of the verandah.

As she had only just arrived 'on holiday' I thought it might have surprised the neighbours if she had gone for an early morning walk. As I went to bed and lay down on the mattress alongside Ruzizi she rather unusually woke up. At that stage in her life she was never without her hard rubber football, carrying it up trees using a leg to hold it clasped firmly to her. She would bounce it, throw it, run after it, play pig in the middle with it, with shrieks of delight if she could get two other people to play with her, so naturally she went to sleep with it clasped firmly. However, now it had rolled some two feet away from her and however far she stretched out her right foot she could only recover it if her big toe could encompass it and she couldn't quite reach. So, she stood up, walked the length of the rope that was restricting her movement and geometrically moved it down the rail of the verandah in order to lessen the degree and give her another inch which might be just enough for her big toe to cover the ball and bring it to her side. Unfortunately, and I was watching all this, alongside on the floor, the extra two inches she obtained by adjusting her collar rope was not sufficient – her big toe just touched it, and it rolled another inch away. One could almost see the puzzled thoughtful frown on her face as she sat down on her mattress and quietly contemplated the problem. She then picked up her mattress in both hands, it was some six feet long and two feet wide, threw it over her head and hurled it forward onto the ball. It produced a pressure on the ball and it was then very easy to pull both the mattress and the ball towards her. Having done so she replaced her mattress in a parallel position, exactly where it had been, and with the ball now clasped firmly to her breast went instantly to sleep again.

On a normal day, back home in Langata, after her early morning mug of tea, a little lie-in, and perhaps a little carpentry she would then move from her house area and go and see what was going on in the workshop or the garden. She would watch intently as the mechanic would rub down a vehicle prior to spray-painting it and she would then pick up the pieces of discarded wet and dry emery paper and start rubbing the old paint herself, copying the mechanic dipping in the bucket of water with the emery paper, as often as he did. On occasions, she wasn't quite so helpful, like the time when a neat pile of wheel nuts were taken one by one and dropped down the hole of a white ants' nest which involved four foot of excavation in order to recover them! Then she would follow her particular friend, the shamba, and if he was cutting grass she would scrape up the grass into huge piles and then jump on it or like as not fling it to the winds again. I can see her now standing flailing away with her two hands, enjoying watching the cut grass blowing in the wind. Often when the mechanics had finished in the yard of an evening and they had all dipped their hands in the liquid soap under the bench and walked across the yard to the tap, to wash their oily hands she would do exactly the same, turning the tap on and off. Taking sodas out of the crates, opening them and drinking even whilst climbing a tree was no problem. She would have a fad for a week on Coke, and then change her loyalties to ginger ale, then perhaps bitter lemon, and then back to Coke again but always hot tea took priority over any other drink.

She seemed to resent being dependent on being fed like a lesser animal such as a cat or dog and she didn't immediately eat any food – banana, paw-paws, biscuits or whatever – that you might give her. She much preferred to rush into the kitchen, open the fridge or the vegetable cupboard door and take out what she chose. That was fair game. It had been gathered and she enjoyed it tremendously. There wasn't a single stalk or blade of grass or berry on any one of the numerous bushes in the ten-acre plot that she didn't inspect daily and invariably she would chew away at berries – these she enjoyed most of all. Feeding could be a social attribute as well. I remember one day when I was returning home after three or four days away on a safari I got there at the staff's lunchtime break and I saw her eating posho and meat, the African's staple diet, sitting joining in a ring of African staff squatting round a bowl. She was obviously included, but the look on her face was a fed-up look with turned-down mouth because of having to rely on what she obviously considered to be an inferior environment of eating with the staff. Whereas when we took her out on picnics on a Sunday afternoon, perhaps with Paul and Rita and all three of us offering her choice titbits like grapes and nuts, she would lie back, clasp her belly, cross her legs and a very different look of total enjoyment and satisfaction came over her face, enjoying being the centre of attraction.

Occasionally she would enjoy a piece of meat and often she would cram chewed-up food into her lower lip and keep it there in a most revolting fashion. Naturally toilet-trained on arrival, if she was in a car for a long period, like a whole morning's run, she would get in the habit of knocking on the side door glass with the flat of her palm if she wished to stop to get out for a pee. She adored a car dashboard; turning on wipers, blowing horns and winding and unwinding windows was one of the greatest delights. That, and climbing trees. Having reached the fork at the top of some huge tree she would then tear off all the adjacent foliage and shove it under her backside which was instinctive nest making, but she never really understood that chimpanzees were only meant to do that once a day when they go to bed, not every time when they climb trees. As a result, several of the trees in my garden were becoming a little bare of foliage.

She loved small animals and small people and she enjoyed taking such people for a walk firmly clasping their hands. Often she would start off down the garden for a walk with me and then spying one of the many African children that hung around the servants' quarters she would abandon me like a shot to play for hours with a smaller person. Then, if a still smaller child appeared she would abandon the first for the littlest.

On one occasion Ruzizi was having a holiday at one of our remote northern camps, and at first the African *bibis* who lived in the village adjoining the camp were absolutely terrified of her but over the days Ruzizi spent hours wooing them, sitting innocently beside them, unravelling knitting wool or whatever and eventually they accepted her. They would be sitting down knitting but if they once put down their babies for a minute Ruzizi would clasp them desperately in her arms and only very reluctantly give them back. Babies and puppies alike seemed to enjoy the feeling of Ruzizi's friendly fur but not so the cat that squawked like a scalded one, when one day she was grabbed from behind by Ruzizi in an attempt to clasp her to her bosom.

Blind Man's Buff was another game, when there were a lot of kids about and even when there were none. I found myself chasing her around the huge table in the kitchen, to her squawks of delight. If she suddenly turned round she would actually giggle in a high-pitched scream that she also used when she was tickled under her neck.

I got to know just about all her sounds and was particularly interested one day when she was sitting on the fence in the yard at Langata and a driver who was driving a pick-up up the drive to take food to a camp passed her. Suddenly three or four of the staff left in the yard started calling the driver's name quite loudly to 'Stop – come back' because they had noticed he had left his jack and spare wheel behind, and because he was going on a long safari they were shouting for him to return. At this point Ruzizi who had watched and been following the whole incident with extreme interest made a sort of a screaming grunt which I had never heard before or in fact since, and assumed it was used by the gatherers to mean 'Don't wander off. Come back here. Here is a super berry that you have missed.' It was a sound that would have been familiar enough to Gret. It was a totally different sound to her 'Danger ahead' call, for example.

Then, in the evenings, she invariably came and sat on the verandah with me. Ruzizi would sit there and reach out and clasp my wrist in her hand and firmly place my hand on her belly demanding a tickle. Grooming, along with car dashboard instrument knobs and switches, climbing trees and playing ball, were her chief sources of delight. Although she enjoyed having her hairy back inspected in a pretence of looking for fleas, never, ever did I find even one flea on her, but grooming is a very important contribution to a chimp's pleasure. She was also very interested in bandages if ever the staff cut themselves and she also loved squeezing out blackheads from unsuspecting visitors with her two index fingers!

Occasionally if she had done something silly like falling off a low branch of a tree, she would repeat the process as if to say, 'There, I did it on purpose after all'. Always, when in a good mood, she would run or lope for about ten paces followed by three somersaults, then ten more . . . .

☆　　☆　　☆

'Shit! Surely that can't be the end of the tape,' he said as urgent bleeps sounded, but it was. Rather crossly he ejected and turned the tiny tape over . . . he repeated himself to make sure . . . .

☆　　☆　　☆

then she would take ten more paces after the somersault . . . . There was one particular day that she taught me pat-a-cake. She had never done it before – she must have been about two and a half years old at the time. I later discovered that the West African ayah who looked after the little girl who lived next door had taught it to Ruzizi on one of her not infrequent visits to the next door neighbours.

Most afternoons Ruzizi could be seen pushing the prams as the ayahs peregrinated along the beautiful leafy lanes and jacaranda-strewn roads of Langata. Ruzizi never walked better than when she had a pram handle to grasp. It wasn't until some years later that I learnt that many negro children in the States play pat-a-cake, pat-a-cake, baker's man, as do some European children but it is seldom played by East African children. Seldom that was, until Ruzizi started the craze. Mind you, she never quite got the sequence completely right, but always squawked with delight when she made an error or striking the incorrect hand of whoever she was playing with.

She was almost innocently cruel to the toads in the pond, the frogs in the grass, chameleons in the trees, and wasn't past absent-mindedly pulling off a leg or two, but with the endless flowers she picked she was less destructive. Over the years she developed a most charming habit. During her day on the shamba if she saw a particularly brightly coloured petal of bougainvillaea or if any of the flame-coloured flowers that covered the wilderness at the bottom of our plot appealed to her, she would often pick it and keep it and when I returned in the evening, she would produce it in rather a crumpled state and offer it to me. This was sometimes particularly endearing because chimps are notorious for giving very little away. Everything available they will grasp with their toes and arms and leg and fingers and mouth even, but seldom will they part

285

with one item once they have it in their possession. It is not suggested that Ruzizi learned to give for the sake of giving but she discovered that when she handed the flower over she received a reward like a tickle or at the very least, praise.

She was tough, with a high threshold of pain and could fall out of a tree, then just shake her head: even after a severe fall she would take no notice whatsoever. On the other hand a tiny prick from the vet for an inoculation which she could obviously hardly feel was a very different matter. That to her meant that someone was attacking her, and it took four people to hold her down for her rabies jab, and every time the vet's Volvo (in particular of the many cars that came up the drive) arrived within her vision she would bolt up a tree and refuse to be coaxed down, and every time we drove past the vet's which was about three miles away she would turn her head away and put her right hand, fingers open, over her face. Very occasionally she would give her equals, like Chomba, or Rita or Paul when they came round, a little nip on their wrists with her teeth, not intended to hurt, but to warn them off, a wholly jealous nip. If, for example, she was sitting in the car with me as I was about to drive off and perhaps Chomba would try to get in, she would grab his arm and close her teeth around Chomba's skin, meaning 'Bwana is mine – you mustn't break up the two of us' – a very jealous possessiveness. But she wouldn't do it if a stranger came because she knew that the stranger would present no threat to the affection between her and myself.

On occasions she took a mysterious dislike to somebody or something. There was one particular staff member, a vehicle electrician who only came on contract work maybe once a month, she really got upset whenever she saw him and we had to tell her very firmly not to bite Joseph. Joseph, of course, became frightened of her but she finally got the message and when they crossed on the drive, he going one way and she the other, she knowing that she wasn't allowed to bite him, would pick up a handful of stones and throw them at Joseph, not very hard and not very accurately but the message was obvious. 'I'm not allowed to bite you but nobody said I couldn't throw stones at you.' The most poignant of my remembrances were of Ruzizi in the evening when she would climb to the top of her favourite tree, squat on her haunches in the topmost bough and look patiently for hours on end towards the Ngong Hills. I was amazed by this prolonged stillness in the otherwise ever-active chimp and thought on what great unknown thoughts so imperative to the plan of creation were passing through her brain. Chimpanzees, I am absolutely certain, are more than just a stepping stone from the primates to the human; they are another independent step forward on the mysterious evolutionary journey. Somewhere there had to be another god, in whose image they were made.' He stopped the tape and returned it a little sadly to the glove box.

He then realized that tape or no tape he couldn't begin to describe some of Ruzizi's characteristics.

Harry always knew that there was something peculiar, extra special – extra-ordinary really – about Ruzizi. An obvious manifestation of this peculiarity was displayed by her when she met a person or an animal for the first time. She would instantly 'tune in' or 'turn off' with every person or animal with whom she ever met. She seemed to Harry to have invisible sensing 'vibe waves' that either meshed or did not mesh with waves from other living beings. Just as she took an irrational instant dislike to some people, to others she showed instant intense platonic affection. By the time Ruzizi worked her miracle, Harry had come to take for granted this strange endowment.

Harry first recognized the phenomenon when she was very young. The first occasion was when a friend of Nicky's came round to Harry's house looking for Nicky, whom he had known since they were at the same kindergarten not realizing that she had gone to live in Australia after her marriage. His name was Zul, a Kenyan of Asian origin whose father owned one of the more luxurious Masai Mara tented camps; Harry only knew him slightly. He was a handsome boy, looking like an Indian Test Match cricket fielder, thought Harry, standing there in his white sweater. Harry and Ruzizi were right down the bottom of the garden at the time of Zul's visit going for Ruzizi's pre-bedtime walk.

When she caught sight of him, Ruzizi was in a characteristic pose, her face very near to the object, her eyes squinting down her flat nose, on this occasion at a lone lotus on the bottom spike of an ornamental sisal bush.

Zul never even knew of Ruzizi's existence at the time, nor had he had any particular experience with primates before. As soon as Ruzizi saw him at the top of the garden, immediately cutting short her interest in the lotus, and in Harry, she pounded up the grassy hill towards the Asian boy her knuckles pressing the ground. In a high speed lope she hurled herself at his neck, two hairy arms held him in a firm embrace, she tucking her chin closely into Zul's neck, a sign of affection Harry later noted, that had until then had been reserved for himself.

For a full half hour Ruzizi clung to the boy refusing to let go as he sat down awkwardly at an invitation to have a 'sundowner' on the verandah.

Resulting from Ruzizi's instant friendship, Harry and Zul saw quite a lot of each other in the following years. Zul would drop in everytime he came back to Nairobi, after a safari, to see Ruzizi. He had to admit that for no obvious reason, Zul was Ruzizi's best friend. 'He's not even small' he used to say completely mystified: he was used to Ruzizi's unfaithfulness when it came to little people, and he didn't at that time understand Ruzizi's 'personal vibration wave frequency selection mechanism'.

The relationship which had existed between himself and Ruzizi was unique. A shepherd's relationship to his dog might be, he reluctantly agreed, a degree of the feeling he experienced. It was complicated, yet simple. He knew, for example, that after the first few times that Ruzizi held her hand to her eyes every time they passed the vet's surgery in the car, she was doing it not for fear of a visit, not to shut out the horror which she had already forgotten, but because she knew it would please him by her doing so. On one occasion she was given a musical box which, like most of her toys, lasted for less than a week before it was torn apart, but for the first two days of that week when it was working Ruzizi mistakenly thought it was her sitting on the box, not the lid shutting, that stopped it playing. When she realized that this was a mistake and it was in fact the lid shutting that stopped it, she still continued to sit on it in his company as a sort of a private joke between the two of them. Whereas for the remainder of the week that it worked she would religiously close the lid with her hands to shut it when she was in Chomba's company who didn't share in that particular joke.

Then there were the mysterious times when she seemed to have a foreknowledge, a sort of premonition of something that she would not enjoy very much being about to happen, and she also seemed to know instinctively that by removing herself from the place where it was going to happen she could avoid it. Harry's clients of course loved Ruzizi, from the most brash types who just wanted to be seen with a chimpanzee – 'You must just take a picture of me with your monkey, Mr Hill.' To whom Harry always gave the standard reply, 'Certainly, Mrs Baboon'. In contrast to them were two sensitive teenage girls from Milwaukee who put off their flight back to the States for two weeks in order that they could have another afternoon with Ruzizi. What an afternoon that had been, thought Harry. Ruzizi had tugged the girls away for a walk down the grassy lawns to what he described as The Jungle by the river at the bottom of the plot. Harry watched the three of them disappear from sight, one either side of Ruzizi holding her hands. She was somersaulting wildly in the middle and stopping every hundred yards or so to drag the girls down to sit on the damp grass for an impromptu round of pat-a-cake. It was almost dark by the time the three of them returned.

Ruzizi's relationship with the big groups of maybe twenty or thirty students that he had had on safari was different again and it astounded him. There could be absolutely no way of her knowing that the group was about to descend on her in her garden but nevertheless long before the coach arrived she would, on perhaps two occasions out of three, disappear completely. The students rather unhappily had drunk their cups of tea, eaten their cucumber sandwiches and were standing aimlessly around the table at the top of the garden which he had provided and just as they were about to depart, having been there for over an hour on their scheduled visit, Ruzizi would appear, loping up the lawn as if to say, 'Well, I suppose I've got to endure them but five minutes is plenty long enough'. Harry knew also that it wasn't just because she did really enjoy being with them – she did, but she loved best of all the terrific sensation it caused when she did appear after the groups thought they had missed her entirely. Probably some of Ruzizi's happiest times were when that huge cheer went up from thirty people when she suddenly appeared.

Chomba insisted that on these occasions Ruzizi disappeared long before the coach had pulled into the drive, so it remained a mystery to Harry how Ruzizi knew when to hive off.

By six years of age female chimps have not yet reached the age of puberty; there was therefore about Ruzizi none of the embarrassment of owning a female bitch on heat when it will grasp one's leg in a passionate sexual endeavour. Platonically Ruzizi was incredibly inquisitive if she caught sight of a man having a pee. She would twist her head on one side and almost scratch her head in incredible interest and amazement at seeing the male organ which she knew she had not. 'What on earth is that for?' you could imagine her saying. Down at the coast on holiday she wasn't above snatching a kikoi off an unwary visitor in order to check out such mysterious parts of the body, but it was all entirely platonic, just a childish inquisitiveness. In fact with Harry's friends like Rita and Paul, Ruzizi had a reputation of being naughty and clownish, always late for everything and although, on the face of it they agreed with Harry when he tried to explain the reasons for her actions, Harry knew that they didn't really understand.

Those evenings with her in her favourite tree, sitting so high in the branches that they would bend and swing in the breeze, otherwise so uncharacteristically still, and so obviously thinking. Harry saw it clearly, understood it clearly, but found it impossible to explain.

When he analysed his thoughts they went something like this: the Victorians hated Darwin because there was no place for angels in evolution, yet the Victorians could not bear the sadness of the world without the hope that angels would carry their dead children to a continuance. Harry, on the contrary, only two generations later, like most of his contemporaries, did emphatically believe in Darwin and his theory of evolution, give or take a mutation or two, and rejected the dogmas of Christianity, particularly angels, accepting only the Sermon on the Mount, and that only, as a sound philosophy for a way of life. Yet during those two generations thoughtful Christians had been attempting to reconcile the best of Christ's teachings with Darwin's teachings. Harry had assumed that there could be some slight meaning and purpose in the obvious survival of the fittest. From the jellyfish to dinosaurs and on to mammals, then the supreme man evolved and now it was the brain of that man that was spearheading evolution, but what then was the purpose, what then was the reason for those species that had fallen by the wayside to be evolving still? The 'dead end' primate groups – the chimps, for example? He refused to believe that the hopes and fears and plans of Ruzizi were totally useless. He knew Ruzizi's actions were not always instinctive. Sitting comfortably in his car just out of Kalolen he tried hard for one last time to make some sense of it. He realized that he had been fortunate to have visited, during his lifetime, such bolder brush strokes on the Darwinian canvas as the Galapagos Islands, the marsupials of Madagascar, as well as the evolutionary star billings like the indigenous and aboriginal offshoots of Oz and above all to have shared a season with the gentle bushmen of the Kalahari. Only last year he had gone 'walk about' and let his business run itself. Harry found it compatible with his logic to accept the unsurpassed organization of a termites' nest as being in the continuing order of things – termites evolved no more and are static. He found himself accepting, too, the survival unchanged in sixty-five million years since dinosaurs roamed the earth of his Nile crocodiles on Lake Turkana. They were the strands that pushed up man the ultimate: the hope the very reason for existence.

One sight he had been privileged to see confounded this comfortable logic. Clients returning from safari would abandon in the buses less valuable objects which they decided would be too heavy to fly home with after all. The result – a hundred collected and rejected animals' skulls lined Harry's Langata wash bay wall; a miniature mountain of semi-precious stones of petrified wood and of flat stones called marji a chumbi with fossilized fern and foliage outlines embedded in them were all piled at the end of the washing area at Langata.

Ruzizi during the day would collect a slab of this flat stone and struggle over to her sand pit with it. By breaking it she might find herself with two pointed triangles of stone and a long thin strip. In the morning when she in any case was most active in building, she did on one occasion stick the two triangles of flat stone point downwards in the sand, and balance the third stone across them to make a bridge. She immediately proudly balanced herself with some difficulty on the wobbly platform eighteen inches off the ground untaught. The question that worried Harry was what in the sanity and logic of evolution is the cause for a chimpanzee to build a dolmen – and plan it by thinking about it in the tops of trees at night? He was even more sure of this parallel development after what he always referred to as 'The Dagoreti Miracle'.

The most wonderful act in Ruzizi's life was known only completely to two people. Why they had told no one was for fear that less well-informed people would attempt to show that it had not been the way that they knew it had been. Harry was particularly afraid that outsiders might destroy his faith. Now with exquisite pleasure just once more, Harry recalled with sheer delight the prelude to his private miracle.

On occasions, many years previously, when the kids were still at school in Kenya and Tilda was still used from time to time, Harry and Jenny would organize a car treasure hunt in aid of Dagoreti Red Cross Children's Centre, which was situated some six miles out of Nairobi. These social events in themselves never raised large amounts of money for the children's centre, but it was amazing how many of the participants became involved for the rest of their lives with the centre, having been introduced to it through the Hills' events; people who would probably not otherwise become involved in the running of the centre for the physically handicapped African boys and girls.

The events were also tremendous fun for the participants. The enthusiasm was such, for example, that it was more common than not for competitors to jump into swimming pools, fully clothed, in order to be the first to recover a horseshoe clue from the bottom of the deep end, for example. For this reason Harry, when organizing the treasure hunts, always made sure that at least one clue would be at the Dagoreti Children's Centre and often ten or twelve of the crippled children were invited to the finish, complete with wheelchairs and crutches.

The buildings which housed the centre were anything but inspiring. Dirty mud-spattered walls, whitewashed long ago, red rusty corrugated iron tin sheds, the baked mud bare playground in which the children played, the filthy torn blankets on the crowded beds, were a gruesome sight.

Philosophically Harry told himself that a ten-year old child,

292

for example, paralysed from the waist down living in poverty in the third world might suffer less than his equivalent in a developed country, because in a developed country there was so much more the child would miss and on balance he concluded it wasn't that much more terrible to be handicapped in poverty. Dagoreti children were financed by a tiny government grant, and with as much charitable income as they could raise. This paid for two full-time qualified European nursing sisters who ran the place. Some of the visitors who first came across the eighty crippled children at the Red Cross Centre found nothing but shame and sadness, others were encouraged because amongst these children playing football in wheelchairs, dragging their iron legs across a hopscotch pitch, there were constant smiles and endless laughter.

The gate was broken down, many panes of glass were missing from the windows and most of the children had open running sores, but nevertheless Harry would wax eloquently when he described to his entrants to the car treasure hunt, that a hundred shillings would buy a month's supply of San Izal just for starters. He could, in fact, think of few other places in the world where a hundred shillings would buy so much health and happiness.

On one occasion Jenny had organized a race between some of the children in wheelchairs and some of the children on crutches. The prize was an exercise book or a biro pen but the enthusiasm generated could be equated with the enthusiasm of clouds unfurling and *Chariots of Fire*. When Jenny managed to get this race on the local cinema circuit's newsreel many would laugh in derision and some would cry in sympathy but few could ignore it. Those days now seemed a lifetime ago, with Jenny and Tilda and the kids, when life was fun in summer weather with green days in the forest and blue days by the sea.

He remembered one Christmas, fifteen years later, when Ruzizi was in her fourth year and he had not even been near Dagoreti children's home for about fifteen years. He wondered if perhaps he couldn't work out something with Ruzizi that would bring the children at the centre a little happiness that Christmas. Harry even remembered how he had impulsively jumped up from his Koinage Street office desk that November morning and strode through the front office shouting over his shoulder to his three sales girls, 'I'm just off to Dagoreti to see how run down it is these days and to check out if we can fix up something for Christmas with Ziz. I'll be back after lunch if anyone wants me.'

As he drove the twenty minutes drive out of the crowded city to the Rural Suburb he decided that he was definitely not looking forward to seeing the centre again after so many years. He guessed the two European nursing sisters supplied by the British Red Cross would have been Africanized long since, and even as they had found it virtually impossible to keep the place clean with the meagre funds available, God only knew what it would be like now.

Pulling in at the familiar broken corrugated iron gate, looking at the half a dozen crippled kids that gathered round his car before he got out, things didn't seem too different. In fact he noticed with surprised that the main admin block was being that very day coated with White Sludge – from the East Africa Oxygen Company in Nairobi, its facing wall dazzling in a most unaccustomed brilliant white. The reception office smelt better than he remembered too, with an impressive hospital ward disinfectant odour.

Sitting at a cluttered desk was the woman he had come to see. An elderly grey-haired African woman. She rose as he entered – 'Sister Doris' she introduced herself, holding out her hand. He just worded his own introduction 'Harry Hill' and accepted the handshake when they simultaneously recognized each other.

'Good God, it's not? Dory!'

They embraced, then Dory stood back slightly awkwardly and confessed, 'I heard about Jenny and Simon when I was living in the States – I just couldn't write to you – I tried a hundred times.'

His instant reply, 'For God's sake, Dory, that was a hundred years ago – and what could you say, anyway?'

She nodded in agreement, 'What could I say? I knew your Simon for what – two or three month when I was twenty-five and he – how old – eight? Yet I have never loved anybody more.' Her eyes misted and she shook her head in annoyance with herself and bit her bottom lip. 'My Simon's a doctor in Washington, DC, now,' she said proudly, noticing Harry's surprise and totally misinterpreting it she added, 'You don't mind – my calling him . . . .'

She left the sentence unfinished as Harry interrupted, 'Mind! It's the most wonderful compliment I've ever received.'

It was agreed that they would meet at Dory's little flat after Christmas and have a long chat. Meanwhile Harry explained what he had in mind: his chimp dishing out Christmas presents to her kids. Dory agreed at once. Then Harry tried, as he often did, to explain the virtues of Ruzizi. When he was describing her, and how she had arrived so soon after Nicky had gone to Aussie and how she had so completely filled the void left by his daughter's departure, Dory looked a little askance at Harry. A month later no one knew better than she exactly what he had meant, as Ruzizi had captured a corner in Dory's heart, a place in her affections on the same plane as that of Simon's – short memories she would cherish for ever.

The Arts and Crafts Fair held in December at the agricultural showground just outside Nairobi has become a Mecca for Whites in Kenya. It has completely replaced the Royal Agricultural Show as their annual meeting place. It is held on a Saturday in early December, the idea being to purchase the White tribal cottage craft produce for Christmas presents. About fifty tents, stalls with handicraft products in them, each manned by a European who is supplementing his or her retirement income by selling handmade jewellery, hand-carved boxes, oil paintings, furniture, cotton toys, candles, cakes, jams, chocolates, armchairs and even cut-glass. Incredibly good value and extremely artistic. Every year it seemed to rain and the thousands of visitors would always be wearing their wellingtons, and carrying umbrellas – few Kenyans own a raincoat. The wind would often lash round the tents causing them to flap enough to blow away. To all intents and purposes it could have been in the middle of the shires of England on a wet August Bank Holiday. They always joked that you would see more black faces at a UK Midlands village fete than you would here, a few miles outside Nairobi in independent Kenya.

Of the several thousand people who visited the fair one would see only three or four black faces. Those of the White Tribe who lived in Nairobi relished the opportunity to see again old friends who had come down from up-country to visit or who had their own stands, who lived in remote farms up-country and who would bring their year's work down to sell at the festival. The previous year, the Christmas of 1983, Harry had bought Ruzizi a huge pink panther bigger than herself which had been a terrific success. Ruzizi and the pink panther were inseparable for all of ten days until it was trailed through the old sump-oil pit at the bottom of the garden and even after Harry insisted that it was thrown away, Ruzizi would lovingly collect one dismembered oily cotton rag arm from the pit and take it up to the top of a tree.

The fete had the air of a festival and it was an incredible sight. The thirty acres of car parks were full, quite large amounts of money changed hands and you would see European children trooping back to their cars in the car park laden with homemade cakes and homemade dolls, their parents carrying homemade furniture and Christmas-wrapped packages of homemade jewellery. The previous year Father Christmas had arrived by helicopter and a gust of wind on landing had nearly caused an accident, so he had been prohibited from landing in a crowded area with a helicopter.

This year Harry had advertised the previous week in the local rag, *The Karen'gate Chronicle*, that all visitors to the Arts Fair would be invited to bring with them their old toys which they did not require, whatever their condition, in order that he might collect them and distribute them to Dagoreti Children's Centre on Christmas Day. Father Christmas would be there to receive them. Father Christmas this year was Ruzizi in a rakish red cap with traditional white snowed hem. She originally had a red cape as well but she didn't think much of that and had taken it off and folded it up, or rather roughed it up, to sit on. There she was, behind the huge box marked 'Toys for Dagoreti Children's Centre', shaking hands solemnly with every child who deposited their old toy in the box.

It was Christmas Day two weeks later. Harry and Ruzizi had just arrived at Dagoreti to give out the presents they had collected for the children and Ruzizi was about to excel herself. There were so many toys donated that Harry had had to use one of his pick-ups in order to get them all to the centre. He had also asked one or two of his friends and acquaintances to be there and help the chimp with the distribution. Some twenty whites, with their families, as well as about as many again of African well-wishers and Board members had all gathered to make a crowd of perhaps a hundred spectators.

All the invalid girls, some fifty of them, were sitting or

standing on one side of the little muddy courtyard. Ruzizi, in her Father Christmas hat and a symbolic red scarf round her neck, looking like a Snoopy Red Baron, would grab a toy, invariably a doll or a furry animal, from the box, rush across the yard and give it to one of the crippled girls and then come back for another one. Occasionally if one present from the box was a very small toy animal, Ruzizi couldn't resist taking another and clasping the first in her toes for herself, as she gave the other away to shrieks of delight. Because the girls were to receive dolls and Ruzizi couldn't differentiate between boys and girls the boys were to be lined up later to be suppled from a different box with different toys. It was a moving scene and some of Harry's friends who were watching tried to hide their emotions and perhaps a tear or two by saying to Harry such things as, 'Good God, Harry, how did you train her to do that? What the hell did Tiny Tim say?'

Harry could remember every detail of that day. Ruzizi at her magnificent best enjoying every second of being the centre of attraction. Kids with sores, kids with runny noses, kids with flies settling unmolested on their encrusted eyelids, generally dirty, most helpless, paralysed or legless or armless or eyeless, many with hideously burnt faces from where they had fallen into cooking fires as babies. Some deaf, some dumb, some blind and all poor.

Jesus H. was there ever such a sad sight? So why the hell was everyone laughing and cheering as Ruzizi grabbed a naked white doll from a little crippled girl and gave it to a bigger neighbour and before the first crippled girl had time to cry out, in her arms was thrust a huge teddy bear which Ruzizi had been dragging along behind her, clasped between the thumb of her toe, a favourite carrying place of hers. Cheering, clapping kids and staff and audience. One of the crippled children had given Ruzizi an empty old dirty black plastic bag and Ruzizi had the bright idea of getting Harry to fill this with three or four toys so that she didn't have to cross the square so often. Ruzizi would tear off towards the children with a full sack and do a somersault halfway across so exuberant was she. And the next time her famous parachutist headroll when she put out her arm to land on, then she would get hopelessly tangled up with the sack of toys and have to abandon it temporarily and run back for it, to the absolute shrieks of delight of the waiting crippled children.

Ruzizi had finished giving out dolls and furry animals and teddy bears to the girls and had just started giving clockwork cars, board games and toy soldiers, to the boys. Harry had left the box of toys and gone over to explain to Ruzizi where the groups of boys were waiting patiently for their presents some fifty feet from the girls when he noticed the incredible delight that an eight-year old girl with her leg in crude irons, was getting from playing with a Cindy Doll. Harry couldn't help wondering how much more pleasure that Cindy Doll was giving to that girl than it would give to most of the toy-saturated children of the developed world.

Ruzizi then did a very strange thing. Instead of filling the sack with the remaining boys' toys and taking it over to the boys, she scampered back to the toy box and picked up a worn white-haired teddy bear, the only toy left in the girls' box, she then crossed the square, past the ranks of crippled children and shinned up the wall of the building behind. She thundered over the tin roof with the teddy bear grasped in one hand and dropped out of sight on the other side of the eave. Rather annoyed Harry shouted, 'Ruzizi, where the hell are you going?' With the weary gait of an overweight sixty-five-year old Harry trotted around the end of the building to get a better view and saw her in the act of climbing through an upstairs window of another tumbledown building of the centre. With a little difficulty he found the open stairs that led up to the ward into which Ruzizi had entered.

In the same way that Harry had never dreamt or even thought of owning a chimp until it happened, he had never thought either about the submerged hopes and fears and hates and love affairs of eighty or so crippled children that are thrown together for so many years. Suddenly he guessed it all. If, in boarding schools for the educated elite or in prisons for criminals or where any collection of people were gathered together, there are such deadly alliances, such bullyings, such open and closed plots and fears, he guessed how much more intrigue there must be in such a place housing, as it did, so many destitute crippled humans.

Dory had organized that each prefect in charge of each sleeping ward would make certain that all the physically disabled children had been carried or helped by those who could propel themselves a little better, downstairs to receive their presents in the playground. For tiny selfish reasons the two boys who had been instructed to bring down Tom had opted not to do so, but who could really blame them? Tom was now four-years old and he had been at the children's centre for nearly three of those years. He was completely paralysed from the neck down and nobody had ever heard him speak or seen him smile. Dory, for one, hoped sincerely that he had no memory either for who could wish the gift of memory on Tom who as a nine-month old toddler had witnessed his demented father chop off his mother's head, chop off also his two-year old sister's head and then receive the blow that should have severed his own head, when the neighbours had burst in and put his father off his stroke. Or had the poor crazed maniac returned to normal for a split second? Whatever the reason, instead of slicing his son's head off with a blow from the panga he was wielding so furiously, he turned it flat on its side and changed his motion from a mighty side-swipe to a downward hammer-like blow with the flat of the blade hitting the baby's soft head with a tremendous force. From that time on Tom had been the cabbage that he was now.

The beds in that deserted room which normally held two children each, head to tail, were made up of the typical strips of inner tube so common to third world beds. A dirty curling uncovered one inch foam mattress was strewn on each bed, together with the dirty rags of sheets and blankets. There, in the one occupied bed halfway down the ward, lay the four-year old boy staring vacantly at the ceiling. It was the job of the other boys in the ward to tug and prop Tom up twice a day and make sure that a few spoonfuls of food and a cup of water were poured down his throat. This act of kindness was not inconsiderable, as an hour after he was washed by the nursing staff he would usually be covered in his own excreta and always a thin slime of snot connected his nose to his mouth and there would usually be a fly feeding off the liquid from either eye – a sight to incite disgust rather than pity. So the scene was set fair for the miracle.

At one end of the nearly empty ward Ruzizi was scrambling through the broken window with the teddy bear clasped in her toes. At the other end of the ward a puffing Harry and breathless Dory had just climbed the stairs and were standing and watching, and halfway down the ward was Tom, hardly visible, lying silently on his bed.

Ruzizi thumped down onto the floor of the ward, jumped across a few beds. She still had her red scarf round her neck in a rakish fashion but her Father Christmas hat had been discarded on the roof. She went straight to the bed where the boy was lying. Placing the teddy bear at the bottom of the bed she then, with her left hand, firmly grasped the boy's neck and with her right hand gave a deliberate and fairly sharp backhanded clip across the back of the boy's head which she had pulled up roughly by the shoulder. Dory, seeing this, started to step forward thinking the chimp was in some way harming the completely crippled child but Harry guessing otherwise, restrained her.

Ruzizi left the teddy bear at the end of the bed and shuffled off down the ward and out of the window the same way as she had come. He and Dory walked towards the bed. At first the head lying on the pillow did look at rather an odd angle and it crossed his mind with terror that perhaps Ruzizi had broken the neck in some impulse to put the child out of its agony and then when he and Dory were still about ten feet away in the corridor looking in towards the sick child Dory grabbed Harry's hand, 'Oh, Harry,' she said, 'oh, Harry look.'

He looked and saw the miracle. One of the previously paralysed legs was raised about an inch from the dirty mattress on which it was lying. The previously paralysed face of absolute vacantness turned into a smile, the like of which neither Harry nor Dory had ever seen, as Tom looked at the departing chimp and the teddy bear at the end of his bed.

A month later the boy was sitting up and six months later took his first step but both he and Dory kept the secret of the miracle cure to themselves. He evolved some theory that chimps in the wild knew just which nerve to touch if their babies had, for example, been dropped from a tree and the resulting blow to the head had sent them into a coma. But Dory was more psychologically minded and thought it may have been the fact that Ruzizi was the first creature that had ever communicated with the cripple in a way that was entirely devoid of disgust but, as Harry said to himself, miracles do not require too close investigation. Nevertheless, since it was Christmas Day he had to admit it did beat watching *The Sound of Music* for the third time round on television and going to bed with indigestion. Yes, Harry was quite definitely very proud of his Christmas 1984.

13

The Finish

As a corollary to the exquisite pleasure of remembering that Christmas Harry found himself, almost against his will, remembering one of the saddest moment of his life. When he had learnt that his wife and son had probably been killed in a plane crash, he had refused to believe it, and it had only dawned on him fully twelve hours later when he had found their bodies. This day was different.

This day was sudden. Harry stopped the car at the end of the drive and peered through the windscreen. That tree-lined drive to his house which had been the scene of so many happy days which had given so much pleasure in his life, up and down which both Nicky and Simon had first been pushed in a pram by their ayah; then toddled up, then walked up, then biked up, jogged up, then drove up and down, and finally flew over in their aeroplanes. That same drive. Now up it was walking Chomba, the shamba, and in his arms what at first Harry thought was an oily, dirty torn black blanket and then as it approached and he saw clearer it turned into the forlorn shape of a dead body of a chimpanzee.

Nothing, Harry thought, then or after is quite so poignant as the dead body of a chimpanzee, head, hands and feet all flopping helplessly. Clasped between two dead toes a little bunch of bougainvillaea with two beautiful blue magnificent petals, the hue of which Harry had never seen the like before.

Poor old Chomba was too dazed to explain what had happened but the details of Ruzizi's last day came in fits and starts in Swahili. It seemed that Ruzizi had been too inquisitive. She had climbed the main electricity pole that carried the 220-volt cables of electricity across the drive and into the distribution point of the house. The bougainvillaea was growing up the pole and had spread out, entwining with a colourful branch, the lethal live wires. On that branch were the two beautiful blue flowers. Chomba was convinced that Ruzizi had reached out to pick them for Harry, like she often picked odd flowers that took her fancy. She reached forward with one hand on the bottom wire, but as soon as she touched the top wire to grab the flower 220 volts of mains current went through her and she dropped to the ground, stone dead, with burn marks on each hand.

Harry tried to comfort himself, being an optimist, with the consolation of the painlessness of so quick a death. Then to further comfort himself he asked himself what he would have done with her when she got bigger, and a hundred other justifications for her untimely death but it was no use. Chomba and Ruzizi had been burning eucalyptus leaves earlier that day. Harry had smelt that so typical tropical garden smell of the smoke a hundred times before – he was never to smell it again without seeing in his mind the dead body of Ziz.

After his wife and Simon had been killed he still had Nicky and he still seemed young with a lot of fight left in him, but now life didn't seem worth living, so bleak was the void.

Harry buried Ruzizi in the Langata garden under her favourite tree, alongside a pony that had died when Nicky had been young and cats and dogs. To the little funeral gathering he invited Paul and Rita and Dory and, of course, Chomba and Joseph were there. Zul was on safari in Tanzania and Harry could not get in touch with him. As Chomba dumped the body of Ruzizi tied up in a sack, into the grave Harry noticed the outline of her small head pressing against the side of the sack. It reminded Harry of when she had been alive and she had loved to put things over her head and run around the table playing blind man's buff and at last Harry said, 'To hell with being maudlin' and actually sobbed as the injustice of her death struck him; the waste of all things, of all people. She, who only wanted to play all day long. She, beloved of all who knew her. She, so innocent. Why? Why? Why should her life be cut off so suddenly, so short? 'Don't worry,' said Dory as she whispered into Harry's ear, 'She's an angel, remember? She's gone to join the angels – I'm certain.'

It was a beautiful day without a cloud in the sky that day

they buried Ruzizi. Harry had often seen it before and wondered about it often since, but never had he received a satisfactory explanation, and yet it is a fact – you can ask anybody living in Langata – that the trees, maybe after a month or two without any rain falling on them, suddenly exuded a water-like liquid from their foliage and quite large wet patches appeared in the grass beneath them. So it wasn't really any great surprise when he felt a drop of water splash on his forehead from the tree under which Ruzizi was so recently buried and in which she had done so much of her thinking. Dory had never seen it before. 'That proves it,' she said, 'when angels die even the trees weep.'

Harry remembered distinctly the protection he promised himself, against future hurt, 'Don't ever love again,' he said to himself. 'No love, no harm, no possibility then of a wounded heart that will never heal – simple,' but even as he thought it, he knew the answer was anything but simple. Never to love again for fear of losing the object of that love, made as little sense as never opening your eyes for fear of damaging them, never walking again for fear of falling.

Harry was sitting stationary in the car and as he came to the end of the Ruzizi story in his mind, it slowly dawned on him why he had wanted to think of her. His first reaction had been not to think about her, as he invariably saddened himself by thinking about her death. There was nothing very happy about that. Then, an eerie feeling came over him, the like of which he hadn't felt since he was a child when he had been read ghost stories by his grandmother in Leighton Buzzard. He felt the physical presence of Ruzizi sitting beside him in the car, although he knew she had been dead and buried for eight years – then the fear changing to feeling her spiritual presence and that was comforting, 'nothing spooky about that,' Harry said to himself. Obviously if he had been concentrating on things long enough like he had, positive thought waves and all that, obviously the spiritual presence is going to appear to be there but he wasn't too sure.

He felt that it was himself that was entering another plane and that he was imagining things in this future plane, but he

304

was still in complete control of his senses, he told himself. He knew that the car he was sitting in was quite obviously of the present. Thoughts of Jenny and Simon were quite obviously of the past, but thoughts of Ruzizi? That was the problem. He could have sworn that they were of the future.

Then fear grabbed him again. What was he doing there, anyway? What force was leading his physical body down to the coast to die? What force was it? Now that force seemed to be controlling his mind. He was thinking of things he didn't really want to think about. 'Mathari for you, Harry my boy' – a reference to the name of the Nairobi lunatic asylum. 'You're losing your marbles, that's your problem,' he said to himself. Because of Harry's new fears that his reminiscences were driving him out of his mind, he stopped reminiscing about the distant past and concentrated on the present and very recent past.

He compared the trip he had just done with a hundred other Nairobi-Mombasa drives which he had done in his lifetime – same sameness really, no towns, no turnings, no roundabouts – just the endless bush. Filling stations and tatty little dusty villages with their day and night clubs and no other dukas. No view of Kilimanjaro – didn't expect that really so late in the year but nevertheless he recalled wistfully that time when he and Nicky had driven down in his Mac Car Transporter one January and had seen the giant snow-capped peak, its head towering over them, nineteen thousand feet in the clear blue sky looking like a giant Christmas pudding topped with cream for all of five of the ten hours it had taken them to get to Mombasa. It just followed alongside. Today cloud cover had been so low he had not even seen it once.

At the start of Harry's drive to the coast that morning – that morning? Only eight or nine hours ago? Impossible he thought – more like a lifetime ago. Extreme fear had caused his thoughts to lose continuity. Now again, towards the end of his drive, just as he believed that he was succeeding in straightening them out, his thoughts started to go haywire again.

☆　　☆　　☆

He was sitting in a comfortable armchair in Dory's Dagoreti corner apartment half-way from the Centre to Nairobi – 'just far enough away to keep me sane' as Dory put it. The block of flats was typical of the desperately needed 'buffer against revolutions and riots' occupied by the working Nairobi Africans who made capitalism work. They could just afford a car and a telly as well as to educate their three or four kids, especially if the wife could find a job as well. Sadly they are a tiny minority, many millions of Kenyans with nine or ten kids rely on one or two acres of subsistence farming, or are nomads, desperately seeking feed for their cattle and goats and daughters, all of which are their currency. Whereas in the opposite camp a hundred of two megamillionaire right-wing Africans build themselves concrete castles for homesteads and surround them with barbed wire and killer dogs to keep the starving at bay. Harry considered both the latter life styles were conducive to revolution, hence he always called the few working Africans 'The Buffers'.

The flat was tastefully furnished and softly lit; heavy curtains – the only velvet ones in the whole block – kept out most of the unbelievable cacophony of Matatu van hooters in the Ngong Road below, trying to induce more clients to climb in to their already over-filled mini-buses.

In the years following Ruzizi's death Harry was a frequent and comfortable visitor and on occasions Dory would spend a pleasant evening at Harry's Langata house. Gradually during these little dinner parties Dory's story emerged. Her marriage to the well-connected son of a Labour politician had lasted fourteen happy years. He was a part of the UK brain drain and their married life was spent in the States. It produced her Simon, the son, and Ann his younger sister, both now grown up. They beamed down on Harry and Dory from their pewter-framed photos on the mantelpiece. Just when she was approaching forty Dory fell madly – no other adjective will do – in love with a twenty-two year old Uganda boy whom her husband was teaching the trade of computer software. Dory was adamant that no tiny blame was to fall on her tolerant loving husband – he even wanted desperately to turn a blind eye to his wife's affair with the young man – but Dory insisted everyone must know of the magic she was so unexpectedly enjoying. The more her well-meaning friends assured her it couldn't last – the more she blatantly, proudly showed off her youthful lover. The month Dory finally 'moved in' with her

Romeo he fulfilled every one's expectations, except Dory's, and just moved on . . . . 'But perhaps it was all for the best,' she ended, still obviously in love with the rat, fifteen years later. 'After all, think what the centre would be like without me.'

'True,' nodded Harry wisely, only later learning about Dory's final little Kenya drama.

Dagoreti Red Cross Children's Centre had welcomed her with open arms when she returned alone to Kenya in the seventies – with open arms and with four thousand shillings a month. This amount of shillings afforded her just her flat but not a car so she took the bus to work every day. Obviously she wasn't looking for a big income so much as a worthwhile way of life doing something she knew she was good at – organizing institutions and looking after the helpless.

She didn't kid herself she was God's gift to the Kenya Red Cross but for six full months she did her best to clean the place up, get more funds allocated, secure more regular doctors' visits, build another long-drop choo and so on. Then the blow fell. One of the all-African Board of Directors found that he had a cousin – a fully trained girl from Kenyatta Hospital Nursing College who would happily take over Dory's job and for five hundred shillings a month less pay – and 'Well, nice as Dory was, she was a Ugandan you know, not quite the same as being a Kikuyu like the director's cousin, etc etc'. The new girl ran the centre for three whole months whilst Dory popped in to help in the evenings for no financial reward, she having quite easily secured a secretarial job with a new computer firm in Nairobi. Then after three months the new girl started running a car and the already meagre food input to the centre decreased in volume to the exact cash volume of the cost of running the car which the girl kept for her own exclusive use. Next, every weekend the girl was never on duty, leaving it all with the hundred attendant problems, to her number two, an ancient Luo lady that had no interest at all in handicapped children. At the start of the fourth month after Dory had been replaced, all eighty children there at that time did what no other institute until that time had dared to do – they went on a hunger strike. The Board was not stupid. There was a suggestion that the President himself was interested in this unique situation of crippled children not eating. Forty-eight hours after the news broke, Dory was reinstated.

Dory had just cleaned away their dirty plates from the little dinner party and sticking her head round the swing door to the living room from the tiny kitchen, she asked Harry that hardy perennial question 'So why don't you?' Harry had had a bad day at work, every month a new Economy Tour company was licensed by the Ministry in competition with Harry Hill's Safari. They all cut their own throats to get in and most fell by the wayside after operating an inferior safari or two but it still meant less turnover for Harry. But that was not really what was worrying him this particular evening. He had been to a Tour Operators' Association luncheon earlier in the day and the invited guest speaker, the Permanent Secretary in the Ministry of Wildlife and Tourism, had directed the main thrust of his speech – not to suggesting cures for the hundred things wrong with Kenya tourism like airport corruption, like unbelievably bad roads, like tightening security, you name it – but instead he had insisted that he was reminding everybody that it was his, and the Ministry's intention, to indigenize the tourist industry. Not Africanize it, that of course was most necessary, not put it in the hands of Kenyan citizens, most of it was already in the hands of Kenyan citizens, not to encourage Africans to go abroad to get more tourists, but to take it away from the efficient white citizens and give it to inefficient black citizens. Indigenization whichever way you looked at it was apartheid – the colour of your skin being the only deciding factor as to whether or not you were allowed to run a business in modern Kenya!

Obviously such speeches always upset white citizens – Harry particularly. His reason told him it was all political shop window dressing and nothing would ever come of it but indigenization was an ugly word. Add to that niggling feeling of annoyance, what awaited him on his return to his Langata home from the town office that evening. There was a breakdown of water supply, common enough – no water. The telephone was off again, not unusual; these days it was more often off than on. And to add to it all there had been during the day the tenth power cut that month so no welding had been done in the workshop and his ten mechanics men had been standing around doing nothing all day. On top of all this, his oldest servant, Sampson, who should have been preparing a meal for him, was blind drunk and there was no tea or sugar left to have himself a cup of tea despite the fact that he had seen both there in plenty the previous day – the sort of petty pilfering that the starry-eyed idealists used to scorn the kali old women settlers for complaining about.

Thus the perennial question, 'So why don't you then . . . ? Pack it all up and live in a "civilized" country, like Australia or South Africa.' Harry looked up from the *Daily Nation* quick crossword – his intellectual limit these days – and replied 'Why don't *we*?'

With a smile of sadness Dory appreciated the implication. She knew it was only because the old widower had had a bad day. Both were too set in their ways for 'we' thinking at their time of life. 'Thanks, but no thanks. I'm still carrying your blooming burden.'

Harry laughed outright. 'We both are really – and it hasn't changed much.' This was a reference to a Jenny and Dory joke when they had both arrived in Kenya. Harry had half-jokingly said he was about to obey Kipling's great imperial decree enshrined in Queen Victoria's Jubilee poem and 'take up the white man's burden'.

Both Harry and Dory got to giggling then, comparing in their minds the pomp and circumstance of the supreme power at the absolute height of the British imperial dream at which stage the phrase 'white man's burden' was coined and comparing the old white man and the old black woman sitting in a tiny flat outside Nairobi nearly one hundred years later. The great empire builders would turn in their graves, but they couldn't deny it; Dory and Harry were the inheritors of just that same burden.

On such days Harry would take the long way home via Karen to get to Langata to reassure himself as he passed the drives of hundreds of houses with their so very English names on their name boards, like his own four adjacent neighbours, for example – Hill, Wood, Fox and Hedges. Such visible proof that the Europeans were not done for yet always cheered him up.

But nevertheless he still muttered to himself all the way home about 'indigenous citizens' having no choice of birth place, just luck, compared to his deliberate choice of renouncing the Queen and swearing loyalty to the Republic.

One thing he didn't mutter about which his black African

business associates would have reminded him about with a good-natured laugh, was the British High Commission 'Right of Abode in Britain' stamp Nicky had insisted he get stamped into his Kenya passport before she left.

Nobody could say that Harry wasn't a trier. There must be a special sign of the zodiac for such characters, who were not failures exactly; they succeeded greatly in many respects but in supporting lost causes they were less successful. When Harry was depressed over the victimization of Europeans in Kenya he would reel off letters to the editor of the daily papers, most of which were too radical for publication but one or two did get through. Only last year his friends were teasing him about this one:

Nairobi, February 19th 1990

Dear Sir

A typical illegal, indigenous tout at Shimoni greets all White tourists with the following opening gambit, pointing to the Arabic slave caves last used over a century and a half ago!

'That's where YOU colonialists kept us slaves – but never mind, we forgive you . . .
'

Well, thanks – but it is not much comfort, being forgiven for a crime you did not commit!

It is currently fashionable for Black men to blame White men for the problems with which the Black men find themselves surrounded.

Most politicians, Black and White, are inclined to bend History a little – but there is a limit! Do not break it!

The piece of land now known as The Republic of Kenya, was placed under the protection of the Great White Queen a hundred years *after* the British Empire abolished slavery.

The first civilizing missions, and early settlers of the British East African company which I suppose could be described as 'You Colonialists' also first arrived around that time, i.e. a century *after* the caves had ceased to be used by the *Arabs*.

The colonialists brought with them many evils and many virtues – like hospitals, railways, education, all buildings over two storeys high, aeroplanes, books, beer and Mr Bonnke!* But slavery was not one of them!

Incidentally, oh indigenous tout, you could also say that the British Navy patrolled the Indian Ocean for the first half of the nineteenth century to ensure that brown men did not buy black people from other black people for a handful of Birmingham beads, and take them to a place across the sea, where white men provided them with a standard of living usually superior to that which they had left behind (and still do) but perhaps that is bending History a little too far the other way!

Yours etc

Harry Hill
Kenyan Citizen

☆   ☆   ☆

What now seemed to Harry like a hundred years before but was really only just before Harry had left Husbands Bosworth with his beautiful young wife and young son. One of Harry's fondest memories of that time had been meeting with Robert Bolt and actually seeing Bertrand Russell as they planned a poster campaign for the newly-formed CND and marching from Aldermaston to Trafalgar Square. The ensuing years of peace and proliferation had dampened, though not completely doused, Harry's convictions.

Harry's last partisan fight against the Establishment had been more spectacular, more personal and more enjoyable than his first. Harry hadn't had much to do with Wilson Airport since Nicky had left. Occasionally he would visit the Nairobi Aero Club, for a cheap lunch or a beer on the way

---

* A reference to the Kenyan Billy Graham

home but the week before the Pope arrived in Kenya Harry was at Wilson Airport all day long and often till late into the night.

Permission for sky banner advertising had recently been granted by a line in that most mysterious piece of Kenyan government administration, the *Kenya Gazette*. It was a fascinating new study for Harry. There was a nostalgic scent of new-mown hay as the perimeter grass of runway 07 had just been cut. In the hot afternoon sun one of Harry's Safari Service pick-ups was backed up to Paul's pick-up of a similar height and stretched between the two flat beds was what looked like a balsa wood lath-like frame of a miniature Zeppelin. The little party of Harry and two of his safari workers and Paul were now proudly inspecting the piece of home carpentry and one or two junior craftsmen from the adjacent hanger had also come across to inspect the strange object.

Harry took out from the front of his pick-up a parcel of two neatly ironed but obviously used white double-bed sheets. Paul produced six tubes of 'Evo-stick' and there and then by the side of the runway they completed the fabrication of their erection. The sausage-like shape was three foot in diameter and the front round wire hoop that formed the open frame was, in fact, one of Harry's mosquito net hoops. Then a fifteen foot long body. They had a twelve volt paint spray gun working off the vehicle's battery and that sunny afternoon they were busy spraying the strange-looking model a light brown colour. It was torpedo-shaped, the flat end being open-framed and on the other end, the rounded nose-cone end, a second cone like a cap had been added. From a distance it looked exactly like it was meant to look – a giant condom.

The next day they tested it for lift off behind Oliver's old Cessna, borrowing the line and hook from the sky banner advertising boys. In the spirit of the Right Stuff, crossed with Heath Robinson, the first attempt to get the cylinder airborne was unsuccessful. It snapped the overload fuse in the banner trailing rope. Oliver and his plane came horribly near to biting the dust or at least having the propeller chew up the tarmac as his nose dropped suddenly as a result of the sudden tug which had in any case reduced him to stalling speed, followed by a hasty bumpy landing and the giant condom looking definitely used as it trailed along the tarmac runway at forty-five miles

312

per hour. It was back to square one for Harry and Paul. It was nearly dark by the time they had it ready for the next test flight. Most inappropriately little holes had to be made in the tit end in order to allow the air to flow through the tube-like body, thus creating less resistance and allowing it to trail without pulling the plane to the ground. Harry was particularly insistent that the holes had to be camouflaged. It would never do to fly the symbolic monster with visible holes in it, he said.

At last the great day arrived. It was completed and tested just in time the previous evening working by camping gaslight. There had been, not surprisingly knowing how cantankerous Paul and Harry were in their later years, some considerable argument as to the exact wording to be written in giant black block letters on both sides of the condom. Paul persuaded Harry that 'FOR CHRIST'S SAKE WEAR A CONDOM' was too offensive. They finally settled for 'KENYA'S ONLY' on one side and 'SALVATION' under it, thus allowing for maximum size letters. But Harry still grumbled it should have been written in small letters all on one line to make the message clearer. As it was, both Paul and Harry could clearly read it as Oliver circled at one thousand feet above the aerodrome.

His Holiness, pink-faced, white-haired, white-capped and white-robed, surrounded on the dais by a sprinkling of purple-robed monseigneurs, looked like one lonely silver star in a velvet black sky. He was surrounded by a hundred acres of black-haired, black-faced, brown-eyed worshippers. A pin-prick of white in a sea of blackness. Harry and Paul were jammed in the traffic on Uhuru Highway lining the park and were amazed to see the crowds stretching literally for miles in every direction. Amazed and sad, because Harry and Paul were genuinely critical of the pantomime that was being enacted before their eyes. They sincerely believed that the population explosion – Kenya's birthrate is amongst the highest in the world – was Kenya's greatest problem, Kenya's greatest evil and here was a man respected by millions, suggesting that nothing be done about it, encouraging the population explosion that could lead to catastrophe, death by starvation or death by violence as a result of the continuation of the rocketing birth rate in the Third World. The Pope was not only condoning it but actually encouraging it, blessing the

313

continuation of the evil.

The Pope and his entourage had been in Ruanda the previous day amid an identical black sea and was to be in Tanzania the next day amid another identical black sea as far as the eye could see. Unknown to Paul and Harry, His Holiness had had a bad day in Kigali the previous day. Some inspired African of the Tutsee tribe, an Assistant Minister of Information, had jumped up uninvited and unplanned from a seat where VIPs had been placed near to the Pope and had asked the question which came out fairly clearly on the Tannoy system, 'How, Mr Pope, do you suggest we control our greatest problem – the population explosion?' The Pope spent some ten minutes on the official party line answer, at the end of which spiel the Assistant Minister incredulously and innocently looked at the Pope in the eye and said, 'You mean, sir, that I am to tell my people not to fuck?' Believe it or not, it was a serious question.

In Nairobi, as the Pope got to the 'Go forth and multiply' part of his speech, Oliver's red and white Cessna appeared from out of a bright blue sky. As he circled overhead, the message on the condom he was trailing was plainly visible – 'KENYA'S ONLY SALVATION'.

Harry and Paul watching from the highway were not exactly triumphant but very satisfied. 'Haven't felt so good,' Harry said to Paul, sitting beside him, 'since we fixed those bloody potholes' – a reference to an occasion the previous year when Harry had had the seats removed from one of his Turkana buses, taken it to Colas in Nairobi's industrial area, and filled it with five tons of steaming asphalt. Then he had driven it one hundred miles down the Mombasa road with six of his staff and filled some twenty giant nine-inch-deep and two-foot-across potholes which had been unfilled for the previous nine months – a startling indictment of the correct authority. 'That will show 'em,' said Harry, arriving back in Nairobi some £300 or £400 the poorer – but of course it didn't. They both knew their messages would be ineffective but that is no excuse for not doing something about it.

He was thinking not about his recent days in Nairobi, but of the recent times he had spent on safari.

Many years ago when Jenny had been alive Ol Donyo Nyiro had been Harry's favourite place. Increasingly, however, these days he also enjoyed being at his Mara Camp. It was the Masai tribe of Kenya who owned the land where Harry Hill's safari company had set up their camp.

Historically speaking, (he would tell his clients) the Masai had had a raw deal. In the days before the railhead reached NI – O – ROBI – ironically now – 'Place of Sweet Water', the Masai tribe spread from the great inland lake, recently named after the Great White Queen, right over the Laikipia, towards the snow-capped giant mountain on the equator, and they were undoubtedly the dominant tribe of East Africa. The mainly British settlers brushed the Masai further and further back towards the lake.

By decree, the Masai were to keep to the western side of the railway-track as the colonists developed the White Highlands. Even after independence, that great warrior tribe did not seem to have very much say in the running of the country, nor did they seem particularly interested in western-type materialism – though they were still pretty rich, with cattle and goats. They love their cattle, they have over twenty words in their language for different shades of the colour 'brown'. Mind you, they used to say that God had given all the cattle in the world to them, and it was their duty to recover them if they strayed into the hands of other tribes!

Anyway, this reserve where we are sitting, was cut-clean out of the middle of Masai land, it was yet another blow to them, and now to make it worse, most of the money the park generates, never seem to get to the Masai who own it!

In fact, the Masai group ranchers get really fed up with the luxury camps, and lodges inside the parks, and you can sense the difference with us here. Here every penny goes into the pockets of the people who owns the land, because I insist we pay them direct.

That way, they are on our side; we are a part of their way of life! They come to us with their problems; only last night our camp vehicle took two Morans – fifty miles to the clinic. One of them had three fingers bitten off by a mad hyena. It is nice to be wanted and that helps the atmosphere here! You'll sense it!'

Harry was very satisfied with his 'recent past' lifestyle. A

315

typical scene would be him sitting in a canvas director's chair, looking out across the Talek River which bordered his Masai Mara Camp. A dozen clients and Harry would be sitting round the camp fire as the African night descended as suddenly as a theatre curtain – ending the day. Everybody who has lived in East Africa – citizens, residents, research workers, tribesmen, and indeed visitors, all have their own bag of 'safari stories' – like all stories – the most ordinary experience can be enthralling if well related, and the most sensational incredibly boring, if badly told.

Then off he would go with a whole gaggle of hair-raising adventures. 'Only last month' (many started 'only last month') 'saw two young lion just over there on the plains' (nodding to across the river) 'chasing an old bull buffalo; the buffalo stopped suddenly in its tracks – spun round, and lunged at the two lions. They skidded to a halt, turned around and began to run away, for dear life – the buffalo chasing them. Climbed up a tree in the end – they did – in the Mara mind! – lion chased by a buffalo . . . .' Harry would shake his head in disbelief.

'Tommy, – a herd of 'em once 'bout thirty or so, I suppose, crossing this river – up the stream with the migrating wildebeests in July, three or four years ago – haven't had a decent migration since then – We were watching them from the river bank, I remember we had some VIP clients with us – not that you are not *all* VIP . . . .' He added quickly with a smile . . . to the attentive clients sitting round the fire . . . .

'Giant crocs standing up on their tails – six foot out of the water, snapping away at the little tommies – the crocs were obviously waiting for the wildebeest calves, but they forgot all about them, and chased these little gazelles; all thirty of 'em scrambled up the bank, followed by the giant crocs. They all got clear, but one! The croc snapped and caught this one's leg, it got away though, never known such a cheer from our group as when it got free – but talking about crocs, you have got to be careful of them – would not recommend you going down to wash in the river, it's got bilharzia anyway!'

And so he would carry on all night long. Usually ending with the story of how his daughter Nicky had been literally taken by a baboon from her carry-cot when she was only six months old, fortunately, Harry had recovered her when the baboon dropped her after dragging her through the bush a hundred yards, 'talk about Ayers Rock!' And so he continued, omitting fear of the species his clients would be seeing in the next few days.

'Elephants, seen 'em carry one of their own sick babies for miles, two matriarch cows, tying each other's trunks together under the belly of the baby to support it – it was too sick to stand on its own. Seen 'em cross the Zambezi when it was twenty feet deep, walking along the bottom with their trunks sticking up like U-boat periscopes – saw two thousand of 'em once in one herd on the Nile, in Sudan in the old days – Leopard . . .' and so he would continue long into the night!

Harry felt that God was in his Heaven, and all was well with the world, as he walked towards his tent on those nights.

Harry found himself becoming a self-styled Guru, he was still remembering those recent evenings around the camp fire in his Mara camp. He now found that his long experience of the situation in which his clients had invariably found themselves so recently, secured for him a certain respect and dependence, and gave him an authority which he would exploit mercilessly.

'Don't worry about being scoffed by a lion' he would say to the eager audience – if you are, it will have been planned – since the – I was going to say beginning of time, but that's wrong – time has no beginning. Look, your very being here, depends on a motorcycle I used to drive in 1938, starting on the third and not the fourth kick. He would hastily go on to explain how he was knocked off his bike that day, and how if he had hit the on-coming vehicle, a yard sooner or later and he would have been killed, instead of injured. Thus no him, and therefore no safari – none of them would therefore be sitting there, etc., etc., etc. The moral being if it is to be, it is to be and the weaver must have worked 'you being lion fodder' into his web the day he saved me to bring you here.

It was not long before he found himself recounting another old favourite of his, which showed the weaver of the web of destiny in startling clarity.

'We were on our way out here, overlanding in 1956,' he would begin . . . 'in an old Army Ambulance which I had bought for £60 in a UK surplus sale. Just the wife, my son, Simon and me. It was only about eight o'clock, but pitch dark, Tilda's headlights had failed; young Simon, about eight at the

317

time, was holding two wires of a portable spot light which we carried, on to the battery terminals under the seat. Jenny – that was my wife, was leaning out the side – no doors as such on Tilda, just rolled up canvas ones – looking for a mission to spend the night. We were about a day's run out of Bangui, still in CAR in Bushongo country – somebody had told us there was a Catholic Mission only about four or five miles away. We had just passed a sort of a notice – Jenny was pointing the spotlight ahead so I could more or less see the track we were travelling on, when she noticed the sign, but couldn't read it.

'I thought it might be a sign for the Mission turning, so I stopped Tilda about twenty-five yards past it. I reversed back, so we could read the sign in the spotlight and surely enough, it pointed to the turn for the mission! It was only about two miles down that turn. Super welcome from an Irish father with two Belgian nuns – hot baths, went to a service the next morning, in a little mud chapel – left the father a bottle of JB – everybody happy.

'Super view from that Mission, looking across the Congo. At its widest, nearly three miles wide, I should think. Five minutes after leaving, we were back at the sign, where we had turned the previous night. It was a dusty corner, you could still see Tilda's track marks clearly in the dried mud. The road which we had been travelling down the previous night showed our tracks continuing on past the sign to the Mission for twenty-five yards after the sign, but it was in fact not just a turn that we had passed as we had approached that previous night, it was a T-road going left as well as right! A T-junction in fact, and do you know what was straight ahead?'

Harry paused for dramatic effect.

'It was a view point – sort of a primitive dusty car park, cut out of the bush. Our tyre tracks of the previous night stopped one foot short of a hundred-foot sheer drop into the Congo River below! Not even a strand of wire! Straight over we would have gone, if I had not stopped that second, and I hadn't seen a thing – and you' – he would say . . . looking at a client sitting in a chair on his right . . . 'are worried about being eaten by a lion?' He would end with a smile – 'if you are to be eaten tonight, it was planned that you should be, that night – because if I was not here, you wouldn't be here – so don't worry!'

318

☆   ☆   ☆

Harry sitting in his Corolla, having driven to within a few miles of the Indian Ocean, suddenly frowned. Then a new wave of fear swept over him, on this occasion, not a fear of his anticipated appointment with death, but a fear of becoming mentally unbalanced. This time he was not imagining a distant Nicky's voice, this time he was literally talking aloud to himself . . . .

'Why didn't you recall that near-disaster with Tilda in the Congo when you were thinking about your overland trip two or three hours ago?' he asked himself. A simple enough question surely – it was the answer which was causing him to doubt his own sanity. 'Because it didn't happen – that's why I didn't recall it,' weakly still to himself . . . 'surely, you must have *known* that it didn't happen? – you persuaded yourself it *did*.

'You had retold the incident so often for years, that you thought it had really happened!

'What about all those hundreds of punters you have comforted with the story? Well . . . ' he said indignantly to himself – 'they were comforted, true or not – talk about believing your own bullshit! So, it didn't happen! Yet, you thought for a moment it had.'

Harry also found himself, as a sort of a duty really, explaining to his clients the current politics of the country. 'It's painfully obvious . .. ' he used to say, 'to anyone who has spent a year or two in any African country, that despite what the BBC, the Human Rights organizations, and the American State Department insist, a Westminster type of two-party democracy would be a king-sized disaster as far as Kenya is concerned. I am all for helping the oppressed, but in any countries where tribal loyalties are paramount, two parties as per UK is not the answer, especially when the two super tribes are numerically about equal.'

'Dualism in Kenya would split it right down the middle and we would have a Biafra-type civil war! What the critics do not realize is that, as things are at the moment, all the tribes *do* receive ministerial positions doshed out by the President which gives them all a certain amount of power, a feeling of doing something. Whereas, if they were sitting in a parliament in

319

ever-lasting oppositions and believe me, that's what would happen if you had an opposition party – the second largest tribe would get no power at all – ever. And another thing,' he would say . . . warming to his point, 'You will always find four or five candidates standing for each seat and although they are all theoretically under the one party manifesto at the moment, their personal political opinion can vary from extreme left to extreme right. So in that respect, you can pick your choice in any case. – The electorate *does* get a choice. No, most people think one party is like one wife – more than enough!

'Take my man for example – Phil Leakey. Did you know we had a white man in Parliament? Returned by a majority of six thousand over all the three other black candidates who stood for the seat at the last election – and only two hundred of his voters were white! And the people standing against them, belong to the two major tribes of Kenya – lost to a Mzungu! . . . Rather amazing actually, I was his agent at the polling booth, all fair and above board, but a tedious old business. The organizers of the election strung string out on poles, to form different queuing lines. The first line being for voters whose names began with A, B and C, the second being with D, E and F and so on . . . . The only problem was that although there were some eight queuing lines, ninety per cent of the electorate queued in two lines – the K, L, M, and the N, O and P line because most Luo and Kikuyu names begin either with K, M, N or O.

'Anyway, into these two mile long queues arrives an incredible sight. It is a hot day, the thousands of Wananchi are good natured, the women with perhaps two babies at their breasts, one more on their shoulders, and two more toddlers clinging to their legs!

'The polling booth, a mud-floored corrugated-iron primary school, and it was hot remember, the sanitary arrangements were hardly adequate for the sixty kids who should have been using them, let alone a crowd of forty thousand voters!

'A Rolls-Royce, one of the two in the republic, stops at the end of the two mile long line of voters – out steps Lord Maston, one of the early white settlers who chose citizenship at independence, in his pin striped suit, rolled umbrella, and a bowler hat. A proud Kenyan citizen – practising his right to vote, so while his chauffeur waits in the shade of a eucalyptus tree, his

Lordship sweats it out from nine in the morning till six at night in the motley queue, to cast his vote. There's democracy for you!

'I reckon that myself in the polling booth dipping the electorate's middle finger in dye to make sure they didn't vote twice, was the only other Mzungu old Maston saw that day – and he didn't even nod to me, that would have implied complicity. Just marks his cross, posts it, picks up his brolly and bowler and strides out.'

He was now entering another village and by now it was quite dark. In his dipped headlight beam Harry noticed the not unusual sight of the outline of two Giriama girls. The black shawl was a final concession to the vanishing purdah practice of strict Muslims of covering female heads and faces completely. A black shawl was a common enough sight. Also the fact that they were waving him down and wanted a lift was a common enough sight. Just about every pedestrian in Africa wanted a lift, thought Harry. They never used their thumbs as did their opposites in Europe but seemed to be patting an imaginary ball two feet off the ground with the open palms of their hand. Harry drove past without a thought. The girls just seemed to him a part of the village, soft and gentle, like the swaying palms.

The village was illuminated mainly by the soft light of paraffin lamps. In the open doorways Harry noticed for the first time a watery full moon in the late evening sky which was beginning to clear a little. He even saw a lone star as dark clouds scudded across the heavens blown by the winds caused by the difference in temperature between land and the sea, a gentle breeze from the sea. Or was it the other way around? Harry could never work it out, especially at Lake Turkana where all the winds are convectional and on occasions they blow with tremendous force from the cool water to the hot land and then, after two or three days, will reverse their direction from the hot land to the cool water. It just didn't make sense!

Harry smiled as he thought of his beloved cradle of mankind again, then of Gret and then of Eve. Then of the girls he had just passed. He had in his pocket a wallet full of two-hundred-shilling notes.

He then thought what sense it would make to be a partner to conceive a child at the end of his life. That would make good sense, some continuance. A life full of learning, a life full of wisdom, a life full of experience, otherwise wasted. 'Yer what!' laughingly from Nicky, her words crossed his mind.

He was only about two hundred yards past those typical call girls, prostitutes, whores, harlots – what's in a name? – when he slammed on his brakes. He looked in his mirror and the sandy track behind him was illuminated now from the bright red lights of his brake lights. He left his foot on the brake and shifted the gear into reverse, not because he intended reversing towards them but in order to see them better in the light from the reverse lights added to the brake lights. It took the girls perhaps half a minute to run from where they were to the stopped car. In that half-minute Harry's mind was working overtime, even by the standards of his now fast-flowing imagination. He smiled to himself as he thought how disbelieving and horrified his few friends would be. Such philosophizing was interrupted when he realized there would be few friends indeed who would ever learn of this.

'Oh, cut the bullshit Harry. It's natural enough isn't it?' he said to himself. 'What you want is a good screw before you go.' Then he started thinking about Ken, an old army friend from his El Alamein days a hundred years ago. Ken was a communist. 'There is absolutely nothing after death' Ken used to quote Karl Marx. 'The only manifestation of eternity is in our children, and their children and their children's children. Their well-being is your life's reason. There is no other purpose.' Then he convinced himself that all his life, all that day's drive it had been planned that he should meet with these two girls. Harry smiled to himself. 'You don't have to make bloody excuses, no one will know.' The girls would welcome the two hundred bob if not his old body.

By now the girls had reached the car. Well, that's pretty standard, he thought. It could have been Fifth Avenue, the Reeperbahn, or Leicester Square.

'How much you give, Johnny?' Then it dawned on Harry that the village he had just passed through was within a day's easy walk of the Great Sin Cities that lined the coral reef – African mud hut 'cities' built behind each luxury beach hotel.

He smiled to himself, at least it was Johnny and not Fritz. He liked that. All the Africans at the coast spoke German these days. Who won the bloody war anyway?

'Two hundred,' he said to one of the two eager young faces peering in the window.

'Each?' one answered enquiringly.

'OK, each,' he said. He wasn't quite sure that he could handle one, let alone two, but he couldn't think what else to say.

'OK, follow me Johnny.' He got out of the car.

One of the girls put out her hand. 'Come,' she said. Soft sand underfoot. At many main events in his life Harry seemed to remember the feel of soft sand underfoot. The other girl was now trailing along behind. By the occasional moonlight flickering between the clouds and the palm fronds Harry was relieved to see that they both were young and fresh with a neat row of white teeth and kind eyes that seemed to understand humanity so well. He put the first girl's age around twenty-five. The soft sensuality of the tropical night engulfed him. He remembered that when Shakespeare had suggested that 'Lilies that fester smell far worse than weeds' he was referring to character, not body odours. Nevertheless it always seemed an appropriate quotation on those rare occasions when Harry found it necessary to explain to hygiene neurotics from the western hemisphere how the native nomads kept so clean with so little use of water and even less of soap. The fresh breath, the shiny ebony limbs of Harry's new friend would compare most favourably with their opposites in the west where deodorants were likely to fail after a night's work, and then, for sure, the festering lily stench of stale cosmetics would smell much worse than the wild fragrant weeds of nature.

How different had been this girl's quarter of a century to that of Nicky he thought, or Jenny's first twenty-five years come to that. Were they sadder or gladder? Better or worse? God knows, but different. This girl had probably known literally hundreds of men in the full Biblical sense of the word, and Jenny and Nicky at twenty-five only one each! He would not judge. Her sensuality was transferring itself from her hand to excite him.

After five minutes walking through the palms they arrived at the walls of a hut, a deserted hut that had no matuki thatch on the roof – a skeleton of a hut open to the sky. By now Harry was becoming aroused. Without hesitation or embarrassment the girl whose hand he had been holding walked into the derelict hut open to the sky, undid her kikoi, placed it on the ground, laid down on it and opened her legs. Harry was fumbling with his trousers when he noticed the other girl in the doorway was beckoning him. It turned out that she had been around the back of the hut to fill a bowl with precious water and was obviously implying that he must wash his penis before performing. This Harry willingly did assuming there was some superstition that it might save the girls from AIDS.

It didn't take long for Harry to realize that his partner was circumcised and with that knowledge a terrific tenderness came over him. Although he was hugely excited he temporarily stopped his attention from between her legs and tried to kiss her. He was rather surprised when she shied away. Then he kissed her breasts. This apparently was more welcome. For half an hour Harry worked as he had never worked before in his life to bring the young girl without a clitoris to climax. His efforts could not have been more appreciated. Harry guessed that it was probably the first time in her life that a man had taken the trouble to excite her and she responded, first by smothering him with kisses on the lips, then clasping him to her and finally by discarding the traditional wedge of seaweed – the only birth control method she knew.

Harry had never made love to a circumcised woman before. The performance certainly took longer than he imagined possible. He was trying to make up, he told himself, for the brutality of his fellow men who had dared to cut the girl's sexual organs so brutally for so horrendously selfish and ridiculous a reason. She threw her arms and legs around his waist and clasped his hand to her lips. Never in her wide experience had she known anything so exquisitely wonderful. She groaned, she giggled, she even laughed a little. Harry's heart pounded. 'Jesus, I'm going to die on the job,' he said to himself. But he didn't. The contact had also given him the most extreme sexual pleasure that he had experienced in the twenty years since Jenny had died. As an eyeless man sees with his stick, so a clitoris-less girl develops amazing muscular ripples and suctions deep inside her body. At one time Harry had felt an astonishing caress like two fingers stroking him where no fingers could have been. He had gasped at the indescribable pleasure of it. Now, as they both lay there looking up at the velvet night he wasn't in the least surprised to notice the full moon come out of the clouds – a complete round full moon, wedged between the mangrove poles of the thatched roof above them.

As Harry was putting his trousers back on again the girl sat up. Harry felt in his pocket for the wallet and was ashamed of himself for thinking that perhaps it wouldn't be there. It was, sure enough, and he was uneasy when he took out a five-hundred shilling note and handed it to the girl. She shook her head and said, 'No thank you, Johnny.' That was a compliment indeed for an old boy of his age he thought, with pride. He walked across the moonlit sand under the palm trees to where he could just see his car lights parked on the track. The other girl was by now standing by the car. Harry pulled out his wallet again, it had several thousand shillings in it and he impulsively thrust it into the younger girl's hand. He was slightly annoyed with himself, because in his satiated sexual state he didn't want his last lay, even in his imagination, to be a sordid affair of prostitution, yet he wanted the two girls to have the money. He knew he had no need for it, and it might at least give his future child a slightly better start in life.

In his imagination both the girls were becoming wrapped in respectability, in the mysteries of the east, exotic, beguiling and romantic. The perfumed garden come to life. He was already thinking of one last mad embrace of the Rupert Brooke romantic type. Then he felt a faint tug at his sleeve from the girl's sister still standing by the car with his wallet now firmly tucked into the top of her kikoi.

He smiled and shook his head at the invitation and she said, very gently, 'Asanti sana.'

Harry frowned and she repeated, 'No, asanti sana for her' nodding towards her sister, who was still framed in soft moonlight. Harry was pleased at the correction. Harry the romantic, Harry the optimist, interpreted the little scene. The girl's sister was offering her body to Harry because she wanted him, not his money, or at least she wanted to give value for the money she had already received. At first he thought the 'Thank you' from her was for the money, but finally everything was put right in Harry's romantic old mind when he realized that the final 'thank you' from the younger girl meant 'thank you' for restoring her sister's faith.

They were by now back at the car. Harry had already put the scene safely into the past and was actually sitting in the car about to move off when the second girl, which he had taken to be the sister of his recent sex partner, knocked on the car window and said, 'Wait a bit, Johnny.' All had been so perfect till then that he was in two minds whether to drive away from the scene but he felt he owed it to the girls to trust them. Five minutes later he had been led back to the derelict hut to the surprise of his life. He smiled to himself – this was the wrong way round – oysters were meant to put lead in his pencil – oh, a refill then. With her back to the wall sat his lover. In front of her a small red plastic bowl, not unlike the one he had so recently abluted in he could not help remembering. It was filled full with oysters, delicious small Mombasa rock oysters. There must have been hundreds of them. The three of them, the two girls and Harry, tucked in, left handful by left handful, squeezing out the salt water. The girl had sprinkled them with vinegar. Harry had never tasted oysters like them, small but tender. Some praise, having tasted his favourite food from Osaka to Cornwall. Popping them into his mouth three or four at a time made a perfect feast, a superb – the hairs on the back of Harry's neck, if he had had any, would have stood on end – a superb supper – a last supper!

He guessed the girl had hurriedly produced the feast, probably from her brother who cycled to the sea every day to bring back to the village whatever was in abundance at the time. He also sensed that the girl was trying to impress her lover with her domesticity – but the last supper image was so terrifying that he could not enter into the spirit of things. He was glad that he had accepted the offer though. A gentle coastal village not short of food was a reasonable enough place to bring an offspring into the world. 'How will those old Hills' genes get on here?' He could not get the thought out of his mind.

In the most leisurely fashion, after he had declined a 'mirrarh' and a Sportsman cigarette, and accepted a cup of tea, they walked back to the car again still under the palm trees by the side of the road in the moonlight with its sidelights on. Leaving parking lights on was an old habit Harry had brought with him from post-war foggy Britain.

His final thought as he parted sadly from the last people he was ever going to talk to was a typical Harry thought. 'Good God, I must really be over the smoking habit' – he had given up fifteen years previously – 'Why else would I reject that last proffered cigarette? It can't do me any harm now, any more than AIDS can.'

He drove gently on through the palm trees for nearly half an hour following the sandy track, when he came to a T-road. Instinctively he turned right. The track became less sandy and more corally and it climbed perhaps thirty feet and there, glittering in the moonlight, jet-black straight ahead of him, was the Indian Ocean. Harry looked out to sea. All evening the clouds had been blowing gently inland, now the heavens were clearing, clear across to India, stars shone down as only African stars know how, and perfectly on cue silver clouds scudding in the breeze revealed the orange moon, already descending towards the black and silver of the rippling sea.

It was a perfect scene. If you have got to go, what a night, what a night to go! Harry thought again about the old J.B. Priestley play where Death's Angel comes into the pub to choose who is to go with him. And all the people who had been so recently grumbling and fed-up with life, had so hastily found good reasons why they could not go with him, and so he picks the hero who says 'Life has always been very fair to me. I've no doubt that the life hereafter will be equally good – take me!' Harry thought to himself that if an angel appeared and you're actually invited, that means invited to somewhere, and so of course you'd go. But no angel appeared. 'Well, OK, I'm not volunteering but if I've *got* to go . . . .'

I do seem blessed indeed, my death looks like being both painless and sudden. Until this morning I had not really thought about it and yet I have been given all the time I want to reconcile myself to it. It was ordained, the trail to Tilda was not my idea. I have been following an impulse – my last sex and my last supper show me this to my satisfaction. There is a weaver of the web all right and she won't stop weaving when I die. She is working on a very intricate piece right now to get me back to Tilda; and that piece will continue to exist without me. So be it: I guess I'm lucky after all. I am not forsaken. 'In that respect I'm not complaining sir. I appreciate how much more blessed I am than was Christ himself. "*Eloi, Eloi lama sabach-thani?*" Not so me – lucky me. In the fullness of life I shrug off this mortal coil, now as useless as a discarded snake's skin. I *am* blessed. I have not had to pervert my logic into accepting other men's dogmas and yet surely somehow some spirit from somewhere has blessed my spirit.'

'True, I have no angel as such to lead me on.' For a split second Harry recalled the spirit of one of earth once whom had loved him the most. He tried to transform that image to clothe it in contemporary religious doctrine. He gave a sudden guffaw of laughter out loud – for a second shattering the silence of the coastal night. Across his imagination flew a white-haired Ruzizi with giant angel's wings flapping as she settled like a marabou stork into the topmost branch of the tallest tree in his Langata plot.

Next he considered the overland girl's ghostly story of the previous night and the reality of Oliver's and Anne's photographs of the resurrected Tilda – coincidence as comforting as an angel proving to his satisfaction that his being was a part of the weaver's web of destiny – and he found his comfort in realizing that he would still be a part of that web tomorrow: his death would not unravel it.

The dipped headlights of the Corolla flashed onto one of the house signs at the end of a culverted drive. Such name boards are common all over Kenya's European residential areas. It read, in black letters on a white background, Oliver and Anne. 'I thought so,' Harry said to himself as he turned up the drive, 'I thought that was what it was all about.' He quietly parked his car near the house and started creeping around the typical single floored house. The boxer dog sprung out at him, looked as if it was just about to bark furiously, then froze in its tracks standing four-square with the hair of its back standing upright. Harry crept around the corner of the moonlit house, across Anne's precious Kikuyu grass lawn. And there she was! The huge red crosses on a new bright white background, shining in the moonlight. He installed himself at the old familiar driving seat, clutching the old steering wheel, looking out of the perfectly-restored windscreen. The dear old familiar feel of the steering wheel that had steered him across minefields, down so many glorious leafy English lanes, along the rock-strewn shores that saw the very dawn of Man – what better device existed to steer him now into the unknown?

It was like a jagged flash of yellow Hollywood lightning going straight to his heart, like the cramp he used to get in his leg, but in his heart and across his chest. Then Tilda seemed to turn completely over and over. Then she was bumping normally, travelling about thirty miles an hour, slowing to twenty in soft sand. Harry remembered that the night had been still and silent, now he heard faint singing. Clearly now, *Waltzing Matilda*, louder and louder. Tilda was moving. He stood up with his foot on the accelerator which he had done so many thousand times in the past, holding the steering wheel, leant out of the open cab to look backwards and upwards and there, against the background of stars, were a pair of army boots at the end of someone's legs hanging just above his head. He saw the outline of many shadows on the roof, shadows drinking and smelt the smell of beer, in long-necked old beer bottles, and then above all the strange swell of the music of *Waltzing Matilda* which was becoming loud by now. He heard suddenly whoops and cries and whistles and catcalls. He looked out and there was Julie whom he had seen at Paul's last night, standing there with a little Tuareg boy. 'I thought she was going to the Masai Mara at Sparrowfart this morning,' Harry said to himself. 'What the hell's she doing here?'

Then the going seemed to get harder in the soft sand as he tucked himself back firmly behind the wheel and peered out at the moonlit sand through the low windscreen. 'All right now?' he asked disbelievingly to himself. 'Don't fuck it up now, don't spoil it, don't expect too much. Something's happening, isn't that enough?' The wind-rippled sand rose slightly to a little dune ahead. The going was getting softer. Harry slammed Tilda down into third, gave her maximum revs, thinking to himself every big end he had would come flying through the sump. Then he could hardly hear the engine noise for the sound of *Waltzing Matilda*.

On top of the dune were two girls leaning against two bicycles. Jenny, he recognized at once, although heaven knows she didn't look a day over eighteen. Her hair was blowing in the desert breeze. It took him a little longer to recognize the second girl astride another bike. Then it dawned on him. It was the original Tilda! – the young Australian's girlfriend. With an arm on each shoulder standing just behind them was

Simon. Tilda turned round and smiled at Simon. He dropped his arm as she pedalled furiously down the slope towards the oncoming vehicle. Harry could hardly see where he was going any more. He had to wipe his tears away with his battledress cuff. Harry knew that the girl on the bike now ahead of Jenny was intent on whoever or whatever was in the back of the ambulance. He also noticed that each person he saw was dressed in the exact fashion in which he himself remembered them, as if it was his mind that was creating them. Julie, for example, was wearing the same clothes that she was wearing the previous evening. Harry particularly recalled the tight-fitting blue jeans, that was the only dress he had ever seen her in. Simon was wearing the red neckerchief Jenny had given him for his eighteenth birthday, over his flying jacket. Harry clearly remembered his own comment on the gift and most affectionately said, 'You'll look like the ruddy Red Baron in that, Si!' Tilda, pedalling furiously on the pre-war lady's bicycle was to Harry very much alive but without colour, except the greys of a 1939 Kodak Brownie box camera. Jenny was naked and unashamed.

The last trite sentence was forming on Harry's lips, 'Journey's end in Tilda's meeting' or was it his first sentence? The strains of *Waltzing Matilda* were much too loud to allow it to be heard in any case. The tiniest flicker of a frown crossed Harry's face for the tiniest fraction of a second! One just didn't frown in Paradise! The accent was Simon's, the style Nicky's, the grammar Jacobean, the disapproval obvious, 'Wouldst thou offend God? For whom doth thou seek?'

ANAGNORISIS

The twins always rose with the sun. For once they had not been sleeping in the playhouse but they were out there long before Anne and I were ready to get up. They both came tumbling across the lawn and burst through our open French window into our bedroom.

'Mummy – Daddy' plaintively, ''ncle Hawry's asleep in my seat' from the first, 'Yes – and he won't wake up,' from the second.

I got up to investigate, throwing a kikoi around my waist whilst Anne splashed off for a shower. And there, sure enough, was old Harry slumped over the steering wheel of Tilda, as dead as a doornail. I wonder why doornail?

I am Oliver and it is I who wrote the previous chapters about the life and death of Harry Hill. I have headed this last section 'Anagnorisis' rather than Epilogue for the same reason that I called the opening chapter 'Before the Start' rather than Prologue and the penultimate chapter the Finish – all to make it sound less finite than do Beginning and End, Prologue and Epilogue. The whole point is that this is *not* an Epilogue – that comes later.

The female overlander Harry and I both met at Paul's place the day before Harry died, was called Eileen, not Julie, and she came from Aussie not from Norfolk. Eileen, like Julie, died tragically but in a motor accident on her way to the Masai Mara about five miles out of Nairobi quite near Dagoretti Red Cross Centre the morning after the little party at Paul's place. So for two of the six of us there present, death was imminent. I changed her name to Julie when describing her in order to capitalize, dramatically speaking, on Kenya's most famous overlander Julie Ward, whom I had previously also met at Paul's place and who had achieved a certain fame by having been brutally murdered in the Masai Mara Game Reserve two years before Harry's death. No connection whatsoever with

Jenny's parents who were also called Ward nor come to that, with the best actor in the world, our own Jimmy Ward.

Also I am *not* screwing my lovely African sec and I am also sure that my wife isn't having it off with that 'gleesy gleek plick' that moved in up the coast – actually he's not a bad chap. Those suggestions, like bringing in Julie, were my attempts at 'poetic licence'. I have no need of such fictitious ploys now. The truth is too dramatic. Now I fear only that my descriptive powers are inadequate to convey the reality.

Harry had, you may remember, come out to Kenya originally to work for my old man in his brake lining business. What also made it easy for me to tell the tale was the fact that there was much similarity between my old man and Harry. Both were born in the English Midlands, both served in the North Africa campaign, both were irrationally prejudiced all their lives when it came to Germans, both spent much of their working lives in Kenya, both had children born or bred in Kenya and both died here.

The comparison ends with Harry and my father. My mother's life for example was very different to Jenny Hill's. My mother was antipathetic to Africa, and was regarded by the Europeans as a hedonistic renegade. Shortly after weaning me, she allowed herself to be carried out of Africa in the arms of a visiting antique-dealer, and has spent the rest of her life not unhappily in the Lanes behind The Old Ship in Brighton.

Harry was perhaps even more pro-African and pro-Commonwealth than my father had been. Harry had hung in his town office a large *Telegraph* political map of the world dated 1920, published when Harry was two years old and when, after the Protectorates were handed out after the First World War, the British Empire was geographically speaking at its largest. When Harry was asked if such a blatant display of Empire might not hurt the feelings of the new aspirants to the independent republic Harry would answer 'No way – they probably think the pink is for Communism any way.'

I have, whilst attempting to describe Harry's character, perhaps included too much of his homespun philosophy, the reason for that is firstly because it helped me relate to him – relate as in American on safari – and also because if you think about it, all the other arts and sciences can flounder without a professional teaching discipline, whereas philosophy I think, improves by being self-taught.

I have recounted an incident where Harry had convinced himself of the truth of his own bullshit – the story he used to tell his punters of the night Tilda nearly fell a hundred feet into the Congo River! I included this, because it shows one of the things that endeared people to Harry.

He would instantly retreat from his exaggerations if anyone challenged him. He would not take offence; he would say, with a good-natured smile at being caught out . . . . 'well, it *could* have happened – couldn't it?'

I also made use of some of Harry's dictated mini tapes which I found in his car and he had actually got one of his Son et Lumière 'Origins of Love' tapes with him in the car. They are to be found all over the place. Anne and I have even got one down here at the coast, because after the show – and it was much better with music and his noises off – Harry used to sell copies to anybody who wanted one and many people were eager for a memento of those magic nights they spent up at Harry's northern camp.

Obviously I made up completely or 'reconstructed' as people more commonly say nowadays, the last thirty-four hours of Harry's life after he left Paul and Rita's dinner party to when the twins found him dead at the wheel of their playhouse ambulance.

His new Corolla was parked neatly outside our house so it wasn't too hard to 'reconstruct' that as I flew down to the coast he had driven down.

Our local 'quack' is a friend of ours called Henry with whom Anne plays golf. It was Henry who issued Harry's death certificate in Mombasa. Anne and I are always teasing him that the one thing he is really good at – in fact the only thing he is any good at – is issuing death certificates.

Hauling Harry across the lawn and into the back of the Volvo estate car to deliver him to Mombasa's morgue wasn't so funny. I had never realized before how heavy a dead body was. (Oh, dead weight I suppose!) The twins had been quite easily persuaded to play down on the beach with their ayah as the macabre shuffle took place. Our night Askari, whom the twins insisted on calling 'Skari', took one of Harry's arms, and Anne the other and me his two legs, like a bloody wheelbarrow. Melodramatically halfway across the lawn his ass dragged a bit

I suppose, and two photographs fell out of his hip pocket, one of Tilda obviously taken the day the Hills and Dory had arrived in Nairobi and the other one of those that I had given him, that Anne had taken, of the kids' playhouse which I had shown him only the day before yesterday. Although I say it myself you really couldn't tell my restoration job from the original. It was then, when I noticed that Harry had no wallet on him, that I guessed how he had spent the cash there must have been in it!

I would like to have suggested that Harry's dictaphone was found switched on at his last 'transfer' as they say in the tourist trade, and that the sweet haunting melody of *Waltzing Matilda* could be heard recorded on it but the truth is that he did not have it with him in Tilda – he had left it in his car.

It was, as usual, 'another bloody lovely day in paradise' three days after we found Harry dead in the playhouse and I was sitting on the verandah of the house; it was gone eleven o'clock and I was enjoying my first Tusker of the day and Anne had slipped away to our new Megamarket – well, eight shops on the ground floor joined together with a sort of arcade to change the 'vids'. The twins came panting across the lawn from the playhouse where they had just gone to play after the morning on the beach – c'est la vie!

'Daddy, Daddy, there's a monkey in our house.' Then, from the second twin, 'Yes, and he's playing pat-a-cake with Skari's old coat.' I jumped up and ran across the lawn following the twins. I think even before I looked in through the little sliding glass window high in the side of the ambulance, that I guessed what I would see. It wasn't a monkey, and it wasn't the Askari's overcoat!

Ruzizi was up to her usual trick insisting on a round of pat-a-cake, this time with a badly wounded soldier in an army greatcoat. I pulled up on my hands on the roof of the ambulance for a better view through the window but then there was a creaking screech and the whole slab on which we had planted the playhouse broke away from the rest of the cliff and fell down to the little rocks and sandpools below as I jumped clear.

Now was the first really worrying thing. Not that it fell but the fact that I did not feel worried. The reason was that despite loving my kids as much as anyone – so certain was I that I had seen what I had seen, that I remember thinking 'Are the twins inside?' – just for a second I wouldn't have minded if they *had* been inside. I felt so certain that it was something I can only call 'Eternal Goodness' that was falling. But they weren't inside, they were standing beside me looking down at their broken playhouse. A piping voice of one of the twins again, 'The monkey's fallen over' and then from the other 'Yes, and our house'.

The next difficult thought I had was that it couldn't have been a hallucination or we wouldn't all three have seen it. The third day and all that didn't worry me then.

It is now seventeen days since Harry died, and fourteen since Tilda toppled down on to the rocks.

The late Harry Hill has been hastily cremated in Mombasa – hastily because the Kenyan morgue deep freezers are notorious for breaking down! Anne, myself, and Paul and Rita were the only mourners present at the incineration but apparently the beautiful Nicky, whom I have worshipped from afar for all my life, will be coming over from Oz with her family to organize a remembrance service in Nairobi All Saints' Cathedral some time next month.

Tilda had once more been hauled up the little cliff at the edge of our plot. She has been temporarily patched up and placed on a much more secure site, a hundred feet inland in line with our house.

Everything is back to normal – except me! It has slowly dawned on me that the inadequate me has stumbled across proof positive of eternal life.

It would have been more helpful for my peace of mind if Ruzizi had been playing pat-a-cake with a wounded soldier of Monty's era. I could have then related it to Harry's story of a wounded Desert Rat, hallucinating about a tailless monkey and thus found it possible to convince myself that I, too, had been imagining things, though how to explain that the twins also saw what I did, they having no prior knowledge, I do not know.

The bigger mental problem is that the more I try to recapture that scene just before Tilda fell, the more certain am

I that Ruzizi was not surrounded by wounded soldiers of the first El Alamein campaign. For one thing, they didn't have First World War type gasmasks in the desert during the Second World War, yet I saw one in the back of Tilda. Also there were not too many army greatcoats on active service around El Alamein, yet most of the wounded I caught a glimpse of and definitely the particular soldier Ruzizi was playing pat-a-cake with, was wearing one such overcoat. The twins also noticed that, you will remember, but most extraordinary and most significantly Ruzizi was not keeping in time with the tune of *Waltzing Matilda* or anything like that. I recall most clearly the little ditty the wounded soldier was repeating aloud as his hands met the chimps – 'Two rows of cabbages, two of curly greens, two rows of early peas, two of kidney beans.' Now I just could not have imagined that – I had never heard those lines before. It wasn't till Paul told me when I asked him about them at Harry's cremation the other day that I had any idea that they were the writings of one of the First World War poets.

A feeling of awe – awful, in its true sense took over my mind. At first, I was afraid that I was doomed to become a despicable religious freak, or at best, a contemporary Ancient Mariner ranting on about a nonsense in which no one had any interest. Originally too, I must confess that like a dusty apostle, I felt a need to share my experience, then I found sense enough not to tell all and sundry.

My revelation of the eternal had given me implicit spiritual assurance and comfort, yet had demanded no allegiance, asked for no sacrifice in return. My second thoughts were therefore more rational. Far from a fanatical desire to enforce the world at large to give my vision credence and pay it homage, like so many other visionaries from Mohammed to Joseph Smith have done, were I to share my experience I concluded that it would dilute it.

I remembered how my father would tease Harry and Jenny when they were reluctant to explain to us, their best friends, how to reach their favourite valley on Ol Donyo Nyiru. Both the Hills' secret valley, and my relationship towards my revelation would suffer were they not kept secret.

I am as certain that I saw Ruzizi in the back of Tilda, as I am certain that her mortal remains, were at that 'time' four feet under the sod of a Langata garden. My logic however finds

336

it much more acceptable to consider this 'second sighting' as a time warp, confirming that time is as curved as are the other three dimensions, as circular as space itself must be.

An even more complicated associated problem confounding my logic was that the surroundings in which my vision was set were those of a 'time' three quarters of a century removed from my own. It would have been much easier therefore to assume that I had seen Ruzizi's double, or an ancestor of her's, but I have no doubt that it was Ruzizi herself that I saw and not another similar chimp.

I have therefore had to assume the theory as upsetting to the metaphysical as Darwin's was to the physical world. I concluded that the recent compounded speed of human evolution is putting the human species at a metaphysical disadvantage as an 'incomprehensible barrier' has fallen, barring our progress. Whereas paradoxically, less-evolved brains can duck the barrier. A result hinted at in Tao's P'u philosophy, is that a less sophisticated mind, as found in a chimpanzee for example, can achieve wonders which are denied a modern human brain – like transcending time perhaps! Simultaneously I was thinking along the lines that she seemed able to collect discarded thought waves.

I am concluding therefore that the vision of Ruzizi in the back of Tilda did not belong to any specific time but to all time. This feeling was strengthened by an incomplete action I saw and most of all by the look she gave me.

EPILOGUE

Nairobi City fathers had once seen fit to post long since dilapidated notices on all their ingress roads, reading ... Nairobi-Green City In the Sun. Lately, although only half the fault can be attributed to the City Commission Commissionaires this description deservedly collects an increasing number of ribald comments. It was a pleasant surprise therefore that the day chosen for Harry's memorial service in Nairobi All Saints' Cathedral was kind to his memory.

The squat towers of the neo-Norman building, although recently over shadowed by mega-storey, 'office and shop' blocks, still caught some shafts of sunlight. It was not old as in 'European listed buildings' old – the type that Harry missed, but its plaques at least did date back to the last century. The Sunday best dressed mourners collected in the car park reluctant to be the first to enter, most of them were in any case infrequent visitors there. Paul and Rita were pointing out, to an 'overland' girl who accompanied them, the plaque dedicated to the memory of Inspector Rhyll of the Uganda Railways who was, so read the script, dragged from his sleeping compartment by one of the Lions of Tsavo during the construction of the 'Lunatic Line' in 1896.

To many of the white deceased, the pause of their coffin beneath the vaulted aisle of that cathedral, is their last resting place before their final safari to Langata. This is where, opposite the main entrance to Nairobi National Park, are both the crematorium and the cemetery. Adjacent is the popular 'Paupers Field' which it is said, though only in its thirtieth year, has already been thrice sown with corpses, which perhaps accounts for the yield of extraordinarily long elephant grass in that portion of the cemetery. Those ex-White Tribesmen who die in foreign parts, as a few do, in Cape Town, Eastbourne or even as in Harry's case, in Mombasa, enjoy (and then only if their next of kin can afford it) a memorial service, or if they

338

cannot, then a small mention in the Personal 'Death' columns of the *Standard*.

Outside the sky was blue and the traffic noisy, but inside the typically stale and silent Anglican Cathedral, under the high arched roof any Brit might have felt at home. Inside were hassocks, cassocks, musty psalters of Psalms, and crumpled books of Prayer and Hymn, an offertory box designed to receive only coin, a whole boxful of which in these days of falling value of the Kenyan shilling, would barely pay for one bunch of altar lilies

Nicky and her two boys, a year or two older than our twin girls, were also on parade. Anne and myself were the first little knot to enter, but eventually the pews were nearly full, mainly with Harry's white associates, the elderly representation of which seemed to be catching the Luo's tribes passionate interest in all funeral and memorial worship. Many of the African tribes of Kenya, particularly those born in the region of the Great Lake Victoria, would go without food if necessary to enable them to afford their departed loved one the little glass peep window in the coffin.

Also present at the service was, a fair sprinkling of Africans and Asians, automatically seeming to segregate themselves by rows.

The day before I had flown Nicky up to the NFD, and when we were over the forest on the side of Ol Donyo Nyiro mountain, Nicky had scattered Harry's ashes out of the cockpit window. It certainly didn't seem twenty-three years since I had flown Harry and her up there to scatter Jenny and Simon's ashes, but it was; I remember I had only had my PPL for nine months then.

Being no corpse, no ashes and no coffin at the service did seem to make it a more jolly and a less morbid affair. Nicky looked absolutely beautiful of course, all in mourning black. Her tanned complexion, and her unaccustomed smart black skirt, high heels and even a fashionable black straw hat, made her look very like videos I had seen of Princess Di at the Cenotaph – and she seemed to radiate a similar charisma.

I was sitting next to the aisle – two rows from the front. On my left were the four impish young children and then Anne, keeping an eye on them. Paul and Rita and the overland girl made up the rest of our pew. With such lively company and with the sun pouring in through the sparse stained glass windows, the ambience was not conducive to thoughts of death, and finite thinking.

Nicky had chosen the Hymns and Psalms and had also decided to read, as an obituary for her late father, a script he himself had written two or three years before he died. Harry had apparently sent his daughter a copy of it at the time he was trying to get it published in a travel magazine – it never was published, one reason being it was much too long and another it was a little anti the UK tourist establishment. Nicky felt that 'The Odyssey' as Harry called it, summed up completely her father's character, portraying as it did how Harry thought of himself. I had read it before, in fact you will perhaps notice I have cribbed at least one of Harry's analogies from it. I found the end a shade trite, but in general, agreed with Nicky that it showed Harry in a kindly light. I enjoyed hearing it again especially when read by Nicky in her most attractive accent into which I noticed there was just a trace of Digger creeping in to merge with the clipped Kenyan. I have noticed that many cultured female voices strike a tone unpleasantly authoritative, domineering even, but Nick's was the perfect pitch for the occasion.

I also find Harry's essay an appropriate 'ending', because Harry's existence seems interwoven with Ruzizi's as well as Tilda's.

In sincere and moving tones, Nicky looking a little out of place as she began to read:

' "I personally listen to the travel tales of two or three thousand of my own clients whom I take on safari in Kenya every year. Coupled to this background, my sales visits to Australia, Japan, the Persian Gulf, Thailand and North America, my recent ASTA Trail through LA, Rome, Budapest and New Dehli, throw in a WTM and an ITB and also my personal family holidays of long ago in the Bahamas and the Alps, and you will appreciate the fact that I am no greenhorn to travel. Add my proud claim to have visited every country in Africa and every game park from the gorillas in the mists of the Ruwenzoris to the oryx in the dust of Etosha, and I thus claim to be at least on a par with your correspondents – no stranger to tourism, sufficiently experienced to be taken by surprise by very little. I labour this point not to seek admiration, I have

340

long since learned that one can fill one's soul as perfectly on a bus trip into your nearest market town as by gadding around the world as I do, but I do claim my comparisons can at least give my story, which follows, the authority of perspective and the credence of a wide experience.

' "Recently (whilst the San Francisco earth was quaking, in fact) I found myself ambulance delivered to the emergency ward of Lennox Hill Hospital, 77 100th Street, New York. The detail of that week – one of the more remarkable of my recent past, is more suited to *The Lancet* than travel trade gazettes. Sufficient must it be to say it would make a superb advert for the plastic card. The last words I croaked before falling into a coma with a temperature of 106 degrees in reply to the infamous USA 100 dollar medical question – 'Are you insured' were 'No, but I have a credit card'. (In all fairness I must add that the best medical attention in the world was lavished on me at very little charge.)

' "The significance of this sickness anecdote is to explain that after a week of soaring fever of tick borne typhus, especially in a not particularly well-worn body like mine that has seen over sixty summers . . .".'

Nicky looked up from the page smiling. 'That's typical Bwana,' she said to the congregation, 'he was nine and a half summers over sixty at that time actually.' She carried on reading . . . .

' "One feels knackered to say the least. Minor travel frustrations, a lens falling out of your spectacle onto the pavement of Fifth Avenue, a zip bursting open from a suitcase and cascading underwear when one is halfway across the 'walk' all assume gigantic proportions after tick-typhus and almost tears of desperation. The waft of cooking from underground New York restaurants instead of making your mouth water, makes you want to retch! Minor irritations like not being able to secure a cab despite hailing them non-stop for twenty minutes and you break out into a cold sweat.

' "I therefore opted to cut short the hurly-burly, the cut and thrust of selling safaris in the States, and grabbed a clipper back to the tranquillity of distant relatives and village life in the old UK before tackling the eight-hour wide-bodied flight back home to Nairobi (being routed via Miami-Paris from New York only put two hours extra on the USA – Paris flight time).

' "It was Paris where things started going wrong. Transferring from the clipper at Charles de Gaul, I was confronted with a contemporary tyrant with carrot coloured hair, and a red and blue neckerchief.

' "She was controlling the forward booking offices for half a dozen airlines, and it was she who heaped scorn upon me for my stupidity in assuming that one could fly Paris/London without a booking – especially at the weekend! No help, no alternative suggestions, and least of all, no sympathy, and no sorrow, just delight in the power she wielded over my weakness.

' "In her office was a replica of a guillotine to mark the two hundredth anniversary of triumph over those other tyrants. I longed for the blade to clack once more, and to see the carrot head, red and blue 'kerchief and all, roll into the basket.

' "I then found myself on the platforms of the unwashed, undecorated, unorganized Gare du Nord, where all the passengers were blatantly waiting in the first class waiting room. In reality it was standing room only all the way to Amiens, first class! But all is forgotten, all is forgiven, I'm on the way to tranquillity and rest at last.

' "Utter and complete disillusionment came at Boulogne, and the first trace of sheer terror. After thirty-six hours of struggle since New York the after-effects of my fever were worsening. Backwards and forwards milled many thousands of weary travellers, at the strike-bound and storm-bound port, possessions clasped under their arms. After interminable delay, and some of them had been there for six hours or more, a cheer greeted the news that one more ship would been sailing for Folkestone shortly. Still crushed to death but cheered a little now by the good fellowship which replaced the desperation.

' "The seemingly two-mile trudge with heavy bags increasingly bowed back against a hurricane was soon forgotten on board. Even the cursory thought that there *couldn't* be enough lifeboats for the thousands lying, sitting, crouching in every gangway, on every stair, on every deck – a day's supply of passengers on one car ferry? I am renowned for my hyperbole (more modernly known as 'bull shit') but even I was amazed to learn on the television report of that night's seas that they were the stormiest of the century! I would have certainly have put it

342

as the stormiest of the decade but it wasn't *that* bad!.

' "Imagine the scene, the biggest gale of the century, the chain-smokers of Gauloise that surrounded me, the mass of humanity at my feet and in the aisle which made it impossible to throw up over the side. You weren't even allowed on deck. It can't be that long – but it could. We were two hours outside the port of Dover, having been diverted from Folkestone. But of course to apportion blame for this latest discomfort was pointless. In fact, most of us, I am sure, were thinking 'God bless the seamanship of the skilful captain' who eventually docked us gently as a kiss in a swell so huge that waves were breaking over the very roof of the Customs House from the quay next door.

' "In a daze I watched the thousands disperse, as if by magic, at so late an hour – it was nearly midnight – through the efficient efforts of the train manager, to London mainly. But I could not face another train journey, and what to do in London at three o'clock in the morning? I just wanted a bed in Dover, or failing that, a hire car to a friend in Hove, to die in peace. The one official had shot his bolt dispersing the millions, the storm was still raging, the rain lashing down. It was now past midnight. 'Hire car sir? Have you booked one? Well, I doubt it sir – no way. A taxi? Just may be if you are lucky and walk down that platform to the end over the bridge to East Dock exit – well, you might be lucky and find one but it *is* one o'clock in the morning.' The length of the platform was such that the rails touched in perspective at the bridge end. I and my cases were now headed, and had been for forty-eight hours out of New York without sleep. That hike was reminiscent of tales I had heard tell of the 'Burma Road' half a century ago.

' "My cases were by now full of old car batteries. I yearned for one of my mighty, proud muscle-rippling members of staff who would never let a tourist carry even a pair of binoculars from car park to camp, or my beloved mighty staff who would not let me carry my briefcase from car to office! (When I am not in the jungle, that is!)

' "A bowed, bedraggled, grey-complexioned old man staggered up the endless flight of the footbridge steps. 'O Brave New World of Miami Airport just a day away; where are your deep pile purple carpets, your glittering miles of moving pavements? A century away more like. Was it a fever-induced nightmare or was it Dover in Dickens's time? It *couldn't* be 'Come to beautiful Britain' of 1989!

' "An endless iron bridge of Telford's era, rainswept and deserted, lit, I could have sworn, by gaslight out of a Jack the Ripper set, finally disgorged the near swooning ancient invalid at an equally deserted black hole in a tunnel bridge wall leading to the East Docks!

' "A tiny grimy notice reading 'Taxis' was, I realized, as near as I would get to a taxi at that hour in the morning. The rain lashed down and I slumped onto my lead-filled cases with the broken zips.

' "Living most of my life leading tented safaris in the African bush I am often asked to recount my most frightening experiences. Lions of course, kill outside my tent nightly, and one always saved the last bullet for oneself when surrounded by a pack of frustrated hungry hunting dogs. A cycle of adventure – you name it – but never believe it!

' "It was a deserted Dover dock gate when a storm was blowing, after forty-eight hours non-stop travelling after a serious illness that required complete rest. I anticipated spending the rest of the night on the wet steps against a wetter windswept wall. I even doubted if I would be alive to see the dawn. A cold bead of sweat was noticed by its warmness as it joined the flow of rain dripping down my neck.

' " 'Come to beautiful' Britain – a ghastly caricature of the words rang through my head. All the efforts of the tourist boards of Great Britain to seduce a tourist to this! I think I prayed forlornly and hopelessly for a miracle. There was a blur of faint light in a window in the bleak wall opposite across the deserted, flooded, rainswept dock road. Was it a door? Feeling slightly like Moley finding Badger's foot-scraper in the wild wood – with my very last reserves of will-power I staggered into the glass-panelled door. I feebly pushed on the door and a swirl of rain entered with me lashing at the old carpet inside.

' " 'Allo mate! Blimey, where you come from? 'Ere 'av a seat – like a cuppa? The missus only gives me evaporated milk I'm afraid. Still, it keeps the cold out'.

' "The night crossing keeper of the Dunkirk Crossing – in the greatest tradition of the greatest country for hospitality – completely restored my faith in the greatness of Britain. A call to his daughter's boyfriend who ran a taxi, who knew of a veritable unfilled heaven of a hotel but, 'I'm afraid it may be a bit 'ighly priced sir'. It was one tenth of the price of my last New York bed and one hundredth the price I would willingly have paid.

' "Ten minutes later saw me performing the sacred Japanese tea-making ceremony, but much more intently than ever a Japanese, with an electric kettle and a Tetley teabag, followed by a steamy hot bath, and not a Yankee shower, and a bed of such a perfection that defies description.

' "It is not my intention to blame the slings and arrows of outrageous fortune that placed me in so perfidious and uncomfortable a situation, but to thank God for a man like the man who mans The Dunkirk Crossing. The value of such a man to The British Tourist Industry is of course inestimable but the great moral lies not there either, but elsewhere again. Being so recently used to paying $2 to every top-hatted bell-hop in the States for his calling a taxi (some two hundred a day it seemed) I offered my saint £1. Of course he refused it: I cursed myself for this insult and thus finally I come to the point of this essay.

' "I was reminded of a small piece of philosophy I first discovered about fifty years ago when my BSA motorbike broke down somewhere between Husbands Bosworth and Newport Pagnell.

' "(In those days Newport Pagnell was not yet only the second Forte's going north.) In an overgrown hedge where some huntsman had fallen to his death was a carved stone and I, Harry Hill, do solemnly swear to pay by debt to the Dunkirk Crossing man and to all the Dunkirk crossing people in all the world by following its dictates. I think it read:

> I shall pass this way but once, therefore any good deed I can do to my fellow human beings let me do it now, let me not neglect it, for I shall not pass this way again".'

Nicky's voice wavered slightly as she read the last two lines of her father's Odyssey. To the minor embarrassment of some of the White Tribe, the old general, one of the late Harry Hill's long serving drivers, started clapping as Nicky finished reading. I felt that he wasn't clapping because he sympathized with his late Bwana's written sentiments, he probably only understood a small part of it anyway, I guessed that his applause was an expression of delight at hearing Nicky again after so many years' absence.

Some of Harry's closest friends were a little moist-eyed, Dory and Zul I noticed particularly were dabbing away at their eyes surreptitiously, but I, knowing what I do, was not in the least sad, blissfully happy in fact. I shed tears of sheer joy. My mind wandered away from the service.

Long before Tilda's resurrection and my vision, I remembered Harry used to talk about 'Morphic Resonance' a questionable suggestion from a respected biologist in UK and expounded by other solid psychologists from Heidelberg, that there exists a mysterious 'field' around all living animals that enables other living things to benefit and learn from each others' passed experiences without physical contact. Harry had always been convinced that Ruzizi had been particularly receptive to such 'field waves'.

It now occurred to me that there might be a collection of such, previously intensely strong 'thought waves' trapped, or stored in the back of the ambulance. The concentrated agony and ecstasy that had occurred in that small space must have produced many such waves of morphic resonance.

It did not put too great a strain on my rationality to conclude that perhaps because of the small space, and the movement of Tilda through the dimension of space the waves had been held in another dimension of time, waiting for a receiver.

My thoughts wandered on – I knelt for a prayer I even smiled at one of the twins covering her wide-open eyes with her fingers, but I was miles away, still thinking finitely. If you can name a thing, you can analyse it: the philosophers suggest that without a 'word' for it, there is nothing – neither the word God, nor Saint would help me rationalize Ruzizi. Finally, I linked her to the word 'Angel'. I did not like the mediaeval dogmatic commutation of the word, but I could think of no other word more apt.

The congregation at the memorial service were now singing a hymn with surprising gusto, considering many of them hadn't heard the tune or the words for half a lifetime, hymns I decided embodied possibly the best of Anglican Christian philosophy. Now to attempt to complete my theory, I had only to irrevocably connect the reality of the Tilda's Angel I had seen, to Harry, and in particular to Harry's death.

I shut my eyes tightly, my ears too in a way. I just let in a line or two of the anthem – 'Changed from glory into glory – of Heaven, to Earth come down' – then I sealed off all external influences. I was reviewing my vision which I had seen only a month ago.

Somehow clearer in retrospect. Back in my coastal garden, at first I remembered Ruzizi had her back to me, then she lessened her concentration on pat-a-cake with the wounded soldier in the army greatcoat on the stretcher opposite her, and turned round to look upwards at where I was peering in at the little side window. First, a trace of a frown which quickly cleared, then a look quite clearly indicating the pleasure of recognition. I knew instantly that she would not be that pleased to see me, but she obviously associated me with Harry and I knew that she guessed that she was about to enter a time where Harry would be.

Then she performed a most characteristic act, similar to that which I had often seen her do before.

She reached down with her foot into the eternity that was the floor of Tilda and caught hold between her big toe and her second, a small branch, and held it up for me to see. It was during my memorial service concentration that I realized what she had found, it was – a twig containing two petals of the most vivid blue bougainvillaea I had ever seen.

Now, I understood the look that came into her eyes, showing a degree of happiness only a chimp can know, just about as happy as it is possible to be. No, a look much, much more happy than ever it is possible to be in, for want of three more appropriate words, in – *This Old World*.